11/13

WILD

FORT

D0541412

Essex County Council

3013020542046 5

WILD CARDS

FORT FREAK

A MOSAIC NOVEL

Edited by

George R. R. Martin

Assisted by

Melinda M. Snodgrass

And written by
Paul Cornell
David Anthony Durham
Ty Franck
Stephen Leigh
Victor Milán
John Jos. Miller
Mary Anne Mohanraj
Kevin Andrew Murphy
Cherie Priest
Melinda M. Snodgrass

Copyright © 2011 by George R. R. Martin and The Wild Cards Trust

All rights reserved

The right of George R. R. Martin to be identified as the editor
of this work has been asserted by him in accordance with the
Copyright, Designs and Patents Act 1988.

First published in Great Britain in 2013
by Gollancz
An imprint of the Orion Publishing Group
Orion House, 5 Upper St Martin's Lane,
London WC2H 9EA
An Hachette UK Company

This edition published in Great Britain in 2013 by Gollancz

1 3 5 7 9 10 8 6 4 2

A CIP catalogue record for this book
is available from the British Library

ISBN 978 0 575 13424 9

Typeset by Deltatype Ltd, Birkenhead, Merseyside

Printed and bound by CPI Group (UK) Ltd,
Croydon, CRO 4YY

The Orion Publishing Group's policy is to use papers that are
natural, renewable and recyclable products and made from wood
grown in sustainable forests. The logging and manufacturing
processes are expected to conform to the environmental
regulations of the country of origin.

www.georgerrmartin.com
www.orionbooks.co.uk
www.gollancz.co.uk

For Mike Fitzsimmons,
a good friend and a true fan

Editor's Note

Wild Cards is a work of fiction set in a completely imaginary world whose history parallels our own. Names, characters, places, and incidents depicted in *Wild Cards* are fictitious or are used fictitiously. Any resemblance to actual events, locales, or real persons, living or dead, is entirely coincidental. The works contained in this anthology are works of fiction; any writings referred to within these works are themselves fictional, and there is no intent to depict actual writers or to imply that any such persons have ever actually written or published the fictional essays, articles, or other works referred to in the works of fiction comprising this anthology.

NEW YORK CITY POLICE DEPARTMENT
5th Precinct
Officers and Support Staff
A Partial Listing

Deputy Inspector Thomas Jan Maseryk, commanding
Captain Chavvah Mendelberg, second

lieutenants (7)
Lieutenant Harvey Kant (joker)

sergeants (19)
Sergeant Jessica Penniman (SERGEANT SQUINCH), lockup, ace
Sergeant Homer Taylor (WINGMAN), desk, joker
Sergeant Vivian Choy (TIENYU), patrol, ace

detectives (6)
Leo Storgman (RAMSHEAD), Detective-Investigator, 1st Grade,
  joker
Michael Stevens, Detective-Investigator, 3rd Grade, nat
James McTate (SLIM JIM), Detective-Investigator, 3rd Grade, ace
Tenry Fong, Detective-Investigator, 2nd Grade, deuce
Joan Lonnegan (RAZOR JOAN), Detective-Investigator, 1st Grade,
  nat
Mitch Moore (SHADES), Detective-Investigator, 2nd Grade, deuce

uniformed patrol officers (123)
William Chen (TINKERBILL), deuce

Francis Xavier Black (FRANNY or ROOK), nat
Lawrence Bronkowski (BUGEYE), nat
Miranda Michaelson (RIKKI), joker
Anna Maria Rodriguez, nat
Van Tranh (DR. DILDO), ace
Benjamin Bester (BEASTIE), joker
Chey Moleka, nat
Sam Napperson (SNAP), nat
Anya Lee Tang, deuce
Lu Long (PUFF), joker
Angel Grady, nat

special details
Thomas Driscoll (TABBY), undercover, ace
Dina Quattore (K-10), K-9 detail, ace
Dr. Otto Gordon (GORDON THE GHOUL), forensic pathologist,
    joker

support personnel
Apsara Nai Chiangmai, file clerk, deuce
Joe Stevens, janitor, nat
Eddie Carmichael, consultant, sketch artist
Joe Mortiz (JOE TWITCH), sometime snitch

AUGUST

THE RAT RACE

by Cherie Priest

PART 1.

Leo braced the phone against his ear with his shoulder while he rubbed at his eyes and groaned. He muttered, 'Jesus Christ, not another one.'

'Another what?' asked the woman on the other end of the line. When he didn't reply fast enough, she demanded again, 'Another *what*, Dad?'

'Another streaker. Tinkerbill's bringing her in.'

The unclothed party in question was pretty, blond, and in her twenties. She was also glowing with a fizzy pink aura, but the aura couldn't be construed as clothing, and anyway, the sparkles had been Bill Chen's contribution. They'd wear off by morning. Probably.

Leo dropped the receiver away from his mouth and hollered past it, 'Somebody get that kid a shirt or something!'

Bill blindly grabbed a squad jacket off a coatrack as he ushered the protesting prisoner toward booking. He threw it over her shoulders but she almost shook it off when she turned around to tell him, 'You're making a mistake! I … I didn't just grab my keys and leave the house like this, you have to believe me!'

'I believe you.' Bill said it deadpan, with his peculiarly childish voice. Speech like that shouldn't issue from a man of his size and shape – six and a half feet from toes to cap, and wide as a fire-house door. He shuffled his beefy shoulders and shook his head, prodding the still mostly naked woman barefoot along the dirty floor of Manhattan's 5th precinct.

They don't call it 'Fort Freak' for nothing.

'Dad?'

Leo returned his attention to the phone and said, 'Melanie, I'm sorry, honey. You've caught me at work, here. You know how it is.'

'Oh, I understand. How can my pitch *possibly* compete with a room full of naked people?'

'Just one. One naked person.'

'Look, Dad. Quit putting this off.'

'But what if I don't want to move to ...' He fished around on his desk, looking for the brochure she'd sent him a week before. He found it buried beneath three or four unofficial 'in' stacks of reports, court documents, file notes, and case reminders. The paperwork drifts smothered everything, including the nameplate: DETECTIVE-INVESTIGATOR, 1ST GRADE: LEONARD STORGMAN.

His daughter impatiently supplied, 'West Palm Beach.'

'Yeah. Florida.' With the vibrant sales brochure finally in hand, he skimmed the tagline: *First planned adult community exclusively for jokers!* And he sighed. 'I know you've worked real hard, pulling this together, but I don't think I'm ready for an old folks' subdivision.'

Leo stuck a finger in his shirt collar. He pulled the sweat-dampened cloth loose and let it fall back against his neck. August's dank mugginess pressed inside the old building, and the precinct's vintage air conditioners valiantly wheezed and rattled, but did little else to address it. He nearly shuddered at the thought of such excessive warmth all year-round.

'You don't think you're ready to retire either.' Melanie's voice shifted, slipping from hard-nosed community planner to wheedling daughter in a snap. 'Dad, I wish you'd just think about it. Come down south! It's nice here, and *I* live here – and it would make me feel better to know you're nearby, in case something were to happen.'

'I'm turning sixty-two, not ninety-two. I'm not going to slip in the tub and break a hip.'

'I'm not trying to imply—'

He cut her off. 'Sweetheart, I know you're trying to help. But I don't need help yet. I need some time to think, and—' His end of the conversation derailed abruptly, distracted by a pair of swinging hips in a pencil skirt, spotted across the precinct floor. He mumbled, 'Hang on a second.'

The hips disappeared behind a column. It wasn't just the shape of the hips that had his attention; it was something about the gait of the walk, and the curve of the body. He knew that walk. He knew that body.

The woman emerged from the far side of the column, her backside facing him for a moment while she paused to speak to someone. Then she said, 'So long, David,' and turned around, and paused. She scanned the room.

Leo watched. He cataloged her like a piece of evidence.

Her hair was shorter now, and smoother, and a little darker – almost a true brunette. The full curve of her cleavage and the dip of her waist were a little more pronounced. One hand on her hip. One hand hanging at her side. Posture off-kilter, just enough to look casual.

Her big black sunglasses were identical to the ones he'd seen her wearing last, but that was twenty-five years ago. Funny, how styles come back around. Funny, how he would've known her anywhere, even after all this time.

The lens-covered eyes settled on him. The corner of her mouth crept up, pulled by a string of nostalgia until it'd drawn her lips into half a smile.

From the phone Leo heard: 'Dad?'

He said, 'Honey, I have to go.' He hung up. Slowly he stood, matching his rise to her approach – so by the time she was in front of his desk, he was on his feet. He said, 'Wanda?'

And she said, 'Leo.' Wanda Moretti pushed the sunglasses up onto her head, then changed her mind and folded them into her purse. 'Been a while, hasn't it?'

'Yeah. You, uh … you look great.'

'Thanks. You don't look so bad yourself.'

Leo Storgman did not often feel self-conscious. He'd had plenty of time to get used to his appearance – two decades since his card had turned. But he fidgeted now, scratching at the back of his sticky, wet neck, jostling the houndstooth newsboy cap he often wore. It sat comfortably between the thick horns that curled out from either side of his head.

'Aw, now. You don't … you don't have to say that. You haven't changed a bit – not a goddamn day. We both know I can't say the same.'

'I didn't say you hadn't *changed*. I just said you didn't look bad.' She didn't bother to hide her appraising gaze. 'I'd heard, and I'd wondered. But you still look like *you*.'

'Eh. Wasn't born looking like *this*.' He made a little gesture with his hands, displaying the way they'd become bone-white, almost translucent except for the scum-green liver spots that speckled his knuckles. Similar patches blotched across his mostly bald head, right down into the ring of graying hair that held his hat like a nest. 'But it could be worse.'

He was careful to pin his eyes to hers, if only to keep from looking over her shoulder, or over his own shoulder at the crowded, chaotic room. Many of his fellow civil servants had drawn much stranger and worse transformations.

By the soda machine stood beat cop Rikki Michaelson, a small, greyhound-shaped woman using her slender, pawlike hand to press for a Dr Pepper. Leaning against the wall beside her was Lu Long, with the bulky, elaborate head and upper torso of a Chinese dragon. He was wrestling with the tab of a Pepsi can, his heavily clawed fingers ill-suited to the delicate task. And beside the captain's office door Leo spied public defender Charles Herriman, his prosthetic hands wrestling with his latest case files. It almost looked like he had the situation under control, until his cell phone rang and the juggling act fell apart.

Wanda reached for the back of the chair that faced Leo's desk and asked, 'You mind if I sit down?' Without waiting for him to respond, she took the chair and settled into it, putting her purse and an expensive-looking leather satchel on the floor by her feet.

'For old times' sake?' he asked.

'For old times' sake, sure. And official business too – something weird, that's for damn sure. But to tell you the truth, I didn't know if I'd find you here. Couldn't remember exactly how old you are.'

'Still have five months on the clock.'

'I hope they're an easy five months. I'd hate to see you go out with a bang.'

'Easy. Sure.' He glowered mournfully at the drifts of paperwork and loose filing, and told her, 'This week alone we've got streakers, inconveniently coincidental burglaries, and an uptick in the usual gang bullshit. The Werewolves and the Demon Princes never did get along, but it's getting nasty out there.'

Wanda shook her head and sighed. 'You remember that case back in, oh, I don't know. Must've been '89 or '90. That gangbang-ing joker who got real high and then ate somebody's poodle?'

Leo let out a short bark of a laugh. 'Yeah, I remember it. Haven't thought of it in years. Did you do the court-reporting on that case?'

She said, 'No, wasn't me. I was gone by then.'

'I heard you got married again.' He'd heard she'd married *up*.

'Yeah, back in '88, but it didn't stick. And I left court-reporting, too. Went into real estate instead.'

'Like you always said you would. I remember you talking about it, but I didn't know you'd gone off and done it.'

She grinned. 'Got my license and started moving houses, condos, what have you. It worked out better than sitting around a courtroom, tapping till my fingers were raw. Kept the kids fed better, too.'

'How're they doing, anyway?'

'Grown, mostly. Moved out, thank God, all four of them. What about your daughter?'

'Melanie.' He cocked his head at the phone. 'That was her, just now. She's gotten into community development planning.' He picked up the flyer again and handed it to her.

Wanda said, 'Hmm. Jokers only. That might have its perks. Or drawbacks.'

'I don't know what to make of it yet. Mellie wants me to move down there, closer to her. Once my time's up here, you know.'

Wanda hadn't lowered the flyer yet. She looked at him over the top of it and asked in a very pointed fashion, 'Just *you*?'

Leo cleared his throat and reclaimed the flyer. 'Just me. Vicki ...' It was strange, saying his wife's name. 'Vicki died of breast cancer back in '98.'

Wanda said, 'Oh, God, Leo. I'm sorry to hear that,' like she meant it.

Wanda had never been the jealous type, as far as Leo knew. And that one ill-advised night they'd shared back in the old days ... it'd never gone anywhere. Vicki had never found out about it either, a fact that Leo considered one of the sole earthly evidences that there might be a God.

Leo said, 'Sometimes it feels like she died a million years ago, and sometimes I forget, and start pouring her a cup of coffee in the morning.' His wife had been good to him – better than he'd deserved. Even when his card turned, all she had to say was, 'I didn't marry you for your looks. I won't leave you for them either.' He changed the subject. 'What really brings you out here, Wanda? It's been a long time.'

'Like I said – partly for old times' sake. And partly' – she reached down to that leather satchel and pulled it into her lap – 'this.' She lifted the flap and drew out an envelope. From it, she extracted thirty or forty singed sheets and spread them out on the desk in a loose, brittle stack. 'Pardon the smell.'

'What am I looking at? Besides burned paper?'

'Transcripts, or pieces of them. From an old case, somewhere between '75 and '79. Most of these are waterlogged or burned beyond usefulness, but the clerk at the courthouse saw *this* and they called me.' She pointed at a corner, where a blue pencil had scrawled 'WM.'

'Your initials.'

'My initials. Other than that, you can only read a little bit, here and there. They asked me if I could tell what case they're from.'

Leo looked up from her initials to ask, 'They don't know?' But before she could answer, he had another one lined up. 'Were these damaged last week, in that courthouse fire?'

'You got it. The fire didn't do much damage, but it made a real mess. And look.' She pulled another sheet forward, and pointed at a string of letters that stood out among the other lines of smudged, smeared, water-destroyed print. 'Right here. I'm pretty sure that says "Detective Storgman." So I was hoping you could help me answer their question – maybe recognize something I'm missing.'

'Huh,' he said, peering down at the document. 'I think you're right. Then this is probably a case from '79. I didn't make detective until December of '78.'

'Okay, that's helpful. Narrows the window quite a bit.'

Leo touched the fragile pages gently, scooting them around with the tip of his finger and hunting for places where the words were not burned or washed away. 'It's hard to tell. Except.' He used his pinky to point at a spot that wasn't very clear. 'You see this part?'

Wanda came forward and craned her neck around, leaning in a way that set her breasts right at Leo's eye level. He struggled not to notice.

'Right here. It says "Augustus."' Then he wondered aloud, 'What the hell was that kid's first name? I remember it was fucking ridiculous.' He snapped his fingers. 'Bernard. Bernard Augustus.'

'It's not ringing a bell,' Wanda said dubiously.

'Because nobody ever called him that. Everyone called him Deedle.' Leo leaned back in his chair and folded his hands behind his head. Wanda sat back in her seat too, which was a goddamn shame.

She said, 'Deedle. Now *that* I remember.'

He bounced slowly, thoughtfully, in the chair. 'These must be the trial transcripts from the Rathole murders.'

Wanda shook her head. 'No, they wouldn't be trial docs. It's coming back to me now. That kid never made it to trial. These are more likely from an arraignment hearing.'

'Yeah, you're right, come to think of it. He escaped.'

'Not for long.' She put her hand up to her face as if to lean on it, but nibbled gently at her thumbnail.

'No, not for long.' He paused, still thinking. 'That was one hell of a case. My first murder, and I was wrong – it wasn't '79. It was the tail end of '78.'

Wanda considered this for a moment, and said thoughtfully, 'You know, those files were all about to be moved out of hard copy storage and scanned onto CDs. They were going to be dredged up for the first time in decades, before they burned.'

Leo said, 'So?'

'So, they were going to be *read*. Dr. Pretorius has a whole new class of happy young lawyer wannabes who were set to scan this old stuff for class credit. And some of the more interesting cases would come to the classroom for teaching materials. History of joker law, such as it's been.'

'This is all that's left?' he asked, indicating the soot-flaking papers.

'Might as well be. But I couldn't help thinking, when the clerk was going on about the fire, how amazingly convenient it was – just *these* years, right where a group of eager young proto-lawyers were supposed to go digging.'

Leo stopped bouncing and gathered up the brittle papers. He handed the small stack back to her. 'What are you getting at?' he asked, as if he couldn't tell.

She began the task of stuffing them carefully back into the envelope. 'All I'm saying is, maybe the Rathole's worth another look. Another *quick* look,' she specified. 'Don't you have a cold case unit around here, or something?'

'The Rathole's not a cold case. It's closed. A credible suspect was arrested—'

She interrupted, 'A *convenient* suspect. Who then conveniently died.'

'He was good for it.'

'Maybe he only *looked* good for it. And you still have five months left on the clock.' She looked so eager, there in her fitted suit with her legs crossed at the knees.

But Leo said, 'Wanda, it's been thirty years. Everybody who isn't dead has forgotten everything important. I'm glad I could help, but don't get worked up about the Rathole now. It's a waste of time.'

THE ROOK

by Melinda M. Snodgrass

I find the first day of anything tough – first day of school, first day of camp, first day of the year. My tendency is to view the unknown future more with trepidation than joy. And now I could add to that list the first day of work.

As I walked toward New York's 5th precinct, a hot, muggy wind off the East River sent trash scurrying down the gutters and wafted to me the scent of garbage rotting in black plastic sacks awaiting pickup. Abandoning me, the wind raced on to seize the American flag on the front of the station house, gripped it, and set it twisting and snapping like a maddened whip.

The four-story building that housed law enforcement for the part of New York City known as Jokertown was pale stone and it came right up to the edge of the sidewalk. There were a handful of parking spaces out front, but they were filled, and it made me glad I hadn't bothered to bring down my car from Saratoga. To either side of the precinct rose two redbrick buildings that were both taller and wider; it left the cop shop looking like a short guy squeezed between burly longshoremen.

I held my hat against a particularly strong gust of wind and picked up the pace. Not just because I wanted out of the heat, but because I wanted to be early. I opened the door, then paused for one brief moment to savor the moment. My dad had worked here. Been captain of this precinct. Died at his desk on a particularly chaotic Wild Card Day that is now in the history books. I had never known John Francis Xavier Black. He died four months before I was born, but his picture is everywhere in my mother's house upstate, and I'd heard the stories from one of his detectives, Sam Altobelli. And now I was about to walk in his footsteps.

Are you proud of me, Dad? I hope you're wa—

I lost the rest of the thought and my hat when I was shoved violently from behind.

'Jesus fucking Christ, get out of the way.'

My hands and knees, rather than my face, met the stained linoleum floor, and I flinched as a pair of size thirteen, thick-soled, metal-toed shoes stepped over me. I tried to regain my feet, but was knocked down again by the long scaled tail that dragged behind my assailant.

Regaining my feet, I tapped the broad shoulder. The back of his head was weirdly misshapen and scaled like the tail. 'Excuse me,' I said.

'This time,' a deep baritone grunted back.

This time I closed my hand on one beefy bicep. 'No, you owe *me* the apology.'

The man turned. I braced myself for what I would see, but I didn't brace enough. I ended up taking a step back. What faced me was a dragon.

He was also a cop. The tail and the head had sort of distracted me from noticing the blue uniform. Great, I was about to start my first day on the job in a fight (hopefully verbal) with a fellow officer.

It was shift change, so the room was bustling. The desk sergeant stood up, and was patting the air in a soothing gesture. Moving his arms caused his drooping and faded brown batwings to jerk too, but he wasn't exactly leaping or flying to my aid. The night-shift cops, now in civvies, paused in their rush for the door. It might be the end to their 'day,' but a fight was always worth a delay.

Day-shift cops were pushing in behind me. One of them – a man with a shock of orange-red hair, the red-veined nose of a drinker, and a missing ear – slapped the dragon man on the shoulder and said, 'Kick the rook's ass, Puff.'

So much for the verbal thing. Maybe I could take him if I fought dirty. I glanced from the grinning razorlike teeth to the clawed hands that were clenching and flexing in preparation, and I had the feeling that he knew more about dirty fighting than I could ever hope to learn.

'Guys, guys, what's going on?' came a basso rumble from behind me.

I risked a glance and found myself staring at a horror. He had to be pushing seven feet tall, with a wolf's snout, bear claws at the end of arms so long they dragged the ground, and bull horns thrusting out of the forehead. And fur.

I was starting to feel like a minnow in a shark pool.

'Dumb-ass was standing in the door blockin' the way,' my nemesis growled. 'I thought he needed a lesson in manners, and now he thinks *I* oughta apologize.'

I found myself gripped in a one-armed man-hug by the furry, horned, giant muppet-thing. 'Hey, give the kid a break. He was probably just gettin' his bearings.' He gave me a little shake. 'Right?'

I looked up and realized the brown eyes on either side of the snout and fangs were warm and very kind. I nodded; it was as good an explanation as any, and it might keep a bad situation from turning into complete shit.

'Aw, Beastie, ever the peacemaker,' said a redheaded woman. Her shoes were polished mirror bright, and her pants crease could have provided a shave. She patted the dragon on the shoulder. 'Lu, it's not the kid's fault you're hungover. Come on, we're going to be late.'

Everyone started to move again. Dragon guy fell into step with the one-eared guy and the redhead and threw back over his shoulder, 'Next time you see me, Rook, step aside.'

'Come on, kid, let's get you to the briefing. Don't wanna be late on your first day.'

'Thank you, Officer …' I let my voice trail away suggestively.

'Bester. Benjamin Bester, but everyone calls me Beastie. You can too. It's great not to be the rookie anymore.'

'Glad I could oblige.' I followed after him, past the winged desk sergeant and up the stairs. 'Who's my other rescuer?' I asked, with a nod toward the redhead.

'Angel Grady, Puff's ... sorry, *Lu Long*'s partner. She'll be captain before she's forty. She's awesome. The other guy is Thomas Driscoll ... Tabby. He works undercover.'

'That can't last long. He's pretty distinctive-looking.'

'No, no, he doesn't go undercover like that. He turns into a cat.'

'Oh,' I said, faintly, as we topped the stairs and entered the squad room.

More chaos there. Phones were ringing, people were talking. Depressed-looking suspects in handcuffs were seated at a few desks while uniformed cops and plainclothes detectives pecked at the dirty keyboards of ancient computers. One old guy had ram's horns growing out of his skull. At the back of the room were two glassed-in offices for the precinct brass. I wondered if things had been remodeled since 1986. They must have been. Somebody would have noticed if my dad had died at his desk in a glass office.

Clashing odors swirled through the room. In addition to gun oil, sweat, and vomit there was the distinctive burnt-nuts smell of very old coffee and very fresh donuts in the air. My stomach gave a growl. I had been too nervous to eat breakfast. *Maybe this is how cops become a cliché*, I thought. I longed to go in search of the donuts, but instead followed Beastie into the briefing room.

Beat cops were settling into chairs. Behind the podium was a middle-aged Asian woman with an oval face and worried dark eyes. Her name tag said CHOY. Behind her was a large and detailed map of Jokertown and a bit of Chinatown where the two intersected. There were wanted posters and updates from the FBI, SCARE, and other law enforcement agencies.

I took a chair in the back. I'd drawn enough attention for one day. The sergeant began the briefing. I took out my iPhone and began taking notes.

'Mr. Lee reports that somebody's been entering his fish market and eating just the mussels and the clams. He comes in every morning to find empty shells. Tabby, maybe you could offer some insight?' The Asian woman looked over at him.

'Love to,' Driscoll drawled.

'Just don't get distracted banging the alley cats, Tabby,' a short, skinny Asian man called. Laughter sputtered through the crowd.

A middle finger flipped up, and Tabby shot back, 'Unlike you, Dildo, I can do more than two things at once.'

More laughter, quickly extinguished when Choy said, 'Okay, okay, moving on. The turf war between the Werewolves and the Demon Princes is heating up. Some of those guys are better armed than us, so *be careful*. And we've got a purse snatcher operating between Elizabeth and Orchard. Keep an eye out, and for God's sake kick your lazy asses into gear and run him down. The store owners are complaining that it's hurting the tourist trade.'

'Are we ever gonna get those Segways?' asked a cop who was busy brushing powdered sugar off the shelf of his belly. I could see why he wanted one of the two-wheeled personal transports.

'In a word … no,' said the sergeant.

'Ah, damn. Then can I get a car?'

'No.'

The new mayor had taken many of New York's Finest out of patrol cars and put them back on foot or on bicycles. He thought it improved community outreach when the police had to walk among the citizens they were supposed to be protecting. I thought he had a point, which is why I had decided to take an apartment in Jokertown. My mother hadn't liked it, and I admit some of my neighbors left me queasy, but all the research indicated that when cops lived where they worked conditions in a neighborhood improved. And when I had been in law school there'd been a lot of discussion about breaking the cycle of gang membership leading to jail, returning to the gang—

'… Black? Is Black here?'

I have this tendency to become fascinated with some thought, and miss what was going on around me. Hence I missed my name being called. I scrambled awkwardly to my feet while thrusting my hand into the air. 'Here. Here. I'm here.'

'Okay, Bill, he's all yours,' said Choy, addressing an absolutely enormous Asian man in the front row.

He stood and peered back at me. I gaped. He looked like an Easter Island statue. He shook his head with its thick mop of jet-black hair and said, 'How did I get so lucky?'

I choked on a laugh. The voice that emerged from that massive body was a ridiculous high-pitched squeak.

'You think his voice is funny, wait till you get a load of his power,' the woman next to me whispered. Her name tag read QUATTORE. Curling black hair brushed her shoulders, and I couldn't help but notice her impressive rack.

At the same time Tabby grunted, ''Cause you're such a fucking sterling example to us all.' My new partner glared at Tabby.

There appeared to be a story there. I just didn't want to become part of it.

'Okay,' Choy broke in again. 'Go out there and catch bad guys.'

There was much scraping of chairs, coughs, and conversations as the cops headed for the door. Bill walked to me. I craned my neck to look up at him, and I'm five feet ten.

'Bill Chen,' he said, and thrust out his hand.

I watched mine disappear into his paw. 'Francis Black.'

'Okay, Franny, stick by me. Keep your mouth shut. Learn something.'

'I go by Frank,' I said. 'And I thought that's what I did at the Academy?'

'Oh, no, no, no, no, no. That was bullshit. *This* is Jokertown.'

It was indeed Jokertown. Bill's beat encompassed most of the famous tourist attractions – the Famous Jokertown Dime Museum, the strip club Freakers, the line of mask and cloak shops on Hester. Interspersed among them were Starbucks stores and – most incongruous of all – a new Hyatt Hotel.

The sidewalks were crowded, worse than even normal Manhattan. Joker body shapes aren't exactly human normal, and many jokers require additional help to get around. So the sidewalks were also clogged with wheelchairs, four-wheeled carts, and other unique forms of conveyance. At one point Bill stepped casually through the scrabbling eight legs of a giant spider topped with the head and torso of an old woman scrabbling down the sidewalk. Bill acknowledged her with his baton. 'Morning, Arachne.'

'Hi, Bill,' the spider-woman responded.

I didn't trust myself not to tread on one of Arachne's legs so I stepped off into the gutter to walk past her.

'First day on the job?' the old woman asked.

I stopped. 'Uh, does it show that bad?' I tried to look at the human face, look the woman in the eyes, but my eyes kept flicking back to the spiky hairs protruding from the spider body, the eight legs culminating in pincers.

She chuckled. 'Yes, you look poleaxed.'

'Franny, come on,' Bill bellowed. I ducked my head at Arachne and hurried to catch up.

Bill strode along, nightstick swinging in the rhythm of his walk.

'Isn't it a little threatening to be carrying your stick? All you'd have to do is slap your palm with it, and you'd be a perfect cliché,' I said.

'It's how I access my power, kid. When I want a critique of my policing style I won't be asking you.'

'Sorry.'

A big hand closed on my shoulder. 'That's okay. At least you have the sense when to climb down. So many of us are macho assholes. Even the girls.'

'So, what is your power?'

'The day is young. I'm sure you'll see before it's over.'

'I noticed that every pairing seems to be a joker and a nat, or an ace and a nat,' I said.

'Precinct policy. Pair a nat and a wild card whenever possible.'

We made a stop at a newsstand at the corner of Hester and the Bowery. An incredibly wide man with blue-black skin and tusks protruding from his mouth was selling a *Times*, a *Newsweek*, and an *Economist* to a multiarmed, multieyed joker. After the joker skittered away on what seemed to be a million centipedelike legs, the proprietor leaned on the weather-worn counter. He and Bill slapped palms and bumped fists. Then Bill asked, 'What's the word, Jube?'

'Pretty quiet.'

'Well that won't last,' Bill said.

'Hey,' said Jube, 'I got a new one. A joker, a priest, and a rabbi are in a lifeboat ...'

But I was thinking about Bill's last comment and didn't hear the joke. It was August. In a month, on the fifteenth of September, Jokertown was going to bust out in a celebration that was half Mardi Gras, half St. Patrick's Day, and half riot: Wild Card Day. For me it was the anniversary of my dad's death.

Bill groaned. 'That was terrible. You need a new writer.' Then added in his absurd voice, 'Let me introduce my new partner. Franny, meet Jubal. He's been watching the world go by from this newsstand, for what? Forty years?'

'Close enough. I don't want to actually count them up.' A broad hand thrust toward me. We shook, and Jube looked closely at my nameplate that read F. X. BLACK. 'There was an F. X. Black at the 5th twenty-five years ago. Any relation?'

The words emerged from between my teeth like pulled taffy. 'Yeah, my dad.'

Bill was staring at me and I felt heat rising up the back of my neck. Mercifully we were interrupted by yelling.

'You ugly son of a bitch! I gave you a goddamn fifty, and you gave me back change for a twenty. I don't fucking *think* so.'

Across the street and on the corner, people swirled like water circling a drain, attracted by the altercation at the pretzel cart. Bill and I plunged between parked cars and into the street. Bill held up his stick like Moses exhorting the waves, and lo and behold, all the traffic stopped.

A red-faced nat dressed in shorts, tennis shoes with calf-high socks, and a green polo shirt that strained across his belly screamed into the masked face of a joker. 'You're a goddamn crook, you fuckin' freak.'

The small joker seemed to be shriveling beneath the barrage of words and profanity. His face might be hidden, but folds of skin sagged down his neck like wattles on a turkey, and the same dangling folds festooned his arms, visible because of his short-sleeved shirt.

'Okay, let's all just calm down. Now what seems to be the problem?' Bill said. It's the standard cop line, and usually presented in an all-knowing tone. Bill's high-pitched voice rather undercut the effect. His bulk made up for it.

'I gave this guy a fifty, and he only gave me change for a twenty,' the tourist repeated, at a much lower volume.

'I didn't,' the joker whined.

'Open your cash box,' Bill said.

I gulped. If the joker refused we'd be forced to get a warrant. But he didn't. And I checked off lesson number one. It never hurts to ask. Cops are intimidating, people usually agree and you avoid the warrant. I could just imagine how Dr. Pretorius, my constitutional law professor at Columbia, would react to my conclusion.

There was no fifty in the cash box. I decided I needed to start acting like a cop and investigate. 'How much for a pretzel?' I asked.

'Buck twenty-nine with tax. Buck sixty-seven if you want cheese. He wanted cheese.'

I looked up at Bill who was glaring at me. I took a breath to help quiet the quivering that had hit my gut and said, 'Nobody pays for a dollar sixty-seven pretzel with a fifty-dollar bill.' I peered into the cash box. 'And he ...' I indicated the joker. 'Would have cleaned out his cash if he'd tried.'

'Which is why he just pocketed my money,' the tourist blustered.

Bill looked from one to the other. Suddenly he unlimbered the cuffs and spun the joker around.

Back at the station Mr. Kuzlovsky had recovered his fifty-dollar bill, the pushcart vendor was in a cell, and I was feeling really, really stupid. After the arrest Bill had patted down the joker, and found the fifty tucked away in the drooping folds of skin around his belly. Bill was laboriously typing up a report using a one-fingered hunt and peck method, and he sensed my embarrassment. He looked up, and his expression was kind.

'Don't worry about it, Rook. Just don't let pity cloud your judgment. And don't overcompensate by assuming innocence just because they've been afflicted and you find them disgusting.'

My new partner was turning out to be frighteningly astute. I decided not to insult us both by denying it. 'I'd quibble with the word choice, but I am finding this harder than I expected,' I said. 'I took an apartment down here so I could try to see the neighborhood as just a neighborhood.'

'That's good. And now you gotta see jokers as people. Which means like most people they're shits.'

I dropped into a chair, and shifted my nightstick and handcuffs so they weren't digging me in the kidneys. 'That's a damn depressing attitude.'

Bill shrugged. 'Just being realistic. We're cops, which means we see the bad, not the good.' He flashed me a grin. 'Cheer up. In a week you'll assume everybody's lying.'

'Great.' I sighed and looked away.

'What else is bothering you?' I was beginning to wonder if Bill's power was telepathy.

'I'm worried that searching a physical deformity qualifies as a strip search. If it does we should have gotten a warrant.'

Bill stopped typing and leaned back in his chair. It creaked ominously. 'You one of those annoying armchair shysters?'

I stared into that broad face and for one cowardly moment considered lying. 'No, I'm an actual shyster.'

'Oh, fuck. That's just great.' He shoved back from the desk, the wheels on his chair chattering across the floor. 'Well, that probably means you can type. Be my guest.' And he stomped away toward the break room. It looked like the bonding moment was definitely over. As I settled down behind the computer I figured the word would be all over the precinct by shift change.

We were back on the street by 10:30 A.M. We broke up a fight outside Squishers Basement at 11:15. The combatants were about sixteen sheets to the wind. As I stepped back, panting and rubbing my upper arm where one of the drunks had landed an ill-aimed punch, I found myself yelling at the bartender who had come outside to observe the fight.

'What the hell time do you open? Or did you ever close? Unless you've got a special license you better have closed at 4:00 A.M.'

Bill slapped me on the back. 'They serve "food."' He put air quotes around the word. 'Which means they can open at ten, and he makes a great hangover remedy.'

After the drunks were sent back to lockup I realized I was famished. Bill was hungry too, so we hit a local diner for burgers. I made the mistake of ordering mine with guacamole and blue cheese. For the next hour I got to listen to Bill talk about my 'yuppie burger,' and I was revising my opinion of his empathy. I checked my watch. It was 1:20 and I had a headache blossoming behind my eyes.

A stir on the sidewalk again drew my attention. I was starting to distrust anything that disrupted the smooth flow of bodies through the canyons of Manhattan. There were youthful male hoots and catcalls.

An old man's voice with a decidedly Yiddish accent quavered out, 'You're a bunch of *pigs*. Just *pigs*.'

This time I led the way toward the altercation, pushed through the crowd, and found a naked woman. She was young, and trying to cover herself with a forearm across her breasts and a hand in front of her crotch. Her arms sported some interesting Oriental ideograph tattoos along with the usual punk girl hearts and skulls. The only other thing on her body, aside from a mop of untidy jet-black hair, was a nose stud flashing in the autumn sunlight. Her cheeks were bright red with embarrassment.

A wolf whistle cut the air followed by, 'Hey, baby, great ass!'

'Oh, bugger off!' she shouted back. The accent was British.

I held up a hand and said authoritatively (I hoped), 'Okay, nothing to see here, move along.' The minute the words emerged I winced because right on cue some wags in the crowd delivered a one-two punch.

'*What?* Are you *gay*?'

'Like hell there isn't.'

There was a clerk from a mask and cloak shop gawking. I shouted at him, 'Bring her a cloak.' He hustled off. I turned to the girl. 'Okay. What are you protesting? Fur? World hunger? The mayor?'

'Listen, Mr. Policeman – if you are a policeman, and not a park-keeper or something – *I* didn't do a thing. I was just walking along, minding my own business when suddenly—' She gestured down the length of her body. 'I'd like to report a robbery.'

The clerk returned with a cloak that the young woman flung around her shoulders and pulled tightly closed to a chorus of disappointed 'Oooh's' from the onlookers.

'Well, that's a new one,' I said. I unlimbered my handcuffs.

'You're arresting *me*!?' Hazel eyes flashed fury.

'Indecent exposure.'

Bill arrived, his bulk scattering the crowd like a polar bear through a seal colony. 'Hold on there, Rook.'

'My clothes just—'

'Vanished. Yeah, I know,' Bill interrupted. He said to me, 'Women have been losing their clothes almost daily. We figure it's some ace perv, but we haven't got a line on him yet. So question some of these pervs.' He raked the crowd with a jaundiced eye. Men started drifting away.

'Hey, hold it,' I yelled, but a lot of them vanished into the bustling crowds. I questioned the few I'd corralled while listening to Bill and the girl's conversation. Now that I realized she wasn't a criminal it had begun to penetrate that she was really cute.

'What's your name, miss?' Bill asked.

'Abigail Baker.'

'What do you do?'

'*I* am an *actress*.'

'Look, we need you to come down to the precinct and make a statement.'

'I have no clothes.'

'We'll give you a jumpsuit.'

'Wonderful. I'll look like a criminal. And what do I do in the meantime?'

Bill called out to the shop owner. 'Hey, Jeannie, we're gonna borrow the cloak for a few hours, okay?'

'Clean it before you bring it back,' Jeannie called.

Abigail's mouth formed an 'O' of outrage, and she emitted a sound like a furious kitten. 'I would *prefer* to return home.'

'And I would *prefer* you come to the precinct.'

◆

'... it was involuntary public nudity.'

We were in an interrogation room. Abigail was making an orange prison jumpsuit look almost attractive. She wore a pair of flip-flops that Sergeant Penniman had pulled out of her locker, and was sipping a Diet Coke. Bill was asking questions and I was taking notes.

She peered down her nose at me and said, 'Involuntary. That's I ... N ... V ...'

Bill choked on a laugh. I felt the top of my ears getting warm. 'I know how to spell "involuntary." I went to law school.'

'Oh, how interesting? As what?'

'As a student!'

Bill restored the peace by asking, 'Okay, where do you live?' She gave an address on the southern edge of Jokertown. Bill leaned back and studied her. 'They pretty much cater to students. I thought you said you were an actress?'

Abigail blushed, and took a quick sip of soda. 'Well, I am ... almost. I'm just finishing up a few classes at the New York School of Performing Arts. But I'm understudying a major role at the Bowery Repertory.'

'Oh, so you're a wannabe actress,' I said.

'And you're a failed barrister.'

'I *chose* to be a police officer,' I began.

'Franny, go get me a soda.' He handed me a dollar bill. 'An orange. And while you're at it ask Apsara for the victim report form.'

I left, grumbling. That girl had really gotten under my skin. I had to ask the old ram's horn detective how to find the file room.

He gave me a very tedious set of exact directions, and I headed there.

Watching too many cop dramas had given me a sense of what a file clerk should look like. An old, male, potbellied, maybe retired cop. What met me was a vision out of an Asian film. The girl looked very young, and she was flat-out gorgeous. Jet-black hair that hung past her ass, skin like honey, an amazing figure. I tried to moisten my lips, but my mouth had gone Sahara dry. 'I need … I need …'

'Yes, officer?' Her voice was like bells. 'What *do* you need?' Long lashes briefly veiled the laughter in her eyes.

'Victim's report form.'

'All right.' I watched her go swaying away to a filing cabinet.

Her path led her past a strange little ornately carved wooden house with a gold leaf roof. I realized I'd seen similar styles in Thai restaurants.

She returned with a couple of sheets of paper. 'I'm Apsara Nai Chiangmai. You're new. What's your name?'

'Fran—' My voice squeaked. I coughed and tried again. 'Francis Black.'

'Francis,' she said slowly, making my name into a song. 'That's a nice name. I like the feel of that on my tongue.' She did that thing with her lashes again, and I thought about cold showers.

'Thank you,' I muttered, and grabbed the papers and headed for the door.

'Come by anytime,' she called.

'Okay,' I gasped.

As I left I thought I heard a cranky old man's voice saying her name in that parent tone that tells you you've really fucked up.

I found the soda machine, bought Bill's orange beverage, and got myself a Coke. I didn't open it right away. Instead I rolled the cold can across my forehead. Having regained control over my anatomy I went back into the interrogation room.

It wasn't deliberate, I hadn't planned it, but I happened to be at the front door when Abigail headed out. She was still in the jumpsuit.

'Do you need a taxi?' I had to clear my throat to get out the last word.

'You might notice that I no longer have a purse, which means I have no money, so no.'

'Uh … right … I could loan you …'

She walked past me, heading for the door. I hurried to open it for her.

'Uh … look … I'm new in town, and you're … foreign, maybe we could have dinner … tonight …' At her expression I modified the statement. 'Sometime?'

'Are you on crack? No!'

The door closed behind her and I heard Sergeant Taylor (whose nickname was Wingman, I had learned) give a snort of laughter. 'You gotta work on your timing, Franny,' he said.

2:10. Back on the street. Bill gave a warning to a panhandling joker whose gig was to offer to wash the windshields of cars waiting at stoplights. He looked like a big octopus from the waist down, and he had an interesting pitch. If the driver was polite and gave him a dollar, the joker would heave his bulk onto the roof of the car, and with a shammy in each of his nine tentacles (I don't know why he had nine tentacles, but he did), he would proceed to wash all the windows on the car. If the driver was rude he still heaved himself onto the roof of the car, but this time he inked all the windows.

As we walked away I asked, 'So, why does he just get a warning?'

'Because Arms washes the captain's car.'

'Maseryk?' I had heard about Maseryk from Altobelli. He described him as a military flat-topped, hard-ass straight arrow. I couldn't mesh that image with him getting free car washes from a joker.

'No, Mendelberg.'

'Ah.' The other captain of the 5th was a joker. It was beginning to look like jokers stuck together. Bill again appeared to read my mind.

'Arms is bipolar. He can't really hold a job. Washing police cars is the only steady pay he gets.'

'Ah,' I said again. 'How long does it take, acquiring this' – I gestured around – 'I guess you'd call it area knowledge?'

'I've been in this precinct for five years, three years before that at the 13th. But I grew up in Chinatown near the 5th. I've got a pretty good handle on J-Town, and in Chinatown I know practically everybody.'

'That isn't very encouraging. I'm going to be ready to retire before I get to know people.'

'Assuming you stick. You strike me as the type to end up down at One Police Plaza at headquarters.'

I watched his broad back, and resolved that wouldn't happen. Then I realized that was probably exactly what my rabbi, Sam Altobelli, was planning. And if I really did want to follow in my dad's footsteps and make captain I was going to have to play the political game. I followed morosely in Bill's wake because I was back to questioning the motivations that had led to this career.

I was a Columbia law school graduate. I had passed the New York State bar. I hadn't been law review material, I was never going to end up in a white-shoe law firm, but I had been in the top third of my class, I could have found a good job. But I wanted to make a difference. Help people.

So, become a public defender, or work for an environmental non-profit, said that inner voice that sounded suspiciously like a cross between my mother and my college advisor.

I will, I promised them. *If this doesn't work out.*

I was deep in thoughtful contemplation of my navel, watching the cracks in the sidewalk, when Bill's radio crackled to life. 'Bill, one of my pooches spotted our purse snatcher. He's running west on Broome over near the Dumpling House.'

'Thanks, K-10, we're on it.'

Bill took off running. I grabbed at my stick and cuffs to keep them from battering my kidney and took off after him. We came around a corner onto Broome and I heard a woman screaming. I had a fleeting glimpse of a young man clutching a large red leather handbag and running as if all the hounds of hell were on his heels.

We gave chase. Bill might be big, but I ran track in college, and the perp was motivated. We had soon pulled well ahead of Bill. The purse snatcher grabbed the corner of a brownstone and spun himself into an alley. I made the turn, and a garbage can came crashing and banging toward me, depositing its odiferous load at my feet. I slipped on a combination of rotting potato peels and plastic wrap. I managed not to face plant, but one hand and one knee dropped into the oozing garbage.

'Yuck.' I bounded up and ran on, trying to shake the garbage off my hand.

The alley ended at a chain-link fence. The purse snatcher had slung the purse over his shoulder and was swarming up the wire. I heard Bill behind me. He was roaring something, but the blood was pounding in my ears, and I couldn't quite hear him between the slap of my feet on pavement and the shaking and chattering of the fence.

I leaped up, gripped the metal, and started to climb. The perp looked back and kicked at me. I yanked my head away just in time, and his foot just hit my shoulder. I was starting to get royally pissed. I lunged and managed to grasp the purse where it bounced on his skinny ass.

I heard Bill whistling as I yanked at the strap. The purse snatcher gave a wail of despair as he tumbled off the fence. I lost my grip and fell too … and realized we were both surrounded by a bright pink aura filled with sparks and floating stars.

'I *told* you to get out of the way,' Bill said.

I slammed the door of my locker and batted irritably at the stars floating in front of my face. I was now, intimately, familiar with Bill's 'power.' There were snorts of laughter from Beastie Bester and Van Tranh, aka Dr. Dildo. 'How long is this going to last? And you better not say forever.'

''Bout six hours.'

'Great. I'll see you tomorrow.'

The route to the front door from the locker room took me past the file room. The incredibly sexy Asian girl giggled, and peered at me from behind the curtain of her ass-length black hair. Apsara, that was her name. I had picked up some forms from her while we were booking Abigail, and had thought I'd ask her out. Now she thought I was a dork, and that was never going to happen. Feeling incredibly sorry for myself, I proceeded to the front door and emerged onto the darkening street. Ten hours ago I had stepped through this door feeling like anything could happen.

Unfortunately that had turned out to be true.

◆

Halfway home a heavy hand descended on my shoulder, and suddenly I was kissing the soot-stained brick wall of a building. 'Okay, you're under arrest.'

'I'm a cop,' I mumbled against the rough surface.

'What's that, scum?'

'*I'm a cop!*' I shouted.

'Yeah, and I'm the pope.'

'My badge is in my left breast pocket.'

Rough hands jerked me around and dove into my pocket and emerged with my badge and ID. I was facing a hideous joker. He had bulging eyes, a unibrow that made his forehead seem even more shelflike, a bullet-shaped head that looked like one side had been smacked with an iron skillet, and all of this crowned with spiky gray hair that looked more akin to a warthog's bristles than human hair.

Standing next to him was a strange-looking girl with shaggy brown hair pulled back in a ponytail. She had the biggest barrel chest I'd ever seen on a human, and a tiny waist that would have made Scarlett O'Hara green with envy. She wasn't ugly just … odd. Her name tag read MICHAELSON.

'Then why you got the glow?' the bug-eyed guy asked. His name tag identified him as BRONKOWSKI. The human whippet next to him smiled, revealing small fangs.

'Bill's my partner. We were apprehending a purse snatcher and … well, he sort of … missed.' The ugly guy guffawed and a small dimple appeared next to the girl's mouth. 'And what the hell were you arresting me for?' I added, aggrieved.

'Walking while pink,' Michaelson said, in a tolerable female imitation of Officer Friday's flat, unemotional tone.

'You mean you just arrest people for *glowing*?' I gestured at the stars and the sparks.

'Tinkerbill wouldn't have whacked 'em unless they were guilty of something.'

'*Tinkerbill?*' Delight over my partner's nickname gave way to lawyerly shock. 'You're arresting people without probable cause.'

'Kid, how long have you been on the job?' asked Michaelson. Which I thought was sort of rich. She didn't look much older than me.

'Today was my first day.'

She and Bronkowski exchanged a glance. 'You'll learn,' she said, and they let me go.

I got arrested four more times before I got home. Each time my badge, and the explanation that I was Bill's partner, got me released. But I sensed I had left a trail of hilarity for the swing shift.

In my effort to be P.C. I had picked an apartment smack in the middle of Jokertown. It was a relatively new building erected during a liberal mayor's efforts to gentrify the area. It was white stone, relatively modern, which meant the living room, dining nook, and kitchen were all one big room. I had a decent-sized bedroom and a full bath with a tub in addition to a shower. I set my hat on the bookcase as I came in, and straightened the photo of my father in his dress blues. 'Well, Dad, I hope you weren't watching today,' I said to that stern, chiseled face.

I was supposed to have dinner with Altobelli that night, and I knew my mother would be waiting by the phone in the house in Saratoga, wanting to hear about my first day on the job. Not wanting to be seen in public, I canceled with Altobelli, but mothers couldn't be postponed.

I put in an order for some Thai food to be delivered, and settled into the recliner with the phone tucked under my chin. 'Hi, Mom.'

'Oh, honey, I've been thinking about you all day. How was it?'

The five-year-old who had run to Mommy with skinned knees and bumped elbows wanted to wail out every slight. Instead I feigned cheerfulness and said, 'Great. It was great.'

'Your father would be so proud.' I heard the sigh in her voice. 'So, who did you arrest?'

I told her about Abigail.

'Never get involved with perps or witnesses, dear. I'm sure Sam would tell you the same.'

'Yeah.' There was a knock at my door. 'Hey, Mom, my food is here. I'll call you tomorrow.'

'Okay, honey, take care. Be careful.'

I slammed down the footrest of the recliner with a satisfying kick, grabbed my wallet, and headed to the door. I opened it to a joker delivery boy. This one wasn't too weird. He just had faceted eyes like a bee, and the usual fan of angry acne across his cheeks and chin that was the hallmark of every teenage boy. The hallway smelled of cabbage rolls and coffee, but they lost out to the sharp scent of green curry and garlic beef wafting up from the bag the kid carried.

'What do I owe you?'

The kid looked at the bill. 'Twenty-one fifty-three.' I dug out twenty-five, and realized I couldn't make a habit of this.

'Thanks.' I started to shut the door, but the kid held up a hand. 'Yes?'

'Uh … if you want anything like for … *dessert,* I can set you up. I've got a *friend.*' He was staring at the pink and sparking nimbus that surrounded me.

'It's a good thing you kept that vague, kid, because otherwise I would have to arrest you. But it's your lucky night. I'm tired and I'm hungry so I'll pretend I don't actually understand what you're saying. But just for that …' I took my cash back out of his limp hand, pulled out the five, and gave him a one instead. 'No tip.'

'Hey! What about the fifty-three cents?' he howled in outrage as I started to shut the door.

'Get it from your *friend.*' I slammed the door.

'Everyone's a winner. Come on, mister, five'll get you ten. Ten'll get you twenty. Easy peasy, just pick the card.'

The singsong patter of a three-card monte hustle reached us. Bill gave a gusting sigh. 'Fuckin' Joe Twitch. Just 'cause he's a sometime snitch he thinks he can pull this shit. Let's go protect the rubes.'

Joe had set up between the Jokertown Dime Museum and Freakers, a spot guaranteed to get a lot of traffic. The citizens of Jokertown ignored him, but there was a crowd of tourists gathered around. None of them had ever seen a man's hands move that fast. They were almost a blur. The man guiding those hands was short, wiry, and ugly as sin. He had faintly mottled skin, curly brown hair, and catlike green eyes that technically made him a joker. Aces and deuces were people who were outwardly unchanged, but possessed superhuman (or totally lame) powers.

The current mark had his cowboy hat pushed well back on his head, and was watching the moving cards with frowning concentration. He made his pick. It was wrong – of course – and Joe took his money. That's when I saw the tattoos across his knuckles – FAST and FSTR.

Before another sucker could step up Bill pushed through the crowd. 'Clear out, folks, you're blocking the sidewalk.'

The crowd moved away with alacrity. Joe had the cards and money in his pocket and the table folded before I had taken two steps. Bill extended his nightstick. That plus a single word, 'DON'T,' rooted Joe where he stood.

'Aww, shit, Tinkerbill, I'm just an honest businessman, making an honest buck.'

'No, Twitch, you're a crook and hustler. I don't want to hear you've moved over one block and set up again.'

'This is like fucking harassment!' His body swayed and jerked spasmodically. 'I'm get a lawyer, take way to the Supreme Court!' He was talking so fast that he was dropping words, and a tiny rivulet of drool had begun to run from the corner of his mouth.

'No, Twitch, this isn't harassment. *This* is harassment.' Bill pointed his nightstick at Joe Twitch and whistled.

The pink glow, stars, and sparks appeared all around Joe's skinny body. For an instant I thought the guy was going to cry, and pity briefly twisted my gut. Now that I was close I could see dark circles under Joe's eyes, and he looked like he'd been missing too many meals. He was also young, probably no older than me.

The moment of naked vulnerability passed, and he settled into bluster. 'I'm somebody! I was on *American Hero*.' He was madly twitching now, popping his knuckles over and over. 'You know Curveball? Babe, right? Well, her and me, we're like this!' He crossed his fingers. 'I can get her number for you.'

For one brief, wild moment I considered it, but then decided dating an ace would probably be more excitement than I needed. 'No thanks.'

'And trying to bribe an officer can get you arrested,' Bill said.

'Yeah, like you're not all on the take.'

Bill's face tightened in anger at Twitch's words. 'Get out of here before I decide to find some reason to arrest you.'

Twitch and his table disappeared.

I spent the rest of the day occasionally thinking about the skinny joker and those desperate eyes. I was beginning to discover that sometimes certain people just get under your skin. Like the old lady whose apartment had been burgled, and she just kept crying because the perps had let her cat out. I had radioed K-10 and Tabby to be on the lookout. Quattore had been sympathetic, but Tabby had told me to shove it, he wasn't the fuckin' ASPCA. And now Joe Twitch.

We got back to the precinct at the end of our shift, I sat down in my chair, and the stench of cat urine rose up around me like an almost visible cloud. I felt the wet go right through the seat of my pants. Puff was laughing, his eyes glittering with malice. Tabby sauntered over. 'Don't you ever give me an order again, *Franny*,' he said in a low, ugly voice.

Like Joe, I didn't know whether to fight or cry. I settled on, 'It's Frank, and I *asked* you for a *favor*.' It sounded lame even to me.

Wednesday afternoon I was typing up a report about a cat fight between two strippers at Freakers that had resulted in assault and property damage charges. Beastie and his partner Chey Moleka, a Cambodian immigrant who was known for sharp elbows and voracious ambition, came through with another naked girl. I assumed she was naked. Her feet and legs were bare, and she was wrapped in Beastie's voluminous yellow raincoat. This was the sixth naked chick in three days. They all told the same story – they were just walking along, minding their own business, when suddenly their clothes disappeared. For my own satisfaction I had stayed late one night, and tried to establish some connection between the women when there had only been four of them. I hadn't found a single point of contact.

'Where did you find her?' I asked.

'On Bowery,' Moleka replied shortly. Ever since she'd found out that my dad had been the captain of the 5th she'd gotten pretty short with me. Competition was a terrible thing – and I was planning on burying her.

And while I was daydreaming about my future victories something suddenly clicked. Frantically I rummaged through my desk and pulled out my notes on the other flashers. I tried to bring up MapQuest on the old desktop on Bill's desk, but it hummed, clicked, and gave me the blue screen of death.

I went over to James McTate's desk. He was new to the 5th, a detective and a joker/ace. If you just saw his face you would think he was normal, but his body was anorexic thin, and his bones seemed to be covered with skin and nothing else. He had immediately been dubbed Slim Jim. He was from Arizona, but for some inexplicable reason had decided to move to New York. When I thought about being a joker/ace in a place like Arizona, I started to understand why he'd moved.

McTate was a detective, but friendly, so I wasn't too shy about approaching him. His partner, Tenry Fong, one of the older guys on the force, gave me a cold glance and went back to his report. Bill kept telling me that the detectives were no better than those of us in uniform, but I couldn't shake the feeling they got the best cases, and I craved one of those shiny gold badges. Slim Jim looked up at my approach.

'Uh … could I use your computer? Just for a second,' I hastened to add. 'Ours is …' I made a helpless gesture.

'Sure.' He pushed off with a foot and went wheeling out of the way. I brought up MapQuest, printed out the page, and highlighted the bus route. It ran along Park Row, then straight up the Bowery to Cooper Union and then continued up Third Avenue. Next I marked the location of the flashers in a different colored ink. Most were along the Bowery, but there had been a number of Cooper Union college girls among them.

I jumped out of my (new) chair, and yelled, 'He's riding the 103 bus. It's somebody on the bus!'

'What are you yapping about, Franny?' Bugeye growled.

'Frank,' I said wearily, knowing it would have no effect.

I found Bill in the bathroom, and poured out my theory. He listened while finishing up. He shook off, zipped up, washed up, and said, 'Let's go talk to the sarge.'

We found Sergeant Choy down in the basement constructing a tiny machine out of paper clips and tin foil. I had been around long enough to learn her ace power. She could control any machine she had built or heavily modified.

'The rook here has a theory about the naked chicks. I think he may be on to something.'

I went through it all again to an impassive Choy. 'I don't have a car here, ma'am. I ride the bus, a lot, ma'am, and I realized all these flashing events are happening along one particular bus line. And it's all pretty girls in their late teens and twenties, ma'am. It's some guy on the bus, ma'am. I'm sure of it.'

Choy ran a hand through her silver-flecked black hair. 'One ma'am is sufficient. It's a good theory. Let's test it out. Bill, you and the rook wear civvies tomorrow. We'll put you both on the bus. I'll contact the other precincts where that bus runs, and tell them we're running a sting that will cross their territory. Now we just need a tasty temptation.'

'Apsara would be perfect,' I heard myself saying.

Bill and Choy exchanged amused looks. 'Yes, I expect a lot of men would like to see that.' She tapped thoughtfully on the table with a bent paper clip. 'If this perv is on the bus she would be hard to resist.'

'And I hear she's not too much in the resistance department,' Bill said, then hastened to add, 'Though she is a civilian ... technically.'

Choy pushed back her chair. 'Let's ask her.'

So, the next morning I found myself riding the bus pretending to read the *New York Times* while I watched my fellow commuters. Apsara was happy to help, so she was set up to parade down the Bowery as the bus passed. All around her were various other officers ready to act, and Choy overseeing the operation.

I was seated at the back of the bus while Bill grooved on his iPod at the front. I focused on men seated in the window seats on the sidewalk side of the bus. I glanced ahead and saw Apsara prancing down the street carrying a shopping bag. Her long hair swayed with each swing of her hips. I forced myself back to watching the commuters instead of the girl. Good move. I saw a skinny teenage boy of maybe sixteen come slightly out of his seat. As I watched, his tongue licked nervously at his lips, and he raised his hand, brought his fingers to his lips, and blew a kiss. Apsara's clothes vanished, and the kid leaned forward watching avidly as the bus went farting past.

I was out of my seat, grabbing the cuffs out of my pocket. 'Got you!' A look of almost comical alarm crossed the kid's face. 'You are under arrest.'

Bill pulled the cord and the bus rolled to a stop.

The kid started yelling. 'Don't you touch me! I can fuck you up bad! I can make anything disappear. I could disappear your dick ... or ... or your *eyeballs*.'

Bill and I exchanged a glance. Clearly he was an ace. Clearly we didn't know the limit of his powers. The heavyset African-American woman in the seat next to the kid handled the situation for us. She swung her incredibly large, and apparently incredibly heavy, purse into his belly. The air *whoofed* out of the kid, and he folded up like an origami figure. 'You took the clothes off that girl? You're a damn pervert,' she yelled. She slid out of her seat to make room for me. 'You arrest his ass.'

I spun the still gasping kid around, pulled his arms behind his back, and slapped on the cuffs. Maybe he had to blow a kiss to use his power. I sure hoped so. In case he really could remove my dick. By now Bill had pushed through the rubbernecking commuters and was at my side.

Unfortunately, Apsara was already wrapped in a coat provided by Choy by the time we got off the bus with our prisoner. I felt a little guilty over my sexist and lascivious thoughts, so to make up for them I called to her as we headed toward a waiting squad car with the prisoner. 'Thank you. I'm sure that can't have been pleasant.'

'No problem, Franny.'

I winced. 'Actually, it's Frank.'

But she ignored me, swept the crowd with a dazzling smile, and added, 'It was fun.'

◆

The kid was in an interrogation room. The handcuffs had been removed and he was nervously rubbing at his wrists. On the other side of the one-way glass a crowd had gathered – Sergeant Choy, Tabby, Puff, Slim Jim, Rikki, K-10, Angel, Moleka, and Razor Joan Lonnegan. The female cops were all demanding blood, the males tended to be amused, and there I was saying over and over in ever more plaintive tones, 'He's a minor. We've got to call his parents.'

The gender bickering abruptly ended. Of course I had my back to the door so I didn't get the hint to stop talking. '... call his parents!' My voice rang out.

A hand fell on my shoulder. I choked on the final word, turned, and looked up into the square-jawed face of Captain Maseryk. With his iron-gray crew cut and perfectly pressed uniform he looked more military than cop.

'Nice work, Black. I hear from Choy this was your idea.' I mumbled something. His pale eyes scanned the rest of the crowd. 'And Black is right. Call his parents.'

'Can we talk to him before they do?' Bill asked.

'But gently,' said the captain in an equally gentle tone.

Bill and I headed toward the door to the interrogation room. I had an itch between my shoulder blades as if invisible daggers were scratching at my skin.

The kid looked up at our entrance. He had a prominent Adam's apple that was bouncing up and down. His black T-shirt had Ge N I U S with a word beneath each letter – Germanium, Nitrogen, Iodine, Uranium, Sulfur, and some numbers above them. His backpack, which we'd searched, had a number of science texts in them. It seemed he was a nerd with power – never a good thing.

'Stripping women. I think a competent D.A. can make the argument that's almost rape.'

The kid went white at the R word. 'I didn't ... it's not ... you're full of it.'

'Maybe my partner is exaggerating, but only a little,' I said. 'You're in a lot of trouble.'

'I know my rights. I don't have to say anything.'

'Oh, goody, now I can make up any story I want, and sell it to the D.A.,' Bill said.

'You can't do that!' The kid's eyes shifted nervously to me. 'Can he?'

'Sure he can, and you won't have said anything to counter his version of things,' I said, though it pained me to do so. 'Look, talk to us. Tell us why you did it. The D.A.'s reasonable. If you just discovered your power maybe you were having trouble controlling it.'

It was the wrong thing to say. It struck at the core of his fragile teenage ego. His face went red, then white, the pimples livid against his skin. 'I've had my power for three years. I tried out for *American Hero*. I'm not just some dumb kid. They said I was too young, but they took that stupid girl and her stuffed dragon! I'm an *ACE*!' And then he blew a kiss at me, and I was sitting there buck naked.

Bill gave a thoughtful nod. 'And a one-trick pony. I can see why they didn't take you. Tough power to put on television.' He said all this while I was holding my file in front of my package, and Bill's behind my ass, shuffling for the door.

I exited to gales of laughter from my coworkers.

The following week Bill and I got moved to the swing shift. Night in Jokertown was a whole new experience. On the Bowery neon ruled, garish as the Las Vegas Strip. Off the main streets darkness ruled.

Even though I had moved into the neighborhood a few days before I started work, I hadn't gone out much. Too busy getting settled. After I started work I hadn't gone out much because I'd been too damn tired. And when I did feel like going out I was probably going to head to the Village or Little Italy. A singles bar in Jokertown didn't look like a real good prospect for a nat like me. And in the privacy of my own head I could at least be honest with myself – I wasn't going to date a joker.

At night the crimes were darker too. The bar fights more vicious. Armed robberies often became assaults. We found some bodies too, victims of the increasingly vicious turf war between the Demon Princes and the Werewolves, and I was proud of myself because I didn't lose my dinner over any of them.

This night the heat lay on the city like a suffocating blanket. A hulking figure wrapped in a voluminous cloak shuffled out of an alley. My hand closed reflexively on the butt of my pistol.

Bill laid a hand over mine. 'Relax. It's the Oddity. They're on our side – sort of.'

I had been on the job for a week and was starting to feel like a bit of a pro. 'I know, I've heard about him. Bugeye, Puff, and Tabby seem to think he's … she's … it's … a good guy.'

'I take it you don't agree,' Bill said in a neutral tone.

'The rule of law is essential to an advanced society. You abandon that, and no one is safe because there's no certainty. The government can seize your person or your property, gangs threaten you and your only recourse is to form or hire your own gang—'

'Aren't we just another gang, bigger, better armed ... maybe, but still a gang?'

'No. We try to adhere to a set of standards that protect people from the overwhelming power of the state. They have recourse when we act like thugs. They have none from a person like him ... her.' I gestured at the figure now vanishing into another alley.

'Yep, you're going to end up at One Police Plaza, Franny,' Bill said.

'Frank. It's Fra—' I started to say when I was interrupted by squealing tires. A beautiful vintage Ferrari convertible came roaring around the corner. Bill and I dove off to each side as the car careened wildly, the driver trying to get control. I had a brief glimpse of long brown hair and a horror mask face before the car was past us.

We took off in pursuit while Bill radioed in our location and the description of the car. It wasn't too hard to follow; there was the sound of scraped metal and squealing tires, and car horns from the other drivers on the street. Our pounding feet echoed off the walls of surrounding buildings. I felt like a one-man band with my handcuffs clinking against my heavy flashlight, billy club banging against my belt buckle, holster thwapping against my thigh.

Brakes screeched followed by a bang and the wail of crumpling metal. A girl, her voice at a supersonic level, screamed out, 'Come on, boys! It's all yours!'

We heard approaching sirens. I pushed harder, but didn't seem to be running any faster. Bill and I finally spun around the last corner to see dark forms heaving all around the car, which had plowed nose first into a building. Not just any building; McGurk's Suicide Hall, the headquarters of the Demon Princes. It was like watching African army ants swarming on the body of a fallen water buffalo. I pulled out my flashlight, thumbed it on, and eyes glittered in the sudden light. Jokers. Lots of them. All holding a piece of the Ferrari.

'*Hey!*' Bill shouted. We sprinted forward. We passed the mouth of an alley, and were ambushed by four rolling garbage cans. One hit me hard on the shin, and I went down. By the time Bill and I fought free, the car was a metal carcass and all we saw were a few backs vanishing into various alleys. Not one of them went into Suicide Hall, which meant we couldn't either.

The girl who had driven the car into the wall was in the top ten of ugly jokers. A pair of tiny arms emerged just below her breasts, ending in hands with only three fingers tipped with claws. Right now they were folded over her stomach. She kicked off her high-heeled shoes and took off running.

I sucked in a deep breath and set off after her. She craned her neck around to look at me. A red fluid dripped from the corners of her eyes and ran down her cheeks like scarlet tears. Her nose was a flattened snout, but beneath them was a perfect cupid bow mouth with full, sensual lips. The incongruity was almost more horrifying than the deformities.

She was fast, but lacked stamina. Bill and I managed to get on either side of her. Her shoulders slumped, she came to a stop, and she folded the extra arms across her stomach. The claws were dripping the same viscous fluid that ran out of her eyes.

'Is that your car?' Bill panted.

'A friend loaned it to me,' she said.

'And told you to run it into a brick wall, and then have it stripped?' Bill's voice dripped sarcasm. She gave the universal teenage response – a bored shrug. 'Let me see some ID,' Bill said.

'I don't have it with me.'

'Do you have a driver's license?'

'Not yet. I'm in driver's ed.'

'What's you name?'

'Joan McDermott.'

'Okay, Joan, we're going over to the 5th and *calling your parents*,' he added with a glance to me. 'Get the registration out of the car.'

I trotted off obediently, rummaged through the glove compartment, and came out with a folder containing proof of insurance and the registration. The car was owned by one Peter Fairbanks. Memory kicked in and provided the title that went with that name. It was Assemblyman. He represented a particularly rich and Republican part of Long Island. A slow throbbing headache began at the base of my neck, crawled up over my head, and settled behind my eyes. It was going to be a long night.

'Take her a Coke. See what she has to say,' Bill tossed over his shoulder at me as he pulled the phone closer and got ready to dial.

'Bill, she's a minor. We're not supposed to interview her without her parent or guardian present. We did that once with that stripper kid, and it made me really uncomfortable.'

'That's 'cause he stripped you.' I just kept staring at him. 'Are you a cop, or her fucking lawyer?'

I stood my ground. 'I'm trying to be an honest cop.'

Bill came out of the chair and this time I did step back. 'Franny, you are really pissing me off. Take her a goddamn Coke.'

'All right, but I'm going to formally register my protest.'

The vending machine ate my dollar and burped out a can of Coke. I continued on to the interrogation rooms. The walls were a particular shade of puke green, and they seemed to hold the scent of flop sweat, alcohol, vomit, and blood. The girl was seated at the table, hands cuffed behind her back. I sat down the cold can of Coke and unlocked the handcuffs.

'Oh, you must be the good cop,' she said sarcastically, but her voice quavered on the final word.

I didn't answer. Just pulled out the chair, swung it around, and straddled it, resting my arms on the back. 'Officer Chen is calling your folks.'

'Just my mom. Dad took off four years ago.'

'Oh.'

'Yeah, it was because of me,' she said, in answer to a question I hadn't asked. Her tone was casual, but I watched the bottom lip of that vulnerable mouth quiver slightly.

Cop Frank saw the opening. 'Want to tell me what happened?'

'Shouldn't I have a lawyer?'

Cop Frank knew what he was supposed to say. *It's not necessary. We're just having a friendly talk until your mom arrives. It'll go better for you if you cooperate.* But Lawyer Francis answered, 'Yes, you should have a lawyer. Are you requesting one?'

She shook her head. 'No, we can't afford it.'

'There are public defenders,' I said. I figured Captain Mendelberg and a D.A. were behind the one-way glass cussing me out.

The joker girl said, 'Yeah, and they suck.'

I couldn't argue with that. There were always exceptions, but most P.D.s were young, overworked, and underpaid. Or angry attorneys from white-shoe law firms forced to do pro bono work. Then I remembered I knew one of the exceptions. He'd been a year ahead of me at Columbia and he was a joker; Charles Santiago Herriman. He was smart and had been inculcated by our Con Law professor Dr. Pretorius with a strong sense of outrage.

I wrote out Herriman's name on my notepad and ripped off the page. 'Here, this guy is good. Have your mom ask for him when she calls the P.D.'s office.'

'Okay, thanks.' The girl took a sip of Coke and glanced at the wall. Her upper teeth sketched her lower lip. 'I was at a party. At Barrington Prep.'

I knew the school. It was a place where wealthy families sent their sons to prepare them for their future positions as legacies at Ivy League universities. 'Sort of a long way from home, weren't you?' Barrington was up the Upper West Side near Central Park.

She nodded. 'I'm on the debate team at school. We debated Barrington last month. I met this boy …' She cleared her throat and tried again. 'We'd been tweeting a lot, and we liked a lot of the same things – books, music – and I beat him in the debate so he knew I was smart. He invited me to a party … Todd picked me up.' Her eyes filled with tears and her snout nose was a vivid red. She rubbed a hand across her nostrils, and snot gleamed on her skin. 'I've never been in a Ferrari before. I felt so special …' Her voice trailed away, and her eyes filled with real tears that alternated with the red gunk. 'But it was a Pig Party.'

My spine stiffened. It had begun at colleges where frat boys invited the ugliest girls they could find, and gave prizes to the boy who brought the worst. It was a nasty game and apparently it had filtered down to the high school level.

'I wanted to leave, but they said I was the Pig Queen, and I had to stay.' *False imprisonment*, my mind supplied. 'They let the other girls leave, then they got in a circle around me and started pushing me back and forth between them. They made the freshmen kiss me.' I made a comforting noise, and she continued. 'It was getting rougher and rougher. I think the punch was spiked. They sure seemed drunk. Then they got this long pin and a fake tail, and they started playing pin the tail on the piggy. They jabbed me a bunch of times.' *Assault and battery*, my mind supplied. She stood up and started to pull up her skirt. 'I can show you.'

'Uh, I'd need a female officer,' I rushed to say, really not wanting to see her bootie. 'We should get a medical examiner and a camera to document your claim.'

'It's the truth!' she said, stung by the word 'claim.'

'I'm not saying it isn't, but we need evidence. But go on.'

She found the thread of the story again. 'Todd and some of the older boys started yelling about how I had to give them blow jobs. They grabbed me and forced me onto my knees. Some of the boys already had their pants unzipped, and they were ... hanging out.' She held up her second set of hands with those long claws and studied the tips. 'I got scared. Real scared. So I dug my claws into a couple of their ... things.' I winced. 'They were all shouting and screaming. I ripped Todd's pocket and got the car key. Then I ran.'

'Why bring the car to the Demon Princes?' I asked.

'As I was driving away I heard Todd shouting. I guess his dad didn't know he'd taken the car. I wanted to make him pay.' She hung her head.

'Okay. So, I assume there'll be a mark on their ... penises.'

She nodded. 'This gunk is like ink. I've done tattoos for some of my friends.' She reacted to my expression. 'Flowers and things. They're pretty.'

'I'm sure they are. Look, uh—'

The door opened and a plump woman who looked like she'd

thrown on her clothes rushed into the room. 'Joanie, honey. What's happened? Are you okay?'

'Oh, Mommy!' Sobs and hugs ensued.

The young D.A. who was on duty came in and indicated for me to leave. 'Your daughter's in some trouble, ma'am,' I heard him say as I left.

Work consumed my waking hours and even invaded my dreams. For some reason I couldn't get the ugly joker girl out of my head. Maybe it was that beautiful mouth. Maybe because the entire neighborhood was discussing the case.

I was discovering that Jokertown was a tight-knit community. People knew of Joan, her accomplishments and goals. I went in to buy tomatoes only to hear Mr. Flannigan the greengrocer talking with Mrs. Synderman about how this might cost Joan her scholarship to Princeton. They both clammed up at my entrance, and I didn't think it was just because I was a nat. I was the man who'd arrested Joan. The old joker men playing endless games of speed chess discussed Joan. Even in the precinct the joker officers occasionally murmured about the case.

I decided to call over to the D.A.'s office and inquire about the case, and I was shocked to discover they were throwing the book, the kitchen sink, and everything else at her. I raised the fact that she had been held against her will and assaulted. It's strange how sometimes you can 'hear' a shrug across phone lines. 'It's her word against theirs.'

'And her daddy isn't a state legislator.'

'That isn't why—'

I cut him off. 'Yeah, right.'

'You're not going to be trouble, are you?'

'Let's just say you better be ready to treat me like a hostile witness.' I slammed down the phone. Bill looked up from where he was shoveling Shanghai spicy noodles into his mouth.

'You gotta learn to let things go, Franny. We arrest 'em. You don't look back, and you don't second-guess the learned counselors.'

'Even if I'm one of them?'

'You do that and then *everyone* will hate you,' he said.

And I had no answer to that depressing pronouncement.

That night I had the opportunity to get out of Jokertown. Sam Altobelli had invited me to a fund-raiser for the police benevolent fund at the Four Seasons. Extra tickets had been purchased by some of Manhattan's richer citizens, and were to be handed out to 'deserving officers.' I didn't know how deserving I was, but I had a powerful rabbi. I also knew there was no way I could have afforded the two grand.

As I struggled with the cummerbund that went with my rented tux, I wondered if I ought to have refused harder, and not let Sam overrule me. The free tickets should have gone to some long-time veteran, or a person who had done something heroic in the line of duty. But Sam had argued that attractive and educated also counted for a lot, and many of those hoary old veterans sported noses with broken veins from too much booze, or trailed a long tail of citizen complaints. I found that depressing, and wondered if that would be my ultimate fate.

There was the strobe of camera flashes as I walked up the wide staircase toward the Pool Room. I hoped my picture wouldn't make it into any of the papers. That would make my life pure hell.

The tables had been removed except for a few at the edges of the room to force people to 'mingle' around the white marble pool in the center. The glitterati of New York society moved beneath a canopy of seasonally changing trees. They were still the bright green of summer. Conversation bounced off the floor-to-ceiling glass windows, and reduced the small chamber orchestra to a strange hiccup of music that occasionally penetrated the roar. There was the faint odor of too many bodies. I could feel sweat forming under my arms, and I hadn't even entered the press of people.

I snagged a glass of champagne from the tray of a passing waiter, and grabbed a shrimp puff thingee off another tray. It was good champagne and a good shrimp thingee. Then I scanned the crowd for a familiar face. Instead I found myself faced with a man wearing an elaborate gazelle mask. 'Francis Xavier Black,' the man said.

'Um, yes … do I know—'

He laughed, a rollicking, deep belly sound. 'No, no, but Sam told me about you. Lucas Tate, editor of the *Jokertown Cry*, and I think you might be worth an article. *Son of Famous Captain Returns Home.*' I could hear the capital letters in the headline, and shuddered.

'No, please don't,' I said faintly.

Tate rolled right over me. 'And we're coming up on the twenty-fourth anniversary of your father's death. I'll send someone around. Or, hell, maybe I'll do it myself.'

'Oh, no, really, please … don't.'

I heard the mayor's familiar nasal tones calling out a greeting.

'Lucas, how the hell are you?' They walked away with the mayor's arm across Tate's shoulders. 'Who do I have to fuck to get your paper to endorse me?'

Eventually Sam found me, and I got introduced to the chief of detectives, the chief of police, and the D.A. for the City of New York. 'I hear we lost you to the thin blue line,' she said. 'If you ever change your mind, come and see me. I could use somebody who's actually interacted with the scum.'

I wondered if she'd still feel that way if she talked to the young A.D.A. I'd basically threatened earlier in the day. Then I realized I had an opportunity to do something for Joanie McDermott. 'Ma'am,' I began. 'There's this case.'

But her attention was wandering, drawn by a passing congressman. 'Excuse me. Don't worry about the case. We'll put them away,' she threw over her shoulder as she hurried after power.

'That's the problem,' I muttered to myself.

Unfortunately Lucas Tate remembered meeting me, and remembered his desire for a story. I demurred. Tate called Sam who called my mother who browbeat me into submission. The story appeared in the Sunday issue of the *Cry*. My hope was that everyone at the precinct would miss it because it was the weekend.

They didn't.

I walked into work, and suddenly I was naked. There was the click of digital cameras and phones snapping photos, and gales of laughter swept through the squad room. Apsara had her hand over her face, but her fingers separated so she could peek through. Bruce Cordova, aka the Stripper, was leaning on a broom handle in the doorway laughing at me while Puff pounded him on the shoulder. I snatched a file off a desk and covered my junk, but not before Captain Mendelberg walked through and gave me the once-over. 'Not bad, patrolman,' she drawled and headed into her office.

The desk sergeant walked up and said, 'Better get some clothes before I have to arrest you for indecent exposure.' Wingman brayed at his own wit.

Once again I had files at my crotch and crack and I was shuffling into the men's room. Bill came in after me. 'It's not smart to stick your head up, Franny. You'll just get it cut off.'

I was in that state between anger and depression. I couldn't figure out which way to fall. I decided anger was healthier. 'Are you part of this?'

'No. If by "*part of this*" you mean planned it.'

The door to the john flew open and Tabby and Puff strolled in. 'You asked for it, Rook. You got a law degree. Your daddy was the captain of this precinct,' Tabby said.

'The kid didn't pick his father,' Bill said.

'Yeah, but he picked to be a cop.'

'And come here,' Puff added.

'And he gets invited to receptions at the Four Seasons.' Tabby again.

'And has articles written about him,' Puff said.

'I didn't ask for any of this,' I said.

Bill took a step forward. He was bigger than either of the other two officers. 'Back off. Now. I won't ask again.' Puff and Tabby left. Bill turned back to me. 'Do you have an extra uniform?'

'Yeah, at my apartment.'

'Gimme the key. I'll go get it.' His face fell comically as I dropped the files and spread my hands.

'What key?'

Days passed. I took to just keeping an extra uniform in my locker. The game was getting really old, but obviously not for my tormentors or for Bruce, whose parents had quickly cut a deal so the kid was doing his community service at the 5th. The cruder members of our force – read most of them – had adopted him as a mascot and my personal tormentor. I knew if I whined to the captains I'd pay, and they didn't seem inclined to ride to my rescue. I considered confronting Cordova and giving him a little 'come to Jesus' talk, but I was feeling so low I figured he'd just laugh and blow me off.

Which meant I was in a really bad mood so when I came across Abigail Baker again, I wasn't inclined to be sympathetic despite our shared nude experience.

It started with a skinny joker that looked like a big ant. He had been racing into coffee, ice cream, and sandwich shops – anywhere there was a tip jar – grabbing the jars and racing off down the street. Bill was in taking a report from the latest victim. I loitered in the door where I could keep an eye on the street.

'How hard can it be to find a giant ant?' the owner, who looked like a giant caterpillar, asked.

I spent a moment picturing a Japanese monster movie version of the ant guy and the caterpillar guy battling over an empty pickle jar filled with dollar bills. It didn't have quite the panache of *Godzilla Versus the Swarm*. But then my attention was drawn to the jewelry store across the street.

Mr. Zamaani, owner of Fine and Rare Things, came barreling out of the door and gripped a young woman by the upper arm. The girl was staring down at her hands, and the sapphire and diamond necklace that lay across them. Mr. Zamaani started screaming, 'Thief! Thief!'

I ran across the street dodging cars and tourists in pedicabs. The girl was bucking like a foal newly broke to halter trying to break Zamaani's grip. Zamaani's round, fat face looked like an overinflated red balloon, and he was still bellowing in Farsi and English. 'Thief! Evil thief!'

'I didn't … I never … I was just admiring it.' I recognized the accent even before I saw her face. Abigail Baker.

I dodged past an elderly woman in a swan mask, pushing a shopping cart full of bric-a-brac with a cat riding proudly on top, and laid a hand on Mr. Zamaani's arm. 'I'll take it from here.'

'Well, thank God, someone sensible,' Abigail said in aggrieved tones. I spun her around and slapped on the cuffs. 'What the hell? I didn't do anything. I was just standing here admiring the jewelry and suddenly it was in my hand.'

'You're just a victim of circumstances, aren't you?' I said sarcastically.

'Absolutely!'

'Guess we'll sort it out down at the precinct.'

'Not again,' she wailed. 'I have an audition.'

At the same time Zamaani said, 'You'll lock her up?' I nodded. 'For a long time?'

'That'll be up to a judge.' I started walking away, towing Abigail behind me.

Back at the precinct I very quickly learned that these kinds of robberies had been occurring for decades. Long before Abigail was born, much less arrived in New York. Apparently Abigail was the world's unluckiest person – unless you counted me. As she was walking out I apologized, and then, to my horror, I heard myself saying, 'Uh, Abigail, there's a jazz festival at a really great—'

'Oh, sod off!'

Three days later I was due in court to testify in the purse snatcher case. It didn't take long, and as I was walking out I saw Mrs. McDermott and Joanie, accompanied by Charlie Herriman, the prosthetics attached to his flippers clutching at the handle of his briefcase. The inevitable happened. He dropped the case, spilling papers. I ran over to help him gather them up.

'Oh, it's you,' Joanie said.

At the same time Charlie said, 'I know you. You were at Columbia.'

'Yeah,' I said, helping him shove the papers back into his case. I stood and looked at Joanie. 'How are you doing?' I asked.

Her response to even that tepid remark took me aback. Joanie's eyes filled with tears.

'Not so good.'

'You shouldn't be talking to my client,' Charlie said in a faintly whining and almost apologetic tone. That's when I remembered that despite being brilliant, Charlie had always undercut the brains with his nervousness and klutziness.

'What's going on?' I jerked my head toward the courtroom.

At that moment the familiar burly figure of Assemblyman Fairbanks hove into sight. He was accompanied by several young men dressed in the Barrington Prep uniforms, and a distinguished silver-haired man whose entire demeanor screamed *counselor*. Joanie buried her face against her mother's shoulder to avoid looking at them. The boys smirked and whispered to each other. They entered the courtroom. Moments later a harried young D.A. came rushing past and hurtled through the doors into the courtroom.

'We've got to go,' Charlie muttered to the mother and daughter.

I stood dithering in the hall for a few more minutes, then slipped into the courtroom and took a seat in the back. Charlie was at the podium dropping papers while he made a motion to compel the young men to submit to a strip search to verify his client's defense.

'How does this go to the charge of grand theft auto?' asked the elderly judge whose wrinkled skin and dark tan created the impression of a lizard squatting behind the bench.

'It's an affirmative defense, Your Honor, going to my … um … client's state of mind when she ran from the Barrington dorm. She was escaping a threatening situation where she was being held against her will.'

'She could have called a taxi,' the judge said.

'She was afraid she was going to be raped—'

The D.A. bounced to his feet. 'Objection.'

Charlie plowed on doggedly. 'She wasn't thinking all that clearly.'

The D.A. was fulminating. 'That's incredibly prejudicial. Where's the proof?'

The judge stared over the top of his glasses at the five perfectly groomed young men. The smirking jerk expressions had been replaced with those of respectful attention. He looked back at Charlie. 'The D.A. raises a valid question, Mr. Herriman. Where is the proof?'

'The proof is on their bodies, Your Honor.'

I winced and watched the D.A. pounce.

'So she's admitting to assault and battery?' His tone was silky.

Charlie opened and closed his mouth several times. 'She had a right to defend herself, and they assaulted her first.' He yanked photos out of his briefcase and tried to wave them dramatically. They slipped out of his prosthesis and went flying like frightened birds all over the front two rows. As he rushed about trying to pick them up he said, between sharp pants, 'They stuck pins in her.'

The D.A. didn't like where this was going. 'Your Honor, granting this motion would be like giving the police a warrant without probable cause. There is no evidence that this pinprick occurred at Barrington, or that the defendant didn't injure herself after the fact to support these claims.'

'And I suppose the wounds on the boys' penises will be attributed to some quaint initiation rite at Barrington?' Charlie pulled out an asthma inhaler and took a hit.

The silver-haired lawyer seated next to Assemblyman Fairbanks stood up. He was very smooth, it was like watching water flow. 'Gerald Pitken for the boys, Your Honor. I will resist any effort to traumatize and humiliate these young men. The public defender appears to be on a fishing expedition.' He sat back down.

The judge glanced at the assemblyman who wore a ferocious frown. He studied the boys again. He looked over at Joanie with her flattened snout and those grotesque arms thrusting out from her waist. He banged down the gavel. 'Motion denied.'

I slipped away.

◆

'Why, Officer Black, what a pleasant surprise. Do come in.'

'Pardon me for imposing, sir,'

Tate chuckled behind his lion mask. '*Sir*, please, you'll have me looking over my shoulder for my father. Lucas, please.'

I ducked my head. 'Lucas.'

The apartment would have been elegant and tasteful if the living-room walls hadn't been lined with masks. There were so many that you stopped seeing individual designs and were just overwhelmed by colors, feathers, and flashing sequins. Tate mistook my expression for one of admiration and launched into an exhaustive and boring monologue about the masks. 'This one is from the court of Louis the Fourteenth …'

My eyes began to glaze over and soon all I was hearing was *'Blah, blah, blah blah, Mardi Gras, blah blah blah blah, Hutu tribal, blah blah blah, Venetian Carnival, blah blah.* I began to squirm because I'd come here with my own agenda, I had limited time, and he'd turned into a pedant.

Tate finally seemed to realize that he was boring me insensible. 'But enough of my particular hobby horse.' He led me over to a couch and gestured for me to sit down. 'Now, what can I do for you?'

'I need a photographer.' And I outlined the situation.

When I finished I could tell Tate was smiling, though I couldn't actually see his mouth behind the mask. 'I'll do it myself.'

When the kid opened the door his mouth dropped open and his eyes began to flick nervously from side to side. 'Hi, Bruce,' I said. 'First, the little morning game is gonna stop.'

'Yeah, how you gonna make me?' The nerd bluster was back.

'I'm going to sue you and your parents. Since I'm a lawyer it won't cost me a dime, but it sure will cost your folks.'

The kid went white again, and he grabbed at my arm as I started to walk away. 'No, please. Don't.'

'Okay, then you're going to do something for *me*.'

They really were a pack. Bruce and I sat on a bench at the edge of Central Park and watched as Todd Fairbanks and his posse emerged from the front doors of the Barrington Prep. The gold embroidered patch with the school's insignia flashed in the autumn sun and glowed on their navy-blue blazers. Little budding Masters of the Universe.

I realized I found them more loathsome than the most deformed joker in Jokertown. 'Them,' I said.

'I've never done that many,' Bruce whined.

'Don't fuck this up.'

He concentrated to the point that the tip of his tongue emerged. Then he brought both hands to his lips and blew kisses at them. All their clothes vanished, except for one boy who still had his shoes and socks.

Tate, muffled in a long cloak with a hood, stepped forward. Over the roar of passing traffic I couldn't hear the rapid-fire whine of the digital camera shooting multiple photos, but it was clear from the boys' expressions they realized what was happening.

I turned to Bruce. 'Okay, you can go.' He jumped up, but I caught him by the wrist. 'But first, play back the deal.'

'I don't say a word to anybody about this ever.'

'And.'

'And I stop taking your clothes.'

I released him and decided to walk through the park. It was a nice afternoon. I could hear the music from the carousel, smell hot dogs and pretzels on the various carts. There were a lot of girls taking advantage of the last warm days before winter, and skating and running past in shorts and tank tops. And Tate would need time to download and print the photos.

The McDermotts lived in a run-down building on the south end of Jokertown. I stepped over a modified tricycle in the lobby and tried to visualize the child's body that could ride it. I couldn't twist my brain that much. Somewhere above me I heard the elevator making its slow descent. I gave up, and instead sprinted up the five flights to their floor.

Sheila had just gotten home from her job at an electronics store, and I knew her daughter had chess club and wouldn't be at home. The mother answered at my knock and frowned, trying to place me, while she pushed a stray lock of hair off her forehead. When she did recognize me the weary irritation turned quickly to alarm. 'Joanie …?'

'Fine. She's fine. I wanted to give you this.' I handed her a business card for Dr. Pretorius. I had considered using Charlie for what I had planned, but Pretorius was the most feared plaintiff's attorney in Manhattan. He was a much better choice, and once I'd outlined the McDermotts' situation he was excited to help. 'Dr. Pretorius is expecting your call.'

'Why am I … I can't afford to pay a lawyer, that's why we have the public—'

'He'll take his fee out of your settlement.'

'What settlement?'

'Joanie's going to be able to attend any college she wants.'

'How? Why?'

'Call him,' I said, flicking my nail on the edge of the card. I left.

◆

You don't approach a public figure in their office. Surrounded by the trappings of their power and position they tend to bluster. Nor do you brace them in their homes. That sets off all the old defending-the-castle responses. No, you catch them in public where they can't easily make a scene.

Being a cop also means you can locate a person pretty damn easily. Especially someone who doesn't know he's being watched or followed. I waited until Fairbanks was playing eighteen holes with three buddies, and I bought myself a tee time. I played golf in high school and college, and I was pretty sure I could outplay four fat old guys. I was right. By the fourth hole I was on their heels. Then I got lucky. Fairbanks sliced one into the trees. I heard him thrashing around searching for his ball. I hoisted my bag higher on my shoulder and called to his companions.

'I'll help him find it. I'm just waiting.' It's always fun to rub it in to bad golfers that you're better. And I was pretty sure that any friends of Fairbanks would be assholes.

He grunted at me as I joined him among the oak and beech trees. 'Sorry. We're holding you up.'

'No problem. I wanted a chance to talk to you.'

His face closed down tight. 'Call my office and make an appointment.'

I shrugged. 'Okay, but you probably don't want these floating around your office.' I took out the photos of Todd Fairbanks and his friends. Todd and two others had the distinctive marks and stains from Joanie's claws.

'You asshole. Is this some kind of blackmail attempt because—'

'No, just reminding you of your civic duty. Your son's a first-class thug. He and his little pals humiliated, imprisoned, and terrified a girl, threatened her with rape, and now you're trying to get her thrown in jail. You're going to use your influence and get the D.A. to drop these charges.'

His face was turning an alarming shade of red. 'Like hell—'

I waved the photos. 'Or else these go wide on the Internet, along with Joanie's story. The best-case scenario for your kid is that people will believe he got a hand job from a joker and she tattooed his dick. Which will make him a laughing stock. Or they'll suspect her story is true, and most Ivy League colleges aren't going to risk admitting a potential sexual predator.'

'I'm asking you again. How much do you want?' The words squeezed between his clenched teeth.

'Not a damn thing. But Mrs. McDermott is going to be suing you and your son. I suggest you settle. She's also suing Barrington Prep, and since you're on the Board of Governors you should urge them to settle too.'

'Whoever the fuck you are, you've made yourself an enemy.'

'Good. I think the kind of enemies a man acquires tells you a lot about his character. I'm very comfortable having you dislike me.' I started to walk away. 'Oh, your ball's over there. Behind the tree.'

I returned to the fairway, smiled and nodded at Fairbanks's companions. 'If you don't mind I'd like to play through,' I said.

The solid feel of the head of the driver connecting with the ball was very satisfying, and watching the ball arc straight down the fairway felt equally great. And then it rolled onto the green and stopped only a few inches from the hole. Heaven appeared to be pleased, too.

The next morning I walked through the precinct unmolested. Bruce looked up from where he was emptying the grounds out of the coffeemaker, then quickly ducked his head and looked away. Tabby and Bugeye, who had been loitering in anticipation of seeing me humiliated again, gaped, exchanged glances, then glared at me. I gave them a sweet smile. A knot of people were reading the *Cry*. The front-page story was all about the huge academic grant made by Barrington Prep to Joan McDermott, enough to fund her undergraduate degree at any Ivy League university. There were also rumors of a lawsuit against Assemblyman Fairbanks, and more rumors that he would settle.

I was a little sorry that Barrington hadn't had their nuts hammered to a wall, but figured Pretorius had wrested more money out of them by letting them avoid admitting culpability. And I had a feeling Fairbanks senior was none to happy with his son and heir right now.

Bill was studying me with a look that was half frown, half calculation. 'You're not naked.'

'Nope.'

'The charges against Joan McDermott have been dropped.'

'Looks like it.' I moved on toward the locker room. He followed me.

I had opened my locker and he peered in. 'You don't have an extra uniform.'

'Nope.'

'What did you do?'

'Solved a few problems.'

'How?'

'Creatively.'

'Do I want to know how?'

'Nope.' I slammed the door shut and headed for the door and our briefing.

'Answer me this.' I paused and looked back. 'Did you have something to do with that McDermott girl?'

'Maybe.'

We measured glances. A slow smile split his face, and he nodded.

At the end of my shift I was packing up to leave when Bugeye came over. I eyed him warily. 'Hey, a few of us are going over to Shift Change for drinks. Want to come?'

Shift Change was the local bar where most of the off-duty officers of the 5th went to drink. I'd never been invited before. 'Sure,' I said. I wondered what new and horrible thing they were going to do to me.

As we walked down the street I realized that Rikki, Beastie, Shades, Wingman, and Lieutenant Kant had fallen into step with me. My nervousness increased, but they were just exchanging gibes and talking about cases.

Wingman held the door for me. I gave him a funny look, but went in. Bill was seated at the bar. Puff was lighting a cigarette with one of his flaming goobers. Tabby had a shot and a beer lined up in front of him. The usual cop groupies, generally older women with lush bodies, had hung themselves on the male officers.

'What are you drinkin'?' Puff said. 'It's on me.'

'Uh.' I wondered who had stolen the real Puff and left this version behind. 'Scotch, rocks,' I finally managed.

A steady line of cops came by to give me a slap on the back and tell me that I'd been doing a hellva job. I looked up at Bill who had an expression like the Cheshire Cat's. He had definitely been talking.

And from somewhere in the crowd someone said, 'Nice work, Frank.'

I cranked around on the bar stool and addressed the room. 'Franny will be fine.'

There were guffaws and Bill pounded me on the shoulder. I turned back to the bartender and ordered another drink. It seemed I had made the right career choice.

THE RAT RACE

PART 2.

Charles Dutton's mansion was a sprawling affair that was normal on the outside and strange as hell on the inside. Stuffed with oddities, antiques, and wild card paraphernalia, the house was almost a museum. In fact, Dutton occasionally referred to it as 'the annex,' by which he implied that some of the Famous Jokertown Dime Museum's displays might hypothetically rotate in and out of his private quarters.

Leo didn't like doing poker night at Dutton's place. He was often consumed by the irrational conviction that the house was bigger on the inside than the outside, but he wasn't about to skip a Society game over such a minor quibble.

He was just deciding between lifting the big, ludicrous door knocker (some kind of animal head, maybe) and pushing the ornately offset doorbell that protruded like an ivory blister when another cab pulled up. This one deposited Father Squid, who paid the cabbie and gave Leo a nod that wiggled his tentacles.

Leo nodded back. He liked the priest – a joker a few years his senior with the cephalopod face and body like a boulder. As the cassock-clad minister climbed the front steps, Leo called out, 'Don't tell me I'm late.'

'Surely not. It's barely even dark.' He reached past Leo and seized the door knocker. He lifted it and dropped it a couple of times – casting forth a low, clattering rumble.

And then the two men stood there, side by side, until the door was answered by Dutton himself.

Charles Dutton was a tall man, thin and perennially well dressed. His death mask was its usual shade of liver-disease yellow, and if he was showing more skin he would've been smiling broadly. He opened the door and spread his arms like a showman with a baton. 'Gentlemen! Or, you two, as the case may be.'

Father Squid said, 'I resemble that remark.'

'I know you do. Come on in. You're not late, but you're last. Everyone else is already upstairs in the sanctum sanctorum, making drinks and starting cigars.' He held the door ajar and kept his arms aloft, gesturing into the corridor with its long red carpet runner. 'Come in, come in. And let the game begin.'

Leo and Father Squid followed Dutton up the stairs to the third floor, where the 'sanctum sanctorum' was set up for entertaining. The detective suspected that the intimate, windowless room had once been a secondary dining area or maybe an inconvenient parlor. Regardless, it was now a place where Dutton brought his friends, shelved his liquor, and kept a felted table with seven seats and as many ashtrays.

Some years previously, someone (and no one seemed to remember *who*) had made a joke about the Tiffany-style lamps, the wood paneling, the smoke, and the hunkered shoulders ... to the effect that their gathering looked like a black velvet painting of dogs playing poker. At the next gathering, Lucas Tate – that aficionado of all things masklike and mask-related – arrived wearing a bulldog mask and toting half a dozen more dog masks to be shared with the group.

Thus, the Black Velvet Society.

And thus the four seated men who raised amber-colored drinks or saluted with freshly lit cigars.

The greetings went around in a circle.

'Doctor' Hendrik Pretorius was not a real doctor, but he sat closest to the bar and doled out the medicine with a generous hand. Lean and permanently tan, the man's silver beard shot to a tidy point, a shorter analog to his ponytail. Many cops couldn't stand the sight of the old civil liberties lawyer. There were reasons. There were also reasons that Leo didn't mind him. 'Detective.' Dr. Pretorius waved with a decanter before leaning back in his chair and sliding the crystal bottle back into its slot on a shelf.

'Lawyer,' Leo replied. Another old joke. 'Journalist,' he carried it a step farther, acknowledging Lucas Tate, editor of the *Jokertown Cry* with a halfhearted shot from a finger-gun.

Tate was seated, masked, and languid, as usual. The elongated skin tags that passed for his hair were drawn back away from his face. 'Cop.' Tate nodded from within his St. Bernard mask, which he indicated with aplomb as he then said to Father Squid, 'Picked this one for you, tonight. I was feeling ... *holy*.'

The priest said, 'Yes, I bet you were. Toss me a stogie, would you?'

'But of course.' Tate fished around in the box and made a selection.

Lieutenant Harvey Kant threw back a slug of whatever very expensive beverage he'd been handed, swallowed hard, and said, 'Leo,' with a friendly address of his long, brown index finger. The rest of him was brown too, and decidedly reptilian. He looked rather uncannily like a burly lizard.

Lucas Tate said, 'Catch,' and tossed the priest something that smelled Cuban.

Father Squid caught it with the snap of a tentacle and motioned for a light, which Dutton swooped in to provide. The priest said, 'You boys sure know how to take care of a guy,' and he settled himself into one of the remaining seats, beside Chaos – who adjusted three of his six arms in order to be more accommodating.

'Oh, and uh ... Sibyl,' Leo added quickly, spying the motionless blue woman standing unobtrusively naked in a corner. 'Good to see you too,' he murmured.

Sibyl didn't have a vocational descriptor like the rest of the players, but then again, she wasn't playing – she only accompanied the lawyer, whose side she rarely left. 'Ice Blue Sibyl,' everyone called her. She never called herself anything. She never spoke at all, and no one knew how much she understood except, perhaps, Dr.

Pretorius. Leo wouldn't have admitted she made him uncomfortable with her smooth, seamless skin and her perpetual silence. But he didn't have to.

Leo shook the nearest hand Chaos offered him. 'How's it hanging?' he asked.

'Let me unfold it and I'll check,' Chaos offered.

'I've heard that one. And for God's sake, restrain yourself.' Leo used a cigar to distort one corner of his grin.

Chaos wiggled in order to better wedge himself into place, so that he could play without elbowing anyone on either side. 'You're the one who set me up, tossing off a line like that. Nobody's fault but your own.'

'I was hoping for new material,' Leo told him.

Charles Dutton said, 'You young lads – always daring to dream. Chaos hasn't learned any new jokes since Nixon was in office.'

'In my defense,' said the six-armed man, 'that man was a veritable *oasis* of humor.'

'If you say so.' Leo turned his attention to Dutton. 'And who're you calling "young"?'

'For a *relative* value of young,' their host clarified. 'Look around you. What's the median age here, you think? We ought to start calling ourselves the Social Security Society.'

More softly than he meant to, Leo said, 'You know, they're throwing me off the force in January, for being old. I guess it's better this than the alternative.'

Chaos patted his shoulder and said, 'All the same, it ain't hardly fair.'

'Not remotely. Look at him – still a spring chick, I tell you,' insisted Dutton, doing his part to keep the mood light enough for cards. He approached the table and drew out his own seat, which was everyone's signal to start. 'So. Shall we?'

Chaos fidgeted, still trying to keep all his shoulders within his personal space. He asked, 'Who's dealing? Host?'

'Always,' declared Dutton, reaching for the pack of cards and tapping them out into his palm as neatly as a cigarette. 'If you'd come around more often, you'd know that.'

'If you didn't have Cosmos so often—'

Father Squid made a sound that cut him off. 'None of that. This is a *friendly* game. You're both welcome here. It's not our fault you two can't play nice.'

Chaos grumbled something under his breath, but he didn't push his luck. Instead he asked, 'What're we playing? Hold 'em?'

Charles Dutton leaned forward and began to thumb a single card, facedown, around the circle. He said, 'Christ, no. This is *man*-poker. Seven card, or nothing.'

'Got it.'

Another card made the rounds, this one faceup.

Leo picked up his offerings and shuffled them between his fingers until he liked the way they looked. Seven of clubs. Ace of diamonds. No matter which way he held them, he wasn't thrilled, but he kept it to himself.

Dutton said, 'All right,' and everyone threw in, starting small.

When Leo's turn came up, he pulled out a George and tossed it on the pile. The next set of cards came around, and he added those to his hand, and added a few more bills to the pot. He still wasn't liking the hand, and was paying too much attention to it when Dutton nudged him by saying, 'Ante up, old man.'

'Sure. Sorry.'

But he escaped that round having lost less than ten bucks, and fared better on the third, wherein he picked up mint with a good old-fashioned dead man's hand. He cackled at the money, and scooped his winnings closer to his chest.

'Time for a drink break. Or a refresher break,' Lucas Tate suggested, and they broke off briefly to address half-forgotten cigars and mostly empty glasses while Dutton shuffled, fiddled, and did a decent trick or two with the fresh, starchy cards.

Harvey Kant said, 'You keep playing like that, and you won't need that pension.'

And Leo replied, 'I'll keep that in mind.'

Dr. Pretorius left his seat to go stand near the inscrutable Sibyl, and fixed himself a new beverage. No one offered Sibyl anything, not out of rudeness – but so far as anyone knew, she neither ate nor drank. Anything. She had a mouth, but Leo had never seen it open.

During the course of this break, the talk turned to work in general – and Fort Freak's line of work in particular. 'I've heard,' Father Squid said with a nod that jiggled his tentacles, 'that the gangs are really up in arms.'

Harvey Kant agreed, but added, 'Same old thing. Big, stupid game of "Who took my drugs?" You'd think they'd try something else once in a while.'

Leo said, 'At least we got all the goddamned naked people sorted out, if you'll pardon my French, Father. But the thefts – scads of 'em, none of it related as far as we can tell. Except they *must* be.'

Head-shaking went around the table, along with new puffs of smoke from Lucas Tate's cigar. But as they buckled down for another hand, Leo cleared his throat and said in the direction of Dr. Pretorius, 'And then there's that thing about the courthouse.'

Chaos said, 'What, the fire? I heard that wasn't a big deal.'

'It was an inconvenient deal for *me*,' Dr. Pretorius griped.

Leo said, 'Yeah – it messed up the doctor's plans for his students. And it dredged up some strange old things in the process.'

'Like what?' Dutton asked, but he didn't pause from his down-card dealing to wait for a response.

'Like …' Leo reached forward when the faceup card came around. 'You remember the Rathole, don't you?' He didn't get an immediate response, so he said, 'All of us were old enough. It was a big deal.'

Dutton paused mid card delivery. 'The restaurant? The murders? That was … twenty or thirty years ago.'

'Nineteen seventy-eight,' Leo said. 'Right before Christmas. Some of the paperwork that survived the fire – it was from that case.' He did a little wave that meant *yada yada yada* and continued. 'Anyway, it was something I hadn't thought about. Not in years.'

'But you're thinking about it now,' Father Squid delivered in his best, most detached-but-warm counseling voice.

Leo said, 'It was my first bad one. Right after I made detective.' He gathered up Dutton's next offerings.

Dutton delivered the rest of the cards, and the players delivered the rest of their bets in silence, until Father Squid said softly, 'I remember the Rathole. My first church – the storefront – was right nearby. A girl named Lizzie worked there. She was one of the kindest people I ever knew.'

'The counter girl?' Leo asked.

'Yes. She died that night.'

'Her and a bunch of other people,' Lucas Tate said, and Leo could hear his frown through the St. Bernard mask. 'The counter girl glowed, didn't she?' he asked, but no one answered, so he kept talking. 'Yeah, I remember the Rathole. It happened right after I came up from that assignment.'

'What assignment?' Leo asked.

Charles Dutton rolled his eyes; everyone could see it, even through the yellow death mask. 'God, here we go.'

Lucas perked up significantly and said, 'So you know I wrote this book, right?'

And everyone around the table groaned good-naturedly except for Leo, who knew about it same as everybody else. But he'd forgotten. '*Paper Demon.* You wrote that right after the Rathole?'

'Yes and no. I was out from undercover, but I'd just begun working on the book when the diner got shot up. *My life with the gangs of Jokertown,*' he mused, supplying the second part of *Paper Demon*'s title. 'I was just getting used to hearing my own name again, instead of "Nimrod." Yeah, that's what they called me. Man. It feels like a hundred years ago.'

The detective said, 'Tell me about it.'

Though it'd only been a rhetorical response, Dr. Pretorius took him up on it. '*I'll* tell you about it. I'll tell you about a teenaged street joker who got railroaded for a crime he almost certainly didn't commit.'

'Did you represent him?' Leo asked. 'I don't remember.'

'He escaped before the trial. I never got a chance to defend him, only to file his paperwork.' The lawyer seemed to be restraining himself when he said quietly, 'I was going to use his case in my class next semester. The kid *couldn't* have done it.'

Lucas Tate spoke up, saying, 'That's a little hard to argue. I mean, he was holding a king's ransom in drugs when they picked him up – and that was after he'd spent a week helping himself to the stash he took from the diner. Everybody knew that cook was dealing.'

'We never argued that point. But—'

It was Kant's turn to object. 'Christ, Storgman. I hope you're not thinking of looking into that case again. No point wasting time and energy on a thirty-year-old crime. We got the guy, and now he's dead. They're all dead.'

Father Squid muttered, '*We're* not.'

'Hey, *Nimrod*,' Leo said, wanting to steer away from the potential disagreement. 'Come Monday, I'll be swinging by the *Cry*. Will you be in?'

'I'll be in,' he confirmed. 'But I won't answer to that anymore, *Ramshead*. Go ahead and come by my office, while you're at it. We'll talk about the bad old days, and I'll slip you a copy of *Paper Demon* … in case you've somehow *misplaced* your own.'

Leo said, 'Good idea. I think I might've … uh … lost my copy.'

Almost everyone laughed.

SEPTEMBER

FAITH

by John Jos. Miller

PART 1.

September, 2010

The catacombs underneath Our Lady of Perpetual Misery, the Church of Jesus Christ, Joker, were not as old as those beneath Rome nor as extensive as those under Jerusalem, but they sufficed. Their only entrance was through a trapdoor in the crypt's floor. The trapdoor and permanent steel ladder had been installed during the tunnel's earlier life as a conduit for since superseded electrical and telephone lines and the bundles of wires and pipes. Father Squid was thankful for the ladder. He was getting too old and, let's face it, heavy, for unsecured stepladders.

When was the last time I've played handball with Rabbi Feldman down at the Y? he asked himself. *Or done laps in the pool? I like doing laps in the pool.*

Father Squid was a shade under six feet, but he was big. When he was what he fondly thought of as being in shape he weighed about two-seventy, but he'd passed the three-hundred-pound mark sometime past and he wasn't looking back. He liked swimming because there was more than a little of the amphibian in him. His skin was thick, gray, and totally hairless. His round eyes were slightly protruding and covered by flickering, nictitating membranes. In place of a nose he had a cluster of dangling tentacles that covered his mouth like a constantly twitching mustache. His large hands had long, attenuated fingers and their palms had circular depressions – vestigial suckers – impressed all over them. He walked slowly, ponderously, making soft squishing sounds as he moved. He smelled faintly of the sea.

He sighed as he stood on the ladder's bottom rung, catching his breath. The tunnel was cool and quiet, and dark. The priest stepped down onto the slightly uneven brick floor and reached up to find the cord that turned on the recently installed fluorescent light dangling from the ceiling. He flicked it on to reveal an ossuary with wooden racks placed against the tunnel walls containing piles of old, clean, neatly stacked bones. Father Squid looked at them and sighed again. *So many gone over the years. So many lost and gone.*

The racks held all that remained of the forgotten and unknown who'd been removed from the first Our Lady's graveyard after they'd been forced to move when the church had been sold out from under Father Squid's mortgage. The bones were sorted by type. Femurs, tibiae, humeri, skulls, and vertebrae stacked in neat piles. The strangely twisted and deformed abnormalities frequently found in joker skeletons were jumbled together in a separate bin. All the bones were naked of flesh but to Father Squid's sensitive nasal tentacles they still smelled of loss, sadness, and death. He went to the bank of votive candles adjacent to the racks and lit half a dozen. He bowed his head in silent prayer for those who had no one to remember them and no one to mourn them but the priest and the old ladies of the Living Rosary Society who met in the catacombs once a month to tell their beads in prayer.

The additional candlelight faintly illuminated a little more of the silent catacomb. Farther down the tunnel were tombs and mausoleums, family and individual. Father Squid passed the mass crypt that held the remains of the victims of the arsonist's fire that had destroyed the original Our Lady and killed a hundred worshippers. Beside the massive mausoleum was the stone coffin that contained Chrysalis's remains. Once a year an offering of Amaretto and a dozen English roses was placed on it by a still-grieving devotee. Beyond that a dark niche held a single urn of ashes with the name Spector chiseled on its base that only Quasiman, the church's sexton, ever dusted clean. Farther back was an unmarked but not unvisited wall crypt that held the twisted and deformed skeleton of a boy caught between two states of being. The skeleton had appeared mysteriously in Father Squid's rectory one day, wrapped in a cloak with an unsigned note reading: 'Came across this while privately previewing an estate sale. Since the prior owner has no more use for him, I thought you could finally put him to a proper rest.' Father Squid had removed the single sequined glove from the one human-shaped skeletal hand, and interred the bones quietly.

The priest waddled farther down the tunnel, taking a powerful flashlight from his cassock. This area hadn't been electrified yet. He preferred it that way. This is where he came to perform his private acts of contrition. He visited the single tomb set in a wall niche several times a year, whenever overwhelming need drove him, whenever memories became too burdensome to bear alone.

Storgman's revelations at the poker game had disturbed him greatly, recalling events from the past that he had thought well buried. He'd had a sleepless night. Morning had brought no surcease to his sorrow or his worry. He realized that it probably wouldn't help much, but he had to talk things over with someone. Someone he had once loved greatly, and still did.

He stopped before the tomb and reached out his finely fingered hand and rested it gently on the small name plaque set into the wall. 'Hello,' he said quietly. He bowed his head in prayer, but prayer could not dim his recollections of that terrible night.

December, 1978

Father Squid sat at his desk in St. Andrew's office, tired but satisfied at the tag end of a long night after a long and busy day. Finally, after a few months of uncertainty, things were starting to go well with his new assignment. The congregation, if not the other members of the parish hierarchy, were starting to accept him, starting to believe in him. He had, he thought, his idea of the pageant to thank for that.

He'd first come to St. Andrew's in the summer, fresh out of seminary. In fact, he hadn't even officially ended his study when he'd been shipped off to the Jokertown parish as part of a special program, an experimental outreach to this most peculiar community that wasn't on any map, nor named in government documents, nor ever given official borders. What it had, in spades, was jokers. And what they had were problems, many of which the local parish could hardly comprehend, let alone resolve. When Father Coughlan, the head of the parish, whom Father Squid found to be a sincere but boozy old relict utterly unequipped to deal with the task of shepherding his malformed flock, had pled for help, someone had the bright idea to pluck Squid out of the seminary, slap a collar on him, and send him out among his fellow jokers. But, being jokers and naturally suspicious of all authority, the young priest had been unsure how to reach the parishioners. Until he had the idea for a Jokertown Christmas Pageant.

Father Squid wanted this to be a total community effort. He alternately cajoled and browbeat Dorian Wilde, Jokertown's poet laureate, into writing and directing it. He tirelessly canvassed the neighborhood for volunteers to play the various roles in the pageant; the three Wise Men, Joseph, Mary, the shepherds, the angels, and, of course, the coveted position of baby Jesus himself. He quickly discovered that there is no mother alive, joker or not, who doesn't believe that her child is suitably adorable to play an angel and that there is no businessman or community leader who doesn't believe he's a Wise Man.

The entire community got involved designing and constructing sets, making costumes, publicizing the pageant wide and far. St. Andrew's was getting publicity outside Jokertown, which was all to the good. Wild card chic was all the rage, and Father Squid hoped to grab a bit of it, not for himself, but for the people of his parish. Even Father Coughlan was happy. Church attendance was up. More donations were coming into the coffers. All this had been achieved without more effort on Coughlan's part and he was that much closer to his retirement and the small cottage in Ireland that he coveted.

Though all the work fell on Father Squid's shoulders, he was young and energetic and enthusiastic. He worked long hours not only on the pageant but at the community center he'd started in a boarded-up old liquor store down the street from the church. Often, like tonight, he'd work all day and well into the night and then end his day by swinging by the Rathole and lingering over a cup or two of coffee.

Maybe, he reflected as he buttoned up his coat and left his office for the chilly December night, the idea of becoming a priest wasn't so crazy after all. There were still problems he had to deal with, of course. Complications. Things he hadn't planned on. But given the difficulties of his past life, these were all small potatoes. Faith, he told himself. Have faith, and it will all work out.

Father Squid was an easily recognizable figure. Many he passed on the still busy street greeted him. A few stopped to chat. It was part of his job, so he humored them all, though he was tired and really wanted to get inside someplace warm, get some even warmer coffee inside of himself, sit, and rest for a while and then walk her home with the dawn.

She was another miracle in his life. He was almost ashamed at the undeserved blessings he'd received lately. He'd come far from the St. Cabrini's orphanage in Salem where he'd been abandoned as an infant by anonymous parents, almost certainly because his card had turned. He'd been lucky to have only drawn a joker, one that allowed him a relatively normal life. He'd been lucky at the orphanage too. The nuns had been good to him. The other kids didn't even bully him, much, because either his natural heritage or the wild card had also given him the build of a baby bull. But St. Cabrini's had never been a real home and of course they'd cut him loose when he turned eighteen. The years of drifting after that had opened his eyes to the ways of a world much crueler than that of the gentle nuns who'd taken care of him. For a while he thought he'd found a family of sorts when he'd been drafted into the army, but that proved to be more of a lunatic asylum than a home. After 'Nam there was more footless wandering until he'd joined the Twisted Fists. That had been the biggest mistake of his life

Father Squid was a block or so away from the Rathole when he realized something was wrong.

Police cars passed him, speeding down the street, sirens flashing, lights punching through the darkness as they slowed to breast the crowd blocking the road. The sidewalks were also overflowing with curious onlookers, though their ranks parted as Father Squid approached.

'Look, it's that priest—'

'Father Squid. Someone must have called—'

'Thank God he's here—'

'Oh, Father, it's awful—'

Father Squid found himself suddenly immersed in a mad scene painted as if by an artist sunk in a nightmare of twisted bodies and deformed faces flashing in the strobing bursts thrown out by the police car's pulsing lights. He advanced on stiff legs, his expression as suddenly frozen as his heart. *Let it not be the Rathole,* he prayed silently. He pressed on when he reached the yellow tape cordoning off the sidewalk in front of the diner. A uniformed cop came forward to stop him as he ducked under the crime scene tape.

'Hey you, you can't go in there!'

Another cop recognized him. 'Let him through. He's a priest.'

'A priest?' The first cop looked astonished. He was a nat. All the cops were. Sergeant Mole was the only joker cop in the Jokertown Precinct, and they kept him down in the basement filed away out of sight, much like the records that he maintained. 'Well, all right.' He turned to his partner as Father Squid, who had not slowed his inexorable pace, marched past with an unreadable expression on his face. 'They're sure making them weird-looking these days.' He shrugged. 'Nobody in there needs a priest, anyway.'

If Father Squid heard, he gave no sign. His first prayer denied, he prayed again, *Let it not be Lizzie.*

He could smell the blood and death as he came through the front door. It was like 'Nam again. Or as if he were running with the Black Dog once more. The stink of death, like the blood, was everywhere. Crime scene techs and uniformed cops were swarming the tiny little diner with their cameras and their notebooks and their normal, brisk, unaffected faces. There were bodies. There was blood. There was, draped on the floor, Lizzie, still glowing faintly. Her skin was a pale, washed-out green.

'Hey, you!' someone shouted. 'You can't come in here.'

'He's a priest.' The young cop who'd first vouched for him was standing by his shoulder.

A man came up to him. He was a few inches shorter than Father Squid and of moderate build, dark-haired, and young. 'I'm Detective Storgman,' he said. 'You are?'

'Father Squid.' He didn't look at the man. He couldn't take his eyes off Lizzie. He'd seen many bodies in his day, and he knew a corpse when he saw one. He was hardly aware that he spoke again. 'What happened?'

'Looks like a robbery gone bad,' the young nat detective said. 'Did you know anyone here?'

Father Squid still couldn't take his eyes off Lizzie's body. He wanted to, but he was afraid that he'd collapse if he moved so much as a single muscle. When he spoke again his voice was without inflection.

'Not for long enough,' he said. 'Not nearly long enough.'

September, 2010

That was how, Father Squid thought, it ended.

Partly, anyway. Because it really wasn't over, not even now, over thirty years later.

The horror he'd found at the Rathole that night still haunted his dreams, and at times would even catch him unaware during his waking hours. He'd never stop paying for his role in the events that culminated in the killings.

He leaned like a sick man against the wall behind which Lizzie was entombed, then pushed himself erect and shambled back down the corridor and up the stairs, the tears drying on his cheeks before he gained the sunlight again.

THE RAT RACE

PART 3.

Wanda arrived promptly at Leo's desk, just as he was swiping up his keys, adjusting his hat, and reaching for his jacket. 'Your timing's great,' he told her.

'I never miss a date.'

'Is that what this is?'

She shrugged. 'It's a lunch date, anyway. And then a trip to the morgue – *very* romantic.'

'The newspaper morgue. And it was your idea.' He couldn't keep the smile off his face. It wasn't every day a pretty woman showed up at his desk, inviting herself into his lunch hour.

'And I appreciate you humoring me. Should we walk it or ride?' he asked.

With a glance down at her very high heels, Wanda said, 'Let's ride.'

'Works for me,' he said.

Just then his partner – a tall, pleasant-looking black man about half Leo's age – dropped a stack of folders onto his own adjoining desk. 'A ride to where?' he asked curiously, lifting an eyebrow at the sight of Wanda.

Before Leo could answer, Wanda said, 'Oh, we're just getting lunch and thinking about a cab. And you are ...?'

'Michael Stevens.' He nearly tripped over himself to make the introduction. 'I'm Leo's partner.'

'A *new* partner?' she asked, giving him an up-and-down appraisal usually reserved for show cats. Apparently the conclusions she drew were good, because she took Michael's hand and shook it.

Leo answered, 'Relatively new. Ralph retired back in 2000, and these days he's laid up with lung cancer. Mike's been with me since last year – after Ralph's replacement transferred out to Seattle. Anyway, Mike, this is Wanda Moretti. She's an old friend.'

'Moretti ...' he repeated. 'I think I've heard the name.'

'I used to spend a lot of time around the precinct,' she said, leaving a thousand hints and implications to flutter in the wind. 'But that was a long time ago.' Then she turned to Leo and said, 'I definitely like the look of him!'

'Um, thank you,' Michael said, and dark skin or no, Leo watched him redden. Wanda'd always had that effect on people. Twenty years hadn't taken the edge off it; the decades had given her time to fine-tune it.

'Are you a family man?' she asked, her eyes flitting across his desk and spying a framed photo there.

He tracked her gaze and said, 'Yes! I mean, *yes*. This' – he retrieved the photo and handed it to her – 'is my ... ah ... my girlfriend and daughter. She's a dancer. My girlfriend, I mean. Not ... um ... not the baby. Obviously.'

'What a lovely family,' Wanda said approvingly. Then she teased in a half whisper, 'And it's just as well. I'm old enough to be your mother.'

Michael rallied through his rising blush and said, 'I don't believe that for a moment!' with just a touch more chivalrous enthusiasm than an unembarrassed man would've mustered.

'Trust me, Sunshine,' she said. 'I've got shoes older than you. But it's nice of you to say so. Leo? Are we ready?'

'Yes, ma'am.' His coat was halfway zipped. He zipped it the rest of the way and told Michael, 'Be back in a couple of hours. Got my phone if anything exciting happens.'

His partner said, 'All right. Have fun. And, I ... um. Nice to meet you, Ms. Moretti.'

'Likewise, I'm sure,' she told him, and falling into step beside Leo, the two of them left to flag down a cab.

Once Wanda was seated beside him and they were on their way, she said, 'I do like him, you know. Your partner.'

'He's an all right kid. Got too many brains for his own good, but I trust him. You wouldn't know it at a glance, but he's actually pretty tough for a goofy-looking nat. Tough and ... young. Jesus. Was I ever that young?'

'Oh, yes. With a picture of your wife and kid on your desk and everything. I remember it well.' But this tiptoed too closely to uncomfortable territory, so she gracefully shifted gears. 'Now this Michael – he's another nat?'

'Yeah.'

They were both thinking about Ralph, so they discussed him for a while; and the trip to the High Hand was short enough that they didn't need much else to talk about.

The restaurant itself was almost too high-end for lunch, but Leo wanted the hour to look good, and it did. The food was great, featuring a pair of aged steaks smothered in mushrooms and caramelized onions. The conversation was better. Photos came out of Wanda's wallet and her three grandchildren were discussed, and real estate came up but only briefly. Leo told Wanda about some of the more peculiar cases he'd seen in the intervening years since last they'd spent any time together; he spilled about his daughter's erratic love life and his own lack of grandkids. And when the check came Leo got it.

Down the street at the *Cry* offices, they were informed that Lucas Tate was in an unexpected meeting – but he'd left word at the front desk that Leo was welcome to make himself at home in the newspaper morgue and he'd be with him in an hour.

A rickety service elevator deposited Leo and Wanda in a subbasement lit with unsteady fluorescent lights covered with ill-fitting plastic shades. The main corridor was lined with doors – mostly glass ones, and mostly they were open. Signs beside the rooms announced MICROFILM MACHINES, SCANNED FILES, AND READING ROOM. In these rooms were filing cabinets of the ordinary size; and a few doors back they found much larger metal cabinets, with drawers as wide as Leo's desk.

The rooms were divided into decades, and the cabinets were divided into years. '1978–79' was penciled onto a piece of yellow paper and held in place upon one such drawer by a strip of Scotch tape gone brown with age.

Wanda reached for the drawer and braced herself, and drew it open slowly. 'It happened around Christmas, right?'

'Just before it,' he confirmed.

Soon they found what they were looking for. The headline screamed loud, in font as big as the detective's thumbs: 'MASS SHOOTING AT RATHOLE DINER.'

They read in silence. And as the paragraphs brought the night back into focus, Leo's memory filled in some of the missing gaps. It didn't take his breath away, not this time. But it made him quiet all the same, restoring that dreadful sense of unease he'd almost forgotten.

In 1978 the Rathole was a mom-and-pop diner beyond the main drag of the Bowery, a couple of blocks down Grand Street. Open all night every night, it was one of those places that should've saved money and left the locks off the doors. It served the expected clientele, off the beaten path in a part of town most kindly described as 'iffy.'

'Elizabeth Allison Wallace,' Leo read out loud. She'd been working the counter that night. 'And she was pregnant – not very far along.' He remembered the girl lying on the cold tile floor behind the register, her phosphorescent skin still giving the shadowed nook a soft, lingering gleam like a low-watt bulb. When she was still alive, she'd hovered a couple of feet off the floor, whether she liked it or not. The neighborhood had called her 'Glowworm' when it didn't call her 'Lizzie.' Nineteen years old, and taking classes to wrap up her GED. She'd had a boyfriend, somebody who was bad news. It was all coming back to him now.

Wanda asked, 'Who?'

He only shook his head and pointed at the paper. 'Donald Richard Reynolds. Went by The Drip. Joker with a face like a half-melted candle. Homeless, with a record. Vagrancy, petty theft, and bigger theft. He also had a daughter living with an ex-wife someplace, and we think he was driving a Mercedes that you can bet your sweet ass he didn't own.'

'What's that got to do with anything?'

He didn't answer right away, but moved on to the next name. 'Maddox Horatio Crowder. Called Hash. Looked a little like a big, beefy alien – with real tight gray skin and four extra eyes. Short-order cook with a sawed-off shotgun. He got into the fray, and got off a couple of shots.'

'What was he doing with a sawed-off?' Wanda wanted to know.

'In that neighborhood, back then? Everyone was packing. But he was packing heavy because he was dealing out the back door. Speed, pot, coke. You name it. Shotgun didn't do him any good, though. By the time we got there, his stash was cleaned out and he was cooling off.'

She suggested, 'Could've been a robbery gone bad.'

'Could've been. Even looked like it – and Deedle looked good for it. When we caught him, he was carrying what was left of Hash's merchandise. The rest had gone up his nose or into his arm. Anyway, who else …?' His finger slid down the typeface, picking up old ink in a soft gray smudge. 'Stella Michelle Nichols, yeah. Bareback, they called her, over at Freakers. She had a …' He made the universal man-sign for breasts, cupping his hands above his belly. 'But on her back too. Worked second shift, showing 'em off. She'd been having problems with an overenthusiastic customer, someone who wanted to stuff more than dollar bills in her panties. But we never did pin him down. Never found her sister either. And then there was that last guy, there he is,' he said, stopping his finger again.

'Joel Eric Arnold,' Wanda read. 'What was his story?'

'A nat, and I knew him, a little. Most of us knew who he was – he was a janitor at Fort Freak, working third shift. That night he was doing laundry around the corner, and he stepped in here for a cup of coffee. Talk about your shitty luck. I remember Ralph took a look at him and started swearing. He recognized him right away. It took me a minute.' After all, half the guy's face had been blown off. Quietly he mused, 'Five people, all shot to death in the middle of the night.'

'And no one saw a thing.' It wasn't a question.

Leo said, 'Actually, that's not true. We got an anonymous tip, that's how we found them so fast.' He hadn't taken the call, but he'd heard the recording later – the frantic, blubbering terror of a man who refused to identify himself, saying only that they were dead at the Rathole, they were all dead. All of them, killed by a man wearing a hawk mask.

'You ever figure out who Mr. Anonymous was?'

'Nope. Never did. And unless he died between then and now, he's out there still.' He continued tapping his gray fingertip on the old newsprint. 'It looked cut-and-dried, Hash – that was the short-order cook, Maddox – had been dealing out the back door, but when we reached the scene, there wasn't so much as a dusting of coke or weed, not anyplace. But there was a hell of a lot of food – like he'd been cooking for a small army right before he died. I mean, the kitchen was *packed*.' The memory of the smell was almost enough to make him woozy. A dozen fried eggs, burning down to charcoal on the stove. Stacks of pancakes heaped on a plate, with another round smoldering on the griddle, and the fryer full of chicken fingers and French fries – all of them cooking way too long, filling the room with the greasy, choking smell of kitchen smoke and ash. 'And there was no money,' he concluded. 'Deedle'd made off with that too. But he was scared shitless when he figured out who all that money belonged to.'

'The mob?'

'Uh-huh. He heard about it in holding, how the mafia higher-ups were wanting a word with him. You know how he escaped, right?'

'Refresh my memory,' she said.

'They were moving him to the courthouse from lockup, and the little bastard got his cuffed wrists in front of him. Bit off his own thumb.'

'Goddamn.'

'Slipped loose, kicked his way out the back door, and hit the street running.'

Wanda wrapped up the rest. 'And turned up dead a week or two later.'

'You got it,' Leo said, though hearing the summary aloud jarred something else loose, another unpleasant fact that he hadn't considered in decades. 'He was beaten to a pulp, behind the old church building Squid was working on back then – turning it into Our Lady of Perpetual Misery. There wasn't enough left of the kid to stuff a pita.'

She considered this, and scanned another paragraph on another page – from a follow-up story printed a few days after the original announcement. 'Deedle had a Mercedes. Or he was driving a Mercedes, wasn't he?'

Leo nodded. 'Stolen. Restolen, actually – the one Don Reynolds had been driving. The kid must've taken it right off the curb. Probably thought it was his lucky day.'

'Is that what you think?' she asked, suddenly very serious.

Leo turned around so he could lean against the drawer and face the room, as if he were giving a lecture. Wanda listened. But he wasn't looking at her while he talked.

'I think this dumbass kid wandered by the Rathole, saw an opportunity, and he took it. Things got out of hand, all those people died ... but Deedle, he was thrilled silly because he'd scored enough money and enough drugs to keep him high for a year. I think he grabbed it and made a run for it – and maybe he wired the Mercedes, or maybe he saw Don's keys lying in a pool of blood, I don't remember how we found the car.'

He paused, and Wanda bit the edge of her lip as she held her breath. She asked, 'What about the bird mask? Deedle was wearing a bird mask, wasn't he? When they caught him?'

Leo grunted dismissively. 'Back in the seventies masks were a dime a dozen and everybody wore one, more or less. The mask didn't mean much. And if Dr. Pretorius had ever gotten a chance to take it in front of a jury, he'd have torn up that point.'

He stopped again, catching his breath or his memories.

And he continued, slower and more certain. 'But someone out there, someone saw it – or saw the tail end of it. Someone who made a phone call.' He considered the newspapers and the burned transcripts.

They closed the drawers and went back up the elevator.

At the front desk, they learned that Lucas Tate had been unavoidably detained and that he would not be joining them after all; but he'd been kind enough to leave a copy of *Paper Demon: My Life with the Gangs of Jokertown* with a Post-it note on the cover, telling Leo, 'Happy reading!'

SNAKE UP ABOVE

by David Anthony Durham

The guy fidgeted constantly. One second he leaned against the doorjamb smoking a cigarette, the next he paced the sidewalk, and then he sat on the steps flicking his lighter open and closed. The only time he seemed to stand still was when ushering a new customer inside the town house or when wishing a departing one a good evening. When he had to send an unwanted patron on his way, he did so with a weird barrage of quick movements, dancing around the guy, not really doing any damage, but untouchable and freaking annoying.

Looking down from a fire-escape landing four stories above, Marcus Morgan yawned and stretched his neck. He'd been up here for several hours, wasting the humid night away, watching the sporadic procession of the malformed and bizarre as they went inside the ramshackle town house. He'd come across the place during his nightly wanderings and figured out pretty quickly what sort of establishment the place was. A brothel. The kind of place the cops would be grateful to him for pointing out.

He'd settled down thinking he'd just gather some information, identify some customers, private eye like. He'd snitch the place out. He wasn't sure what he'd get in return. Some praise. A pat on the back. Maybe make it a regular thing, doing a little bit of good in this place.

For that matter, it would just be good to have a reason to

connect with some people, make some friends. He didn't want to be sulking around alone, but since arriving in New York a couple of weeks earlier he'd been wary to interact much with others in the city. There had been that kid who started following him yesterday. The joker's mouth was crowded with teeth, all pressed together and crooked. He was nice enough and talked a mile a minute, but Marcus ditched him. What sort of friend could he be? Better to get in with the cops.

That, at least, was what he intended when he began his surveillance. But watching the johns exit twenty or thirty minutes after they entered he wasn't so sure. They looked just as monstrous, but they were also more relaxed. More at peace with the world, looking like they'd just had a breakthrough at a really good therapist's …

'Hey, you!' It was the sketchy guy from the brothel, looking up from below Marcus. 'You slithery fuck. What, you think I can't see you?'

Marcus pulled his coils in closer, trying to get them into shadow.

'No use hiding now. You been spotted. Bull's-eye. *Pow!* Shot dead. Come down. Let me get a look at ya.'

Marcus hesitated a moment and then slipped through the opening in the landing and descended the metal stairs. He went headfirst. His arms helped him on, the long stretch of the rest of his body flexing against the steel as it slithered audibly across the rusted structure. He took the gap from the lowest landing to the ground at speed, curving his torso up just before he would've touched the asphalt. The rest of his body flowed down around him.

And there he was, in full view under the harsh spotlight above the brothel's entrance. Marcus's torso and arms were those of a well-muscled eighteen-year-old African-American kid. Normal enough. But beneath his belly button his body was that of a snake; thick, muscular, scaled in a vibrant pattern of yellow and red and black stripes. His snake portion stretched about twenty feet. He'd only been this way about a month and still found his reptilian length more embarrassing than anything else.

The sketchy guy stroked a sparse beard and studied Marcus, green eyes wide. He had letters tattooed on his knuckles, but he moved his hands too fast for Marcus to read them. He looked kinda familiar. 'Jesus,' he said, 'the snake man cometh!' The guy vanished and reappeared right beside Marcus. He tweaked his bicep and then zipped away. 'Strong kid, huh? Like them muscles? Work out?'

Marcus shrugged. He had never been particularly strong before, but he had to admit that his chest and shoulders had thickened. The muscles in his arms cut contours he had only dreamed of a few months ago. His back flared and his abs were chiseled into neat compartments.

The guy pressed in near him. 'You looking for a taste of ... tail? I could probably arrange something. I got a girl – you're into girls, right? – that could handle your length, big guy like you.'

'You have somebody like me in there?'

The guy popped his knuckles and flicked his gaze down Marcus's serpentine body. 'Not exactly. She doesn't need to be "like" you, if you know what I mean.'

Marcus didn't.

'You got cash?'

Marcus shook his head.

'You must have a bill or two, tucked up safe behind a scale or something.'

'I don't,' Marcus began. 'I'm not here for ... I was just ...'

Whatever denial he was trying to fish up proved unnecessary. A commotion inside snapped the guy's attention away. An angry female voice shouted, 'Give me a break here. Spasm! *Spaasssmmmm!?*'

'Cripes,' the guy said. 'Not again. Stay here. Don't let anybody in until I'm back.' He zipped inside.

Marcus stood a moment, alone on the street. People and cars passed on First Street. Somebody was looking through the garbage cans half a block away, but nobody approached him. What would he do if they did? Was he working? Unsure, he twisted around to face the street, arms folded and looking quite a bit more menacing than he knew.

A moment later a young man stomped out, a white guy, looking like a frat boy with his tousled blond hair. Behind him came a woman. She looked like a nat, pretty and dark-skinned, wearing a short nightgown she had clamped in place beneath an arm. 'Spasm,' she said, 'did you *not* hear me shouting, "*Oh, yeah, yeah, yeah! I'm gonna, gonna, gonna* …"' The temporary look of rapture with which she said these words disappeared. 'What part of that didn't you hear? When I say that, you give the john an orgasm. Quick as possible. That's your tiny little part in this. It is your one talent.'

'Look,' Spasm said, 'I'm sorry, Minal. It's got nothing to do with you—'

'I know that!' she snapped. 'Master of stating the obvious …'

As she set her hands on her hips, her gown flapped open, revealing a torso covered in small, tentaclelike things. There might have been hundreds of them, all of them wriggling as if they had minds of their own. They looked so soft, delicate, like nipples, but nimbler than tongues, each of them dancing sensuous invitations. Marcus shifted his torso back a bit, pulling coils around in front of him. He couldn't keep his eyes off the prostitute. Man, he wanted to touch them, to feel them under his palm and caressing the side of his face. A weird pressure throbbed against a portion of his scales. Whatever was down there, it wasn't like the type of erections he used to get.

Spasm shook his head, exhaled, glanced at the fidgety guy. 'Twitch, this is freaking me out, bro. I didn't think it would matter, but each time I go to make the guy come I can't help thinking about … you know … boils and flippers and' – as if of their own accord, his eyes darted to Marcus – 'slithery things. Half these guys don't even have the right parts in the right places.'

'That's the point, Spaz,' Twitch said. 'You and Minal can take all comers. You can serve Jokertown's sexually challenged population. Think of the untapped clientele!'

'That's the problem,' Spasm protested. 'I can't help but think too much. I thought joker sex would give me a rise, but there are better ways to make a buck. Dude, I could be working Vegas or something.'

'You couldn't handle Vegas,' Minal spat. '*I* should be working Vegas!' She stepped back inside and slammed the door.

Suddenly Marcus recognized both men. Spasm and ... Twitch. From ... '*American Hero*,' he said. 'You guys were on *American Hero*! The first season. I watched the whole thing. You ...' As quickly as his enthusiasm came on him, it morphed to perplexity. 'What happened? You guys were famous.'

Both men looked at him, annoyed. Twitch wiped a line of drool from the corner of his mouth. Spasm said, 'Shit happens, dude. A half-snake black kid should know that.' He started walking away.

Twitch pestered Spasm all the way to the end of the block, snapping in front of him again and again. Until he got tired of that and resorted to tripping him, pulling his shirt up over his head, tying his shoelaces together.

Marcus uncrossed his arms. 'Hey, Twitch, you still ... need me?'

Twitch appeared in front of him. 'Need you? What I need is a new way to make a living. I need a break. Nothing's been going right lately.' He paused a moment. 'Hey, what's your name, kid?'

'Marcus.'

'Marcus, my man. Marcus, you ever think of using that tail of yours for something?'

Sliding back slightly, Marcus asked, 'Like what?'

'Like ... doing some high-rise work. Snake burglary. Slither yourself into a penthouse. They got shit just lying around there. Stuff they don't need – not as bad as you and I need it, at least. We could partner on it. Make a stack of bills in no time.'

'No, I don't think so. I'm not a crook.'

Twitch pulled a face. 'Nah, but you can evolve,' he said. 'Give it time. Tell you what, you change your mind, come on back and find me.' He snapped away again.

A couple of hours later, Marcus slithered through dockside crates, containers, and nautical debris. He stood for a while looking over the Hudson. Beyond its glistening blackness the stark geometries of apartment buildings loomed, many already twinkling awake to face the coming day. Imagining the regular families living in them made him physically sick in the stomach.

Wrapping the tip of his tail around the nearest beam, he flowed over the edge and down the wall of cluttered cement and steel and tar-plastered wooden supports beneath him. He found the hand-holds he already knew by heart. A few seconds later he swung his body into a cavelike slot that ran back underneath the docks. He couldn't tell what it had ever been for, but it certainly wasn't in use anymore.

Marcus coiled up on a rug and leaned back against a soiled bean-bag. He tugged his MacBook close. He flipped it open and looked at his face on the display screen. That was all he was going to see. During his first few days in New York, when it still had power, he'd stared at the collage of photos on the computer's screen saver: family shots, their vacation in Jamaica, photos of snakes and lizards, a few sports stars thrown in, a head shot of Mos Def looking deeply introspective, and more than a few screens of Alicia Keys. He just had to imagine them now.

Problem was that it was all too easy for him to imagine things about his life before his card turned. In his dreams he had it all back again. He'd be at home in Maryland, driving his new Versa through his old neighborhood in North Baltimore, a semisuburban community that stretched out toward the county line. Kids he knew played on their lawns. Folks waved as he passed. He slowed going by Tish Reynolds's house, just in case she happened to be out … Or he'd be struggling to get a word in at the dinner table as his brother talked basketball, and his sister gossiped about what Kelly Gaines's sister Michelle did when she found Monique Packer's iPhone and figured it was payback time, and his mom dished out complete meals even though she'd just gotten home from work, and his dad took it all in, his ownership of all of them resting in the curve of his lips.

In some ways they were the Huxtables. Dad a gynecological surgeon. Mom a therapist. Theirs was a prosperous mixed neigh-borhood, but their family friends tended to be upwardly mobile African-Americans, doctors and professors, a politician or two. In their house it wasn't about being equal to whites and having the same privileges. It was about having the same privileges and being a bit better, deserving them a bit more, protecting their status and carefully shaping the direction of their children's lives.

And it was all crap, Marcus now believed. The Huxtables didn't do well with change, with acceptance, with a joker in the family.

Okay, about the only part of what happened that he did admit was his fault was that it was his stupid idea to get Baby Girl. Since his mom was allergic to anything furry, he'd kept fish and lizards, and finally snakes as pets. Quiet and calm. Slim and beautiful and dead-eyed: he liked snakes the best. Garters got old pretty quick, though. His milk snake wasn't much different. The golden boa he bought with an entire Christmas season's gift money was crazy cool, but when a guy that got fired from *Lamont Got Lizards!* told him he could score him a coral snake, Marcus didn't even ask how or why or concern himself with legality.

He called her Baby Girl. For weeks he kept her hidden in one of the basement tanks. He stared for hours at her rings and her eyes. Only gradually did he ease a gloved hand into the tank, so, so gently, not even touching her at first but just being there near her. When he finally got up the courage to pick her up his heart thumped wildly in his chest. The feeling of danger and trust and deadly power afterward left him sated and dreamy.

All totally awesome, until the day he held her near to his face, feeling sure she loved him as much as he did her. She kept licking the air with her tongue. So – thinking snaky thoughts himself – he stuck out his own tongue. Baby Girl didn't hesitate. She opened her mouth and bit the tip of the proffered tongue. He fell unconscious knowing something serious had just happened.

When he awoke his mother was standing over him, her face ashen above a hospital mask. Still, relief flooded him. He was in the hospital. He'd been bitten by a coral snake and lived! If he was waking in the hospital he must be all right.

But then he realized they were in his bedroom. His father's back was to him. He had on his smock and mask, and when he turned he held a curving sliver of surgical steel that looked positively demented. Marcus tried to shout, but his tongue felt strange.

His mother slipped some sort of mask over his face. She said something comforting, but her eyes betrayed disgust. He followed the flick of her gaze and took in the scaled horror that was his body below the waist. It spilled off the bed and trailed across the floor and over his desk, pulsing like a living creature that he was no part of. But he was a part of it. It was him! He knew, even through the haze the gas mask started to induce, what his father planned to do with that scalpel.

As the surgeon moved in, Marcus's arm flew up from under the covers. He slapped his father across his lower jaw. The scalpel flew into the air. His mother screamed. Again, he tried to speak, but his father was scrabbling for another instrument, and his mother was climbing the wall to get away from him. Marcus rolled off the bed, his lower body all muscle, seething with power, pumped full of adrenaline. His father had another scalpel in hand now, but his intent looked more like murder than surgery.

Marcus didn't plan what happened next. His tongue shot out of his mouth. It stretched incredibly long and punched his father right between the eyes, snapping his head back. Worse still, he'd put anger in the strike. He put poison in it. He felt a sharp joy in the taste of it and in the sight of his father going down.

The Cosby Show had never been like this.

Asmodeus wore pin-striped trousers and suspenders over a sleeveless white undershirt, which was moist with sweat down the front and under the armpits. A riot of acne wrapped his jawline like a red beard. Short horns ringed his head in a jagged crown. A heavy inverted cross hung from a thick silver chain on his neck, and curving barbs – like metallic thorns – pierced through his earlobes and cartilage.

For all this there was something comforting about his face when he smiled and said, 'Welcome, young truth seekers.' He considered them a moment, looking one to another as if he were measuring them up. 'Young ass-kicking warriors.'

Marcus lifted his chin, squared his shoulders. He stood as his father had told him military men do, proud and disciplined. A few hours ago he hadn't even heard of this guy. He'd been snaking through the Bowery, trying to pretend he wasn't keeping an eye out for a Dumpster to dive. That kid had found him again, the one that had too many teeth. Marcus stayed close-lipped at first, little more than grunting answers as the guy stuck to his side.

The kid followed Marcus around as if he had nothing better to do, talking the whole time. At first he seemed to be rambling with no direction, but after a while he began mentioning Asmodeus again and again. The things he did for young jokers were fucking straight. Taking them in. Schooling them about fighting and shit. Hooking them up with whatever they wanted. Getting them laid. Getting them strapped. Whatever. He was a fucking Demon Prince! He knew Lucifer personally.

Marcus had no idea what a Demon Prince was and wasn't convinced knowing Lucifer was something to brag about. Still, when he realized the kid was leading him toward this Asmodeus, he didn't fight it.

That's why he was standing at attention before the crown-headed joker. He was one of a group of ten, most of them young, all of them jokers. There were two scrawny brothers, thin and dark like urchins of some Indian slum, both of them with a third eye on their foreheads. Another guy kept pulling things that looked like jelly beans out of his nose. A muscle-bound man stood at the edge of the group. It was hard to say that he was definitely a joker. He might just have been one of those sicko bodybuilders, but Marcus couldn't help thinking he had *more* muscles in *more* places than any nat should have. Another looked perfectly normal but had breath so foul when he grunted a hello that Marcus nearly passed out.

'Look at you,' Asmodeus said. He didn't give any sign that he saw anything but good things in each of them. 'Each of you a warrior awaiting a cause. Each of you cast adrift by the cruelties of the nat-dominated world. Am I lying? Tell me that every shit-fucked thing you've suffered wasn't inflicted upon you by a nat.

A friend, maybe. A sibling. Parents even. Parents! And they call us unnatural. What's more unnatural than turning out their own children?'

The joker wasn't looking at him when he said that, but it grabbed Marcus like it was intended for only him. His parents had turned him out after their thwarted surgery attempt. His father wasn't hurt that bad, but they'd accused him of attempted murder. Even called the police on him. That's when he fled.

'Yeah,' the man said, 'I know where you been. Question is – where you going now? And you going alone? Or you going with brothers who got your back? Cops will shoot us in the back for loose change. That's what we're worth to them. Seems to me we all need brothers in a time like this, in a city like J-Town. And then the question becomes – what does it take to become a brother?'

The guy had a lot of questions. He didn't exactly answer them, but Marcus believed he was working toward it. That why he was still with Asmodeus and the others two hours later, frying beneath the late summer sun and looking down from the rooftop of a tenement building. The space below them had that run-down look typical of abandoned lots. Litter-strewn dirt and clumps of grass, debris. An old bathtub and a stack of railroad ties. That was all normal enough. What wasn't was that a swimming pool occupied the center of the lot. It was figure eight of glass blue, as pure-looking as an Alpine lake.

'Look closely, friends,' Asmodeus said. 'Behold Werewolves at rest.'

Marcus swallowed, partially because he was parched, partially because among the dozen or so jokers lounging on the wooden decking around the pool or bobbing in that amazing water was a girl in a white bathing suit. From a distance she looked kinda like Tish Reynolds. There was something on her face, but he couldn't quite make it out.

'That's not a pool,' one of the twins said. 'It's a couple of Dumpsters filled with water, with a deck built around it.'

'Yes,' Asmodeus confirmed. 'You see, even they – deep down – believe they are trash. Instead of being ashamed of it they thrive, flaunt it. There is no end to their arrogance.' After a moment he added, 'Unless we put an end to it.'

It wasn't the jokers who were out of touch with the workings of the world, he said. It was the nats and those who supported them. It was they who hadn't kept up with the changes the wild card had wrought, an evolution that could never be erased or denied, no matter how much they tried. Some who were brave enough – like the Demon Princes – had fought to protect jokers, to carve out turf and keep it all joker. Why not? Was it so much to ask that they have one place in America that they could feel proudly joker in?

Marcus hadn't thought of it that way before. Being proudly joker. But why not? The shame and confusion and self-hatred and wishing for the past: he could shake all of that off and simply be himself. It seemed perfectly reasonable when Asmodeus explained it. And intoxicatingly attractive, like the girl in the pool.

Marcus couldn't take his eyes off her. Such grace in the way she hung with her arms stretched out on the deck behind her, kicking her legs before her. Yeah, Tish definitely had a suit like that. It was the main reason he spent so much of last summer at the municipal pool, watching her, working up the courage for the few short conversations he had with her. Tish Reynolds ... She'd never know how much he'd thought and dreamed and fantasized about her. He hadn't even said good-bye to her. She'd never seen him like he was now.

Someone pointed out that the Werewolves in the Dumpster were jokers themselves. 'Yes, they are,' Asmodeus said. 'They call themselves Werewolves, but they wear masks to cover their faces. Look at them! Each and every one of them so ashamed of themselves that they'd rather pretend to be nats than show the world their real faces.'

Oh, that's what was on the girl's face, and on all their faces: masks.

'Someone should teach them a lesson,' Asmodeus said. 'Someone should have the guts to go in swinging.'

They came out of the night like commandos in some video game. For a few moments Marcus felt the pure macho adrenaline testosterone buzz of intentional, surprise brutality. They were the shit. The stunned, dumb-ass-looking Werewolves who looked at them as they roared into the lot were proof of it. Marcus had never been a violent person, but if violence was what it took to make it on his own he was up for it. These Werewolves deserved it. Asmodeus was watching them from above, and Marcus and the others had psyched themselves into putting on the best show they could.

It started beautifully. He didn't even use the ladder. He just surged up and over the railing. Bare-chested, his arms out to either side, he came in swinging. He clocked one Werewolf across the temple, laying him out on the deck. Another he missed with his first strike. He twisted his snake portion right around, bringing the same fist back to smash the masked face he'd missed only a second before. He surged toward the next guy, his tail moving him with power and speed he'd never known he had. The guy drew a knife, but Marcus tagged him with his tongue and then slapped him over the railing with his tail. That felt good.

The fight went on down below also, among the lawn chairs and folding tables set up for the evening's festivities. The overly muscled guy had a brute of a Werewolf down and was whaling on him with everything he had. The twins knocked a chest crowded with forty ouncers over, started picking up malt liquor flavored shards of glass and hurling them at Werewolves with ferocious speed. The guy with the bad breath made good use of it, facing his opponents with his mouth gaping, blowing his stench and attacking when they cringed away from it. One of the Werewolves down on the lot pulled a gun and started firing wildly. He got the muscle-bound guy in the shoulder, and might have hit one of the twins. Marcus wasn't sure because both of them darted around like they had springs on their feet.

Marcus realized he and the girl in the white bathing suit – wearing a robe over it now – were alone on the deck. Thing is, she wasn't lounging invitingly on an air mattress – as he'd fantasized she would be when he arrived. She didn't look up at him with a mixture of fear and excitement, a captive among brutes and he her scaled savior. No, instead she stood with her legs set firmly. Her silk robe flowed about her, her mask the same innocuous nat face as the other werewolves. One hand waved a knife; the other was cocked back with an elongated middle finger standing upright like a thin, angry soldier. Not the reception Marcus had hoped for at all.

'Hey,' Marcus began. 'Ah ...'

'Fucking Demon!' the girl said. She rushed him, slashing the knife in front of her in a furious pattern.

'Wait,' Marcus said. 'We don't have to ...' That's as far as he could get before defending himself. He snapped his tail out to intercept her, just under the knife's arc, and clipped the girl's legs. He lifted her as she tumbled over and swatted her out into the pool as gently as he could manage. 'Sorry,' he said as she went under.

Just then a new player arrived. Marcus noticed him because he came from the alley behind the girl. He strode in without the slightest hesitation at entering the fray. Marcus tried to ignore him, intent as he was on turning around his prospects with the girl, but something about the way the guy moved pulled his eyes away from her.

The new arrival was large, cloaked in a heavy, hooded jacket, face covered by a fencing mask. He was incredibly fast, but his strides weren't uniform. He seemed to sprint and hobble and amble, convulse and trip and recover all at the same time. Each step looked like it might send him crashing down, and yet instead each step propelled him forward in great leaps.

'No way,' Marcus said, recognizing the notorious joker. 'Oddity?'

Marcus forgot all about the girl and turned to watch as Oddity collided with the brawling gang members in the lot. For a moment it wasn't clear what the jokers within that one body were trying to do. They slammed a gloved hand down on a Werewolf's head and pulled him back from the Demon Prince he was beating down. Then they leaped forward and smashed a closed fist into the chest of the guy with jelly beans in his nose. He flew back from the blow and skittered to halt in a heap, looking broken in the way of a rag doll.

The Werewolf with the gun began firing at them, but only got two shots off before he ran out of bullets. Both missed. Oddity caught him by the ankle as he began to run and flung him across the lot. He screamed until he smashed into the edge of the building. That silenced him. But the action seemed only to enrage Oddity.

It was an incredible, horrible, fascinating thing to watch. The body hidden in that cloak shifted and trembled. The arms and legs were mismatched, torso bulging, shapes pushing against the fabric, looking like limbs and faces trying to burst through. The masked head groaned and ranted. Sometimes it snapped back to bellow into the sky as if in agony. But despite all that, they managed to inflict incredible damage. They were fast, unpredictable in movement, changing direction and target seemingly at random. They threw their fists around like mallets. Grasped and snapped arms and legs with crushing force.

The muscle-bound Demon Prince wannabe managed to leap onto Oddity's back. He yanked off the mask and drew back his bulging arm to smash the unprotected face. That's as far as he got. Oddity reached back with both hands, grabbed the guy, and slammed him down with all the force they could muster. The guy hit the pavement on his back and instantly went limp. He stayed that way as Oddity lifted and smashed him down several more times.

Marcus suddenly felt sick to the stomach. He wanted to look away, but he couldn't. That's why he was staring right at them when Oddity looked up at him. Marcus found their eyes, set lopsided among a bubbling stew of features. Their nose and mouth shifted, twisted, changing shape and character constantly. Ripples tore through their flesh as if an unseen knife were slicing through it, with an equally unseen needle sewing the gaping tissue closed a moment later. It wasn't just the horror of the faces that most transfixed Marcus, though. It was confusion in the eyes, the animus in one and – somehow – the piteous compassion in the other. At least, that's how Marcus read them in the brief moment their gaze held. Then it was over.

Oddity cocked their head, listened to something, and then

snatched up the mask and bounded away, leaving a battlefield of destruction behind. Bodies strewn about, low moaning, chairs and glass shattered along with heads and bones. Marcus cast around for the girl, feeling he'd like to say something to her. But she was gone too.

He heard the sirens at just about the same time he saw the flashing lights, which was fast on the moment Fort Freak's Finest roared in. Marcus flowed over the railing. He hit the lot and zigzagged through the debris and broken bodies, heading for the nearest alley. What met him there caused him to recoil, almost knotting himself up as he did the serpentine equivalent of backpedaling.

A demon lumbered from the alley. Behind him the discordant chaos of police lights cast it in silhouette, making him a hulking shape, two massive horns curving up from a boulder of a head. When he strode into the light the sight of him was even worse. As furry as any grizzly bear, with the fanged snout of something else, he came in growling. He walked hunched over. His long arms trailed the ground, claws scraping across the asphalt as if he were sharpening them. For a moment Marcus thought he was another vigilante like Oddity, but he wore what must have been a custom-made flack vest squeezed around his torso. A beat cop's hat – ridiculously small – nestled on his head, framed by those horns.

'Hey now, party's over!' he said. He had a smooth voice, funked-out and honey-rich, like Isaac Hayes on *Black Moses*. 'Let's have some order up in here.'

Guy must weigh six hundred pounds! That was a few hundred more than Marcus wanted to tangle with. He put his slither in reverse and darted for another exit.

Two more cops awaited him there: an older guy holding something in hand, smiling like he knew a joke and was dying to tell it, and a small woman who looked mixed race, kind of Asian and kind of black. The woman spoke with a lilting accent. 'We gonna go easy, Snaky-Man?'

'Sure. You get out of my way and things will be real easy.' Marcus set his course, ready to smash through and over them.

The woman fell forward abruptly.

'What the …'

She stood on her hands, and her legs twisted about in a sudden blur. She kicked Marcus in the face. Hard. Twice. He swung for her, but she wasn't there. She was on her feet again, spinning low to slam another kick into his abdomen. He grabbed for her, but she fell backward, caught herself in a bridge, twisted away and came up with her pistol in hand.

The white cop also had a weapon fixed on him, a beam of red light targeted on his chest. It wasn't a gun, but he held it like it was. 'Give me a reason, kid,' he said. 'Blink or something. Breathe heavy, how about that?'

Marcus could feel his tongue rock hard in his mouth, ready to dart out if he let it. But these were the police. He wasn't ready to cross that line. He'd have some explaining to do, but he had to call it quits.

Speaking to the other cop, the white cop said, 'That was that Brazilian shit again, wasn't it? You're too much show, Tang. Too much show. Watch and learn.' He turned back to Marcus. He smiled, though his voice grew suddenly alarmed in a manner that didn't sit right with the pleasure on his features. 'Wait? What'd you just say? That a threat? I can't have you threatening …'

Before he finished the sentence, darts shot out of the weapon, punched Marcus in the chest, and sent every inch of him into a spasming world of hurt. Marcus went down hard, screaming.

Marcus spent a few hours in the dank little holding room, having pushed the chair offered him aside and coiled himself into a seat of his own. He'd had an entire speech prepared pretty quickly, but as the minutes ticked by he increasingly focused on the cold seeping up from the concrete floor. When his public defender finally arrived all he said was, 'I didn't do anything.'

'Ah …' the man said, slapping a briefcase awkwardly onto the desk between them. 'I believe you. What amazes me is that Jokertown's law officers always manage to pinch the wrong guy.

It's an incredible record. Statistically out of this world.'

Marcus thought the guy meant to be funny, but his delivery was flat. It remained so when he said, 'Name's Charles Santiago Herriman. You may hear someone refer to me as Flipper. You shouldn't but ... it might happen. I'm just saying that's me, Flipper.' He lifted his arms, but not enough for Marcus to verify whether the name referred to a deformity in them. He didn't offer a hand to shake. He looked more like a goth kid than an attorney, tallish and rail-thin, with skin that suggested olive but somehow looked pale and brown hair that hung limp around his face. 'As you may have guessed, I'm your public defender.' By the sigh that accompanied this, it didn't exactly sound like good news.

'They Tasered me,' Marcus said.

'Yeah, I heard. You shouldn't have fought them.'

'I didn't fight them! I was just standing there!'

The lawyer didn't dispute this. 'You still feeling the effects?'

'I'm sore.' Marcus rubbed his chest. 'Feel a little ... weird. Has anyone come to bail me out?'

'Anyone like who?'

Asmodeus, Marcus almost said, but caught himself. 'Just anybody.'

'No. All you got is me.'

'You gonna get me out?'

'Sure. Like you said, you didn't do anything. The boys in blue dragged their feet a bit in getting me in here. They ran a check on you and didn't come up with any priors. Seems you've lived a virtuous life. Wasn't what they were expecting.'

Maybe his parents hadn't really called the police. Or maybe they hadn't checked as far as Baltimore yet. 'I didn't do anything,' Marcus repeated.

'Well, that's the thing,' Flipper said. Marcus had forgotten his real name already. 'There's a police report here that says you were involved in gang violence, assaulted an officer ...'

'I did not!'

'Take it easy. The cops don't want you. Not really. What they want is information. They need a full report on Oddity, when they

showed up, what they said, did, et cetera. They want to know everything you know about what the Demon Princes are up to. They
want the goods on Asmodeus, something they can get warrants on.
They want to take him down, and then go a step higher. You help
them do that and they'll make things easy on you.'

'"Easy on me"?'

'It's an expression.'

'A stupid one.'

Flipper sighed. 'You don't want to be mixed up with these guys.
Demon Princes. Werewolves. They take, Marcus; they don't give.
Think about where you are now. You were nothing but a day's
amusement to them. You're on your own. Don't get me wrong.
I'm not saying the cops are your pals, but it don't hurt to pretend
sometimes. Just tell them what you can.'

Marcus left the station just after 3:00 A.M. Two days later.

The alleys seemed particularly alive, the rats running in swarms
that barely parted as he glided through them. He followed a dis-
used train track for a bit and then climbed up to get to the rooftops
as he worked his way east toward the river. It was good to get up in
the higher air. He'd often taken in the expanse of Jokertown from
on high, the rank upon rank of lights, shadows, and bulk of sky-
scrapers, the thick sludge of a brown night sky above it. Tonight
he kept his eyes down and moved steadily, though. He was different from when he'd gone into police custody. He needed to find
Twitch. The guy was shifty, but he knew his way around. He could
get his opinion, at least. A little advice from the streets. That's what
he needed.

The last two days sucked. Seriously sucked. Damn if they hadn't
grilled him something serious. Officers Napperson and Tang,
those were their names. Just beating him down and Tasering him
wasn't enough. They had interrogated him for hours as well. He
didn't know much of anything about Asmodeus, but they wouldn't
believe him. They kept asking about the drugs too. He kept saying,
'What drugs?' and Officer Napperson would respond, 'The ones

here on my palm, see?' And then he would smack him. Happened three times before Marcus caught himself.

Tang didn't exactly play the good cop, but if he'd known anything he might have spilled to her, especially one time when Napperson left and she came around the table and touched a finger to his cheek and turned his face toward hers. Her wide-set eyes blinked as they took him in, full of sympathy, and her voice bounced around with its own wonderful rhythm. Didn't last long, though. Just a show. When she couldn't get anything from him that way, she dropped it.

They took their sweet time fingerprinting and booking him. Wouldn't even let him run a comb through his hair before they mug shot him. The whole thing was a jumble, a nightmare of glaring bright rooms and questions and being on the wrong side of the bars with a guy who liked to take long dumps while looking at him, smiling every time he pushed one out. The cops talked a lot about procedures, about how lucky he was the system was so benevolent and all that, but by the time the dude showed up with his bail he felt filthy dirty, as if every inch of him was tainted, grime under every scale. *Fuck!* He couldn't go back to that. No fucking way.

Marcus skimmed along the rooftops a few blocks south of the brothel. He had crossed the gap between the two buildings and was sliding his rear half over before his mind registered that he'd seen something down at ground level. He twisted his body back around and peered over the edge. In the alley below, well to the back and hidden from the street, some figures stood. Not exactly the place for a casual chat. He slipped farther back along the roof to get a better view.

There were three of them. Two uniformed cops hemmed a third person in. Aggression etched every angle of the cops' postures. The male cop was a joker, with a Chinese dragon's head. He was bulky in the chest, with a scaly tail dragging the ground behind him. The other cop, female, looked to be a nat.

The focus of their attention stood against the wall, palms held up, looking jittery, managing to move about the hemmed-in space at a frantic rate without actually going anywhere. It was Twitch.

Marcus slid over the edge and down to a lower landing, along it and then down again. When he peeked over again, he was directly over them, a few stories up. He could hear them talking – Twitch trying hard to explain something and the cops interrupting him every few seconds – but he couldn't quite make out their words. He could, however, see that whatever he was saying wasn't what the cops wanted to hear. They both drew their weapons out. The female cop kept snapping her head around, checking the alley, but the scaly guy moved in closer, reaching out with one claw as if he wanted to get a hold of Twitch's shoulder.

Marcus opened his mouth and shouted, 'Hey,' but he didn't hear 'Hey.' He heard a sudden pop. Gunfire. The dragon cop tried desperately to get a bead on Twitch. But the ace danced about, frantic, faster than anything Marcus had ever seen. No way the cop was going to hit him. But then the female cop opened up. She shot high, but it must have distracted Twitch. The dragon kept shooting, and an answering spray of blood fanned out in the air, seemed to hang there, disembodied. A second later Twitch was on the ground, one arm flopping sickly, his legs trying to push him away but seeming uncoordinated, something wrong with one of his feet. The dragon cop moved in, gun low, to finish it.

For the first time in a long time, Marcus acted without hesitation. He surged over the roof edge. He dropped with the full speed of gravity as he yelled, 'Nooooo!' Hitting the asphalt hard, he squirmed toward them.

The female cop spotted him first. She stood with her legs planted, gun supported in both hands, and aimed at him. 'Back the fuck up! Police business.'

Marcus feinted to one side. His tongue concussed out of his mouth, as rapid as a bullet. He tagged the woman on her chest. By the resistance there, he knew she was vested. He aimed again. In the face this time, hard enough that her feet kicked out from under her. Her red hair lofted in the air as she went over backward. It felt good to see that. Good to taste the tang of venom hot on his tongue.

The dragon cop didn't shoot, but he lumbered toward him.

Fast for a big guy. Flame erupted in the air between them, a quick blast that vanished in an instant. When it cleared the cop was on him. He turned to his side and cocked his tail back, bouncing and twirling it like a baseball player warming up. *Shit*. Marcus's snake portion surged in, tangling the guy's feet in scaly coils of muscle, tripping him before he could swing that tail fully around on him. The dragon went down, cursing, scrabbling across the asphalt.

Marcus almost went for him, but fuck him. He grabbed for Twitch instead. He got his arm under him and hefted him up, balanced on his side, under his arm. A doctor. He'd get him to a doctor. He started to squirm away.

He'd nearly reached the street when the next shot came. He felt it thud into Twitch's chest. The ace cried out in pain, instantly slick from the blood. Marcus lost his grip, dropped him, and stared down for a moment as a red-black bloom of death spread through the man's shirt. He was still breathing, but it wasn't real breathing. It was just the motions, growing weaker every second.

Another shot. A bullet skimmed his ear. That was enough. Marcus turned and slithered for it.

THE RAT RACE

PART 4.

'Why here?' Leo asked as he shoved the double doors and let himself into an antiseptic-smelling corridor that was brighter than a photo studio. 'Why not one of the newer joints?'

'The clinic has the closest ER,' Michael told him. 'And we know—' He dodged a nurse with a gurney by doing a swift little slalom and swung back to Leo's side.

Leo completed his partner's thought, since he'd already heard it over the radio. 'The joker who laid her flat is poisonous.'

'Venomous, actually. Snakes are venomous. But yes, time was of the essence.'

'What room again?'

Before Michael could respond, a doctor appeared on the verge of halting the two detectives – but Leo flashed his badge and asked, 'Angel Grady?' The doctor nodded and pointed with a clipboard, around the next corner.

Leo and Michael took the turn like a school of fish darting to avoid a predator. Around that turn, they saw Lu Long sulking with his massive arms crossed, standing beside a closed door. From the other side of the door, machines pinged and chimed, and urgent voices discussed what should happen next.

Michael gave a head bob to the dragon-headed joker, and Leo asked abruptly, 'Puff, what the hell happened out there?'

Puff snarled, but then again, it always looked like he was snarling.

'Slinky motherfucker, giant snake. Black, with red and yellow on him. He stuck out his tongue' – and here, Lu Long mimed a popping punch – 'and brained her. Fast as ... fast as ...'

Michael supplied, 'A striking snake?'

'I guess.'

'How's she doing?' the younger detective asked.

The bulky, reptilian shoulders of the Chinese joker shifted in a wave that could've been a helpless shrug. He jabbed a thumb at the window on the closed door. 'They're still deciding.'

'Son of a bitch,' Leo said, to no one in particular. Then, to Lu Long, 'What about Joe?'

'He resisted – and then that snaky fucker interfered, and things, things ... they got out of hand.'

'Out of hand.' Leo frowned. 'That's all you've got to say?'

'You implying something?'

Michael took half a step forward, almost putting himself between them. 'Guys, let's not compound the situation by picking fights. This is a delicate situation—'

'*I'm* not picking anything,' Lu Long muttered, but his stance suggested he might be ready for one, just in case.

'*I* just want to hear the facts. And God damn it, I wanted to talk to Joe,' he grumbled, more under his breath than to either of his fellow cops, or any of the fretting, fidgeting uniforms who were cluttering up the hall.

The dragon man said, 'He's down in the morgue. Knock yourself out.'

The hallway around Angel's room was growing crowded with a halo of uniforms and plainclothes. Rikki Michaelson was standing next to Bugeye, and they were talking with their faces close together, almost whispering like they were loitering in a library. Beastie was occupying one large corner, doing his best to keep his exceptional brown bulk out of the way and not doing a very good job. He wrung his big paws together and shared a few awkward words with Tabby. The undercover cop was holding a brown paper bag and treating it to furtive swigs between his nods of agreement.

Both the big guys straightened sharply when the brass arrived, but not everyone in the hall even noticed right away.

Captain Mendelberg squeezed through what space was left, weaving side to side to pat the occasional back and grunt an 'excuse me' when it was required. She shoved up to Lu Long and pinned him with her eyes. 'How's she doing?' she asked.

He gave her the same answer he'd given Leo, but with a better posture. 'She's alive. They're working on her.'

The captain nodded, her lips crushed tightly shut. 'That's a start. And that's all the press is saying for now, which is fine.'

Tabby made a face like he wanted to spit, and asked, 'They're here already?'

She responded, 'Of *course* they're here. The whole lineup – the usual suspects. *Times*, *Daily News*. The *Cry*'s made it at least as far as the lobby and I've been fielding phone calls from TV crews.'

Sergeant Choy jammed her way through the crowd, sweating from running, or maybe taking the stairs. 'We'll have to issue a statement,' she noted.

'And we will. But not yet. First, we've got to get our thumbs out of our asses and *clear this goddamn hall!*' the captain all but shouted. When no one seemed to know where to go, or what to do, she added, 'Doctors, nurses, gurneys, and chairs need to fit through here, people – now either flatten against a wall or find someplace else to worry. We can't help her like this.'

Lucas Tate chose this brief lull in the nervous hum to mani-fest by the far stairs. He was wearing gray suit pants and a white button-up with the sleeves artistically rolled, plus a flat black mask just barely too large to call a domino. 'Could I—' he began, and all eyes snapped to him. Unsure if he should be anxious at the at-tention or delighted to have commanded it so easily, he continued regardless. ' – get a statement for the *Cry*? A Fort Freak cop goes down, hovering between life and death—'

Captain Mendelberg's skin began to blush hard, almost match-ing the color of her ruby-red eyes, as if she were a kettle prepared to steam. '*You!*' she said, and everyone assumed this would be fol-lowed with an order to get the fuck out, but everybody was wrong.

Her face relaxed from fury to cunning. She pointed at him, then drew her finger back, summoning him close. 'Are going to make yourself useful? Get over here.'

He scampered between the flattened rows of cops, ducking like he was running a gauntlet. When he reached her side, standing squashed between Lu Long, Leo, and Michael, the captain laid out her plan. 'All right. Here's what we're going to do. We're going to get this snaky motherfucker, and we're going to get him *fast*.'

Chey Moleka crossed her arms and complained, 'If we hadn't let him go the first time ...'

The captain said, 'I know, but we *did*. And now we'll catch him again. We're going to do it like this: Tate, I want you to get together with our sketch artist Eddie and run whatever he gives you on the front page of the *Cry*. Hell, stick it on lampposts and telephone poles while you're at it. I want this snaky bastard's face on every doormat and driveway for twenty miles, and I want it there in a special afternoon edition.'

'I'm on it,' Tate replied, scribbling on his trusty flip-pad with amazing haste.

'Tabby, put down the goddamned bottle and do your thing. I want you on four legs and on the street in half an hour, tops. Likewise, K-10, put your nose in the air and have a word with every lap dog, guard dog, and stray dog in Jokertown, and, Tienyu, if you've got something mechanical up your sleeve that can gather any scrap of information, I want you to turn it loose.' One by one, the cops she named began to peel themselves out of the corridor and scuttle for the elevator banks or the stairs. 'And that's just for starters,' the captain growled.

For a split second, Leo almost felt a tiny sliver of pity for the snake. But then he glanced through the long rectangular window of Angel Grady's hospital room, and he got over it.

Just as he was getting himself good and worked up to hit the streets, a pissy complaint began by the elevators. It rolled like a wave at a baseball game, jumping from unhappy cop to unhappy cop.

'Ratboy,' somebody bitched.

Vincent Marinelli smiled – or possibly grimaced, it was hard to tell on a hundred-pound rodent – at the assembly. His whiskers twitched and he cleared his throat. 'I'm afraid I'll need a word,' the Internal Affairs investigator said slowly.

Choy asked with great prejudice, 'Now? For fuck's sake we've got an officer—'

'Stow it,' the captain commanded, never taking her eyes off Ratboy, who had not taken any further measures to approach. 'He's doing his job.'

'And we're trying to do ours!' Lu Long rumbled.

Despite Ratboy's hunkering shape, long nose, small clawed hands, and narrow shoulders, it would be inaccurate to assume he ever sniveled. He spoke clearly and without backing down. 'We're on the same side, here.'

The captain sniffed, though whether it was disdain or something else, no one could say. She said to the entire corridor. 'That's fine. It's *fine*. You all know how this works.' Then, so softly under her breath that only those closest heard her, she said, 'You don't have to like him, you just have to *work* with him.'

... AND ALL THE SINNERS SAINTS

by Victor Milán and Ty Franck

PART 1.

Late again. Charlie Herriman stood up fast and spun away from his carrel. And smacked hard into something.

His case files went everywhere. He clutched at them, then converted the movement into a last-second save of his ironic Hello Kitty backpack, which was suicide-diving off his shoulder with netbook inside. He dropped to his knees, grabbing for wayward sheets and folders that flew everywhere like autumn's last leaves.

'I'm so sorry. Here, let me help you.'

He looked up. His racing heartbeat seemed to stumble. A pair of bright blue eyes looked at him from a concerned female face. A very beautiful face, framed by long pulled-back black hair above a dark purple cardigan.

'Thanks,' he mumbled.

I'm sorry I banged into you, he wanted to say. *I'm just a bit flustered here, since after a morning's research I just finally logged onto the news and found out that one of my clients is wanted for attacking a police officer. Oh, and murder.*

But he couldn't get anything but the apology out past his tongue, which seemed to have swollen to fill his mouth like a sponge dropped in water.

He had *excuses*. His ironic skinny tie had gotten askew and threatened imminent thoroughly nonerotic autoasphyxiation. The ends of his bangs had stuck in one eye and dug in like broken glass, making him blink so hard his whole face twitched.

Worst, his right-arm prosthetic had slipped, and its intricate array of straps and sensors was pinching his flipper fiercely. Which in addition to being uncomfortable was a *real pisser,* because it reminded him that no matter how expensive his myoelectric arms might be, under them he was still a flipper boy.

The young woman was kneeling right by him, almost touching him, scooping up papers and feeding them to him. He tried not to snatch them like a cartoon miser for a spilled pile of dollars.

She smiled at him. His stomach did a slow roll. 'I'm so sorry I ran into you,' she said. 'I'll be more careful next time.'

He looked at her, blinking furiously at his dagger-tipped bangs, nearly choking on saliva.

'Are you all right?'

He nodded spastically. 'Yeah. Fine. Uh, thanks.'

She smiled and stood up. Surreptitiously he made sure both mechanical hands still functioned. Pressing a wad of legal papers to his bony chest he managed to heave himself up onto his black Converse sneaks.

'Great. Later,' his benefactor said, and walked away.

He staggered back and dropped like a bag of laundry into the orange plastic chair he'd just vacated.

Why oh why am I such a chickenshit? he lamented, watching her walk down the whole line of carrels toward the door. In his head. Where he lived most of his life. *Why couldn't I even ask her* name?

Oh, that's right. I'm a dork. Plus I'm a joker freak with flippers for hands.

She vanished from his view. And likely his life. Which that was the story of.

◆

'Charlie!'

He stopped on the library steps and looked around. He had gotten the evil hair out of his eyes, splashed water in them, taken a hit from his environmentally friendly asthma inhaler that held half as much as the old ones did, and was generally back in as much control of himself as he'd ever been. As always the midmorning Manhattan sunlight dazzled him even after what seemed overly stark fluorescents inside.

'Mr. Herriman! Up here.'

He turned and looked up past the entrance roof with its weirdly flared corners. Its convolutions sported an extra feature: a face so black and shiny it might've been an obsidian inset. Except it blinked. It was the face of a kid. A late adolescent who was scared and out of his depth.

Again. And way farther out than he'd ever managed to get before. Which was saying something.

'Marcus!' he hissed back. He looked around frantically. No one seemed to be looking their way. 'What the fuck? You're, like, *this* far from starring on *America's Most Wanted.*'

'We need to talk.'

'No shit we need to talk! Get your ass down from there.' And winced furiously. He was no good at hiding his emotions. He'd just made thoughtless reference to a joker's deformity. The very thing he hated most when it was done to *him*.

But the kid was oblivious. 'No can do, Mr. Herriman. Meet me in ten in the place you'd go to confess to a cephalopod.'

'Wait—' But the face had vanished.

He had the Church of Jesus Christ, Joker to himself. He sat in one empty pew halfway between the door and the altar. Although he'd never been a fan of church he found himself tempted to be soothed by the quiet cool, lit more by the sunlight pouring in through windows at the top of the tall circular apse and the stained-glass panels at the front than the candles flickering vigorously before the Peace Altar – as effectual at bringing light as peace, really. The effect was somewhat lessened by the twisted Jesus hanging on a strand of DNA, while a two-faced Dr. Tachyon looked on. Still, for all its twisted brand of suffering-based theology, the church did tend to strike a chord with those who suffered the joker's curse.

This is lame, he thought, shifting and scratching a fin with the myoelectric wonder of his other fake hand. He'd gotten everything back in place, he thought. But he still itched.

He wasn't even sure he was in the right place. But young Marcus Morgan had been raised a churchgoing lad by a good upper middle-class black family. He knew Charlie's mom was Puerto Rican, so reckoned he was raised Catholic. But Charlie wasn't big on his sins. *Inadequacies* were something else. While no one would mistake Father Squid's chapel for a Catholic church, the combination of piety and irony was probably irresistible to someone like Marcus.

An odd rustle-thump came from behind. He twisted in the pew. The hard wood bit into his back.

Down the aisle slouched a joker. The hood that covered its face appeared made from a burlap sack. Its upper body was swaddled in grimy rags that had maybe been coats in a prior lifetime. The lower half was stuffed lumpily into an army-surplus duffel bag faded near gray. It bunched and hunched like a thalidomide inchworm.

Everything about it suggested that if those strata of decaying cloth were removed, Hieronymus Bosch would puke.

The figure painfully hunched its way up alongside Charlie and poured itself into a pew. The hood turned toward him. He caught a faint glimmer on skin that shone like black glass.

'Nice disguise,' he muttered despite himself. Charlie was wondering how the kid made it around in daylight without being busted. His unnaturally dark complexion was bad enough. But a twenty-foot-long serpent body, in coral-snake colors of red, yellow, and black, was hard to miss.

Marcus had found a way. *This one's smart,* Charlie reminded himself. A lot of his clients weren't. The teenager was too smart for his own good.

White teeth flashed. 'People don't want to see you when you look like this. Their eyes slide right past, even here in Jokertown.'

'Listen, Marcus. You are in a metric buttload of trouble.'

'Don't I know it.'

'This is worse trouble. This isn't getting in a street fight. You attacked a *cop*. And you're liable to be charged with the murder of that Twitch guy.'

'But I didn't do that! The police shot him. The police say that!'

'The cops say you were his accomplice. Joe Twitch tried to shoot a cop. He died. You're looking to get hung with it.'

'I was trying to prevent him getting killed in cold blood.'

'Felony murder rule, Marcus. If you're in on a crime with some-body, and somebody gets killed – even one of your accomplices – you're on the hook for homicide.'

'Fucking cops are lying! Listen. Joe Twitch met with those two cops, the scary dragon dude and that redheaded woman. Next thing I know they're pulling out their pieces and blasting him. Just like that!'

'If that's true, you need to get it to a jury. Trust the system.'

'Like Joe Twitch? No way! I saw two officers of the NYPD commit murder. I saw what I saw. Please, Mr. Herriman. If I give myself up they'll kill me too.'

Charlie slumped against the smooth unforgiving wood. *What if he's right?* This wouldn't be the first time it was hard to tell the good guys from the bad guys. 'What do you want me to do, Marcus? I've given the only advice I legally can.'

'Help me.'

'I can't harbor a fugitive.'

'That's not what I mean. You need to help me clear my name. *Somebody* must know something. There had to be a reason they murdered Joe Twitch. Help me find it.'

Charlie sighed. 'If I do you'll give yourself in?'

'Yeah. You know I'm one of the good guys, Mr. Herriman. All I want to do is uphold the law.'

By whacking people with that ten-foot tongue of yours, he thought. 'I'll do what I can,' he said. 'Keep in touch.'

'I'll do that. Thanks, Mr. Herriman! You won't regret it.'

And he was gone. Shuffle-thump, shuffle-thump.

Charlie rubbed his eyes with plastic palms that tried to feel like skin and failed. 'That's a lie, kid,' he said quietly. 'I already do.'

Embrace suffering, Charlie told himself. It had been his mantra since childhood.

'So you not only shot him, you cut up the corpse. A process which took so long that the cops arrived and caught you in the act.'

The Demon Prince gangbanger nodded his malformed joker head and grinned. It was hard to tell, because instead of eyes the man had two long white horns growing out of his eye sockets. He also had no ears, and only the barest hint of a nose. When he wasn't speaking, he clicked his tongue constantly. The file on him said that his horns were actually extremely sensitive organs for detecting sound. The clicking allowed the joker to echolocate like a bat.

He paused his clicking and said, 'Werewolf had it comin', fuckin' skag. Gotta make a statement, you know? The next guy decides to try and steal our shit, maybe he thinks twice.'

'"*He had it coming*" is not a legal defense, Clyde,' Charlie said with a sigh.

'My name is Nergal.'

'No,' Charlie said. 'Your name is Clyde Drummond.'

'My slave name,' Clyde said loudly, followed by a barrage of clicks.

Charlie chose not to point out that Clyde was a fifth-generation white boy from New Jersey, and instead said, 'It will not help you if you appear before the judge and demand to be called' – Charlie glanced at the known aliases section of the file – '"Nergal, Lord of the Secret Police in Hell."'

Clyde shrugged and grinned again. Or, possibly threatened Charlie with his mouth full of sharp teeth. Again, it was hard to tell.

It had come as an unwelcome surprise that most of his clients were guilty. That bothered him. To his surprised chagrin it didn't bother him near as much as how self-destructively irrational they were, innocent or guilty. The real crotch kick, though, was how *fucking annoying* they could be – trying not to think of Marcus.

And sometimes he got one who was just plain scary. Like, oh, *now*.

The door opened. A horsy, café au lait face stuck in. 'Hey, Flipper, there's a rat to see you.'

Charlie clenched. He hated the name. But it had clung to him his whole life, like a psychic smell of dogshit he'd stepped in when he was five. The bitch about working Jokertown was, no way could he win a harassment beef against a guy with sorry-ass half-functional bat-wings sprouting from his shoulders.

But he wouldn't retaliate by calling him 'Wingman' back. Because he took the high road. And also he feared getting stomped. The joker cop was a head taller than Charlie's five-ten. Wingman could take him.

Who couldn't?

'Thank you, Sergeant Taylor.'

The door closed. And Charlie thought, *Wait – rat?* He couldn't figure out why a police informant would be visiting him at all, much less here.

'Mr. Herriman?'

The guards had taken Clyde back to lockup. Charlie was hanging around doing a quick review of the notes he'd just taken. He found little to comfort him. On any level.

He looked up to see a giant rat in the doorway.

'I'm Detective-Investigator Second-Grade Vincent Marinelli, NYPD Internal Affairs Bureau, Lower Manhattan office,' the rat said. 'There are some questions I'd like to ask you, if you got a few.'

His voice sounded normal, if a bit nasal. The accent was pure Brooklyn Italian. He wore a black Ripstop belt around his furry middle, encrusted with the usual police pods and mods, most prominently his gold shield and blocky black handgun.

'Internal Affairs? Whoa, isn't that kind of ironic—'

Too late, as usual, he caught himself. *Way to be sensitive to a fellow joker, asshole.*

Foot-long whiskers twitched. 'Go ahead and say what you were gonna say.'

'It wasn't important.'

'Maybe not. But please reflect on this: isn't the real irony that you reflexively think of IAB as "the rat squad," when we're the ones working to protect you from the worst criminals of all?'

'Worst—'

'Cops who betray their trust and abuse their power.'

'Oh. I guess I never thought of it that way.'

'Well, now you got no excuse, do you? So can we talk, or what?'

'Huh? Sure.'

'Then let's take a walk.'

The glares seemed even harder than Charlie was used to walking out through the precinct house, the half-heard mutters more venomous. But this time nobody jostled them. It was like an invisible ten-foot bubble surrounded them.

It was a clear, cold early afternoon when they started walking past the white police vans, the garbage bags, and the Blythe van Renssaeler Memorial Hospital branch next door to the cop shop. Elizabeth Street still showed a lot of influences from the days before the wild card, when this was the heart of Chinatown. There was a lot of red, a lot of gold, a lot of Chinese ideograms. And throngs of people, mostly jokers.

It was a long way from the Central Park and Long Island swank of his upbringing. But it was where Charlie Herriman felt most at home. So he kept telling himself.

It was a place where you could walk side by side with a four-foot rat with five feet of naked pink tail and nobody would notice. Comforting, in its way.

'*Rattus norvegicus.*' Marinelli said.

'Huh?'

'The unspoken question in your eyes. I was born like this. A joker in the shape of a giant brown rat. We're the ones won the war with the black rats like 150 years ago.'

'I – I know what it's like to be born a joker.'

'Yeah. I know. Charles Herriman Hermosa, your family calls you. Kids called you Flipper growing up. You didn't much like it.'

'How do you *know* all that?'

'Dossiers. So, like I said, I need your help.'

'With what?'

'You got a client. Marcus Morgan, of the infamous poison tongue. I need to talk to him. Or at least, I need information from him.'

'I don't understand. Does Internal Affairs investigate homicides?'

'We do when we suspect a cop is involved. Or, in this case, two. I was the IAB investigator who caught the call for the Joe Twitch shooting. The gun by his hand might as well have had "throwdown piece" stamped on the slide. And Twitch wasn't the sort to carry a gun. He was the sort of small-time ace who'd figure his piss-ass power would get him out of anything his even-feebler wits wouldn't. It got him on TV, for Christ's sake.'

'It did?'

'*American Hero*. Ace reality show?'

'I don't follow reality TV.'

'So, well. Morgan's your client. Has he been in touch with you since the crime?'

Charlie hesitated. 'Yes.'

'And did he give an account of what went down?'

'I'm not at liberty to tell you. If he was involved, I can assure you he would only have taken action to prevent an illegal act.'

The pink nose twitched. 'You tell him to turn himself in?'

'Of course. It's my duty as an officer of the court.'

'He blow you off?'

'Of course.'

Marinelli paused to scratch an ear with a long hind foot. 'Listen. I believe laws are to be obeyed, and enforced. It's why I'm IAB. At some point your client's going to have to answer to a jury for his actions in this case.'

'That's what I told him, Detective.'

'That said, and this is strictly off the record, I think he's wise to lay low for the time being. Coming in right now might prove hazardous to his health.'

'What do you mean? Surely he'd be in police custody.'

'It's the police who're suspected of doing murder, in this case.

By me and Mr. Morgan, if nobody else. A lot of good officers believe in street justice. They'd see Morgan as a joker – a black one, to boot – who was accomplice to the attempted murder of two cops, and who almost killed one. You think one of them might not look the other way while your client suffered a fatal accident? Or hanged himself in his cell out of remorse? Also, keep this in mind, Mr. Herriman: no matter how dirty we think a cop is, we're always worse. The blue wall will try and protect him even if only to screw us over.'

Naturally you'd think that as a member of the – of Internal Affairs. Charlie thought. Then he remembered his own take on Fort Freak.

'I just don't know,' he said. 'Officer Grady was decorated for bravery under fire with the Marines in the Caliphate.'

'Hitler won the Iron Cross twice in the First World War.'

'Goodwin's Law—' Charlie blurted.

'Give me a fucking break, if you'll pardon my French, Mr. Herriman. I use the Internet too. I'm a rat with the brain of a human, not the other way around.'

'Sorry. But what can I do for you?'

'First, you can get me everything Morgan knows.'

Charlie felt his face stiffen.

'All right.' Marinelli waved a hand. First impressions notwithstanding, Charlie saw it *was* a hand, not a paw, though unusually long and slender. And furry. 'You can give it to me as the statement of an anonymous informant. Whatever. At this stage we're not talking formal, we're talking data.'

'I can do that. Yes.'

'Also I need you to talk to some of your other clients for me.'

'Other clients?'

The detective shrugged. 'Jokertown's got a million eyes, even if it's got a lot less than half a million jokers, like the old joke says. This went down in Jokertown. Some of those eyes saw *something*. But however mouths are attached to those eyes, a lot got a prejudice against talking to the cops.'

'What are you looking for?'

'At this stage? Anything. Forensics shows dick about whether Twitch was actually pulling a piece. Officers Long and Grady shot from too far away to leave powder residue. We got squadoosh.'

'Shouldn't you be questioning your shooters instead? Seems like they're the place to start. Not my client.'

Vincent rolled his eyes. 'Thanks for telling me how to do my job. But yeah, we start with them. Except that Angel's in a hospital bed and the union rep and her doctor are talking about how questioning would be too stressful. Endanger her life. Lu Long's talking shit, but he won't crack without something to throw in his face. Without two stories to compare and poke holes in, I got nothing. Maybe you can help me find my second story.'

'How do I know you're not angling for some cheap collars on my clients?'

'Listen, Charlie. Your mother's family's Spanish. You were raised Catholic? I was raised Catholic. As a Catholic, you know the name of the game is *sins*. And while I don't go to confession as much as my mamma and Father Bonifacio would like, I still operate according to an intricate internal hierarchy of sins.'

Actually Charlie had not been raised Catholic. His father was Anglican. His mother was complaisant. He himself was agnostic. It was a perfect metaphor for the intricate internal hierarchy of doubts *he* operated by.

But Vince was on a roll. Which, it struck Charlie, was a *really unappetizing* visual.

'So, see, the worst sin you can commit is to murder another human being. Right? Right. Maybe the second worst is to abuse trust. These so-called cops may have done both. So while in principle I'm committed to busting all the scumbags on Earth, even I have to prioritize. *Capisce?*'

'Um, I – I think so,' Charlie stammered, desperately trying to recall such Catholic lore as he'd taken in through osmosis. 'You're all about the mortal sins, and haven't got time for the venial ones.'

Vince reached up to tweak Charlie's cheek with a black-taloned finger. 'I knew you were a smart boy, Mr. Herriman.'

And Charlie tried really hard not to think, *Ew, I've been touched on the face by a giant rat.* But then he already had.

To cover any possible look of disgust that had slipped past his sketchy self-control, he said, 'Call me Charlie. I mean, if we're going to be working together informally and everything.'

'All right, Charlie. Call me Vince. Or Ratboy.'

'*Ratboy?* That doesn't bother you?'

Vince laughed. 'Everybody called me that since I was a baby. Even my own brothers and sisters. Especially them. It quit bothering me when I was eight. What I can't stand is being called fucking *Vinnie.*'

◆

'I know your reputation, Marinelli,' the Chinese woman said across the interrogation-room table. She wore a businesslike pantsuit, dark blue, with a pale blue blouse. 'I won't help you bust my boys' chops. Or girls.'

Vince sat back in his chair. It was one of those bright orange plastic ones, uncomfortable as hell, slid you right off on your butt if you didn't pay attention. If you were a nat or a more-or-less normally shaped joker. If you were a giant rat, on the other hand, your tail fit right through the hole in the back and helped anchor you.

'You're refusing to cooperate in an official investigation, Sergeant Choy?' he asked.

Vivian Choy pressed her lips tight shut. She had what looked like an Erector set spread across her desk. She was halfway through building something resembling a mouse with wheels and a camera on its back. 'No. I just know you think even the slightest infraction makes a cop *wrong.*'

'If you break the teensiest little law,' he said, 'you're a lawbreaker. Right?'

'But we're the only thing standing between decent people and the animals out there,' she said. 'You need to cut us some slack. We're the good guys.'

'Good is what you *do,* not what you think about yourself. Anyway, I'm not here to pinch people for skeeving free meals from New Big Wang. We're talking murder, Sergeant.'

'Homicide. Clearly justifiable.'

'That's what I'm here to find out. You were the duty sergeant when the shoot went down. You were one of the first on the scene. Tell me what you saw.'

'It's in my report. Talk to Lu Long and Angel if you want more. By the time I got there, the thing was over.'

'We've got Long's statement, and it stinks to high heaven. Angel's out of action for the time being.' He pushed his pointy muzzle over the table. 'Don't you want the truth to come out? If you think I'm head-hunting here, fine. Then help find the facts to prove me wrong. And if I'm right – are you *really* down with fellow officers committing murder?'

She looked at him as if trying to set his fur on fire. Then she deflated. 'I can't condone that,' she said. 'But to the best of my knowledge, everything happened the way Officers Long and Grady said it did. Moritz pulled a weapon on them. They drew theirs and in defense of their lives, shot and killed him.'

She gestured at the camera mouse on the table. 'None of my toys were there, if that's what you're asking.'

Vince just sat regarding her with big black eyes. He knew the basic fact of interrogation: if you just sit and *wait* long enough, people will blurt.

'Don't think I'd cover for them on something this heavy,' Choy said at last. She knew the trick too. But she couldn't help herself. Especially not looking into uncanny animal eyes, when she knew a human intellect was looking back. 'Grady's an ice queen. Thinks she's better than anybody else in the precinct. Then again, she's got the medals to prove it.'

'Yeah,' said Vince. He was unimpressed with what jarheads called heroics. In DEVGRU they called that *practice*.

'Long, now – he comes on a little strong. More than a little, if you're a woman, if you know what I mean. Sometimes he needs to be reminded what *no* means.'

'He tried to press it with *you*? A superior officer?'

'Listen, he's a dick, but I am not interested in getting embroiled in any kind of sexual harassment beef. I'm a stand-up cop, Detective. And I handled it.'

'I'm not an HR ween looking to stick somebody in sensitivity training here, Sergeant.'

'All right. Let me put it to you this way: I'd go through a door with Angel Grady backing me in a Jokertown minute. Lu Long, not so much. Do I think that makes him a murderer? No.'

'So does Grady say yes to him?'

She laughed. 'This is not for attribution, Detective, and anyway is just surmise. I don't think he's got the right plumbing. And it's got nothing to do with his joker.'

'My *paisans* back in Brooklyn might take that as a challenge to their manhood. Lotta these local Chinese boys like Long think a lot like the Guidos, that way.'

'Think you're telling me something? Lu thinks he's tough. Angel *is* tough. She'd break him in two, that fire-spitting trick of his or not.'

'Okay.' He stood up, knowing the way his naked pink tail slithered from the chair would disconcert her. He wasn't trying to make friends here.

He knew better.

'I got just one question to leave you with, Sergeant Choy. This Twitch was a superfast ace. Why would he throw down on a pair of cops with a POS Raven .380, which according to everything we know about him he hardly knew which end the bullet came out of, instead of just *running the fuck away*?'

'Hunting heads for your trophy wall, Ratboy?'

Like most everybody above the age of twelve, the uniformed officer blocking the hallway stood taller than Vince. He wasn't wide. But he was lean and tough as jerky.

'Got no time for this, Napperson. Act like a pro and stand aside, all right?'

'You're trying to put it to my partner.'

'Your former partner. The Department finally figured one bad apple per pair was enough and split you up. Remember?'

'Lu's still my boy. And you're coming around trying to get people to lie about him.'

'No. I'm investigating an incident he was involved in. It's the truth I'm trying to get from people.'

'It was a right shoot! Lu's innocent.'

'Then as we cops so like to say, he's got nothing to worry about, does he?'

'Listen up, people.' Snap raised his voice. 'Nobody's badge or ass is safe with this rat in the house. He'd frame somebody just for the credit!'

'You'd know a lot about that, wouldn't you, Snap?'

'Your heart bleeds for the skels. I know. And you'd throw a brother officer to the wolves.'

Vince smiled. 'Why would I want to share with a bunch of mangy wolves, Snap?'

'Hey, bro,' a voice said, coming up behind Napperson. 'Take it down. We all got work to do. This isn't helping anybody.'

Snap turned his balding head to look at the burly red-haired man. 'But, Tabby, he's looking to take Lu's and Angel's scalps! He's a fucking rat!'

Vince was aware that the cop they called Tabby was a shape-shifter who spent most of his time as a big orange cat.

'Yeah, he is, ain't he,' said Tabby with a toothy grin. Apparently, the irony was not lost on him, either. 'But Puff can take care of himself. And you getting loud won't change a thing. So do us a favor and shut the fuck up and let the rat go away.'

Face fisting, Snap started forward. As he passed he gave Vince a sharp elbow to the ear, accidental-like.

It hurt like a *mingia muerta*. Napperson had a black belt in hurting people without leaving marks. Vince toppled to the side, where a passing cop caught his arm. As if to regain his balance he lashed out with his tail.

It clipped Napperson's ankles right out from under him. He dented a wall with his head.

'Oops,' Vince said.

The cop holding his arm helped him upright then let go. Vince looked up at him to say thanks, then kept looking up, hoping there was a head at the top of that mountain of beef. There was. An angry Chinese face six and a half feet off the floor.

'Looking to make friends, aren't you?' the giant said in a comically high and squeaky voice.

'Yeah, thanks for stopping me from falling on my ass, officer?' he trailed off.

'Chen. Bill Chen.' The giant tipped his head toward the retreating Napperson. 'Snap's an asshole, but watch yourself. Nobody's going to be in a hurry to save you if he decides to kick your teeth in.'

And up goes the blue wall, Vince thought. *I'm standing right next to it.*

SANCTUARY

by Mary Anne Mohanraj

PART 1.

Kavitha eased her way out of her daughter's room, closing the door quietly behind her. It had taken longer than usual to get her toddler down; Isai had insisted on telling her a long, incomprehensible story about Daddy and dragons. When Michael got home from the station, Kavitha would have to ask him if he'd said something to Isai. In Jokertown, it was entirely plausible that Michael had encountered real dragons in the course of his detective duties – or at least something close enough to pass for real. He was going to have to stop reading his daughter police reports; Isai was getting old enough to understand them. And even though the child appeared to be fearless, some of the things Michael dealt with on a day-to-day basis terrified even Kavitha; Isai didn't need to hear all the gritty details of Daddy's job. Not yet. Isai might be an ace, with fearsome shapeshifting abilities, but she was also only two and a half years old. Michael was just going to have to learn how to make stories up. *Appropriate* stories.

Kavitha was startled out of her newfound determination by a knocking on the door. Not loud, but somehow frantic. *Who in the world ...?* They didn't get a lot of visitors.

Kavitha took a few quick steps down the hall to the apartment door and peered through the little circle of glass. Her eyes widened as she took in the brown-skinned woman on the other side of the door, her face covered in blood and darkening bruises, her arm bent at an angle that was just *wrong*. Kavitha hesitated a moment, mindful of the child sleeping in the other room – but this woman was small and soft and broken. Kavitha couldn't just leave her standing in the hallway. It wasn't as if Kavitha weren't able to defend Isai, if the need arose – in theory, anyway. Michael kept urging her to practice using her powers as a weapon, but she hated weapons. Ironic, considering her boyfriend carried one every day.

Kavitha opened the door, managing to smile at the woman on the other side.

The woman said softly, 'I'm sorry to bother you. Is Michael here?'

Kavitha raised an eyebrow. 'You know Michael?'

She hesitated. 'It's been a while. My name is Minal – he probably wouldn't have mentioned me. But we were ... friends, once upon a time.'

The way she said *friends* made it clear that they'd been more than friends. The woman was wearing an oversized T-shirt and a pair of jeans, nothing glamorous. The bloodstains didn't help, or the glorious black eye. But Minal was still undeniably sexy. Smooth brown skin, waves of wild midnight hair falling down her back. Hair longer than Kavitha's, and Michael did love long hair; every time Kavitha said something about cutting hers, he had to visibly bite his tongue to keep from begging her not to. Minal's body was curvy, generously gifted with both tits and ass. Neither of which Kavitha had much of, which was a good thing for a dancer, but not so great when your boyfriend's ex showed up at the door.

She said curtly, 'Michael's at work.' Kavitha saw the panic rise in the woman's eyes, and repented of her harshness. Even if he *was* dragging his feet about actually proposing, she and Michael were solid – they had a child together, for gods' sakes. She could afford to be more gracious than this. 'But you can wait for him inside, if you want.'

Minal swallowed hard. 'Yes, please. Thank you. Thank you so much.'

Kavitha stepped aside and let the woman slip inside. It was strange – even with a bloodied face and terror in her eyes, there was a palpable heat rising from the woman, some sort of sexual signal, like pheromones. Kavitha didn't think it was just in her head – something about Minal seemed to whisper *sex,* just under the surface. God, Michael must have *loved* her.

Kavitha closed the door, and then studied the woman with cool eyes. 'That shoulder looks dislocated.'

Minal shrugged, and then winced. 'It is. Not the first time.'

'May I?' Kavitha asked, gesturing to the shoulder. Minal nodded, and Kavitha reached out to probe the injury with light, gentle fingers. 'It looks like an anterior dislocation, luckily, and I don't think there's any additional fracturing, though I can't be sure. You should go to the hospital, get that fixed.'

Minal shook her head. 'No hospital. I can't.'

'A clinic? A doctor?'

'No, no. I just – I just need to talk to Michael.'

'But you have to be in terrible pain.' There would have been endorphins at first, blocking the pain, but they'd have worn off by now. Kavitha hesitated, then said reluctantly, 'If you want, I can try to fix it.'

'Are you a doctor?' Minal asked hopefully.

She shook her head, not without regret. 'No – a dancer. But I spent four years in med school before dropping out to dance professionally. I can try to fix it, if you want. It'll hurt a lot, and I can't guarantee it'll work. And I have a kid who just fell asleep, so no screaming. I don't want her to see … this.' Kavitha gestured at Minal's entire body, her battered face.

Minal nodded. 'I understand. I have a high pain threshold – I can take it.' She smiled wryly. 'I can take a lot of abuse.'

Kavitha didn't want to think about what that simple statement meant, the history it implied. Instead, she said lightly, 'Someone sure wanted to test that today, huh? Okay, brace yourself.' If she was going to do this, fast and smooth was the only way to go.

She reviewed the procedure in her head, just once, and then reached out to take hold of Minal's arm. Upper arm in resting position, check. Bend elbow at ninety-degree angle, check, ignoring the flash of rising pain in Minal's eyes. Rotate arm and shoulder inward, toward the chest, to make an L shape. And now, a quick, deep breath for nerve and luck, and slowly, steadily, rotate arm and shoulder out. Kavitha couldn't ignore the pain that blanched Minal's brown face, but she kept going anyway. Seventy, eighty, ninety degrees out and there, there, she could feel it in her hands, the shoulder coaxed back into its joint, back home again with a sudden *pop*. And there it was, the immediate relief from pain making Minal's face ten years younger and surprisingly beautiful, glowing as it turned up toward her in warm gratitude. So beautiful that Kavitha caught her breath, suddenly knowing that she was in deep, deep trouble.

All this time, worrying about Michael, and how *he'd* react to Minal. She'd been so stupid.

Minal tried not to wince away as Michael's girlfriend bent down and dabbed at her face with a wet paper towel. The woman's fingers were very careful and gentle, but it still hurt. They were on the last stages of clean-up; Kavitha had already strapped her arm into an immobilizing sling and applied antibiotic cream to the open cuts. She'd even stitched up the deepest of them, the one right above Minal's cheek, where the Demon Prince's ring had cut her when his fist slammed into her face – no, no. Don't think about that, don't think about any of it. Time enough for that when Michael came home.

Kavitha had filled him in, tersely, when he'd called. He'd be here as soon as his shift was over. For now, Minal would just try to relax and enjoy the beautiful girl whose lips were so close to hers, so close that she could have just reached up and kissed them, hardly needing to move at all. Michael had certainly picked a pretty one, slender and graceful; Kavitha smelled nice too, like sandalwood. Minal was happy for him. Really.

She asked, trying to make the words casual, 'So, you and Michael have a kid? I always thought he'd make a good father; he seemed the daddy type. Have you been married long?' It couldn't be that long; it had only been four years since Michael had worked the vice squad. He'd started out being protective of Minal, then dating her. She'd broken it off when he'd started talking about moving in together. Michael had claimed that he'd be okay with it if she kept working, but it just hadn't seemed wise to get serious with a cop.

Minal had been eighteen when they met, not quite nineteen when they broke it off. Michael had seemed like a good guy for settling down with, but she hadn't been ready to settle down, not with the virus setting her blood to boiling. No one guy, or girl, could be enough for her back then, and the job had seemed a perfect fit. She was awfully popular, so the money was good. Really good. She could fit Michael's entire apartment into her living room. Not that that made up for it all, in the end.

'We're not married,' Kavitha said simply. She finished with Minal's face, and sat back on her heels to consider her handiwork. Minal was sitting on a low futon, and Kavitha was still only a few inches away. If it weren't for this stupid shoulder, Minal could just reach out and pull Kavitha down onto the couch, onto her. That would be a fun scene for Michael to walk in on! But with the shoulder, any such attempt would likely be disastrous.

So they weren't married. Minal wondered what that meant. She was tempted to apologize for her assumption, but thought that would probably make things worse. Michael was probably just being a typical guy, afraid of commitment. You'd think he was smart enough to figure out that having a kid together was the ultimate commitment. One way or another, he was tied to this woman for life.

Kavitha asked, 'So, you two used to date?'

Minal wasn't sure how much to say. Best to downplay it, probably. If this girl got jealous and threw her out, she'd be back in real trouble. She didn't know where else to go. 'Four years ago, for a bit.'

Kavitha nodded, looking thoughtful. 'That was just before we hooked up. I didn't plan on getting serious with a cop, but I picked him up in a bar, we had a great one-night stand, and then, three weeks later, I called him and told him I was pregnant. Contraceptive failure, damn it.' She hesitated, and then continued. 'I was going to abort, but chickened out the last moment. And then Michael got all noble when I got too big to dance and was having trouble making rent. So we moved in together, and then we had a baby, and as it turned out, eventually we fell in love.'

Minal felt an odd stab of jealousy, which stung much worse than any of the cuts on her face. Weird, when she'd been the one who didn't want kids, didn't want a boring, bourgeois life. 'So it all worked out for the best. That's nice.'

Kavitha said soberly, 'We got lucky. When the baby and I caught the virus, I thought he was going to leave. But Michael stuck around, despite not knowing how it'd all turn out. I think that's when I started to fall for him.'

Minal was startled, and again jealous. 'You look … normal.'

Kavitha shrugged. 'It only manifests when I dance, and it's under my control.'

'Must be nice.' Minal couldn't keep the bitterness entirely out of her voice.

Kavitha raised an eyebrow. 'You look normal too.'

'If I took my shirt off, you'd see different.'

Kavitha smiled and said lightly, 'Well, don't go trying to take your shirt off now! With that sling, you probably should keep that shirt on for a day or two. Give the inflammation a chance to subside. And go easy on it after that – it's going to take a long time to really heal.'

It was odd – Kavitha was telling her to keep her clothes on, but something about her body language was off. She was sitting a little too close, leaning in. Her breath was a little too fast. If she'd been one of her clients, Minal would have said that she was begging for it. Minal decided to take a chance. What the hell.

'Are you *sure* you want me to keep my shirt on?' It was her best hooker voice, the come-and-get-me huskiness low and dark.

She couldn't be certain, with Kavitha's light brown skin, but Minal was pretty sure that was a blush. Kavitha ducked her head down, but not before Minal caught the smile on her face. 'For now,' she said, softly. And then she was springing to her feet, graceful as a gazelle. 'I think I hear Isai waking up. I'll be right back.'

Minal hadn't heard anything, but she bit her tongue and kept her peace, wishing that she hadn't said anything. Stupid. She didn't need complications right now. What she *needed* was safe haven, and if she was smart, she wouldn't do or say anything to jeopardize that. Even if Michael's girlfriend did have beautifully long legs and a limber body. A dancer. In all Minal's years as a working girl, she'd never slept with a dancer. Minal squeezed her eyes shut and took a deep breath, digging her long, red fingernails into her palms. This wasn't going to be easy.

Michael felt thrown off balance even before he opened his apartment door. The place smelled wrong. It smelled ... good. Like something delectable was cooking. Which was impossible, since Kavitha was a terrible cook. Michael could grill a decent steak, roast a chicken, steam some veggies. Nothing fancy, but decent; his mother had made sure of that. Kavitha burned rice. And pasta. And water – or at least she let it boil off until it was entirely gone and the pot scorched beyond all redemption. So he knew that his girlfriend wasn't responsible for the complex blend of scents seeping out from under his front door. A savory blend of meat and spices and maybe something sweet – oranges? He'd come home braced for trouble, but suddenly all he could think about was how hungry he was. He took a deep, delicious breath and opened the door.

'Michael, we can't let this girl get away. Taste this!' Kavitha was bent over the stove, stirring something in a large pot.

'Daddy, Daddy, Daddy!' Isai ran across the apartment and hurled herself at him, half shifting midleap, so that for a brief moment he was enfolded in wings – and then she was herself again, naked and squirming.

'Little girl, you *know* you're not supposed to shift without asking first. How many times have I told you?'

'Sorry, Daddy!' she proclaimed cheerfully, not sounding sorry at all. And then she was off, babbling a long story about ducks and chickens and oranges and limes and too much pepper and sneezing and how she got to play with the water and Aunty Minal said that she was very pretty and she was a pretty princess, wasn't she, and Mommy did cooking! The last delivered in a tone of absolute astonishment.

'Your mother cooked this?' Michael asked, raising an incredulous eyebrow.

Kavitha shook her head, laughing. 'I did some chopping and stirring, but under strict supervision. This is all Minal's work. And you still haven't tasted anything.'

'In a minute, I promise. Where is Minal, anyway?'

'Here, Michael.' She stepped out of the hallway shadows, and even though he was happy with Kavitha, *very* happy, almost-ready-to-propose happy, Michael was hit once again by the sheer sex of Minal, tightening his groin, sending his thoughts spinning off in a dozen directions. That's why she was so good at her job, of course. The wild card had left her a curse, but also a gift. If you chose to take it that way.

'It's good to see you again,' he managed to say. And then he took a step closer to Kavitha, still holding Isai in his arms, a domestic talisman. He bent to taste the spoon his girlfriend held out to him. Some sort of pan-Asian duck stew, sweet and hot and mind-numbingly delicious. Just like Minal. 'That's – nice.'

'Michael!' Kavitha scolded him, smiling. 'Damning with faint praise, and you know she doesn't deserve it.'

'I'm sorry. This is all a lot to take in. And I think it's this little girl's bedtime, isn't it?'

'Overdue,' her mother admitted. 'Good night, princess,' she said, bending to drop a kiss on Isai's forehead.

'I want Aunty Minal to put me to bed!'

Kavitha asked, 'Are you sure, princess?'

'Yes! Yes yes yes!'

Kavitha turned to the other woman. 'Minal, if it's all right with you? She doesn't need much – just a trip to the potty, pajamas, a story, and a song.'

'That sounds lovely,' Minal said, coming forward to scoop the little girl into her good arm, coming disturbingly close to Michael as she did so. 'Just what the doctor ordered, at the end of a very long day.'

Michael said softly, 'I'm going to want to hear about that day when you're done.'

She hesitated, then nodded. 'Why don't you eat your dinner first? I'll be back soon.' And then she was turning, walking away down the hall carrying his daughter. Looking oddly comfortable doing so, even despite the awkward sling. It was funny – he'd never thought of Minal as the maternal type. Although he supposed that wasn't surprising, given the circumstances under which they'd met.

He turned back to his girlfriend. 'We have to talk.'

Kavitha handed him a plate laden with rice and duck stew. 'We'll talk while you eat. I think I've gotten most of her story out of her, though she won't tell me exactly who beat her up. And I have an idea to run by you.'

♦

Minal sang softly to the little girl, a Tamil version of 'Are You Sleeping' that her dad had sung to her. She hadn't thought of her dad in quite a while; her card had turned when she was fourteen, and he'd been completely unable to handle what it had done to her. He'd basically kicked her out of their apartment, and with her mother dead for over a decade, there hadn't been any reason to try to stay. She'd hitchhiked her way up to New York, and ended up in Jokertown. Went hungry for a while, when she couldn't get any real jobs, and then, when hunger and her own sex drive got too much for her, she'd started turning tricks.

Still, it hadn't been so bad. She'd become a hooker, sure, but a high-class one. No drugs, no pimp – she'd been lucky enough to meet some other girls who invited her to join their co-op, so essentially she worked for herself. And if she got beat up occasionally, she made damn sure the client paid for the privilege in advance. She even got to be friends with some of her clients – like poor Joe Twitch.

He'd been so scared, when he showed up at her door. Not her real door – she kept her apartment safely separate from the house she rented along with some other working girls. It was a nice house, with a bouncer within easy call and panic buttons built into the headboard of the beds. A safe place. Maybe that's why Joe seemed to relax when he stepped in the door, or maybe that was just her, the pheromones she couldn't help emitting anytime she got aroused. She got aroused so easily, since the virus. It was a nuisance a lot of the time, but the clients liked it. Especially Joe – he was so quick, at everything. He really appreciated that she was ready and willing at pretty much a moment's notice. With Joe, a few steps across the room and he was pulling down her skirt, turning her around, bending her over. Sliding one hand under her shirt, across the tiny nipples that spread across her torso, the wild card's gift and curse. Just the brush of his hand sending her arching back, pressing against him, wet and ready. And then he was dropping his pants, sliding into her – one, two, three, and he was done, but that was okay, because by then, she'd usually come too. The easiest of her clients, and sweet too – one of the ones who liked to cuddle afterward.

She'd actually fallen asleep next to him, something she rarely did, but it had been a long day, followed by a long night. One of the other girls was sick, so she'd pulled a double shift; Joe was her sixth client. When she woke up, it was to find him almost in tears. *What's the matter?* she'd asked. But he'd just shaken his head. Said, *Never mind – better if you don't know any details. I'm going up against someone, someone big. But I can take him. I've got the four-one-one on him; he owes me, and I own him. He's going to pay up. He's going to pay plenty for what he had burned, or he's gonna be the one burning, burning in hell. As soon as I get that money, I'll come back here and pay you first, sweetheart, I swear* – at which point, the conversation took a sharp turn, because even if Joe *was* a regular, extending credit was not normally a part of this business, and he should have known better. He *worked* at a house himself, although granted, a much lower-rent version. Joe had apologized so profusely, and seemed so freaked out, that in the end Minal sighed and let him leave without Jimbo marking him up any. Just this once.

And then she'd gone back to sleep, and woke up to find herself paying for her mercy. A stranger stood at the door to her room, his face and arms covered in angry red blisters, some of them popped open and weeping. His body was wrapped in black and silver leather. Another man was standing much closer to the bed, dressed in pin-striped pants and a white undershirt, his head wreathed in a crown of jagged horns. Demon Princes, from the garb – Minal had just enough time to figure that out, and then the horned man was grabbing her arm, hauling her up to her knees in the bed, slapping her across the face, back and forth, rhythmically, demanding to know what she knew. *C'mon, bitch. We know he was here. What did Joe tell you? What do you know?* And she was trying to tell him *nothing*, but he didn't even give her a chance to catch her breath, much less say anything. And his partner saying, *Hey, hurry up, someone's coming,* and then, thank the gods, there was Jimbo, all nine feet of him ducking down into the room, flailing with all four of his extra-long arms, slamming the door guy into the floor.

The sight of Jimbo must have made the horned guy holding her go a little crazy, because that was when he punched Minal in the face, hard, before he dragged her off the bed with a sharp yank, dislocating her shoulder in the process. He held her naked in front of him like a living shield as he backed away from Jimbo, pulled her back across the room until he reached the open window, and then he shoved her away, to the floor, and he was gone, out the window. But she didn't know when he'd come back, and as it turned out, Jimbo had hit the other guy a little too hard, and he wasn't going to be answering any questions for anyone. Minal knew his friends would be coming back, with reinforcements. If the Demon Princes were after her, her safe place wasn't safe anymore.

So here she was, and now the kid was asleep. One side benefit of her card turning had been that she healed a little faster than normal; the throbbing of her face and shoulder had already calmed down. She wouldn't be up for serious acrobatics anytime soon, but she was closer to healed than a nat would be. No more excuse for lingering in this quiet sanctuary – it was time to go out and face the music.

Michael shook his head at the end of Minal's dry recitation of events. She'd covered everything from the moment Joe walked in her door to Jimbo telling her the second Demon Prince was dead. Michael frowned. 'I can't figure out what this was about. Joe was blackmailing someone, going to meet them for the payoff – listen, did he have a gun on him when he left you?'

Minal shook her head. 'Joe never carried a gun.'

'And is there any chance any of this was drug-related?'

She said, 'I don't think so – Joe didn't use, and he never sold drugs.'

Michael's frown deepened. Hell, this was getting ugly. 'What about the dead guy? You called that one in?'

Minal nodded. 'Yes, of course. We run a respectable house.'

He said slowly, thinking out loud, 'Jimbo will do okay; it was self-defense, and you said they broke down your front door?' She nodded. Michael paused, then said reluctantly, 'I don't think you should go back there.'

Minal squeezed her eyes closed for a second, then opened them again. 'I was hoping you could arrest me? Keep me safe in the cells until you figure out what's going on?'

Michael shook his head. 'I don't know what the hell is going on. All that talk about burning in hell – maybe Father Squid is involved in whatever this is? I'll have to talk to Leo, see if he has any idea what this is all about. But I don't know that the station is the best place for you.' He paused, before continuing on, not sure how she would take the news. She'd been pretty stable, back in the day, but it had been four years since they'd been together, and four years on the street could be hard on a working girl. 'Here's the thing – Joe is dead. He was found with a gun in his hand and crack in his pocket. And there are two cops testifying that he resisted arrest and opened fire on them. One of them is Lu Long.'

Minal's face went still, all the life draining out of her. For a frightening moment, she looked like an old woman. 'Puff?' She swallowed and asked, 'But shouldn't I go in? Testify? Isn't that the right thing to do?'

He hated to say it, but it was the truth. 'Your testimony against theirs isn't worth shit. It wouldn't change anything.' Michael hesitated a moment, and then said, 'Kavitha thinks you should stay with us for a while.' He wasn't sure this was the smartest idea in the world – but what else could they do? He wasn't about to just throw an ex-girlfriend out into the cold. He just hoped Kavitha knew what she was getting into, because while he wasn't normally the cheating type, there was only so much a man could reasonably be expected to take. Even scared and injured, Minal sitting there was an open invitation to sin.

Minal turned to the woman sitting next to her on the small red love seat. Kavitha had been silent all through the recitation, but her warm body beside Minal's had somehow felt supportive, had helped Minal get through all the gory details. 'Are you sure?' She couldn't stay – could she? Honestly, she really didn't know where else to go. Minal wasn't even sure why she'd come here – the memory of someone who'd once been nice to her. She hadn't expected a girlfriend and a kid; she hadn't expected Michael to turn so domestic. Minal didn't belong in this cozy familial scene, but even the thought of leaving it left a tightness in her throat. 'I won't be in the way?'

Kavitha smiled. 'I know the apartment is small, but we can squeeze you in. You're great with Isai – if you don't mind doing a little babysitting, then I could use some extra practice time at the studio. I have a show coming up, and I'm underprepared.'

Minal shook her head, bewildered. 'No, of course I don't mind. I'm happy to cook too, and clean – this is so nice of you.' Was this really happening?

Kavitha shook her head. 'Oh, no. It's not all that nice. See, I have ulterior motives …' Her face flushed, and her voice trailed off.

Minal had seen that look too many times not to know what it meant. Desire. And if she were honest with herself, that desire was definitely returned. *What would happen if I …?* It might be wiser not to answer that question – but wisdom had never been Minal's strong point. *Passion,* on the other hand … It had been a really long day. She was entitled to a reward for surviving it.

She leaned forward and very gently touched her lips to Kavitha's. Kavitha froze for a second – and then was kissing her back. Minal closed her eyes again, this time an involuntary reaction to the shock of electricity running through her. It was just a kiss, the merest brush of lips against lips. Just a kiss, but all her nipples were tingling, a wave of heat racing across her torso. If it weren't for the sling holding her arm rigidly still, she'd have slid forward and pulled Kavitha against her. Well, the sling and Michael. What the hell did he think of his ex kissing his girlfriend?

Minal pulled back and opened her eyes to see Michael staring at them both, looking as if someone had taken a sledgehammer to his head. Utterly stunned. Minal opened her mouth – and then realized she didn't know what to say.

Kavitha spoke up then, with only a hint of apology in her voice. 'We probably should have checked that with you first.' She was looking at Michael as she said the words, but her hand slid blindly across the couch to touch Minal's. Minal curled her fingers around Kavitha's.

Michael shook his head, his eyes wide. 'No, no. That's okay.' He hesitated, then said firmly, 'But, Minal – you don't have to do this. You don't have to do anything sexual in order to sleep on our couch for a few days. That offer had no strings attached.'

Kavitha looked horrified. She said quickly, 'Oh, God, I'm sorry. I wasn't thinking. I forgot about your …' she trailed off, clearly embarrassed.

'… my profession?' Minal found herself smiling. 'The fact that you actually forgot that I'm a whore – that's the nicest thing anyone's done for me in a long time.' She squeezed Kavitha's hand reassuringly. 'Don't worry – I didn't kiss you out of any sense of obligation. I kissed you because I wanted to kiss you.' She grinned. 'And if Michael's okay with it, I'd very much like to kiss you again.' She took a deep pleasure in the way Kavitha bit her lip at her words.

Kavitha started to lean toward her, and then paused, turning back to Michael. '*Are* you okay with that?'

Michael grinned. 'Anytime you want to go kissing hot girls, it's okay with me.' He hesitated, then added, 'Well, maybe not just any hot girl. Not without checking with me first. But this one ...' Michael now looked completely bewildered. 'Umm ... am I allowed to kiss her too? I have no idea what the rules are here.'

Kavitha laughed then, shaking her head and setting her long braid bouncing. Minal found herself wondering what her hair would look like if she set it free. 'I don't know what the rules are either.' Kavitha hesitated. 'And – I'm not sure what I think about you kissing her. But it'd be pretty hypocritical not to let you try it, I think. If it's okay with Minal.'

'Is it okay with Minal?' Michael asked, softly.

Minal wasn't sure what exactly she had done to deserve such a confusing day – but she didn't want to stop now. She didn't know if it was the wild card urging her on, or just the memory of Michael's strong hands on her body. But she leaned forward as he came up out of his chair, dropping to one knee in front of the couch. Their lips met in a kiss that was first tentative, then sure. Memory blazed a trail and yes, that was how it was, how it used to be. Michael's breath cinnamon-sweet, his mouth hot and urgent against hers, and it seemed like forever until they finally disengaged.

Michael turned to Kavitha then, a query in his raised eyebrow. She was biting her lip, and for a moment, Minal couldn't read her. Was that jealousy, anger in her eyes? Was she about to throw Minal out on her ass?

And then Kavitha was against her, pressing her back against the couch, heedless of the injuries to shoulder and face, and Minal probably should tell her to be careful, but if there was any pain remaining, it was lost in the heat of Kavitha's mouth ravaging her own, Kavitha's hands, digging into her ass, pulling Minal's hips up to grind against her own. One knee sliding between Minal's legs, urging them apart, and Minal was suddenly sure that this wasn't Kavitha's first time with a woman. This girl had done this before. And now Michael was sinking to his knees beside the couch, his hand tangling in her hair, pulling her head back, so that as Kavitha started to slide down Minal's body, her teeth tracing a sharp, wet trail along her neck and collarbone, Michael's mouth came down onto hers again, and she moaned helplessly in response.

Minal's last thought, before she sank more deeply into the couch and gave herself up to pleasure, was that she had chosen the perfect sanctuary after all.

THE RAT RACE

PART 5.

In the hospice's lobby Leo Storgman ignored the signs pointing to the cancer ward. He already knew where it was and how to get there, and even if he didn't, he could've just followed his nose. The whole fourth floor had that strange, off-color stink that cancer centers sometimes acquire. Room 419 in particular reeked gently with the smell of cigarettes long-ago smoked, fresh flowers, and antibacterial solution.

The door was ajar.

Leo put his hand on the door and pushed it far enough to admit him.

Propped on the adjustable bed, lying lashed to needles and bags, was Ralph Pleasant. He opened one eye at the sound of Leo's footsteps, and the soft squeak of the hinge. He said, 'Well I'll be damned.'

'How's it going, Ralph?'

The older man twisted himself on the bed, arranging himself so he was slightly more upright. He coughed, a guttural sound that sounded like boiling tar. When he'd finished expectorating, he said, 'Been better. First time I've seen you here in … in a while.'

'Yeah. Sorry.' Leo approached the side of the bed, noting the chrysanthemums, the good bedding, and the menu beside his supper tray. He *was* sorry, about a lot of things. His failure to visit his dying ex-partner was just one more thing on the pile. 'But it looks like you've got a good setup here.'

'Can't complain. Even got a pretty nurse for my sponge baths.'

'Right on,' Leo said lamely. 'So. Um.'

'Did you bring me a present, kid?'

'Course I brought you a present. What am I, some kind of barbarian?' He reached into his pocket and pulled out a slim glass bottle of Ralph's favorite fifth – old-fashioned stuff with a black label and a smell that would melt rocks. Leo palmed it to Ralph, who grinned wide and slipped it under his pillow. 'Don't let the nurses take it away.'

He hacked, swallowed, and said, 'It won't last long enough for them to find it.'

'It'd damn well better not.' Leo smiled too. He knew it looked awkward, and it shouldn't have. He'd spent a decade and a half next to this guy. It hadn't always been good, but it wasn't always bad, either. They'd smiled a lot together. Ought to be easy, after all this time. But it wasn't.

Ramshead turned to nab a chair and paused, looking out the window. He was on Staten Island, a nice long way from Jokertown. Ralph was a nat, after all. He could get good health care anyplace, and the place he'd picked was pretty damn nice.

'You here to check the view?' Ralph asked.

'Just noticing it,' Leo told him, pulling his eyes away from Kill Von Kull and tugging the chair closer to Ralph's bed. He cleared his throat. 'How you been, anyway? They treating you all right in this dump?'

Ralph laughed. It was a horrible sound, old gum from the bottom of somebody's shoe. 'Yeah, it's a shithole, ain't it?' he jokingly agreed, both of them knowing that money couldn't buy much better. 'But I don't have a lot of time left in it, anyway.' Before Leo could muster some kind of polite protest, he also said, 'I hear you don't have much time left either. On the force, I mean.'

Leo took a deep breath, and let it out slow. 'Birthday's in January.'

'Then what?'

'Then … I don't know yet. You remember my daughter, Mellie?'

Ralph nodded, but coughed. He gestured for a Kleenex box. Leo handed it to him.

'Well, she's got this thing – this planned community, down in Florida. First jokers-only retirement neighborhood. She's trying to con me into buying a house down there.'

'You won't last six months.'

'Maybe an alligator'll get me. Or a shark.'

'Naw.' Ralph shook his head. 'You'll die of boredom.'

Leo said, 'Yeah.' Then, rather than leave it on that note, he said, 'Hey, you remember Wanda Moretti?'

'Hard to forget, that one.'

'She's coming back around again.'

'What for?' Ralph asked.

'For … for me, I guess. And, you know. Vicki's been gone for years. Mellie's down south. Sometimes I get tired of eating alone.' *And drinking alone, and sleeping alone.*

Leo was pretty sure Ralph knew about the ill-advised one-nighter back in the eighties. But he'd never said anything about it before, and he didn't start now. 'You could do worse. She could do better.'

'Amen.'

Ralph spit into the tissue box and wiped his mouth with the back of his hand. 'So how'd Wanda get back in the picture? She'd been gone a while, even when I retired.'

Leo hemmed, then hawed. 'It's a funny thing. There was a fire over at the courthouse, down in the basement where they keep all their old shit. The clerks were going through the mess, cleaning it up, and found her initials on some old hearing transcripts – and my name was on 'em too. They were from the arraignment hearing for that guy we picked up on the Rathole case. You remember that, don't you? That diner shoot-up, back at the end of '78. Right before Christmas.'

'Sure. I remember the Rathole.'

'Dr. Pretorius was going to give the case another look, doing that justice project stuff with the law kids. But the fire happened first, and Wanda thought it was pretty convenient. She thinks … and Pretorius thinks too … that the kid we nabbed didn't get a fair shake. Neither one of them thinks he did it.'

Ralph scowled deeply. 'Pretorius never thought anybody ever did anything.'

'I know. But I looked at it some more, and maybe, now.' He shrugged. 'I'm not as sure as I used to be.'

'You're only second-guessing because of your new girlfriend. Maybe you should go down to Florida after all, if you're going to let some woman get in the way of your judgment—'

Leo cut him off. 'Okay, but let me ask you: why wouldn't you look into it? When that kid got killed, why'd you make such a stink about leaving it alone and calling it a wash?'

'The kid was good for it,' Ralph insisted.

A scene flashed through Leo's mind: a body, covered in rust-colored hair and blood the shade of port and strawberry syrup. Its bones so broken that one arm appeared to lack them altogether, and it hung in a coil from his socket. A rib cage pounded flat on the right side, as if an enormous foot had stamped it like a bug. He recalled the smell of the alley, piss and wet newspaper, and rotting crates and yesterday's garbage. He remembered the colored lights, filtered kaleidoscope-style through the windows at the old church building.

Leo said, 'You could've pointed him out.'

'To who?' Ralph asked, squeezing the corner of the tissue box until it began to crumple in his hand.

'I don't know. Mob boys, maybe. They wouldn't have given a shit about the people in the diner, but they were mad about Hash's stash – Deedle definitely took the money and drugs.'

'I don't like what you're getting at.'

'Oh, come on,' Leo said, sitting back and leaning his elbows on the armrests. 'Getting someone else to hunt him down and wipe him out, even I could see – even back then – it looked easier than booking him.' He could've said, *'And it's not like you never did that before,'* but he didn't. They both knew about Ralph's inherent laziness, just like they both knew about Leo's long-ago infidelity. But between old partners some things stay off the table, for old times' sake.

Ralph said, 'Fuck you.' The words slurred through the black

phlegm that filled his chest, and came out with a spit. But it was not a protest, and it wasn't even personal. He just didn't want to talk about it.

Leo tried to make him anyway. 'Is that all you got? It doesn't even matter anymore, no one could tie you to it. No one's going to yank you out of your cushy deathbed.' Something about the room bothered him, but he couldn't put his finger on it. Not right then.

'Like you said, it doesn't matter now. Everybody's dead.'

'Except for you,' Leo pointed out.

'Except for me, and it's not like I shot anybody. It's not like *I* killed a diner full of nobodies for cash and blow.'

'I didn't say you did. I'm just saying, I think you fingered Deedle – and you did it knowing that someone would off him sooner rather than later.'

'Well ain't you something,' Ralph said. The gummy muck in his chest fought the words. He paused to wheeze and spit. His arm dragged an IV line over to a fresh box of tissues, and he coughed up more goop before speaking again. 'Everybody knew he was going down for it, and I might've mentioned it here or there. You can't prove it though, not after all this time.'

'I'm not trying to *prove* it,' Leo said. 'I'm just trying to sort it out for myself. I want to know who really shot up the Rathole, and you're the man who got our suspect killed, when he might've only been some opportunistic jackass passing by. Hell, Ralph. The kid could've been a witness. He might've told us something.'

Ralph's bloodshot eyes brimmed with tarnished contempt. 'He didn't tell anybody *shit*.'

'Maybe he didn't *know* shit. But *you* know something, Ralph.'

Ralph sneered, ugly and imperious. He settled back against his pillows. 'I know a lot of things. None of 'em are any good to you. And none of 'em matter, not anymore.'

'Ralph,' Leo used his name again. He tried not to make it sound too much like begging. 'What happened at the Rathole?'

'Damned if I know *that*,' he answered. 'Damned if anybody left alive knows anymore. All right, I know why that joker kid got done in – you can have that one, on the house. But the rest of it ...' His gaze wandered from his old partner, to his flowers, and back again. He went on. 'There isn't any *"rest of it."* Not that matters to anyone but me, and I'll be dead before New Year's.'

'Don't be an asshole.'

'Who's being an asshole? I'm just looking out for Number One. Now get out of here. Let an old man die in peace. And,' he added, just when it sounded like he'd said his last, 'congratulations on your retirement. I hope they give you a goddamn watch or something.'

HOPE WE DIE BEFORE WE GET OLD

by Stephen Leigh

PART 1.

On Wild Card Day, the stinking, twisted pustule that was Jokertown burst open and spilled its gruesome contents on the street for display.

Just find the snake kid ... What'd the Cry call him last issue? Black Tongue? Find him. That's why you're here. Remember what Snap told you. Said that the snake kid was in with Joe Twitch, that he sent Grady to the hospital after he attacked her.

[John?] a voice interrupted his thoughts. [Are you okay?]

On Wild Card Day, even Oddity wasn't odd. They mixed in with the throngs on the streets, and no one stared at the hulking, tall figure in their black, cowled cloak, their face obscured by the wire mesh of a fencing mask. No one remarked on the mottled, piebald, and mismatched nature of the arms and hands that emerged from the sleeves, no one commented about the strange, furtive movements under the clothing, as if something were writhing and changing underneath. No one glanced about as the creature moaned and clutched itself suddenly, as if someone had just shoved a knife into its side.

Oddity: three bodies and three minds merged horribly into one grotesque. Patty Roberts, John Sheak, and Evan Crozier, who had once been lovers in what they'd called an expanded marriage, and whom the wild card had cruelly bound together for life.

They were on Chrystie Street at the north end of Roosevelt Park.

Most of the people moving by and past them were heading to the park. Most of them were jokers as well, young ones. John didn't remember their names, though Patty or Evan might. John didn't remember names well at all anymore. There: the woman with the peacock feathers for hair and fine down covering her skin, who was she? Or the kid with the bright red and orange carapace, scuttling down the sidewalk on crablike claws; or that one oozing gelatinous streams from a quartet of pores around his neck, his clothing soaked with the snotlike substance? There were hundreds on the streets, all of them wearing their deformities for the world to see.

In the days when Oddity had first walked these streets, it had been fashionable to wear masks. Now, few did that. It was not a change John preferred.

The crowds were spilling over onto Chrystie – both Chrystie and Forsyth had been closed between Delancey and East Houston, due to the audience expected for the Joker Plague concert in the park. Oddity had passed Tinkerbill and Francis Xavier Black, two of the Fort Freak beat cops, lounging at the traffic barricade at Delancey. Chen had nodded as Oddity passed, as if they shared a secret, but John had no idea what. He'd ignored the gesture.

Find the snake kid. Go to … Go to … John couldn't remember the street. How could he have forgotten it already? Another spasm of pain rippled through their abdomen, like a fist trying to beat its way out of their skin.

'Fuck,' Oddity said. The body doubled over briefly. Somebody bumped into them from behind and stumbled away with a muttered apology. 'Jesus bloody Christ.'

[John,] Evan said, [do you want me to take over? Patty can come up to Sub.] Evan was Sub-Dominant at the moment, as Patty rested at Passive far below, where the eternal agony of Oddity's three merged bodies was only a faint prickling. It was John, in control of Oddity's body, who bore the brunt of the pain, though Evan could feel it as well.

[No, damn it! I got it. Just give me a fucking second, would you?] *The alley off Rivington …* Yes, they'd talked to Ears, one of the hundred informants Oddity had in J-Town. Ears, named for the huge, batlike flaps of flesh on either side of his face, heard everything for blocks around him, and retained it all – if you could manage to coax it from his addled brain. *I hear the snake's living in an apartment in the alley of Rivington. Talk to Skeleton Key; he rented the kid the room ...* The names floated through his consciousness again and John reached for them, saying them over and over again in his head, trying not to repeat them so loudly that Evan or Patty could hear him and notice his forgetfulness. *The alley off Rivington ...*

[... please let's not fight among ourselves ...] Patty whispered, down in Passive. [... we only have each other only each other remember don't argue please ...]

John gave a throaty snarl that might have been a response or might have been simple pain. Oddity straightened and glanced around, disoriented momentarily. *Weren't we on Bowery? Weren't we going to see Hart – No ... What are you thinking? No, he's long dead ...* John shrugged away the errant memory; they plagued him more and more often, like dead autumn leaves blowing eternally in his face. He looked around at the crowds, half expecting to see Peanut or Gimli, Chrysalis or Tachyon, all those people he remembered so well while the people around them now seemed more wisps and ghosts. Reality was increasingly less real than the past.

Have to find ... He couldn't remember who they were supposed to find, only that it was important and there was a righteous anger involved. He roared to the night sky, and this time the jokers passing him did look. 'That's Oddity,' he heard one of them – a young woman whose face was studded with wriggling cilia – say to her companion, who had no legs at all, only a slug's tail emerging from under her dress, leaving a trail of slime on the sidewalk. 'Poor thing ...'

As Oddity paused, spotlights flared in the park, tossing the shadows of trees over the street and pinning the stage erected on the tennis courts in their glare. The crowd packed onto the grass outside the courts roared, and a roll of drums echoed from the buildings. 'Hey, fellow freaks! You ready for a show?' someone roared, the voice heavily amplified. The spotlights followed a six-armed, muscular joker striding into the center of the stage. He beat on his chest and a cascade of thunderous drums followed. Three more jokers followed him onto the stage as the crowd screamed in response: a guitar shrilled, a bass thumped, and a synthesizer hissed and shrilled. The band kicked into a song, a deep and powerful voice singing with them.

Gasping, slack-jawed, spittle-dripping:
Rise, Fenris.
Padding the spine of man's serpent,
Urban Midgard encircled.

In the reflected light from the stage, Oddity could see a sea of heads bobbing in time to the music as the crowd rushed to barriers set in front of the stage. Jokers – masked and unmasked – were moving across Chrystie, trying to push into the crush. They could smell the scent of pot, heavy in the breeze. [That's not fucking music. That's just shit.] John nearly said it aloud. [Just goddamn noise. No one makes good music anymore.]

Thinking of music, John remembered other nights, and the world seemed to shift around him. For a moment, he saw himself as he once had been, alone, sitting on the grass of Central Park with Patty between him and Evan, listening to Simon and Garfunkel playing while the three of them passed a joint back and forth. But the memory slid away in the cacophony dinning in his ear, and he cowered back into the shadows, afraid that one of the cops would see them – another memory, another time, when the police were after them – something about having killed a kid they said was a 'jumper.' [Bastards. They don't realize we're just trying to protect our own.]

[John?]

The present snapped back with the roar of the ending chords of Joker Plague's song, and he realized they'd been standing there too long. *Have to find the snake kid. The alley off Rivington ... The snake kid was in with Joe Twitch ...*

Oddity snarled and moaned as they moved southward down Chrystie, turning right at Rivington. Joker Plague was only a low rumble here, and there were fewer people on the street. Oddity glanced around at the grimy, small shops and the equally dingy apartments over them. They turned into the alleyway between a sandwich shop and a convenience store. A single bare lightbulb over a doorway halfway down the narrow lane was the only illumination. Rats glanced up from rummaging among the trash cans and slunk away. Something had died not far away; they could smell it through the fencing mask's screen.

What was it Snap said about the snake kid? He warned us about something ... I can't remember ...

Oddity stood there, frozen. [John? You want me to take us?] Evan asked again.

'No!' John shouted the word, not caring that he spoke aloud, the word tearing at Oddity's throat and sounding disconcertingly like Patty's voice. As the call echoed, audible even over the bass grumble of Joker Plague a few blocks away, Oddity saw movement at one of the windows farther down the alley: a flick of a curtain and a moment's light. John thought he saw a young African-American face.

He forced Oddity to stand stock-still in his black cloak, his head angled down so that the mesh of the fencing mask didn't catch the light of the bulb. From under mismatched eyebrows, he watched the face – the youth didn't show any alarm, and a moment later, the curtain slid back over the window.

Oddity moved to the door. A hand – partially Evan's, partially John's own – grasped the knob and turned. Locked. He knocked, and someone opened the door from inside. 'You're late,' a voice said. 'Told me you'd be here an hour ago.' The voice came from a thick-framed figure. Hands moved in the dim light of a small office: the fingers were silvered, each of them ending in a knobby, intricate protrusion like door keys from the 1920s.

'Sorry,' John said. 'Ears said ... Snap ...' Oddity's head shook. 'Snake kid,' John grated out.

'Yeah, I know who you mean. Up on the second floor. You ain't gonna do anything physical, are you? I mean, I gotta keep this place up, y'know.'

The fencing mask shook, a quick back-and-forth negative.

'Okay,' Skeleton Key answered. 'Then come on, I'll open his door for you ...'

They followed the joker through a back door of the office, down a hallway, and up a flight of stairs to another, equally dimly lit hall. John's thoughts were as murky as the atmosphere of the apartment building. Why were they here? Was this another one of the drug labs of the Demon Princes, another intervention into the ongoing gang war between the Princes and the Werewolves? Snap had sent tips about them often enough recently.

There was so much to do, so much that had to be done to keep Jokertown safe.

'The snake kid ... Black Tongue ...'

'What?' Skeleton Key asked.

John wasn't aware he'd spoken aloud. He scowled, grinding their mismatched teeth together. 'Nothing,' he answered. 'Where's the kid?'

'Just down here ...' Skeleton Key stopped in front of a battered, warped door with scratched, peeling paint. He stuck a finger into the keyhole and rotated his wrist. There was the snick of a lock opening. 'Now remember, I don't want ...'

John wasn't listening. He turned the doorknob, felt it catch on a chain. He put their massive shoulder to the door and pushed; the wood gave around the screw of the chain holder as Skeleton Key gave a 'Hey!' in protest. Oddity saw a flash of red, yellow, and black scaled rings in the light of a lamp inside. Oddity's hands pushed the door wide open; hinges shrieked in protest.

'*You!!*' he yelled. '*Snake kid!*' John's head was filled with a red rage. He ignored Evan and Patty's protests. [John, we have to be careful. Snap said the kid's tongue is poisonous; that's why Grady's in the hospital ...]

Oddity pushed through the remnants of the door. Something hit them hard in the chest, and they felt a stab of pain, though the blow wasn't hard enough to stagger him. Oddity was already reaching for the movement even as the blow came: the snake kid's tongue. John had hold of it just below the fist-sized protrusion at the end; he heard a muffled, strangled scream from the kid. Something green, foul, and wet splashed over their multitoned hand. John yanked hard on the tongue; the snake's tail lashed at him, sending Oddity reeling into the wall hard enough that they broke through into the next apartment. Someone screamed; John saw a pale white form fleeing on what looked a deer's legs. 'Damn it, I didn't *do* anything ...' the snake kid shouted, but John only heard the sound, not the words. A bloody rage filled John, and he wasn't certain who they were fighting. There was only the fury. Oddity shouted as he staggered back into the apartment.

The snake kid was already fleeing. John saw the tail slithering out from the door, and he pursued the joker, pushing past Skeleton Key. The kid was halfway down the hallway, heading for the stairs. Oddity followed: down one flight, and down the next into the basement of the building. As they entered the basement, John tore a cast-iron pipe from the wall as a weapon. Water sprayed everywhere.

[John – that's the water line! What the hell are you doing?]

John could feel Evan trying to wrest control of Oddity from him, and that only made him angrier. Oddity waded into the basement, glimpsing the snake at the rear near the octopus arms of an ancient furnace. The tongue lashed at him again; he swung the pipe like a bat, striking the lump at the end and causing the kid to scream. The snake's tail lashed out, knocking them from their feet. Oddity flailed at the tail with the pipe, heard the joker scream again as he connected. He saw ebony skin, and he dropped the pipe to grab the kid's torso, tossing him bodily backward. A plasterboard wall cracked and broke. The water soaked their heavy cloak, already a few inches deep and rising.

[John, we have to get the hell out of there! John!]

The kid stared at Oddity: his tongue was hanging from his mouth like a piece of frayed rope, dripping blood. Faintly, John heard sirens over the subdued din of Joker Plague. The snake body below the torso writhed, and the kid dove for a casement window, crashing through. Oddity pursued, tearing through the frame with a shout, but it was too small for Oddity's massive body. He turned them back to the stairs, slogging through the water and up to the ground floor and outside.

He saw the snake at about the same time that the tongue hit them square on the fencing mask, crumpling the steel mesh and staggering them again. Venom bit at their disfigured flesh.

The impact was enough that Evan was able to wrest the disoriented and confused John from Dominant, taking control of Oddity, who slowly pushed up from the ground, assessing their body and glancing around. The boy was gone. As Oddity stood, Evan could see the pulsing lights from a police cruiser at the end of the alley. He turned Oddity and limped away down the alley, moaning now not only from the eternal torment of their shifting form, but from the pains of their newly bloodied body.

Evan saw the scowl of Dr. Finn's face as he bandaged Oddity's uncloaked body in the Jokertown Clinic. Evan imagined he saw disgust there. He couldn't blame Finn; it's what all of them felt when they looked at themselves in a mirror.

'I've stitched up the worst of the cuts, and put ointment on the scrapes,' Finn said, 'and this' – he held up a syringe – 'is antivenom, since you say the Black Tongue's poison splashed all over your face and body.' The centaur's tail flicked as he spoke: an angry back-and-forth, and he jabbed the needle into Oddity's arm. Pulling it back out, he tossed the syringe into an orange-colored box on the wall. 'Not that any of my needlework will stay, with the way your body changes, but it's the best I can do.' He took a long breath, exhaling loudly through his nose.

'I'm more worried about the way John's been behaving than any of this,' Evan told Finn. 'He's forgetful, he's getting more aggressive and stubborn. His personality's changing, Doc, I swear it is.'

Finn scowled again. 'Tell me more,' he said.

Evan related everything he and Patty had noticed in the past few months with John's behavior, with Finn nodding and frowning as he spoke. Down below, he could hear John in Passive. [… shut the fuck up you asshole it's none of his business none of this …]

'I swear, Doc, sometimes I don't think he knows what year it is. He talks about Hartmann or other people who have been dead for *years* like they're still there.'

Finn's hooves clicked on the linoleum. He made a note on the chart he was holding. 'I can't make a true diagnosis without more information and tests.'

'But?'

Finn took a long breath. 'But the symptoms you're describing sound like early onset Alzheimer's, and from what you're telling me, it's progressing fast.'

[... fuck him fuck him he doesn't know what the fuck he's talking about ...] Evan heard John muttering.

Patty, in Sub-Dominant, almost seemed to sob. [Evan, if that's true ...] She didn't say the rest. She didn't have to. They both could feel it. The truth was that they'd both suspected it for a while now; they simply hadn't dared to vocalize it or even think it.

The examination table was cold under their rear. Evan longed to put on their clothes again, to cover their twisted form with the cloak and fencing mask. 'What can we do?' Evan asked Finn.

The lift of Finn's shoulder was visible under the lab coat. 'I can give you information to read. There are drug treatments for behavioral and psychiatrical issues: antidepressants like Prozac, or Ativan for anxiety and disruptive behavior, antipsychotics like Abilify ...' The shrug came again. The tail flicked. 'But I'm hesitant to prescribe anything. Given your situation, the drugs might only affect the dominant personality, or all of you equally. I don't see a way to treat John alone.' Again, there was a long hesitation. Evan could hear John still muttering and cursing down in Passive. [... full of shit the bastard I'm fucking fine screw him ...]

'Unless?' Evan prompted. He closed their eyes and grimaced as something – an elbow, a leg, a section of someone's skull? – thrust up from their abdomen, pushing against the piebald skin and submerging itself again. The kid's tongue seemed to have cracked ribs. He fisted the hand on their lap against the pain: the hand was mostly his, but the last three fingers were Patty's, and that was John's thumb.

'We could try the trump virus,' Finn said. 'It's been improved – there's a forty percent cure rate now.'

[... no fucking no don't let him do that to us ...]

'And it kills, what, one in five?' Evan said. 'And the rest it doesn't touch at all. That's our choice?'

[Evan, we should think about it,] Patty whispered. [Maybe that's the best way.]

Finn shrugged. 'Honestly, the odds might be worse than that,' Finn admitted. 'You're three people in one body. If I inject the trump into Oddity ...' He lifted his hands; let them fall again. 'Well, I don't know what the trump would do with you. I don't know if it would kill all three, or maybe spare one of you, or two, or all. And what happens if it just cures one of you? There's no way to—'

Finn's head jerked around as loud voices came from beyond the curtains of their examination room. 'They're in here? Where?'

The curtain was yanked aside. Two of the Fort Freak cops were standing there, with Troll, chief of clinic security, just behind them: Tinkerbill and Franny, who'd been at the traffic barricade earlier. 'Jesus!' Tinkerbill said as he stared at Oddity's naked body. Evan knew what he was seeing: the wide, distorted torso with its mixture of three skin tones, with portions of each of their bodies visible and slowly moving across it, the face with its mismatched features, the way his arms and legs were of varying lengths. At least there was a towel over their lap; their genitalia was more often than not confusing. When Evan stared at the cop, Tinkerbill just glared back. Black simply appeared amused, giving them a wide, toothy grin without saying anything, letting the larger, older cop take the lead.

'Nice bandaging job, Doc,' Tinkerbill said. 'Very impressive.' Chen looked like a poster cop; Evan noted the way the uniform pants were creased, the fact that the shirt was buttoned all the way up over the Kevlar vest, the muscular body that the uniform couldn't hide, the regulation hat, but the voice ... His voice was high-pitched and thin: a voice that could cut glass.

'What the hell are you doing here, officers?' Finn demanded. 'The two of you are interfering with medical treatment.'

'Oddity here looks awful banged up,' Tinkerbill commented. Six and a half feet tall, he was nearly as intimidating a presence as Troll.

'I slipped and fell down,' Evan said.

Both officers laughed at that. 'Yeah, and you did a hell of a lot of damage to the apartment building at the same time,' Tinkerbill said. 'They're still pumping water out of the basement, and Skeleton Key's pressing charges over the damage to doors and apartments. Not to mention that we already have Angel Grady here at the clinic because of the guy you were tangling with ... and thanks to *you*, we've lost him. You've been warned about vigilantism, Oddity. Way too many times. All you're doing is making it harder for us to do our job. Get dressed – we're taking you to the station. You're under arrest. You have the right—'

'I haven't released him,' Dr. Finn interjected. Tinkerbill just looked at him; Black grinned again. 'I mean it,' Finn told the two. One of his hooves stamped against the tile floor. 'You can wait outside. Troll, make sure they don't bother us. I need a few more minutes with my patient, then you can have him.'

'Sure,' Tinkerbill said in his falsetto voice. 'We'll be right outside the curtain.' He nodded to his partner, and they both stepped back. Black swept the curtain around them again as Finn shook his head. 'I want you to know that I didn't call for them,' the centaur said.

'S'okay, Doc,' Evan said. 'We'll phone Pretorius when we get to the station. It's nothing particularly new.'

[... damned cops can't trust cops except maybe Snap and a few others assholes not like it used to be not like it should be ...]

'Evan, I want you and Patty to think about what I said.' Finn glanced significantly at the curtain. 'You need to be very careful. If ... if it's what we think it is, he's only going to get worse and more erratic.'

'I know,' Evan answered. 'And we will.' He moaned as something shifted inside, sending waves of pain down his side. One of the cuts that Finn had stitched gaped and broke open again. Blood streamed sluggishly toward their – Patty's – hip. They both looked at it. 'Can you hand me our clothes, Doc?' Evan asked. 'I suppose I should get dressed ...'

◆

The trip in the squad car to Fort Freak was like a carnival ride. There were fireworks being set off right and left from the rooftops and down the dark alleyways. The streets were crowded with revelers, surging across the roads so that Franny Black, driving the car, had to stop frequently with a curse. An impromptu parade was marching along Canal Street, hundreds of jokers walking or limping, crawling and flying, slithering and lurching down the middle of the street. Atop a float that was a cardboard and aluminum foil replica of a Takisian ship, a quartet of jokers was tossing plastic DNA strands as if they were Mardi Gras beads, the onlookers cheering. Oddity saw a woman lift her blouse to the neck as the float approached, showing six individual breasts in two lines down her chest like the teats of a dog; the float riders showered her with colorful DNA strands.

Just down the street from the station, a spiderlike joker was running wildly back and forth across the street between the parked cars, while a dozen other jokers clapped and applauded. As their cruiser approached, they saw – too late – that nearly translucent thin ropes sagged across the blacktop where the joker had been running. The cruiser plowed into the ropes. They clung stickily, but when they broke, green fire sizzled and sparked and hissed, sending off fierce, blinding bursts that flew into the air and dripped onto the pavement as the jokers laughed and applauded, then fled between the nearest buildings.

'Great,' Black said. Where the strands had touched the car, waxy lines remained behind. 'Now the captain's going to make us clean the damn car.'

Given that it was Wild Card Day, the station was even busier and more chaotic than usual: uniformed cops, both joker and nat, hauled in a steady flow of people – also both joker and nat, some (usually the nats trying to 'pass') with masks around their faces – for public intoxication or exposure, for selling drugs, for prostitution, for assault. The lobby of the station looked as if a roving street party had invaded it.

Sergeant Vivian Choy had the desk; she glanced up wearily at Tinkerbill, Franny, and the looming, massive form of Oddity. Behind her, the station was a loud cacophony with frenetic movement: cops on the phones, cops talking with one another, cops with suspects. 'Room two's open. Stash them in there, then come see me.'

Oddity shuffled along behind the two officers, and took a seat at the bare table in the center of the room. The metal chair with its frayed seat groaned metallically as they sat. Evan brought their hands from behind their back as Oddity sat: the links of the Black's cuffs had been pulled apart. 'Sorry,' he said to them. 'Cheap metal.'

Tinkerbill sniffed; Franny grimaced and took the remnants of the broken cuffs from their wrists. 'Stay put,' he said. 'They'll be in to talk to you soon.'

'And my lawyer?' Evan asked. 'Since you've arrested me, I get my call, right? If you've changed your mind, then I have places to be.'

'Yeah, so do we. I'll have someone bring in a phone. You stay here, or we'll have Squinch put you in lockup. Got it?'

Evan lifted their shoulders in showy nonchalance. 'I'm thirsty too,' he said.

'Sure, we'll have the waiters bring in our dinner menu with the phone,' Tinkerbill answered. 'C'mon, Franny, we've wasted enough time with them already.'

The door slammed and locked behind them. Oddity stared at the mirror on the opposite wall, wondering if there was anyone there watching. Evan could hear John muttering at the edge of his consciousness. [Patty?]

[I'm okay Evan. Can you stay in Dominant? I'll hold John down – he really wants Oddity back and we can't risk it right now.]

[I've got us.]

[What are we going to do, Evan?]

[I don't know. I really don't know.]

One of the clerks, a too-thin kid with blue skin, knocked and brought in a cell phone. 'Sarge says to make your call and give me the phone back,' he said. Evan dialed Pretorius's pager – they all knew the number by heart – and handed back the phone. Evan didn't know how long they sat there after that. He could hear the faint roar of activity outside the door, an occasional snippet of voice. The cheap fluorescent lights flickered. He let Oddity rest, though the body released the intermittent, involuntary moan as the body shifted and changed. He watched their hands go from being mostly Patty to a fair amount of John, to Evan's mocha skin coloring, the joints, bones, muscles, and ligaments sliding painfully past one another underneath the flesh.

The door opened and Leo Storgman – Ramshead – walked in, a forefinger scratching at the ram's horns atop his skull, a thick file in his other hand. He tossed it on the table; Evan wondered if that was a file on Oddity as he saw the detective glance at their hands. 'Evan?' Storgman asked.

'Good guess, Leo,' Oddity answered. 'Yeah. Patty's Sub at the moment.'

Ramshead nodded and took the chair opposite them. 'John had the body when you went after the Black Tongue kid?'

'What's this about a Black Tongue? Why, I don't know what you're talking about,' Evan said.

'Right,' Leo said. He sounded tired, and he scratched again at the base of the ram's horns. 'You were out listening to the Joker Plague concert and hoping to score some backstage passes.' His finger came off the horns and tapped the folder. 'Look, I don't give a flying fuck about the Black Tongue, Evan. I've been thinking about something else. Something a lot older.'

'Like what?'

'Like who murdered Deedle.'

'That's ancient history, Leo. We still miss the diner, though, and poor Lizzie. Deedle ... he got what he deserved.'

'He claimed all along he didn't do it, and there was never a trial.'

'Because he chewed off his own damn thumb and ran. Just like any innocent person would do.'

Leo nodded. 'Uh-huh. Still, not many people could have done what was done to Deedle.'

'Only about a couple dozen I can think of, just off the top of my head,' Evan answered. 'The wild card virus loves superstrength. It's almost as common as jokers with animal parts.'

A trace of a smile slid across Ramshead's mouth. It wasn't a pretty sight. The door opened then, and Dr. Pretorius swept in, looking elegant and dressed as if he'd been out to a society affair, his white beard perfectly trimmed, his long hair pulled back in a ponytail, his genteel face tanned. His lithe movements gave no indication that his right leg was an artificial limb below the knee.

'That's enough talking,' he said to Oddity, then turned to Leo. 'My client is done here,' he informed Leo. 'I've talked to the assistant D.A.; it seems she isn't inclined to waste the city's money and time yet again with the Oddity, especially with the Black Tongue being the one you people actually wanted. Oddity saw the kid and tried to apprehend him long enough to call the station – Oddity was only trying to be good citizens. A shame about the damage, but that was the Black Tongue's fault. My clients were just defending themselves. So unless you're planning to charge them with something else ...' He lifted one eyebrow.

Leo shook his head. 'Not at the moment.'

'Good. Then we're out of here. Oddity, please ...' Pretorius gestured to the door with a sweeping hand. Evan pushed Oddity's hands against the table and rose, the table bending slightly under their weight. They walked to the door, held open by Pretorius.

'Oddity. Evan,' Ramshead called out as they reached the door. Evan turned to see the detective tap the file folder in front of him. 'I'm not finished with this yet.'

Evan shook their head. The grid of the fencing mask slid over Leo's figure. 'That was finished a long time ago,' Evan said. He turned again, and Pretorius shut the door behind them.

THE RAT RACE

PART 6.

'Another morbid lunch date,' Wanda observed. The sign above her head read, SUPERGYROS. The restaurant was half empty, but it was past lunch and not yet supper. 'How long has it been this Greek place?'

'About ten years. But it used to be the Rathole.' If Leo closed his eyes he could almost see it, that night in 1978 – or so early in the morning that the distinction didn't matter any. Small and rectangular, the whole diner had been barely the size of a boxcar and only half as appealing. Sloughing paint, chipped steps, vinyl seats scored with splits and tears from too many heavy asses on too many nights. The stools up at the bar would spin if you kicked them; one had lacked its cushioned round head. Neon signs once advertised Coca-Cola and some brand of chili Leo couldn't remember ... and those signs had only been half lit, half burned out or busted.

All the old details straggled into focus.

He rubbed at his eyes, and his knuckles were cold. Everything was cold, same as it had been that night, when the filthy little dive was splattered with blood from floor to ceiling. But today, the sky was pale and sterile and streaked with gray like dirty gauze.

Wanda said, 'Whatever happened here – back then—'

The detective recalled stepping over Lizzie Wallace, and seeing the blood pooled around her mouth on the nasty tile floor. He remembered the window that'd been taken out by a shotgun blast, and the tinkle of shattered glass still dropping, one dull icicle at a time, from the frame. Like it was yesterday, he saw Don Reynolds lying half in the window and half out of it, his throat cut by the glass. That wasn't what killed him – it just added insult to injury. And there, in the doorway that separated the dining area from the kitchen, Hash Crowder had been splayed. His body propped the door open and let the kitchen smoke billow into the rest of the establishment. The whole place smelled like burned burgers, gunpowder, and blood.

'It was a mess.' It was all he could think to say.

She told him, 'It's still a mess. Are you going to clean it up?'

'I'm trying,' he insisted. 'But the leads are stale, and they aren't getting me anywhere.' He kicked at a small chunk of concrete and tried to look away, to look at Wanda, but he couldn't. 'Everybody's dead. And the people who aren't don't remember anything.'

'Who have you talked to?' she asked.

He sighed. 'I found Stella Nichols's sister, buried upstate. Stella's daughter was just a first-grader when her mother died. The guy she'd reported, her stalker or whatever, his name was Fred Winney. She filed a restraining order a few weeks before she died. But he fell off the map fifteen years ago. I'm still asking around, still trying to find some trace of him. And I'm not meeting a whole lot of luck.'

'That's a start.'

He continued. 'Joel Arnold wasn't long away from retirement himself. He was a widower, and he lived alone – no kids. He'd been working at the precinct a long time, and a lot of cops trusted him. He could've seen a lot of stuff he shouldn't have, but I'll be damned if I can tie any of it to what happened here. I found his supervisor in an old folks' home. Had nothing but good things to say about him.

'Then I moved on to Lizzie Wallace, the counter girl. As far as I can tell, everybody everywhere loved her. No one wants to talk about her asshole boyfriend, though. I'm still working that angle.

'Poor Don, the Drip – when his card turned, his wife left him and took their daughter too.' He shook his head. 'He ended up on the streets, got picked up for a bunch of petty stuff. And they think he was driving that Mercedes. The whole thing,' – he stuffed his hands into his pockets, even though they weren't cold – 'it's impossible. The Rathole could've been a robbery like everybody thought. Or maybe it wasn't – maybe it was a hit that went wrong. Any one of them could be the key, I can't find anything that makes any of the victims look like a specific target, except maybe Hash. He's the one I keep coming back to – he was definitely mixed up with real trouble. Could've been a rival dealer wanted to shut him down, or it could've been the mob. But if that's the way it went down, why wouldn't the mob have taken its stash back? Doesn't make any sense for them to have left it behind for Deedle to snatch.'

He wiped his fingers on the end of his coat and then rubbed at his eyes, and adjusted his hat. Thirty years after the first murder of his career, he stared at SUPERGYROS as hard as he could, and strained to recall anything else.

But the smoke of that night colored everything; it smeared against the glass and left a greasy film on every surface. He remembered the feel of broken glass crunching beneath his shoes as he tried to find someplace to stand that wouldn't be in the way, and wouldn't compromise the scene. He'd looked out through the shattered window and he'd seen a crowd gathering, pushed back and strapped onto the sidewalk by the crime scene tape someone was just then getting around to unfurling. The faces had lined up behind it, curious and concerned, interested and disgusted.

And one face, standing out from the rest. Its tentacles billowing in yesteryear's brisk, frigid air. 'Squid was here,' Leo said suddenly.

'What?'

'He was in the crowd. I talked to him. Huh. I'll have to ask him about it later. But for now,' he said, slipping an arm around Wanda's waist, 'I've got to call it a lunch, and get back to the precinct before they miss me. See you later?'

'Later,' she said, and she leaned in to kiss him.

Back at Fort Freak, Michael was at his desk, alternately chewing on a pen and tapping it against a photo of his daughter, who was smiling and chewing on something else. When Leo dropped himself back into his seat and shuddered, his partner looked up with a soft frown and asked, 'How was lunch?'

'It was great. Why?'

The younger man shrugged and said, 'You look ... pensive. And not in a happy way.'

Leo levered himself out of his jacket and let it fall over the seat's back, pinned by his shoulders and spine. He rubbed his hands together. 'Just the usual. Look at all this shit,' he said, gesturing at the paperwork rising in small heaps across his workspace.

Michael made a point of looking back down at his own tidier desk. 'But that's not what's bugging you, is it? Not really. Where'd you go for lunch?'

'Out,' he said gruffly.

'Didn't run by Supergyros, did you? Isn't that what the Rathole is, these days?'

'Stuff it, kid.' Leo reached for the most pressing folder and opened it, then smacked it shut again with a puff. 'Actually, maybe you can help.'

'Help?' Michael looked up again. 'What do you need?'

Leo appreciated how he didn't say no outright, even though he probably should have. He said, 'So you're not an idiot, and you know I'm fiddling around with that old case.'

'Thanks. And yes, I know.'

'Plenty about it bugs me,' he went on. 'But right now I'm trying to sort out if any of the victims might've been a target zero, you know what I mean? Maybe it wasn't a robbery that went bad, but a personal gripe that got out of hand.'

'All right,' Michael said, and he pulled out a notepad from his top drawer. He clicked at the pen that had only moments ago been in his mouth. 'Hit me.'

'The Mercedes. The Drip was driving it, they found his shelter card wedged in the driver's seat cushions. We've been assuming he stole it, but from who? You think you can look into that for me?'

'Shouldn't be too much trouble. Just a little file-surfing ought to turn it up. What's *your* next move?'

'I'm going to scare up a name for the counter girl's asshole boyfriend. Either no one knew in '78, or no one was talking. And maybe, while you're at it,' he amended his request, 'could you dredge up the old ballistics? We know Hash squeezed off a few shots before he went down. I want to know who he hit. Maybe we can chase that. Maybe someone ended up in an ER peppered with shot. I should check that too,' he mumbled, jotting it on the corner of whatever was closest.

Captain Mendelberg chose this moment to swan past his desk, her ruffly little fish-fin ears flapping against an updo that kept her hair off her collar. Wispy ears or no, they could hear like hell – and the captain didn't look happy. 'Detective,' she said unhappily, and without slowing down. 'A word with you?' She continued swanning, right into her office.

Leo lifted his eyebrows, then dropped them again. Michael looked worried, but said, 'Good luck.'

'I'll need it,' Leo muttered as he rose from his chair and followed in the captain's wake.

Inside her office with the door shut, she didn't quite yell at him. Instead, she stood behind her own desk and looked one part annoyed, one part exhausted, and completely short-tempered. 'It's the Rathole again, isn't it?'

'What?' A careful answer that admitted nothing.

'Don't pull that shit with me, I know what you've been up to. The case is thirty years old, Leo – what the hell do you think you're going to prove?'

'I'm not trying to—'

'Look, I don't give a good goddamn what you do in your spare time. I don't care if you plant roses, or take up dancing, or build stupid little boats in bottles – and I don't care if you peek into old cases *on your own time*. But you're burning office hours on it, and that's where I draw the line. I sure as hell draw the line before you drag other people into it. We're up to our asses in right-now, happened-today, extremely pressing crimes that we actually have half a hope of solving! Look out the fucking window – we've got a gang war we can hardly dent, a veritable *tidal wave* of phony DVDs all over the street, a bunch of weird-ass burglaries that nobody has a hint about … never mind the usual rapes, murders, robberies, and car thefts. Do you hear me?'

She paused, and he stood there, arms crossed.

Finally he said, 'I hear you. And I get it, yeah.'

'You get it?'

'That's what I said. I'm sorry,' he tacked on, because the situation seemed to call for it. 'It won't happen again.'

'It damn well better not. We're swamped here, and you're not off the force yet. We need you, you know. We need everybody, working together, and working on the stuff that's eating us alive right now. Okay?'

'I said I heard you. Are we done here?'

She leaned forward and put her hands down on the desk, looking tired more than furious. 'Yeah, Leo. For now. We're done.'

OCTOBER

THE RAT RACE

PART 7.

Leo looked up from his hand and folded, dropping the cards faceup onto the green and conceding that he was out. It was only forty bucks, but he would've liked to keep it. He said, 'My luck tonight is nothing but shit,' and Cosmos laughed.

Lucas Tate observed, 'There seems to be a lot of that going around.'

But Father Squid promised, 'Next hand, things'll be different, I'm sure.'

And Harvey Kant grumbled, 'Easy for you to say. You've won the last two.'

'Heaven is smiling down on me tonight, indeed.'

'More like, the sun shines on a dog's ass every once in a while,' said the lieutenant. He was only joking, and no one took the losing too seriously. Everybody knew Father Squid's take went straight to the poor box at church.

Tonight they were losing by divine providence at Tate's sprawling apartment with its bay window view of the Bowery. Everything was clean and most of the surfaces were glossy, with sharp, modern angles; except for the profusion of masks, the place looked like a show condo. But the masks were ubiquitous – mounted on every wall, stacked inside display cases and running along bookcase shelves in every corner. He must've had thousands, and all of them stared, the empty eyes following, watching, like a funhouse painting. Some were expensive and beautiful, porcelain-painted pieces that must've cost a mint; on one wall, a harlequin and its lover were seated side by side, while a king of hearts looked on. Some were cheaply made or old and yellowing around their brittle edges. They could've been picked up at any street vendor – a bulldog and a tomcat hung together, and a wise old owl perched alongside an off-color domino with black and silver squares. Frankenstein's monster hung next to Cthulhu, just above the Phantom of the Opera.

The Venetian blinds were open, so the multihued city glow oozed inside, complementing the dimmed compact bulbs and the orangey shimmer of the lit cigars.

Their host was wearing a collie mask with a long, pointed nose that made his voice sound more nasal than usual; Cosmos was in his usual unflappable spirit, hovering at the table's edge in a lotus position, shuffling his cards without touching them – and of course Chaos was absent. Charles Dutton, in his ever-present death's-head mask, had brought the cigars. Dr. Pretorius had contributed enough Guinness and champagne to make Black Velvets for everyone, but only Lucas and Kant were partaking. Sibyl lurked by the bar, playing with the glasses, making drinks and setting them aside, or pouring them out while no one was looking.

Leo pushed his cards back toward Tate, who gathered them all up and began to shuffle. Pensively, as Tate's fingers flipped through the cards, he asked, 'Hey, Leo, did you ever get around to reading my book?'

'Yeah,' he only halfway lied. He'd read most of it over the last few weeks, here and there. Before bedtime, and over lunch. 'I don't know what strikes me as crazier: that you ran undercover with the Demon Princes, or that you went and wrote about it afterward.'

Tate shrugged and said, 'I was young and stupid. I wanted to jump into journalism feetfirst. But the reason I ask is, did you get to chapter seven, the one about the mob?'

'Yeah,' Leo told the truth this time. 'All that stuff about the families providing the drugs and guns. Nothing personal, Tate, but that's not news. It wasn't news in the seventies. It's not even news tonight.'

'I only bring it up because Harvey mentioned you were still chasing Alice down the Rathole.'

'Yep. Running into a lot of dead ends, but a lot of interesting stuff too.' Leo shifted in his seat. He tried to keep the sourness of Ralph's quasi-confession out of his voice, but didn't altogether succeed. 'There was a lot that didn't get checked out back then.'

Lucas spoke, 'I was thinking, the other day. I was wondering if the name Raul Esposito ever turned up in your investigations – past, or latter-day.'

It hadn't. Leo said so, and then added, 'But it rings a bell.'

'He was a *family* man,' Lucas said. 'And I'm fairly certain he was around in '78. To make a long story short, I heard through the restaurant grapevine that he's back in town.'

'Through the restaurant grapevine?'

Lucas waved a little shrug and said, 'Apparently he's out of the killing business, and moving into food service. He wholesales rare mushrooms and aged steaks and the like.'

Dutton's interest was piqued as well. He asked, 'They used to call him the Button Man, didn't they?'

'Yes.' Their host pointed the pack of cards at Dutton and said, 'He was one of Gambione's triggers, but there was an incident in Vegas, years ago. For the longest time, everyone thought he was wearing concrete shoes under a pier someplace, but he's living a couple miles from here, in an apartment off Crosby.' Lucas Tate began to deal.

Leo said, 'And you think he had something to do with the Rathole?'

A card landed facedown in front of the detective. The dealer said, 'It's possible. Esposito was an enforcer and Christ only knows if Hash was dealing honest. If you asked me to speculate – you didn't, but please permit me to do so – I'd guess that Hash was the real target all along. And even if Esposito's clean, he might know who's dirty.'

'Thanks,' Leo told him. He asked for a few extra details, and he got them.

The next night after his shift, he went wandering down Crosby

Street to the address he'd pulled off Tate, augmented with the information he'd gathered from Jack Dobbs, a chef at High Hand – a high-class joint that was, in some ways, the spiritual successor to the dearly departed Aces High.

He reached a nondescript gray brick building that was neither high-end nor low-end, and generally well kept. He stood in the glass-fronted foyer and ran his finger down the call buttons, settling on one that was labeled merely 'R.E.' and pushing it. After a moment of buzzing, a voice answered, 'Hello?'

'Hey. I'm Leo Storgman. I think Jack told you to expect me,' he added, because he was pretty sure that Dobbs would've passed it along.

'The detective,' the voice confirmed. It was a low voice, and it probably once was smooth. Now it cracked very slightly.

'That's right. I'm looking into an old case, one from '78. Lucas Tate thought you might be able to—'

'Tate,' grumbled the voice. 'Might've known.'

Leo waited.

'You may as well come up.'

The buzzer sounded, and Leo pushed the door to let himself inside a hall lined with age-fogged mirrors and tile-work floors. He took a cage elevator up to the eleventh floor and found apartment 1129.

He knocked.

A slender man with salt-and-pepper hair answered. He was quite tall – and he'd acquired a slight stoop when addressing shorter people, or perhaps he was only getting old and his posture was failing him. He wore a turtleneck that covered his flesh up to his chin and down to his wrists, and wool slacks with shiny black shoes.

Again he said, 'Hello.' Then, 'Yes, Jack said I should expect a visit. Should I assume this is a courtesy call? You haven't flashed a badge.'

'I'm off the clock. I just want to talk.'

His eyes narrowed. He asked, 'Do I need a lawyer?'

'Nope,' Leo said.

With a sigh, Raul Esposito stood to the side and held the door open. Leo stepped through it, into an apartment that was sparse and tidy. Although the curtains were open, he could see that they were thick – the kind that could block out all traces of light when closed and sealed. Through a cutout in the nearest wall, he could see a kitchen with a coffeepot on the counter and a teakettle on the stove. The whole unit smelled dimly of something compostlike and alive. Topsoil or mulch.

'Have a seat, if you'd like.' Raul gestured at a mid-century style couch. While Leo sat down in the middle of it, Raul settled into a leather wingback chair that looked as worn as a saddle. 'And what can I help you with, Detective?'

Leo wasn't sure what he'd expected, but this wasn't quite it. He didn't feel particularly nervous, but something felt *off*. He said, 'I'm taking another look at the Rathole murders. Do you remember the Rathole?'

If Raul was startled by the question, his lean, thickly lined face did not betray it. 'I remember hearing about it. That was a long time ago, Detective.'

'Nineteen seventy-eight. Right before Christmas.'

'Then we must be coming up on its anniversary, shortly.'

Leo hadn't thought about it like that, but he was right. Another couple of months. 'Yeah. Some new evidence came to light,' he exaggerated.

'And it somehow brings you to me.' Raul crossed his legs at the knee, and the leather chair squeaked beneath him.

'Indirectly. And look, I'm not going to tap-dance or snow you. I know what you were doing back then, and who you were doing it for – but this isn't about that.' It was half a lie, but Leo'd been doing a lot of that lately. 'I know Hash Maddox was dealing dope out of the diner's kitchen, and I know he was getting it from your bosses.'

Raul's fluffy white eyebrows sank to a line that pointed at the bridge of his nose. 'My *former* bosses,' he corrected. 'I'm … retired from their employ. And anyway, the Gambiones are all in Cuba now.'

'Yeah, I know. And my mistake. But you were here in town, or that's what I've been told. And I'll go ahead and assume that a professional like yourself wouldn't have made such a mess of the place; but I was hoping, since you're no longer with the mob's employ, as you put it, that you might be willing to point me at' – he almost said 'the button man' but he stopped himself in time to say, – 'the trigger man.'

Raul considered this. He folded his hands in his lap and tapped his thumbs together. 'Let me be clear, Detective. I did not learn about the Rathole until after the fact, but yes, I was acquainted with Hash and his activities. As you've implied, they weren't a secret. And when the money and merchandise went missing from the diner's kitchen, my employers were quite interested to know what had become of it. To the best of my knowledge, family in-volvement occurred only after the murders.'

'Are you sure?'

'No,' Raul admitted. 'But I was only an employee, not a man-ager. I wasn't the kind of man who made decisions, I was the kind of man who followed directions. So I can't tell you that Don Gambione had nothing to do with that crime. I can only tell you that if he did, I was unaware of it.'

Leo sat forward, putting his elbows on his knees. 'You seem pretty open about this. Pretty willing to talk, for a man with a résumé like yours.'

He shrugged, a slow, apathetic gesture. 'I'd never be so bold as to say that I'm beyond their reach or their concern, be they on an island or Mars – but on this matter, I have nothing to hide.'

The detective sat back again, unsatisfied. 'It doesn't make any sense,' he mused. 'Somebody, somewhere, has to know what hap-pened. People don't randomly walk into—'

A key wrestled with the front door lock.

Raul Esposito did not appear concerned. 'Don't worry, Detective. It's only Maggie.'

She stepped around the door sideways, opening it as little as possible. She froze when she saw the detective on the couch, and Raul in his leather chair.

Raul said, 'Magdalene, dear. This is Detective Storgman. He's come to ask me some questions.'

'About what?' she asked, and even in those two short words, Leo knew she wasn't local.

The girl had a corn-fed look to her, with the wide cheekbones and slim shape of a Midwest farmer's daughter. Her hair was brown with a wide blue streak that began at her bangs, and her skin was freckled. She was perhaps as young as fifteen, perhaps as old as twenty. She was wearing a strange outfit of black spandex and a faux-leather overcoat, plus a pair of fitted black gloves that looked more expensive than everything else she was wearing put together.

Raul answered her. 'About something that happened a long time ago. I'm afraid I'm not much help to him.'

'It may have happened a long time ago, but there's no statute of limitations on murder,' Leo said flatly, eyeing the newcomer.

'That's true, of course. But as you said at the beginning, I don't need a lawyer. This is only a conversation,' Raul said, more to the girl than to Leo, or so the cop inferred. 'Nothing more.'

The girl hadn't moved. One hand remained on the interior doorknob, as if ready to whip it open and flee. But she released it, and turned to flatten her back against the wall beside the entryway – never once taking her eyes off Leo. Never even blinking.

'Your ... granddaughter?' Leo chose to make a polite guess, and not jump right to *jailbait*.

'My ... ward,' Raul said, clarifying no further. Then, to Magdalene, 'It's all right, dear. I promise.'

She didn't appear to believe him, not really. But she forced herself to assume a more relaxed posture, her hand sliding to her side. That's when Leo saw the plastic grocery bag. He recognized the logo from a nearby hippie store, one of those joints that sells everything organic, free range, and hormone-free. She said, 'I brought ... supper.'

'Excellent,' he said, rising from the chair and meeting her, taking the bag and walking it around the corner to the kitchen. 'We'll take care of this later, or in the morning.'

Leo thought that was a weird thing to say about supper, but for all he knew they ate at midnight. He stood up as well, feeling like his welcome there was nearly worn-out, given the rabbit-scared look the girl continued to give him. 'One more thing,' he said. 'Just real quick. You admitted you knew Hash. Did you know any of the other victims?'

Raul's cool demeanor didn't crack, but it became more carefully blank. 'I'm sorry, Detective. But I'm afraid I can't help you.'

'I don't believe you.'

'That changes nothing. Please,' he added, and opened his arms, spreading those long, thin limbs into an ushering pose that urged Leo back toward the door.

Giving up for the moment, Leo pulled out his wallet and removed a business card, palming it to the man and then shaking his hand. 'Well, thanks for your time,' he said. 'And if you think of anything, or hear of anything, I'd appreciate it if you'd let me know.'

'Of course. And Maggie, dearest. Would you kindly see Detective Storgman out? These corridors twist and are dark, in places. Please see to it that he reaches the lobby safely.'

She did see him out.

And unless Leo was mistaken, she saw him downstairs – from behind him, behind corners. And she saw him into the street and down it; he could hear, every once in a while, the girl's soft footsteps keeping time with his, until he finally lost her on the crowded sidewalks of the Bowery.

MORE!

by Paul Cornell

I didn't mean for any of this to happen. Let me make that clear right from the start. It all happened *to* me. And I'm glad it did. In the end. But there were points there where it all got a bit choppy.

Honestly, it seems you can get arrested for just about *anything* in this city. Even involuntary public nudity. When I'd just been going about my business, walking down the street, and suddenly there I was, au naturel. I had to spell the word 'involuntary' out to the arresting officer, who was about twelve. He looked at what he'd written and said 'oh' like he'd just realized what an oaf he was being, and then said he'd 'been a little distracted.' Then he and his fat, laughing partner hauled me off downtown for, basically, the crime of being in the theatrical profession.

The involuntaryness of the offense ought to make a difference, I feel. The police finally told me that my sudden nakedness in the street had been because I had been the victim of some perving ace called the Stripper. And that time, I can only assume they were right, because, just for once, I didn't feel like it was the fault of my own special talent. It's a shame I didn't have time to realize what was going on and give him a taste of his own medicine. I was finally released without much in the way of apology, despite being the victim rather than the perpetrator. Maybe I just *look* guilty? Maybe I protested too much.

And then there was that business with that valuable necklace that was in, and then suddenly out of, that shop window. Just as I was admiring it. The same officer appeared at the scene of the crime: the twelve-year-old. He remembered my face, made the connection, and acted like he was the great detective, until various wiser heads started pointing out that I'd initially stood there gawking at the jewelry that had appeared in my hands, that I had started waving to the jeweler and pointing at it, and that involuntary nudity was hardly the best preparation for a stealthy jewel heist. Once more, I told the truth, and let them draw their own conclusions, the wrongness of which, this time, I felt guilty about not in the slightest. They assumed it was because of someone else's power. And that must have been true this time. Sort of.

After I was told I was free to go, the twelve-year-old followed up his police brutality with another invitation to go on a date with him. Presumably because he felt that, having already seen the goodies, he felt he was some way into the process already. Needless to say I declined, quite vocally. Aren't there rules against that sort of thing? I was on my way to what turned out to be a disastrously failed audition for a dog food commercial. Following my public humiliation, I couldn't quite summon up the confidence to assert that my little Jack Russell had become supercharged with health. I think if I were American, I'd be suing someone as we speak.

So that's the summary of my previous encounters with the law. Before I get to what I'm about to recount, that is. Which is all sorts of legal hoo-ha. So far, at least, I haven't had to call my mum and ask her to send over bail money.

But those are old wounds, and I have quite a lot of new ones to get to. So. Right. Sorry. Anyway—

Hello. My name is Abigail Baker.

I am a serious actor.

I'm also basically a serious person. If you're looking for a coquettish sense of humor or, it turns out, delirious enthusiasm about dog food, I am not your go-to girl. One of my tattoos even says 'serious person' in Korean. Or at least the tattooist said it did.

If I get laughed at by the staff and customers of one more Korean restaurant, I swear I'm going to get that laser thing done.

Sorry. Anyway—

During what I'm about to relate, all of this ... havoc ... that I did not seek or cause, I really can't emphasize that enough ... I suppose I was being even more serious than usual, because I was doing my damnedest to get into character for a role that I'd been understudying. That of Anabeth Grey in *Grey Hearts*. Everyone knows the story. She falls in love with a secret joker. On their wedding night, he uncovers his secret, that he is, well, not quite as other men, let us say, but rather more ... insecty. In disgusted horror, she kills him. She manages to cover up the crime, but, echoes of Lady Macbeth, his ichor is on her hands, and she keeps making slips that could give her away. Until, on her next wedding night, to a humane and tolerant man, her guilt, or perhaps something more solid, bursts from her and flies off into the night, forever damned.

She is not a bundle of laughs.

I work in the theater. Guilty as charged. To be specific, I worked in *a* theater, the Bowery Repertory, the lovely Old Rep. Though it hasn't run real rep for decades. I was, and thank God still am, just about, on a work placement, which was initially just over the summer, but ran into my new term, at the New York School of Performing Arts. Yes, like in that movie, which I still haven't seen, and people still mention all the time, weirdly enough. The School's great, but it was the placement I was after, and thanks to what I gather were some gentle words to the School from the theater owner, Mr. Dutton, I'd been able to hang on to it. I don't know if you can tell by the accent, because when I go back home they all think I've turned into, I don't know, Popeye, but I'm not from round here. I'm British. From deepest rural Dorset. Though I'm the sort of British person who, I suppose, regretfully, would rather stare at the old country with some horror from a safe distance from over this side of the Atlantic than actually trudge through it every day. I suspect however that, emotionally, I've become a bit *more* British, now I'm seen against a different background. Perhaps sort of pretend British. *Billy Idol* British. I'm sure Quentin Crisp, for example, was *capable* of the occasional use of 'guy' or 'truck' when across the pond, but as soon as he pitches his tent here, it's all English muffins and having his toast done on one side, neither of which I'd even *heard* of before I got here—

Sorry. Anyway—

I came here for Broadway. Okay, so there's the West End in London, and that's great, wouldn't kick a job there out of bed for farting, but it isn't Broadway.

And neither is the Bowery, I know. But at least it's on the right continent.

I mostly did odd jobs for the Rep. I worked in the office, I re-filled the water cooler, I emptied the wastebaskets. But that was awesome. Because I was emptying the wastebaskets *in a theater*. And during the production of *Grey Hearts* I also helped out during set building, got shown the ropes, literally, by the stage manager, Jan, and got to watch Alfre use the lighting and sound decks, with all those arms of his. I'd been up in the rafters with the riggers, who were … just a bit too spidery for me, actually. Sorry. I'd actually *been* prompter, which is a highly skilled task, I'll have you know, for a couple of matinees, with Klaus looking over my shoulder. With that eye on the end of his finger. Which did rather freak me out.

All of this was solid gold for me. The fulfillment of my dreams. Almost since I was old enough to think of what I wanted to be when I grew up (when I was five I wanted to make chocolate biscuits and that would have been a damn sight easier as a life's ambition, let me tell you) I've wanted to act professionally.

I mean I've wanted to act. Professionally.

So, when Eliza Baumgarten, the lovely Liz, went down with chicken pox, I was ever so slightly delighted. Liz had been under-studying for Anabeth Grey, watching Shauna Montgomery's performance, matching her tic for tic as it were, having learned the lines, ready to step in. Shauna, of course, is here from *Accident!* on Fox, taking about a hundredth of her normal paycheck, keeping the theater alive with a short run as a favor to Mr. Dutton, who, a few years back, put her joker son through exactly the sort of on-the-job experience I'd gone through. But she's also a proper trooper: full of stories; respects the craft; nothing but kindness for noncombatants, seems to love jokers, really really *nice*.

Which made it all the more awful when that enormous light fell on her.

Thank God I wasn't up there at the time. Because I do seem to get blamed for things. Usually things that, as I may have mentioned, I did not do.

The chicken pox was nothing to do with me either. I mean, how could it have been?

Sorry. Am I starting to sound guilty because I keep protesting? I mean, because I doth protest too much? I suppose I may still be a tiny bit in character, then, after all these months, because I really did have nothing to do with—

Sorry. Anyway—

I was, however, the (unwitting) beneficiary of said accident. Because with Shauna in the hospital having bits of stage picked out of her and her ankles reconstructed, and Liz looking like Jackson Pollock was her beautician, the Rep were suddenly desperate for someone, preferably someone nat, to play Anabeth. As in that very night. Because a full house had been sold, the show must go on, as Shauna had said before they put the oxygen mask on, and the hole in the stage was very easily repaired.

'I can do it,' I said, stepping forward, perhaps a bit too hastily, but I got the feeling every other female actor in the building was about to do the same, and Kevin as well, who's a bit slight with those bendy bones of his, and could have got the frock on. We'd all been brought up on those MGM musicals with sudden dance routines about how nice it would be to be in sudden dance routines, and we all always rather hoped for something like this to happen, and, well—

I suppose I was the one young enough and foolish enough to get the dream out of my mouth first.

I suppose I didn't exactly *say* it. I bellowed my availability.

'I've memorized the part,' I lied, and chucked a few random lines at them that I recalled from the prompting.

'You're a child,' said James Clark Brotherton, who's been called the finest joker actor of his generation, despite, or perhaps because of, his ability to look entirely nat, and who was playing Nick Grey, the unfortunate victim, a role so made for him he's done it on three continents. He's rather more British than I am, but is from Chicago, so what does that say? 'Anabeth is—'

'A much younger woman than her husband,' I said, 'trying too hard, out of her depth even before she learns who he really is. Or at least she will be, just the once, tonight. And possibly for the matinee tomorrow.'

Vita, the director, made a sudden squeal with those throat pouches of hers, and she pointed at me like I'd got the answer in charades, and everyone looked at her like she was mad, but then she rushed over and hugged me. And I tried to hug her back. At a slight distance. And one press release about Shauna urging between grating breaths that the role be recast from within the company and me being her personal choice later (gosh, she *is* a trooper)—

I was *in*!

So.

I had a day to learn the part.

I went back to the office, and leaned on the door, and tried to stop myself shaking.

I took a look at the script. To tell you the truth, I was surprisingly undaunted. At the time. It's not the width of Anabeth Grey that actors find alarming, it's the quality. She's on and off and sitting at tables that could have scripts glued to them and spends quite a bit of time actually *looking at her palms,* for goodness' sake, and I do have very tiny writing.

It was my big chance. And I was so not going to blow it.

I sat there in the big wicker chair writing notes in the margins of the script, and Vita kept everyone out of the office, and I let Buffo the cat leap up onto my lap and was completely oblivious to anything—

Until I started to wonder if Buffo was putting on weight.

As in, putting on weight in that second. Having got suddenly heavier.

I looked down. And saw that it wasn't just Buffo sitting there now. But two of her. Exactly the same. Looking at each other with startled cat expressions that were half 'Hey that's another cat, I must defend my territory' and half 'Who is that charming stranger?'

And then, suddenly, there were four of them.

I realized that Buffo was touching my bare arms.

I leaped up, and all four of them went flying ... but they stayed being four and ran into the corners of the room, alternating between hissing at each other and looking intrigued.

Not that I couldn't tell which was the original. She was the one who was displaying a full range of startled cat expressions, while the other three were looking more absent, less *real*, somehow.

I stood there. I knew what this was. And it was absolutely not what I needed right now. Not with curtain up on my big night a mere ten hours away.

But I could fix it. And I had to. As quickly as poss.

I dropped the script and ran out of the office. Out of the theater. Into the smelly alley behind it. And I should mention how brilliant and somehow surprising it always is to walk out onto a New York street, too hot in summer, too cold in winter, and right now, in the first week of October, just right and bright with promise. To live in this city is like you're living in the roots of the most tremendous magic forest, but made by people, really *for* people. With breath coming from under the street and music echoing round every corner and the trees in the park gold, and everyone talking to each other very loudly all the time. And *you* can find sleep if you want to, but the city will always be here ready for you.

None of that was in my head at that instant, though. But I put it here because it really should have been. Because of the magic of what was going to happen next.

I stood in the alley and looked up at the buildings.

I'd never even thought about what sort of place the Old Rep might back onto, what sort of room might share a wall with the theater office. Whenever I call Mum, she has another *Daily Mail* scare story about what happens in 'Jokertown.' She's not keen on me being here. But I didn't give a stuff about who or what our neighbors might be. Or I tried not to. I often failed, actually. I still looked twice at jokers I passed in the street, I still found myself moving into different cars on the subway when something that looked, frankly, like a monster out of a fairy tale got on and sat down with its newspaper. And I hated myself for it. Mr. Dutton was an entrepreneur in the joker community. He employed lots of jokers. And he'd been willing to take me when all the other theaters had turned me down. I kept telling myself that the theatrical community has always been a haven for those who are different, for those who needed to hide, be they gay people, transvestites, Gypsies, Jews—

Or … me. I suppose. Sorry. Should have mentioned that. Probably rather obvious now. I think maybe that was the last thing I had to get past, me being proud of—

Sorry. Anyway—

I worked out which was the building in question, and saw that it was a nondescript block of cheap lodgings. Which made sense, because sometimes when I was working late I heard music through the office wall. Old music, rather lovely, very New York: jazz and swing tunes. There was an intercom with five empty name tags, an ancient indication of a Mr. Saunders in flat six, and a big red scrawl in Magic Marker pointing to flat four that said if I wanted a good time I should try Paris. Which I might, on another occasion, have found wry.

I tried every button. None of them answered. Not even Paris.

I tried them all again.

So I did the only sensible thing.

I kicked down the door.

Even with my DMs, it took a few hefty thumps. But honestly, it's not my fault that building standards in this part of the city are so lax. And I was positively looking forward to getting the Rep's enormous carpenters to pop by and make this place an actually better door, and pay for the materials, so don't look at me like that, okay?

I really must get round to doing that.

I realized, as I sprinted up the dingy stairwell, that, judging by the height, I was actually after one of the flats on the third floor. Or the second floor, or the fourth or something, if you're from this side of the Atlantic. So it was Mr. Saunders or one other.

I got to that landing, not even noticing how out of breath I was. I pounded on the door of the other flat, got no answer, then realized I was facing away from the theater.

So. My problem was definitely being caused by Mr. Saunders. So I knew he had to be home. Progress!

I pounded on his door. And I may have screamed a little.

After a few moments, I heard movement inside. I stopped pounding. 'Please!' I yelled. 'Please, I need your help! I know you're an ace, and you're doing something terrible to me, I mean terribly inconveniencing, and you're doing it without knowing you're doing it, and I need your – !'

I realized there was a shadow and a sense of terrible movement behind me.

I turned round and saw—

Ten copies of the door to the apartment opposite, that I'd pounded on with my bare hands. Filling the landing. Lined up like dominoes.

Falling on me.

Something grabbed my arm and heaved.

And I was through the door and into the apartment and the many doors crashed against the door that had been quickly slammed on them.

And I was face-to-face with the most peculiar man.

Although I was relieved, at the time, and a little ashamed to be so relieved, that he was actually quite normal-looking.

Well, better than normal, really.

He had old eyes in a very young face. Dark, curly hair, mussed up, stubble, a jittery look about him, like he wasn't sleeping too well. A hooded sweatshirt that looked like he lived in it. He had one hand on the door, and the other was still holding mine.

I grabbed it away from him. 'Sorry – !'

'It's okay,' he said. 'I'm stopping the door from multiplying, and my own powers don't work on me, I mean, try touching yourself and you'll see – I don't mean *touching* yourself – Hey, look over there.' He was pointing into his tiny bathroom. I looked over there, saw nothing, and looked back just as he closed the door onto his tiny bedroom, the room that was next to the theater office—

Just quickly enough to see the enormous piles of identical DVDs that occupied every surface.

He grinned nervously at me, unsure whether I'd caught that or not, his eyes darting back and forth. 'Oh, it was nothing. You're copying my power. I can see how that might inconvenience you, and you can't stop this because – ?'

'I can't ever stop it! I pick up other aces' powers like ... Wi-Fi! And I can't control them! But if you *are* in control of it, and you just think for a moment about how it works ...' I put a hand on his face and let the information ... sort of flood into me. He looked at me as I did it, as if he were assessing me with those ancient eyes. As if he was somehow understanding me. And somehow, just the tiniest part, asking for something. Without being vulnerable enough to ever ask for anything. The smell of his cologne was like some old military club, all deep seats and brandy and polish, and old wounds smiled at.

I had to find something else to look at before I took my hand away. Because I was suddenly feeling what the Americans call 'inappropriate' and we call nice work if you can get it. Very quickly, by my own standards, which previously have ... actually there's not much to talk about there, and it's all rubbish. I am rather new at this, you know. People say I'm self-assured, and so they don't get—

Sorry. Anyhow—

Then that was done. Now I could control it. And switch it off if I wanted to. Which I did. No more randomly copying stuff.

But he was still looking at me.

'Mr. Saunders—' I began.

'Croyd Crenson,' he said. Telling me his real name. Just like that.

'Abigail Baker.'

And we didn't shake hands or anything.

'Lunch,' he said. 'I'm buying. To make up for your trouble.'

And before I could tell him that I really needed the time to learn my lines, he was heading out of the door.

And, well, it would have been rude not to follow.

I have never seen anyone eat such an enormous lunch. Seriously, five sandwiches. And those are American sandwiches, so that's about twenty-five on the UK sandwich scale. And soup. And a stacked salad bowl. And one of those malt things. While I had a mineral water and a chicken Caesar. He didn't eat like a pig, though, but with an old-fashioned decorum, dabbing at his mouth with his napkin, and making the sheer speed with which he got through that lot seem like the most natural thing in the world.

'My family first noticed it on a shopping expedition to London,' I told him. 'We passed this odd-looking man, and suddenly I was flying. Dad had to catch me by the ankle and walk me along like a balloon. It wore off after a day or so, and I fell onto a pile of carefully prepared cushions, just as my parents were about to crack and call the doctor. They hadn't wanted to, you see. Neither of them had any idea they carried the wild card gene. I had an auntie in Somerset who was supposed to be able to summon field mice, but that was it. Mum cried for days. They talked about taking me out of school, because I was a danger to people. It was only when I got older, and, you know, entered a rebellious phase, hence the tattoos, that I realized I wanted to be near people, to be in a big city, to actually … show who I was to people, get up in front of people. Which still feels a bit … wrong. Sorry. Anyway—' I looked up at those eyes again and realized I'd been going on and on. And that what my day was leading toward had made me tremendously vulnerable. And a bit gushy. 'What it comes down to is this: I can't control it. I'm at the whim of whatever powers I get within twenty feet of. And today of all days—'

'So I can understand wanting to be in a big city, even though there are more aces. But why the hell pick Manhattan, ace central?'

'It has Broadway.'

'You're into musical theater?'

'I love the old show tunes. You know, it's funny, people do make assumptions, with the short hair and the tattoos, for a moment there I thought you were asking if I was gay—'

'Obviously not.' His gaze danced over my face again, half a smile. 'So you like the old tunes?'

I found I was smiling too. A bit too long. I looked at my watch. 'I really can't take up any more of your time, I've got to get back to learning my lines. As for your secret, I mean your ... business, well, I can't condone copying any artist's work, but since it was just that terrible new version of *Thirty Minutes Over Broadway* with Milla Jovovich – Hey, listen, perhaps I should get your phone number. Just in case ...' I realized I didn't have an in case handy.

But it didn't matter. Because he was looking over my shoulder now, and his face had fallen.

I turned to look, and was surprised to see, striding into the diner, all of them rolling their arms like they were pretending to be little trains, all of them in white vests and tight red pants, all of them carrying heavy truncheons that they swung with deft musical precision ...

No, it wasn't another duplication thing, as I had initially thought. It was not actually fifteen copies of Freddie Mercury (as he'd been two decades ago, not the whiskery knight of the musical profession he is now). It was fifteen gang members, all wearing a rubber mask of his face.

'Mr. Crenson!' enunciated their leader, like he was about to ask a stadium if it was ready to rock, 'We are the Werewolves, and we are so pleased you have come out of hiding! Because you' – he slid the end of his stick under Croyd's jaw – 'have been selling your DVDs in our territory, without the slightest little cut for us.'

Croyd took another bite out of his sandwich, considering. 'I heard this was Demon Prince territory,' he whispered at last.

The Werewolves made a collective sharp intake of breath, all turning to look at their leader, who tapped his stick rather forcefully under Croyd's jaw once again. 'Don't say that, Mr. Crenson, that is very very bad of you, to bring up a subject of such personal displeasure.' He pushed harder on the stick, forcing it up into Croyd's throat.

I realized that the staff and customers of the diner had melted away. Either out the doors or under the counter. I hoped someone was calling the police, but I doubted it.

But suddenly, the gang leader took a step back, surprised—

That he was holding, trying to hold, failing to hold—

A dozen sticks, all of which fell to the floor. Taking his dignity with them.

Croyd grabbed the coleslaw and threw it—

And a tsunami of cabbage and mayo threw the entire gang off their feet.

And suddenly he had my hand again and was hauling me toward the door.

We burst out onto the street, and I was certain we'd got away—

Until Croyd came to a skidding halt in the vast pool of mayo that was pouring out of the door, Werewolves skidding and falling over themselves, trying to get to their feet behind us. I spun round at the sound of gun … bits … being … well, whatever they are. Made ready to shoot. Which surprisingly sounded just like it does in the movies.

In the low autumn sunlight, silhouetted figures stepped forward. Their presence had made a crowd start to gather, jokers coming out of local businesses, watching warily. The newcomers wore black and silver, inverted crosses, serious boots, and nice tats, frankly. They were carrying a range of automatic weaponry, and now the noise from the diner had changed too, as the Werewolves had obviously seen them as well, had produced their own guns, and were taking up firing positions.

'We're the Demon Princes,' growled the hairiest of the men. And now I could see that he not only had the one central head, but two tiny others, one on each shoulder.

'Tell it like it is, Ginger,' said one of the heads, in rather a high-pitched voice.

'Crenson,' said the largest head, 'you've been selling your DVDs in our territory, without giving us a cut.'

I might have remarked that a man with three heads going by the nickname 'Ginger' showed either great sensitivity, a certain cunning, or an enormous lack of imagination, but I did not, because I was busy being petrified. You don't get much in the way of gunplay in Dorset. All my mum's worries about Jokertown were coming true.

Croyd looked sternly at the gang. He took a step forward. 'I heard,' he said, 'that this was Werewolves territory.'

I really wished he would stop doing that.

I looked between the armed gang in front of us and the armed gang behind us, and made a decision. I looked at my watch again. 'Well,' I said, 'this is all *very* interesting, but I'm in this play—'

'What play?' asked Ginger.

'*Grey Hearts.*'

'Oh,' the other small head squeaked, 'how fabulous!' I was charmed for a moment that while the central Ginger seemed to be of Polish stock, the heads were respectively Irish and Scots.

'It is, rather,' I said, 'and this particular production, at the Bowery Rep, I think you'd really like, because—'

'Right now,' said Croyd, loudly interrupting, 'I have the power to multiply things. I'm ready to multiply bullets. If you guys open fire, the guys behind me will open fire too. And I'll make it so that in the second the two of us die, so will all of you.'

'But—' I said, 'I thought you could only do it if you were touching – ?'

I was aware of everyone suddenly looking at me.

'Oh, bollocks,' I said.

Croyd looked sighingly at me.

Ginger laughed and raised his gun to aim at Croyd's head.

Desperately, I did something I'd never done before. Something that it took immediate peril to make me do. Because I found it deeply embarrassing. Frightening, even. I took whatever mental muscle tension I felt about the possibility of picking up an ace's power—

And I reversed it. I relaxed it. I reached out.

And, from farther away than a power that *randomly* affected me would be located ...

There it was. Coming from that dull-looking shopkeeper over there with the swooshed-back hair. I held it in my head. I understood it. If I let it happen, I still wouldn't be able to control it. And that frightened me terribly.

But okay ... needs must.

'Sorry,' I said to Croyd. I grabbed his hand. And I let it happen.

The pavement suddenly became something like an ice rink. Immediately under our feet.

I grabbed Croyd's hand and let out one big breath over my shoulder, and—

We were off! Barreling down the street, absolutely out of control. I think the man could make tiny surfaces absolutely frictionless. And no, I hadn't considered this plan one step farther than our immediate getaway.

We sped over a crosswalk, narrowly missing a cab. It lazily blared at us.

We'd left the diner behind. We'd escaped.

Only now, coming up at us—

The bank building jutted farther out into the street than the diner had. Beyond another street full of speeding cars going left and right, its huge gray wall was flying at us!

'Stop it!' yelled Croyd.

'I can't!' I screamed.

And then our feet hit sidewalk.

And we tumbled, head over heels.

And suddenly a fruit stall reared up out of nowhere and I was going to die—

Until I landed in an infinity of melons.

And exploded them with a great fruity burst of impact.

We lay there in the goo.

'We got out of range of the power,' I whispered.

'I'm sorry I got you into this,' said Croyd, quickly getting up. 'I'll come to see your show tonight, okay? Don't look for me at the

Saunders place, I'll tell you when I've got a new hideout.' And he stuffed a big fold of bills into my hand. 'Cab fare. Go learn your lines.' And he was gone.

I slowly stood up. I shook melon from my clothing.

I realized that a joker shop owner, looking like a horrified orca, had run out of the shop and was yelling at me in something that sounded Eastern European. I started to leaf through the truly enormous sum of money Croyd had given me, wondering how much would satisfy him and leave me enough to get quickly back to the theater—

And then I was looking into the trying-to-be stern faces of that twelve-year-old policeman and his fat sighing partner again.

'Oh, come on,' I said. 'He must have ended up with more melons than he started with.'

The boy cop took the money out of my hand and actually tutted at me. 'Destruction of property *and* counterfeiting,' he said. 'Are you going for some kind of a record?'

'I only want *one* thing,' I said to the doll-like policewoman in charge of the cells. She paused for a moment at the door of my one.

'You've already turned down your phone call.'

'A copy of *Grey Hearts*. Actor's edition, if poss. Please?'

She gave me a look and moved on.

'Is that so much to ask?!' I yelled after her.

I'd been in there for nearly three hours. They'd be looking for me back at the Rep. Wondering if I'd done a runner. Maybe even starting to measure Kevin for that frock. I just hoped my mum would never hear of this. Here was I, in Jokertown, among jokers and aces, having been arrested on ace-related charges. I couldn't help but feel ashamed of how ... acey everything was getting. Even though no part of me wanted to be.

Two figures appeared at the door of my cell. The first one, old and grumpy, was looking at me like he was deciding whether I was an irritation or an abomination. Beside him stood his younger, kinder-looking partner. But I wasn't paying him much attention.

Because the first cop had two enormous horns curling round his head. 'So,' he said, 'how you feeling?'

'Rather sheepish,' I said.

I think by the time they got me to the interview room, I'd managed to explain just how much I hadn't meant anything by that.

I didn't want to wait for a lawyer. I thought it was best to tell … well, almost the whole truth, from the top. I felt bad for Croyd, but really I'd only just met him. And he'd said he wasn't going back to the apartment. And somehow I knew he could get out of any trouble I might send in his direction.

'So,' said the older detective, who'd introduced himself as Storgman, 'you got no family over here—'

'Right,' I said, 'I'm the only one without a safe, steady job. You could say I'm the black' – I saw his expression start to change – 'cat of the family! It's an expression. We have. In Britain.'

The younger nat cop, who was called Stevens, actually laughed. Which was a relief. But then his expression hardened. 'I heard "black,"' he said, 'and I so wondered where that was going.'

I put a hand over my eyes. If this was good cop/bad cop, I'd managed to piss off the good cop too. 'Sorry,' I began. 'I'm not in the least bit—'

'You should be quiet now.'

'Yes, I promise I will be, apart from, you know, answering your—'

'*Now,*' said the older man.

And I was.

He gazed at me a moment. Then continued. 'So tell me more about this guy you say "zapped the cash into your hand."'

'The Sleeper,' said Stevens. 'That's what we call him. That's what cops have called him for a *long* time.'

So I told them. I mentioned the warring gangs and the enormous meal. The latter seemed to make Storgman perk up. It was like he'd got a sudden idea in his head, and it was a lot more interesting than I was. Stevens looked questioningly at him, but Storgman waved him away. This was obviously something they weren't going to discuss in front of me. 'And do you know where he is now?'

I gave them the address.

They paid no attention to my desperate pleas about having to learn my lines. I ended up back in the cells. With no indication of when this situation might change. Though I was told a public defender was on the way.

I waited another half hour.

And then I got to the end of my tether.

This lot might be a bit puzzled about how I came to encounter those melons at such velocity, but they still saw me as someone who happened to be round powers, maybe aiding and abetting the Sleeper (why did they call him that?) and not as an ace myself.

I would return to face them tomorrow. Well, tomorrow night, after the matinee. And maybe I could fit in a press conference. But return I would. Afterward.

Hesitantly, I did what I'd done earlier that day. I reached out. For only the second time in my life. And tried to feel what powers there were in the police station.

Aggh! Loads!

It felt like they were grabbing for me!

I managed to take a mental step back. Ye gods. I'd never done this deliberately before. I'd always been kind of ... *taken* by this stuff. Now it felt like I was deliberately ... well, offering an *invitation* to an intimacy that seemed rather ...

Phew, hell of a day all round, eh? Shall we just get on?

There were two powers that felt useful. I picked one of them ... and teased it into coming away with me. Leaving its host none the wiser.

Just as well the owners of neither of these two powers had wandered close to the cells earlier. They'd have given the game away. I'd been aware of the power of the doll-like officer affecting me, but thankfully hers was one of those powers that, even with it running wild in me, I'd need to be touching a person for it to do anything.

I concentrated on the new power until I understood it. I knew it would change me. I listened to hear if that sergeant was coming back, then—

I let it. And suddenly—

I had a different shape! I was a lot smaller. I was furry. And it was dark. I was covered in fabrics. Fabrics that smelt fantastically interesting!

I got my head out into the light. I saw the gaps in the bars.

I leaped for one. Instinctively.

I squeezed my body through it.

I got about halfway. I heaved. I got my back feet down. I hauled my head forward—

And I was out! Trotting along the cell corridor. Bounding along the cell corridor.

Which made me feel suddenly very aware ... of these two *vast* lumps that were bouncing back and forth between my legs. I slowed down. I tried to tiptoe. I couldn't.

I settled into the cat equivalent of a vaguely constipated saunter. I couldn't help but wonder if this was what it was like for human men. Because if it was, I really could forgive them *so* much.

As I was starting to become aware of these ... objects, I also suddenly felt that ... I really wanted to make *use* of—

Oh, this really did explain *such* a lot.

I harrumphed that sensation away, and hoping I didn't en- counter any female cats, and thus find myself in a situation the mere inkling of which would give my mum a seizure, I made my way through the station, moving between people's feet, getting, obviously, now that I think about it, calls of greeting. I got a huge wave from some guy with enormous hands, who'd been tapping away with surprising dexterity at what to him must have seemed like a toy typewriter. And someone who looked like a whippet in a uniform bared her teeth at me, which I kind of hoped was in the way of friendly badinage, because at that point every single aspect of me agreed that I wanted to run.

I did not, however. I continued my blokish saunter. And hoped that I wouldn't knock these enormous ... things against anything on the way to the door.

I finally got to the street and bounded happily off in the direction of the theater, trying not to be distracted by the sight of the sun reflected in puddles.

I made it about six blocks. So far that I started to worry about what was going to happen when I encountered Buffo. And kind of, well, fantasizing about—

Sorry. Anyway—

All thoughts of potential feline sexual harassment were put out of my head as suddenly I was out of range ... and big and human and standing up suddenly and ... naked in the street ... again.

If this had been Dorset, I could have expected cries of outrage. This being New York, what I got was some offhand stand-up comedy, a handful of compliments, and a lot of laid-back staring. But it could only be minutes before—

There was a shout from over my shoulder. Okay, make that seconds.

A patrol car had swung to a halt on the pavement beside me, and a short young female police officer with curly black hair was leaping out of it. 'Have found suspect – !' she was yelling into her radio.

I wanted to yell about how unfair this was.

Instead of which, I threw my hands up in the air and ran. Pursued by the police. And several onlookers who wanted to keep being onlookers. Like something out of *Benny Hill*.

I swiftly decided to stop worrying about the naked bit and just sprint. But not straight for the theater. That was too obvious. I ran into side streets, up alleys, always expecting to run into one of those high mesh fence things that for some reason people put up in alleys in movies.

The sounds behind me kept up with me. Thankfully, the onlookers kept shouting as they ran. I thought I was being clever, doubling back, ducking behind a pile of rubbish bags and letting them go past, but always, within seconds, the sounds followed me.

Not so surprising, I guess, that I was so noticeable. But then I realized—

Everywhere I went, there were dogs looking at me. Looking at me with hopeful oh-I'll-get-a-treat-for-this expressions on their faces. And I could feel a power connected with them, something egging them on, asking questions of them.

That bloody copper. Honestly, you couldn't tell.

Ahead of me, a whole pack of strays suddenly rushed out into the middle of an alley. They growled and lowered their heads at me, all the different mangy breeds.

But I had two advantages. I could nick this power, and I was the child of country folk.

I raised a finger commandingly. As if I were in Mum's kitchen, and her eight dogs were acting up with a squeaky toy. 'Sit!' I bellowed. With all the force of my purloined power behind it.

They did.

I told them they were very good dogs, and had served an entirely new pack by helping me, and if they told their old pack leader I hadn't been this way, there'd be—

I visualized my mum's yard, full of lovely muck and rats.

And they just about swooned and let me on my way.

Now, that was a power that I'd love to have on a regular basis.

I turned right and left, and realized that I was standing outside a church of some kind. The sign outside said it was Our Lady of Perpetual Misery. The noises of pursuit had thinned out round the area instead of being right on my, erm, tail, but it wouldn't be long before they came through here. The most urgent thing I needed was clothes. Such as might be kept in a place like this and given to the poor.

I was considering stealing from the homeless.

Damn right I was, this was my opening night! And okay, so I was now losing track of all the things I had to pay back, but I'd get there.

I saw a side door was open and ran inside.

I failed to find any office or storehouse or anywhere with clothes. So I kept making my way deeper and deeper into the building. The beauty and rather pointedly joker character of the architecture stopped me when I entered the church itself. But I didn't have time to feel awed or less than welcome. Toward the altar a figure in a purple hooded cassock was sweeping up, humming to himself.

Okay, I was desperate. I was going to have to appeal to a man of the cloth, and hope he'd do this my way instead of asking me to give myself up.

I hid most of me behind a pew and called out, 'Excuse me? Reverend?'

He turned and pushed back the hood of his cassock.

I'm not proud of what happened next, okay?

Father Squid was, in the end, very kind about me screaming like that. 'You're obviously in a very vulnerable position,' he said, as he found me a sweater and an enormous pair of jeans.

'Obviously,' I said, still hiding behind the pew.

'It strikes me,' he said, handing me said items, 'that you may well feel recompense has to be made. Above and beyond you paying for the things you have to pay for, and returning to the police after you have completed this quest on which you have embarked.'

'I do,' I said, dressing. And, oddly, I did.

'I think the nature of that recompense might have to do with the uncertainty and fear you feel around jokers, around everything that is beyond your previous experience.'

I frowned. I heaved on the belt to get the jeans round my waist, and found I could loop it round twice.

'The annual Christmas pageant at this church could do with some help from those in the theatrical profession,' he continued. 'Lights, costumes ... and actors. Especially someone who is about to become a cause célèbre, such as yourself.'

'I'll bring these clothes back,' I said.

He looked at me as seriously as his voice was deep.

'And I'll help out with your Christmas pageant,' I said.

'Very good,' he said. And he put some money in my hand. 'Cab fare back to the theater. Break a leg, as they say.'

I closed my eyes for a moment, thankful that he'd anticipated my next problem. 'I do want to make it better,' I said. 'I mean ... everything.'

'Good.'

'The way I've had to lean on everybody, it makes me feel so ... shellfish. I mean, selfish!'

I got out of there rather too fast. Apologizing all the way.

I think he might have been amused by that. Either that or horrified beyond description. I couldn't read his expression well enough to tell.

♦

'I've been arrested by mistake,' I told Mr. Dutton, striding into his office at the theater. Actually, *bursting* in would probably be a better way to put it. I was lucky: he keeps one of his many offices at the Rep, and he happened to be there. He's not the most unspooky of jokers, in that he wears a black cloak and a death's-head mask all the time. But I'd gotten used to that. So there was no screaming. This time. (He really shouldn't step out suddenly backstage like that. Especially not near a trapdoor. Especially not just after I'd been to see that musical.)

'I'm already aware,' he muttered, not looking up from whatever he was signing. 'The police have been in touch, and I've been told to alert them immediately should you arrive.' He seemed to enjoy my discomfort for a moment. 'So much for that. I've told everyone who knows to remain silent about your presence. We'll get one performance out of you, and no matinee tomorrow, but oh, the headlines.'

I thanked him profusely. And wondered whether to question his decision concerning the matinee, but finally decided against and left.

On the way out, I noticed Buffo, now in the singular and looking slightly disappointed at this change in her circumstances. 'You don't know what you missed, sweetheart,' I told her, and with only a few hours left, raced to my dressing room.

Vita yelled at me for precisely one minute, then said she'd heard what had happened, and if I could at least make an attempt at learning the script, she'd appreciate it. Klaus would be ready with idiot boards, and most of my lines were indeed going to be secreted round the set.

I'd just sat down with a cup of tea and the text when there was a knock on the door. And before I could yell at whoever it was to sod off—

In came Croyd. 'Hey,' he said. And he already sounded *fond* of me. In such a calm and certain way. Which made me feel like it was a good thing he was here.

'You shouldn't be here—'

'Relax. I took the very pretty way in. There are cops watching the doors.'

'So how – ?'

'If I can touch a fire escape, I can make *more* fire escapes. And the, ah, owner here seems to have got the staff locked down. Nobody's talking. I told you I'd come see your performance.'

'I need to learn my lines—'

'Here,' he said, 'let me help.' And he picked up a copy of the play.

It turned out he knew it inside out. He read my cues to me, not acting them, but like a director. He gave me all kinds of *aide memoires* about where we were in the play, what everyone wanted, where my character was going.

'I've always loved it,' he said, when we took a break for coffee. Which he took insanely strong. Just this once, I did too. 'It's personal for me.'

'Really?' I said. And I confess, my mind went swiftly to what exactly that might mean, vis-à-vis human anatomy and thoraxes, mandibles, et cetera.

He heard the sound in my voice, and laughed. 'I mean,' he said, 'that I might wake up as ... anything.' And he told me about how his own powers worked. About how he slept and awoke with randomness in his life, a new power every time. About why they called him the Sleeper. 'I could wake up *looking like* anything.' And his face had that questioning look on it again.

'That's okay,' I said, automatically. And then I thought about me screaming at Father Squid and what he'd said afterward. About what I'd said to Storgman. About all my nervy reactions. And my distaste for my own power, that certain distance I had from it, that I'd never quite gotten over. 'Actually,' I said, 'listen. I grew up somewhere where there were no jokers or aces. So I still … get it wrong a lot. I still blunder into doing terrible things. When these days, in this city, that rather means you're doing them deliberately, meaning to hurt people's feelings. But I don't. I want to get it right. I promise that when you go to sleep, I mean, when you wake up, I mean, if I'm … if I'm there, or if I happen to see you, after … I mean, after you've changed … for some reason …'

He grinned, and thankfully interrupted me. 'Maybe you should have played Anabeth from the start.'

'Oh, thanks!'

'I didn't mean—' He saw I was laughing and stopped. 'I meant that seriously, because you're thinking about this stuff, and it's in you, but you're new to it.' His gaze was dancing all over my face, as if I were some part of nature that he was newly appreciating. And that was a great look, actually. It felt like something I'd been missing for the longest time, without knowing it. 'I look forward to seeing you handle it all. 'Cause you're going to. But there is … one thing I've got to say.'

And then he told me how old he was.

'Oh,' I said. 'Right.'

And he looked wonderfully worried about how I might react.

I couldn't find any modest way of saying that was okay. That that was fine by me. That I'd suddenly realized how much I liked older men. Much older men.

It would have been assuming so much to do so.

Because what had happened here, really? We'd had lunch and chatted. And seemed to be making grand decisions about each other. Which could be entirely mistaken.

Then Vita popped her head round the door and precisely yelled at me again, and hustled Croyd out of there.

'I'll be out there,' he said.

And then it was time for makeup. And this half a romance and half a classic nightmare of extraordinary New York was actually going to happen.

I'm tempted to say that if I'd known about who was going to be coming along that night, I wouldn't have gone through with it. But that's not the case. I don't regret any of it really. Hideous, hideous hoo-ha that it turned out to be.

Vita stayed with me through makeup and costuming. She didn't fuss. She led me through my cues, and was pleased by how far I'd got. 'Everyone knows the circumstances,' she said. 'Just look them in the eye, and go straight for a prompt if you need one. As long as you're honest up there, they'll love you.'

'What if the police arrive?'

'Mr. Dutton says he can hold them off until the end of the performance. And hey, you'll have a very receptive audience out there tonight.'

'How do you mean?'

'The Miami Classics have booked the first three rows. They're in the city to see the sights and take in a show. They're a social club for, you know, mature guys who are also aces.'

I suddenly found that my mouth had gone very dry.

'Problem?'

I managed to shake my head. And perhaps make some sort of squeaking noise.

Anabeth is the first onstage. In this production, she's there, wandering about, as the house fills, before the stage lights go on. Vita had told me to ignore anyone in the audience who tried to communicate with me, to stay in the part. And I did, pacing, nervous, waiting in what was meant to be a big empty park for the man I'd just met.

And so I was looking out at the audience and saw the man I'd just met take his seat. He made quick eye contact, and smiled at me, in a way that somehow said he knew I couldn't smile back and that was okay.

So that was good.

What was bad was the row of uniformed police who took their places right behind him. And they weren't so careful with the meaningful eye contact. I got the feeling Mr. Dutton had struck a deal that lasted only until the end of the show. But at least they seemed to be looking right past Croyd. He was sunk kind of low in his seat.

What was worse still were the Miami Classics. They came in laughing and joking, and calling out things to me like 'Hey, your boyfriend's a bug!' until their organizers imposed some order. They were kindly looking silver-haired guys in leisurewear, some of them with wives, some of them displaying ace signifiers like glowing eyes.

The front row of them were sitting just far enough away so that if I really concentrated, if I wasn't taken by surprise by it . . .

Or if I stayed at the rear of the stage . . .

I might just be able to fend their powers off.

But the worse thing of all was what was going on at the back of the theater, moments before the lights were due to go down. The Bowery Rep has always had a 'gangs welcome' policy, which has kept it out of trouble. But tonight, marching in down different aisles, looking quickly round to see if they could find a certain someone in the audience . . .

There came the Werewolves and the Demon Princes. Many Freddies and much leather, with Ginger leading the latter pack. They'd obviously reached some sort of agreement that allowed them to do this together.

Thankfully, in the few seconds before everything went dark, they didn't spot Croyd.

And then they had to quickly get into their seats. It seemed they'd all bought tickets. It's amazing what the sheer ritual of theater can do.

Tonight, it was going to have to perform miracles.

'Hi,' whispered Klaus from the prompt box, stage left.

'Hi,' I mouthed to him, thinking that this was a bit daring of him.

He looked sighingly at me. And I realized.

I looked quickly to stage right, where James Clark Brotherton was waiting for his cue, with much the same expression on his face.

'Hi!' I called to him, waving.

And we were off.

It's a surprisingly happy play to start with. The sense of new romance, of spring, of the lovers remarking on the buzzing of fateful, ironic bees. It's meant to remind the audience of a sort of innocence that's meant to have existed before Wild Card Day. That's how this version was costumed, so what happens to our tragic hero seems to come out of nowhere. I've heard that for survivors of that day, the play can be either a very intense or very depressing experience. Which was one reason, considering the guys in the first three rows, that I was determined to keep it serious. I found myself locating the lines, either in my head, or on the picnic basket, and I think I managed to stay in character, and I was damn well doing it for them. The reviews, up to this point, offer wildly differing verdicts on just how I *was* doing, by the way. I did find myself improvising a bit, because it felt so easy, because what I was playing so far was … how I was feeling that evening. And, weirdly, representing it onstage made it seem even more real.

But I soon realized that both Klaus and James Clark Brotherton got that look on their faces again whenever I wandered off piste. I grabbed a paper plate and read out that there was a chill in the air, and perhaps we could go for a drink … someplace warmer?

The lights went down, and we exited.

Scene two involved the hero's sister and her own spouse, who know about our hero's circumstances, and fret for rather too long I personally think about whether or not to tell Anabeth.

James took me aside in the wings, and for a moment I thought he was going to slap me, but instead he took my hands in his. 'Well done,' he said. 'We'll get through this. Just follow my lead.'

I nodded, rather than saying that actually I'd been doing fine without, or anything like that.

'Do you know who's out there?' he said.

'Yeah, I saw!'

'Lucas Tate, the editor-in-chief of the *Jokertown Cry*. He didn't just send his theater critic, he came down as well! Abigail, we have to show that great man something *extraordinary*.'

I could only manage a thin smile. I was rather hoping for the opposite.

It's act two where *Grey Hearts* really gets going. Anabeth starts to suspect her husband isn't telling her everything, and she tries to figure out what the nature of his secret is, suspecting everything but the truth. There's a scene where the two of them are caught in flashbulbs, just happening to be on the spot when Fortunato's about to exit a club, and Anabeth sees, standing in the shadows round the stage, lit up only by the strobes (and hence there was a big warning on the posters about epilepsy, fainting, and the distant possibility of interdimensional travel for certain aces), all the different things her husband could be: gay; cheating on her; a criminal.

I just had to throw my hands up and strike poses, so I had a moment to see what was happening in the audience.

My gaze found Croyd.

And I saw that he was crying.

I guess he'd want me to say that it was in a very manly way. But it was what I wanted to see at that point. Because I'd been thinking, as we got into the scene … I knew so little about him. Except that he was a criminal. And an ace. A very *variable* ace. And so, after this was over, and I'd been … well, *arrested* … maybe I'd have to wait until I'd calmed down from this hyper-excited state I was in before embarking on any romance, especially with someone who my mum would regard as—

But then the tears. That moment of him being illuminated. The experience on his face.

There was a man used to being misunderstood. And somehow, stupid me with all my phobias and hurdles, I'd gotten straight to the real him.

But emotional epiphanies apart, and heaven knows this play was becoming a bit of a roller coaster on that front, it was going rather well so far. The audience were watching an actual play rather than a media spectacle. And judging from their applause, they seemed to be enjoying it. The gangs were keeping quiet, even. Maybe because, like with everything the Rep did, this was very much about them. When James made his big speeches, in a Jokertown accent that was period-specific, even he got calls of support from the gang rows, and when they heard that was okay, from the elderly aces in the front rows too. I thought that just added to the atmosphere.

Most of all: in my state of teeth-grinding concentration, I was actually managing to keep all those powers out there at bay. The first time I'd had to do that for any length of time. And dealing with that stuff didn't feel at all ... tarty ... but just like doing away with the sort of shyness an actor naturally has to shed to go onstage. So this was actually turning out to be an incredibly pivotal evening in my life, in all sorts of ways.

Which, I think was the thought in my head, that I was living in a tremendous moment ... when actually I should have been thinking ahead.

We'd got to the point when James's character, discovered in all his beelike glory, rips open his shirt to reveal a rather impressionistic version of a striped, furry thorax. Lost in the part, James shoved me as hard as he was used to shoving his regular leading lady, with whom he'd choreographed the move. Despite Vita telling him to take all the physical stuff down a couple of notches tonight.

He shoved me toward the front of the stage.

I staggered on the edge, my arms wheeling in midair, making

the audience gasp, rather wonderfully actually, with that sensation of is it real or is it an act?

And I realized, horrified, a second before it happened—

'You don't understand anything about what it's like to be me!' he yelled.

At which point, overcome by one of the powers in the front row— I burst into flame.

The audience gasped.

Then wildly applauded.

I heard, weeks later, that Lucas Tate, who, doubtless succumbing to long hours fighting for the rights of jokers, had fallen excusably asleep, woke up at the sound of my inflammation.

'Abigail Baker is on fire!' his theater critic gasped to him as, behind his ceramic white cat mask, he blinked his eyes open.

'That good, eh?' he replied.

'Fire!' yelled someone at the back of the crowded theater.

Nobody moved.

I was *that* good.

At being convincingly on fire in a theatrical, as opposed to a realistic, way.

I flapped my flaming arms violently, terrified, trying to some- how roll my center of gravity back onto the stage.

I failed. And plummeted, I thought, homicidally, into the front three rows.

But by then the Miami Classics had had time to get their act together. I found myself caught and held up by a giant rubbery (and I presume fireproof) hand.

I was held there long enough to illuminate the audience.

Long enough, I learned afterward, for the Werewolves, cops, and Demon Princes to look across the theater and see Croyd.

My flame cut out a second later.

The ace that had caught me heaved me upright.

I fell forward, all rubbery now, bounced back upright off my rubber nose, and pitched back helplessly into the audience again.

Where I was caught this time by a burst of warm (and rather stale) air.

Which again pitched me forward.

With air bursting from every orifice.

I bounced across the stage on my face. I slammed into James, fell at his feet, and started levitating slowly away on my back like an air hockey puck.

I realized that I was glowing a bright, sparkly pink. I looked into the audience again and saw that the gangs and Croyd were all doing the same. And that a hefty policeman was waving his nightstick round his head like it was a magic wand, throwing off the pink sparkles in waves, like he was the enforcement division of fairyland.

At least I remembered my line. I bellowed it at James. 'I understand pretty well now!'

Which brought the house down.

Which was hardly the desired effect, and I believe a first for the play in question.

I grabbed the curtain at the back, and managed to scramble to my feet, slipping on the air under me, trying to see what was happening in the auditorium.

Silhouettes were climbing over seats. Pink glows were converging. People had started to shout and cry out as feet landed in faces, and scuffles began.

The gangs had used the confusion to leap up and go find Croyd. The cops had leaped after.

I wantonly grabbed hold of the pink glow power, and switched it off from where he was. Which caused a pleasingly sudden yell of exasperation from somewhere nearby.

Vita was yelling from stage left for us all to get off the stage, to get the safety curtain down.

'No,' I yelled. 'The show must go – !'

James narrowly missed me as he sprinted off.

And looking out at the theater, I could see his point. The Werewolves and Demon Princes were fighting their way toward the middle rows, where I now couldn't see Croyd. The police had waded in. And some of the more game Miami Classics had joined in, throwing ice bolts and doing rubbery-handed kung fu against the gang members with a kind of square-jawed glee. Where else but in this town can you see three Freddie Mercuries trying to escape an old man who's throwing handfuls of explosive dandruff at them? Lucas Tate was standing up, his mask reflecting the pink glow, seemingly dictating an on-the-spot account to his frantically scribbling theater critic, who looked like he was considering alternative employment. Ginger was busy thumping a Werewolf as the two gangs contested over getting to Croyd, but one of his heads was looking over to me onstage. 'Bravo!' it squeaked Scottishly. 'I'll be back for the next show!'

I sincerely hoped the other two heads agreed.

The violence, thank goodness, was very much one on one. Nobody had started to rip up the seating.

As I may have already indicated, none of this was my fault. So how was I feeling, as the air gradually drained out from under me, and I watched the Miami Classics move farther back into the auditorium, and thankfully out of range?

Complicated.

I looked at my hands. They were covered with the remains of ignition products, and still felt a bit rubbery. I thought about what my mum would say, about me having got so thoroughly involved with so many aspects of aces and jokers, in so many different ways, in such a short space of time.

To just start to be properly involved. To look at a riot in a theater and feel bad that these were … *my people.* Who I owed things to, and had responsibilities to, and was caught up with.

I felt a sort of triumph that had nothing to do with the production.

But this had been going to be my big debut, and I was going to be so blamed, and I felt selfish for even thinking about how it was going to look like I'd ruined something while just trying to do my best—

The safety curtain came hurtling downward and the house lights came up. And in the second I had to see the audience clearly before my view was blocked—

I still couldn't see him.

At the sound of heavy boots, I looked to stage left. And saw a new group of uniformed policemen running at me. The twelve-year-old was leading them. I looked to stage right, and there came another bunch of them, led by his fat partner.

They definitely seemed to have got the idea that I was somehow responsible for this.

Entirely wrongly. Look, can I take it as read that you get that now?

Sorry. Anyway—

I was about to start arguing my case, and rather hoping the cop who could turn into a cat wasn't among them, when suddenly I was falling—

Through a trapdoor that had opened underneath me.

Into the arms of Croyd Crenson.

Who had to hold me down to stop me bouncing right back up again with residual rubberiness.

'Hey,' he said. 'You were great.' And he slammed down a lever to close the trapdoor, just as the cops above leaped for it. 'But I got another role in mind for you.'

♦

I hear that Leo Storgman was mightily pleased to get the two of us back into custody. That he'd spent the rest of that day going over lines about 'separating the sheep from the goats' and us not being able to 'pull the wool over his eyes.' I got a lot of this from Lucas Tate, who took up our cause, rather, after he'd worked out what had been going on while he was asleep.

The riot at the theater came to a halt mostly because of the arrival of a truly huge number of uniformed police officers, who carted off everyone involved, including some of the Miami Classics, who'd gotten rather carried away, but were just as gleeful to be in the back of police vans and still mixing it up. So it's good to know their night out wasn't ruined, and they had, as they'd been seeking, an emotional time that reminded them of the good old days. But a contributing factor to the violence winding down was the appearance in one of the theater boxes of Croyd Crenson, with me beside him. Bows were taken, to even some applause from those in the fighting audience still minded to appreciate such gestures. Ginger's little left head even shouted for an encore. Which I thought was pushing it, rather. Croyd called upon the police to arrest him, which would settle the matter for the gangs, and the police, affronted that they hadn't already managed to do that without his permission, arrived moments later to do so.

I heard that Leo Storgman took great pleasure in marching up and down in front of the separate jail cells, his two new prisoners put in different corridors so they couldn't talk to each other. He interrogated Croyd about many matters entirely separate from anything to do with counterfeiting, about a murder case he was working on. He tried to discover from his female prisoner if she had powers herself, or if this was all something Crenson was doing, and how much she knew about the Sleeper, and whether or not she was willing to give him up in return for the charges being dropped over her 'fleecing' that shopkeeper.

She simply told him that the powers were hers, that she was an ace.

He realized, after a while, that neither prisoner was stalling, exactly, or playing dumb. That their relative simplicity and dull straightforwardness extended to the way they talked to their legal representatives also.

The truth of what was going on suddenly came to Storgman as he was about to go home the next day and heard from a fellow officer that an entire stack of seized pirate DVDs had gone. He raced back to the cells, and discovered that they were suddenly—

Empty.

The copies of the two of us having vanished.

By that time, the original versions, so to speak, had relocated to Croyd's new safe house. On the way there, in the back of a cab, I'd read on my phone about all the arrests, and the first reports from people who'd said that the whole experience had summed something up for them, about how disparate and divided this community still was, that the riot had been, well, art. And among all that was Vita, saying that when the authorities stopped harassing me she hoped I'd come back and play a lead, and Mr. Dutton, saying that the theater would be open again for business the very next day, and that far from the incident putting people off, he was wondering how he'd be able to fit everyone in, considering the demand for tickets. And behind him in that news report, there was Shauna Montgomery, making an entrance on crutches, yelling that she was damned if she was going to let this grand old theater go under.

And yes, that last bit did look slightly planned, rather.

I looked up from the display vastly relieved. My debut hadn't been a disaster after all.

Which was when I realized Croyd was looking seriously at me. 'It'll work out for you,' he said. 'Dutton will get his lawyers on it. It'll end up being the first line in your autobiography.'

'I hope so,' I said. 'I have a terrible feeling that Mum may already have read about this.' I felt an angry text message in my hand, checked, and found that this was indeed so.

'Do you want me to drop you off somewhere?' he said.

'No,' I said, and switched off the phone.

'When I wake up with some new power—'

'I'll have it too.'

'So let's hope it's not the power to explode the thing nearest to you.'

'Yes, let's.'

'When I start needing sleep, when I start having to keep myself awake ...' He sighed. 'I'm pretty *variable,* Abigail.'

'Well,' I said, 'aren't we all?'

And I saved him the trouble of worrying about whether or not he could kiss me.

THE RAT RACE

PART 8.

Leo sat at his desk, leaning forward on his elbows and forearms, swearing at the paperwork he didn't want to do – and thinking about Croyd, and how he should've known. Hash had been making that preposterous stack of food when the Rathole murders went down; but all the customers and their meals had been accounted for. The smoke – the eggs, the burgers, the chicken fingers. All of it cooking down to greasy ash. All of it for Croyd, who had vanished from the scene.

He was a witness. He'd been there, inside, when the triggers were pulled. And he'd made it out alive.

The prospect made the detective downright itchy. And he suddenly thought about yanking Croyd's file. It'd be a mile long; he'd been out there since 1946, and he wasn't always the kind of guy who walked the straight and narrow. But it might be useful.

He muttered aloud, 'December 1978. What were you doing then, Croyd?' Was he a joker or an ace? Enormous? Tiny? When the Sleeper awoke on that night and went out searching, hunting for food – any food, and lots of it – and he'd found the Rathole, what new power was he using?

It must've been something good, for him to get away so clean. In the years that followed the Rathole murders, Croyd sure as hell hadn't been lying low. He hadn't snuck off into hiding, fearing retribution. He knew he'd gotten out unseen.

'Invisibility?' Leo guessed. When it came to Croyd, nothing was truly improbable.

Lieutenant Kant bustled by, carrying a folder as thick as his thumb. Leo reached out a hand to snag his attention, and said, 'Hey, you got a second?'

'One or two,' Kant said, stopping in the aisle to stand over Leo's desk.

'Anybody pulled the Sleeper's file yet? Or would it still be in the back?' he asked. Croyd'd had his run-ins with the law over the years, and any arrest formalities would have made mention of his joker or ace traits at the time.

'I think it's still in the back, but you're talking about a hefty fucking volume.' Harvey Kant adjusted the folder in his scaly hand, and shifted his weight when he asked, 'Hey, Leo, this isn't about the doubles, is it?'

'What?'

'Is this about the Rathole again?' Kant asked point-blank.

And here we go again. 'Yeah, so?'

Kant leaned forward, putting his hands on Leo's desk and leaning in. 'When you bring this shit up out of the office, like you're dicking around with old cases on your own damn time, that's one thing. But for God's sake, man. Look around – we've got more pressing problems around here than a thirty-year-old murder that no one gives a shit about anymore.'

'I'm not—'

'You're not *what*? Burning tax dollars on shit that doesn't matter? Look, I know you've only got a couple of months left, but if you're not going to keep your eye on your job, you may as well hang it up now.'

Leo could feel the skin around his collar warming up. 'Now listen, I'm not wasting anybody's tax dollars or time. And I don't think it's fair to say that nobody gives a shit.'

'It isn't on the docket anymore, and you've got gang feuds to sort out during your office hours. Leave thirty years ago back where it belongs, and do your goddamn job.'

Leo was probably imagining the threat he heard, but he didn't like it anyway. 'Yes *sir,*' he said in exactly the same tone he would've used to tell Kant to fuck right off.

If Kant heard it, he didn't react to it. He only retreated with his folder, and when he was out of sight, Leo scowled down at his desk. The lieutenant was right about that much: the gangs weren't kissing and making up, and things were looking nastier than ever. And the burglaries, Christ. What was going on out there?

Leo sighed and scooted the loose pages together, stacking them and tidying their edges like he was preparing to shuffle a deck of cards.

He looked over his shoulder and, not seeing Kant or anybody else, he set his paperwork down and picked up his desk phone. He thought about calling Lucas Tate directly, but figured it wasn't strictly necessary to buzz all the way to the top, so he dialed the *Cry* and asked for the Classifieds department instead.

A woman answered with a greeting that might've been read off a screen.

Leo told her he wanted to place a personal ad. He asked, 'How many words do I get for free?'

'Three lines,' she told him. 'Or twenty-five words, whichever is less.'

'Okay. How about this: "Sleeper: 1978, a bird mask, and an all-night diner. I know you were there. I want to know what you saw." Will that work?'

'That'll work just fine, sir.'

'When will it run?'

'Tomorrow's edition,' she assured him.

He thanked her and hung up, then twiddled his thumbs for a few seconds before standing up and heading toward records in search of anything the force might have on the Sleeper. He didn't find much he didn't expect – and nothing that might give him a hint about what he looked like in 1978, or what he could do – or what ability he must've had that left him the only survivor of a massacre.

Or the perpetrator? Couldn't rule anything out.

So Leo went back to his desk and he opened a drawer, pulling out a small brown notebook and flipping it open.

He picked up his phone again and began to dial. And in the next twenty minutes, he'd left messages for every old snitch and hustler he could think of – anyone who might have the faintest idea where Croyd was, and what he was up to now, never mind 1978.

He was on the verge of hanging up for the final time this afternoon when he felt very distinctly like he was being watched. He looked around. He checked over his shoulder. He lowered the phone slowly, wondering if Kant was peering out an office window and shooting daggers.

But he didn't see Kant and he didn't see Wanda, who'd promised to meet him after work. When she promised these things, she often showed up early – and he didn't mind. Let the whole station see her arrive to meet him. It did his ego good.

No, not her.

However, at the edge of his peripheral vision, he thought he saw someone dart behind a column. It was a smallish someone with long brown hair and a blue streak, but that's all he caught.

He watched the column for five minutes, all the while pretending not to – pretending to concentrate on the forms and figures that made up his inbox. And finally he was rewarded with the sight of a teenage girl slinking away, looking over her shoulder and darting into the hall.

Wanda appeared moments later, smiling and breathless. 'Sorry I'm late,' she said, 'slowest goddamned cab in the city.'

Leo stood up, pulling his jacket into his hand. 'You're right on time,' he said. 'Let's get out of here. I need a change of scenery.'

'Sure. You got anyplace in mind?'

'How about my place?' he asked. He reached into his top drawer and pulled out a notebook he'd been working on in private. It was cheap, blue, and well worn, with curly corners. It shed a spray of confetti from the spiral binding, where sheets had been torn out in haste.

'I finally get to see your place?'

'It's about time, don't you think? And I want to show you what I've been doing about the Rathole. Christ knows they won't let me work on it here. I swear to God, it's like they don't want me fighting crime or something.'

On the way back to his apartment, Leo filled her in on the bitching-out by Kant. 'But I've pulled together everything I've got,' he told her. 'And you and me, we're going to sift through it.'

When they stepped off the elevator into the hallway where Leo's apartment waited, his phone rang in his pocket. He fished it out and checked the number, then made an apologetic face at Wanda. 'Mellie,' he said. 'If I don't answer, she'll just keep calling.'

'She worries about you,' Wanda said.

Leo didn't answer that, because he wasn't sure if she was right or if he'd accidentally raised a control freak; but he accepted the call and said, 'Hey.'

'Hey, Dad. Is this a good time?'

'For what?'

'You left me a message – about your racket,' she said.

'Oh, yeah. Can you make it?' he asked, holding the phone with his shoulder while he rummaged around in his pants for his keys, then opened the door. She didn't answer right away, and he had a feeling he knew what that meant, so he added, 'Some friends of mine pulled strings. It's going down at the High Hand, a real nice place.'

'I'm not sure. I'm tied up in some property problems down here, and I just don't know. I'm going to try,' she amended quickly. 'It feels like I haven't seen you in ages.'

He said, 'Yeah, it does.' He opened the door, and dropped his keys into a small brass bowl atop a small table immediately inside.

'But this time of year – the weather's going to be awful. I may have a hell of a time getting a flight.'

'You might,' he agreed, pointing at a coatrack where Wanda could unload her outerwear.

He tossed his own coat over the back of a recliner, drew back the living-room curtains, and flipped on a few lights – revealing the clean clutter of a man who'd lived alone for a while. An assortment of *National Geographics*, *Consumer Reports*, and *Popular Mechanics* teetered in unstraightened stacks. They accumulated in piles like leaves, alongside well-thumbed copies of John le Carré and James Rollins paperbacks, which toppled here and there to the floor, or gathered in the crevices of his couch and on the kitchen table. The walls were covered with framed postcards from Greece, artifacts of a long-ago honeymoon; beside them hung a smattering of photos – shots of Vicki and Melanie, and one of them as a family when she was yet an infant. Leo was wearing a butterfly collar, which Wanda pointed at with a smirk.

'Dad, I'm really sorry,' she said, and he knew that despite her waffling, she already knew she wasn't coming. 'But it's a huge hunk of time – it's a miserable trip—'

'If you're not coming, you're not coming. That's fine. That's up to you. You're a grown woman, and you don't have to come if you don't want to.'

'It isn't like that.'

'It doesn't matter,' he said, and it sounded like a sign-off. To make it more official he said, 'I have to go.'

'You always have to go. That's how it always is.'

'I'll talk to you later,' he said, and he hung up.

Wanda stood over by the television, where a large white board was set up and stocked with red, blue, and green dry-erase markers. 'Everything okay?' she asked.

'Everything's fine,' he said flatly. 'Mellie's not coming to the racket, but that's her call. I uh …' He gazed around at his home, crowded with the accumulated things of a lifetime. 'I should've cleaned up a bit. Didn't think about it. I've really had my head up my ass.'

'Oh, don't worry about it.' She smiled, picking up a red marker and popping the cap off, then putting it back on. 'You've got a lot of stuff, but—' She craned her neck to see through the wall cutout that showed the kitchen. 'It's only … *busy*. Not dirty. No dishes in the sink, no food left out. It's a nice little place.'

He joined her beside the white board and took the blue marker. 'Thanks. Hasn't had a woman's touch for a while, but I can pick up after myself if I have to. Anyway, what we have here' – he tapped the marker's tip against the board, leaving tiny blue rectangles where it touched – 'is a murder.'

He opened the notebook and removed a few loose sheets, then

handed it to Wanda. 'I'm tired of taking shit about it at work, so I'm taking this home. It's a dossier on the Rathole murders. I need to think about it without worrying some asshole brass is going to stare over my shoulder. And I'm ... I'd be happy for your input,' he said, stuttering a little to find her suddenly so close.

Holding the notebook in one hand, she fiddled with the marker with the other. She appeared to be thinking, but what she was thinking about, Leo wasn't detective enough to guess, or confident enough to speculate.

Wanda looked down to read the top sheet, covered in handwritten notes. 'Stella Nichols,' she said. 'The stripper.'

He cleared his throat, and uncapped the red marker. 'Yeah,' he said, and he squeakily scrawled her name on the white board. 'And everybody else – they're all in there, everything I've got so far.' He began writing the rest of the names – Don Reynolds, Lizzie Wallace, Hash Crowder, Joel Arnold – all in a line. 'It's been driving me crazy, trying to figure out if any of the victims was connected to any of the other suspects.'

'You have other suspects?'

He wrote on the other end of the board: *Esposito, Croyd, Deedle,* and *Boyfriend???*

'Croyd and Deedle I know about,' Wanda noted. 'But who are the other two?'

'Boyfriend' – he used the marker as a pointer – 'was Lizzie Wallace's partner. He was a gangbanger, but that's about all I know. I have an innate distrust of gangbangers, and if I could figure out what his name was, I'd add him to the suspects list. Esposito is an old button man. Worked for Gambione back in the day. Admits he knew Hash, but' – he drew a dotted line between Raul's name and Stella's – 'but he *didn't* admit he knew Stella Nichols.'

'Do you know for sure that he did?'

'I'd be amazed if he didn't. Freakers payroll says he worked the shadows at the strip joint at the same time Stella was dancing there. Listed him as security, but that could mean anything. Maybe he kept an eye on the door, or maybe he kept an eye on the girls – or their admirers. And,' he added, checking the sheet in his hand, 'there's Fred Winney. He was the one Stella accused of stalking her. Winney's dead, by the way.' But this didn't stop him from writing Fred's name on the board, with a dotted line connecting him to Stella. 'Died in a drunk driving accident in 2000.'

Wanda said, 'Hmm.' And she leaned a little closer.

Leo could smell her, warmly and faintly. Pricey shampoo and musky perfume with an undercurrent of vanilla. Sweat from her scarf, dried on her neck when she took it off. After all this time, still familiar. Not the perfume – that was different. And not the shampoo either; but some essence of her that had lingered on him, all those years ago. Until he'd taken a shower and prayed that everything washed off, and his wife would never know.

'This is all very interesting,' Wanda said, the coolness of her words a stark contrast to the heat that beamed off her body. And she didn't actually seem very interested in the white board. 'But.'

She touched his arm, and gently took the loose sheets of paper from the notebook out of his hand. She set everything on the nearest surface, a round table with a landline phone atop it. Her marker went into the aluminum tray at the board's bottom edge.

He handed over his own marker without complaint, though he made a point to cap it first.

She slipped her hands to his waist, and drew him incrementally forward as she said, 'But here's what I really want to know: am I going to have to do all the work, to get you to show me the bedroom?'

... AND ALL THE SINNERS SAINTS

PART 2.

Charlie had rushed home from a client meeting at his Jokertown office to make his scheduled 5:30 P.M. phone meeting with Vincent Marinelli. The phone started ringing while he was unlocking his front door. He managed to juggle his briefcase, keys, and a foam cup full of coffee and answer it without dropping any of them.

'Charlie,' Detective Marinelli's voice said. 'How's tricks?'

'You got my report?' Charlie had been quietly asking his clients and the other petty criminals about the Joe Twitch shoot in general, and their run-ins with Officer Lu Long, aka Puff, in specific. He'd had his write-up sent to Marinelli's office that morning.

'So Long's a sadistic fuck,' Vince said. 'Old news, kid. Give me something I can use.'

The air in the little bodega on the ground floor of Charlie's building was redolent with cumin, allspice, and paprika, and the mouthwatering smell of whatever Mamma Maria was frying on her grill. The scents drifting up into his apartment were the only advertising Maria ever needed to use. Charlie glanced at his watch and wondered if he'd be able to get Vince off the line in time to buy some of whatever she was making before the rest of the block descended on it like jackals.

'All the jokers on the streets are afraid of him, Vince. He half burned one dude's face off.'

'And you shoulda heard the jokes about how it improved his

appearance. Even at IAB. Shit, even public defenders – uptown, not from your office. CCRB threw that beef back in our faces, even though it was classic excessive force.'

'No shit!'

'The victim was a bad actor. Paroled rapist, liked to hurt women. Plus New York loves its cops. They see all these movies where cops have to bend the law to catch the bad guys. All these TV shows. It's hard enough to get more than harsh language for excessive force if the victim's a fucking law professor. This scumbag? Fuggedaboutit.'

'You said "*fuggedaboutit*"? Really?'

'Hey, I had this accent before they put it on TV. Don't bust my balls.'

Charlie swallowed. He felt inadequate enough without the joker detective mentioning his testicles. They were body-proportional for a hundred-pound male rat. 'So you're telling me I just wasted a couple weeks collecting information that doesn't help in any way. This sort of thing seems a lot easier on TV. What about you?'

'Got the same as you. Dick. Long isn't exactly popular with his brother officers, and maybe less with his sisters. But the blue wall stands firm for assholes. If it didn't this job'd be a shitload more rewarding. I may've found some chinks, though. Even the Fort Freak cops admit Puff's a dick.'

'And that helps us?'

'Being a dick? Naw. Bein' a dick got you canned we'd lose ninety percent of the force. Starting with me. But Puff has a way with the ladies. The hard way. He even comes on strong to sister officers.'

'Whoa.'

'Yeah. So what I'm saying is, he's got girlfriends on the street. He has trouble hearing "no" from women, but he sure loves to hear 'em cry. Do the math. Forget all those forensic fantasy TV shows: after perps running their own heads, the greatest investigative tool is pissed-off exes. Or currents looking for the exit.'

'So I should track down Long's girlfriends?'

'Smart boy. I can tell you went to college. I'll send you a list of names. Being Lu Long's girlfriend appears to be a short-term and high-cost proposition. Most of the names on the list are strung out or in jail. A lot of the rest have moved out of the state. This guy just leaves a trail of destruction behind him wherever he goes. One girl jumps out at me, though. Hooker named Minal. She was in a hassle with the Demon Princes last month, and seems to have vanished.'

'Why her?'

'Well, seems sweet Minal had filed an assault complaint four years ago against a cop she says roughed her up after a trick. Guess who's the rougher upper?'

'Okay, I'll ask around I guess.'

Vince said, 'Oh, also I need a sworn statement from your snake boy.'

Like I can snap my fingers and summon him out of the air! Charlie whined in his mind. He didn't do it aloud. He didn't think Detective Marinelli had much patience with whiners. And he found he ludicrously craved the joker cop's approval. 'I'll see what I can do.'

'Great. So long as what you do is get the goods. I'll keep boring from within. It's what rats do. Later.'

The connection died. Charlie slammed the phone into its cradle and rushed downstairs to buy some dinner.

Charlie spent his morning working on a motion to exclude the gun in his Clyde Drummond case. While Clyde had in fact been found *next* to the gun when the police caught him carving up the dead Werewolf, there was no evidence that it was *his* gun. In a stroke of luck, Clyde hadn't left any usable prints on it. So, while the police could testify that Clyde had been cutting up a dead rival gang member with a kitchen knife, the gun lying in the gutter nearby could not be connected to his client in any way.

It was a ridiculous long shot. He would be surprised if the judge didn't laugh him out of the courtroom. Sometimes the necessity of providing a vigorous defense gave Charlie a deep sense of shame. Not because he defended awful people, but because he had to play the law like a game to do so.

Unfortunately, when he arrived at the Tombs to meet with Clyde, the desk sergeant told him that his client was currently being held in lockup back at Fort Freak, and was facing new assault charges.

Jessica Penniman, the sergeant in charge of the lockup at the 5th precinct, was a petite blue-eyed blonde who, under normal circumstances, would have been pretty enough to activate Charlie's stutter reflex. Fortunately, she was soon angry enough to defuse his normal awkwardness. 'Mr. Herriman,' she said, thrusting one slim finger at his chest. 'I am about five seconds from squinching your client down to an inch tall and sticking him in a shoe box for the rest of his stay here.'

Charlie wasn't sure what 'squinching' meant, but the shoe box reference gave him an idea, and this *was* Jokertown. If someone claims they can stick you in a shoe box, safer not to force the issue. 'I don't understand,' he said. 'I was told that Clyde had assaulted someone?'

'He attacked a fellow prisoner in the bus when they were both being returned from the courthouse to the Tombs.'

'Sergeant Penniman, you have my apologies for any inconvenience this misunderstanding may have created. If I could meet with him, I'm sure we can straighten all of this out.'

'He tried to stab someone with his eye-horns. That's not a misunderstanding.'

'I will be sure to impress on him the importance of not doing anything that could be interpreted as' – Charlie paused a moment so he could say it with a straight face – 'attempting to stab people with his face.'

The sergeant gave him one last glare, then pointed him toward a cell at the rear of the basement lockup. 'I separated him from the others in there. Yell if you need me,' she said, then headed off in the other direction.

Charlie walked down to the cell at the end of the row, and found Clyde pacing back and forth muttering and clicking up a storm. One side of his face was completely black and blue, as though he'd had a disagreement with a sledgehammer and lost.

'Clyde,' Charlie said with a sigh. 'Picking fights on the bus from the courthouse is really not going to help your case.'

'It's *Nergal*,' Clyde said. 'And that motherfucker had it coming. He killed one of my brothers!'

'Your brother?' Clyde's file hadn't said anything about siblings.

'One of the Demon Princes! Goddamn gorilla punched one of the Princes to death! We can't let that shit stand!'

'When did this happen? In here?'

'Naw. Last month. Couple days before Wild Card Day,' Clyde said, then pulled a pack of cigarettes from his pocket and tapped one out. He stuck it in his mouth but didn't light it. 'You got a light, Counselor?'

'Don't smoke. So where did this killing happen?'

'Eh, I dunno. Some whorehouse or something. That ho Minal will get what's coming to her, but we don't have anyone inside now but me, so when they put me on the same bus as the fucker Jimbo—'

'Wait? What?' Charlie interrupted. *She's vanished,* Vince had said. Minal was not exactly a common name. How many hookers with that handle could there be?

'I gotta do Jimbo. I'm the only one who can as long as he's in here.'

'Forget Jimbo. Leave him be. You said the hooker's name is Minal?'

'Yeah, so? Who cares? You get me back with the other prisoners so I can finish Jimbo off. They're talking about sending me to Rikers when Jimbo goes to the Tombs.'

'Clyde,' Charlie said, pausing a moment to press his fingers against his eyes. 'You are aware that if you tell me you are about to commit a crime, I am *required by law* to inform the police?'

'But you're my lawyer, you can't tell stuff I say.'

'I can't talk about crimes you've *already* committed. I can, and must, tell about crimes you are *going* to commit. So, to aid in your future defense, *stop telling me you are going to commit crimes.*'

'Fuck me.'

'You,' Charlie agreed with a nod. 'Are certainly doing your best to try. I can probably get the assault charge waved by kissing ass, but you are definitely going to Rikers to keep you away from this other prisoner.'

Clyde sat down on the jail cot with a thump, and gave a few halfhearted clicks. 'Shit,' he said.

Charlie turned to leave, then was struck by a sudden inspiration. 'Hey, Cly – I mean Nergal.'

Clyde seemed to perk up a bit when Charlie called him by his Demon Prince name. 'Yeah?'

'So, that guy they caught you cutting up, that was over drugs, right?'

Clyde nodded. 'Yeah, the Werewolves have been stealing our shit. We had to teach them a lesson.'

'Did you know a Joe Moritz? Called himself Joe Twitch?'

'Everyone knew him. He was kind of an asshole. Jittery freak.'

'You ever hear of him dealing?'

Clyde laughed. 'You kidding me? Twitch wasn't an idiot. He ran scams, small-time cons, I think he might have pimped some. Worked his hustles at a whorehouse anyway. But no drugs. That's Demon Prince turf. Twitch gave our guys freebies with the tail. He knew who to take care of, and who not to fuck with.'

'Did he ever carry a gun?'

'Not that I ever saw. He had a little knife. Gotta give him props. He was quick, he could definitely cut you up if shit went down. But no guns.'

'That,' said Charlie, 'is *very* interesting.'

Charlie walked back to Sergeant Penniman's desk, dutifully informed her that his client would not be safe with the other prisoners, and had made additional threats against Jimbo. Penniman's eyes narrowed at this news, and Charlie suspected Clyde might find out exactly what 'squinching' was before the day was over.

'One last thing, Sergeant,' he said with what he hoped was an ingratiating smile. 'I'd like to speak to the prisoner you say Clyde attacked.'

'Why, he your client too?'

'No, but I would like to apologize to him anyway. If that's all right.'

Penniman shrugged. 'I don't care. He's down at the opposite end of the row.'

Charlie smiled his thanks and hurried down to Jimbo's cell before Penniman could change her mind.

Jimbo, as Clyde had called him, was an enormous joker with four long arms. Charlie had a pretty good idea where Clyde had gotten his mashed-in face now. The big joker looked up at him with vague disinterest and waited for Charlie to speak first.

'Mr., um, Jimbo is it?'

'Yeah,' said the joker in a gravelly voice. 'Who wants to know?'

'Mr. Jimbo, my name is Charles Herriman. I'm an attorney with the public defender's office.'

'Got a lawyer,' Jimbo said.

'I'm not here to represent you. I need to ask about someone you worked with.'

Charlie saw the joker's face close up and the eyes narrow.

'No,' he said. 'Don't misunderstand. This is not in any way an investigation into your place of employment. I just need to ask a couple of questions about a man named Joe Moritz. There was a girl—'

'Minal,' Jimbo said. 'She was with Joe the night he got whacked. Good luck finding her. She's in the wind. Fucking Demon Princes are still sniffing after her, I hear. She won't be sticking her head out anytime soon.'

'You don't know where she'd go?'

'Not a clue. I'm kinda pissed too. She used to have cops as clients. Vice guys. I'd hoped she would get them to help me with this bullshit manslaughter charge.'

A cop's house would be a good place to hide if bloodthirsty gang-bangers have a contract out on you. 'Thank you very much, Jimbo. If my office can do anything to help you in your defense, please don't hesitate to call.' Charlie slid one of his cards onto the crossbar of the jail cell. Jimbo nodded, then put his head in two of his giant hands and leaned back onto the far too small cot in his cell.

A phone call to Vince, and twenty minutes later a courier was delivering Minal Patel's file to Charlie's office. A number of police officers showed up in connection with Miss Patel, including the notorious Puff, Officer Lu Long. She'd filed an assault charge against him four years before. The officer who'd taken the report was named Michael Stevens, who was working vice at the time. Not the guy a hooker would bring an assault report to unless they knew each other. Stevens had appeared in court on Minal's behalf in that assault case, and also in a couple of prostitution charges. He was the only police officer Miss Patel had ever interacted with who'd done so.

Officer Stevens was now working as a detective out of the 5th. A quick Internet search netted Charlie the detective's home address and phone number. He was three numbers into dialing it when he hung the phone up. If Detective Stevens was protecting Minal in his home, there was a reason he wasn't doing it through official channels. Which meant he'd never admit it on the phone or allow anyone to talk to her.

Before he could think better, Charlie threw his coat on and caught a cab to Michael Stevens's apartment.

The woman who opened the door after his second knock was not Minal. She was a slender and beautiful dark-haired woman. She looked at Charlie with the guarded politeness of someone who is waiting to be offered *Watchtower* magazines.

'Ma'am, my name is Charles Herriman. I'm an attorney with the public defender's office.' He held out his card. Her eyes paused briefly on his prosthetic hand, but she made no comment. 'I know this will sound like a strange question, but do you know a woman named Minal Patel?'

The guarded look disappeared and was replaced by outright fear and suspicion. 'My boyfriend is a police officer. If you don't leave right now, I will call him and have you arrested.'

Charlie smiled and tried to look nonthreatening, which was a first for him. He'd never actually *felt* threatening before. 'Please, ma'am, I would happily wait for you to contact Detective Stevens if that would make you more comfortable. I'm working with Detective Marinelli in Internal Affairs. I could call him too.'

Her face fell, and Charlie felt like the world's biggest creep for delivering the implied threat.

Before she could answer, another voice said from behind the door, 'It's okay, Kavitha. I'll talk to him.'

Kavitha stared at Charlie a few seconds longer, then stepped aside and let the door swing open. As Charlie walked in, she turned to the other woman and said, 'I will go check on Isai,' and walked down a hallway to another room.

Minal sat on a bar stool next to the apartment's small kitchen. On the bar sat an open netbook. Her hair was pulled back from a face scrubbed of makeup. She wore baggy CSNY sweats and big round glasses. She was gorgeous. Better-looking than her call-girl poster shot. Much better than the mug shots in her police file.

Charlie's mouth went Novocain numb. His breath started hitching. Reflexively he fumbled for his inhaler, then quelled it.

This wasn't asthma. This was cowardice.

Fucking great, he thought. *First, I'm talking and thinking like Vince. Second, I'm the one who can't introduce myself to the nice woman who helps me pick up my stuff after I blunder into her. How am I supposed to talk to a gorgeous prostitute?*

He cleared his throat. This wasn't a hookup, he reminded himself sternly. This was … business? Something like it, at any rate. 'Ms. Patel?' he asked, using his best interview voice and trying to ignore the tickle of sweat running down the back of his neck. 'My name is Charles Herriman. I'm a lawyer with the public defender's office, trying to help out a client of mine. Could I talk to you for a few minutes, please?'

He flashed his card at her. As she accepted and read it, frowning, he realized he'd mimicked the way Vince flashed his shield. *I'm such a whore,* he thought.

She looked at him over the tops of her glasses. 'What does this concern, Mr. Herriman? I won't do anything that endangers the people I'm staying with.'

'Dealings you might have had in the past with a police officer named Lu Long, out of the 5th Precinct.'

She recoiled. 'Puff?'

I'm losing her! 'Please,' he said. 'Please, Ms. Patel. A man's life depends on this. A fellow joker. I understand you were with Joe Moritz the night he was killed. My client is being implicated in that murder, and Puff ... I mean, Officer Lu Long ... is one of the men who shot Mr. Moritz.'

She eyed him like a rabbit eyeing a creature with a long snout, orange fur, and a black mask who's just claimed to be a fellow bunny. *She doesn't trust me,* Charlie realized. *And why should she?*

Charlie held up his right hand, letting gravity pull his cuff down to reveal the universal joint and the gleaming alloy rods that worked the hand so painstakingly tinted to match his own light olive complexion. 'Not many nats work the Jokertown office,' he said. 'They don't last. My, uh, my joker name is Flipper.'

She looked at his eyes. He tried to stay professional, looking back at her huge, dark almond eyes. She nodded, shut her blue netbook with a decisive snap, and swiveled on the bar stool. 'Either you're sincere,' she said, 'or the world's greatest actor.'

He sighed. 'I can't deliver a line to save my life. But really, it seems shocking to me that no one has asked you about this already. I mean, you knew both men. You supposedly saw Joe the night he died.'

She laughed. It was a lovely laugh utterly lacking in humor. 'You say you're a lawyer. So tell me, what court would take the word of a whore over two decorated police officers? They wouldn't even take my word over Puff's four years ago.'

They wouldn't take her word over Lu Long's. That meant she'd told Michael Stevens something that contradicted Long's version of events. Charlie tried very hard to keep a poker face. 'Please understand, I need to ask some questions of a pretty personal nature. I can't make you answer them. All I can do is remind you what's at stake.'

Minal shrugged. 'Ask away. Just understand that I won't say anything that puts me or my friends in danger. Michael won't get in trouble for telling me to stay quiet, will he? Because if he will, this conversation is over.'

'No, no. I'm working with the Internal Affairs officer in charge of this investigation, and I can guarantee that he is not interested in Detective Stevens. Only in finding the truth about Joe Twitch, and how he died.' Actually, Charlie couldn't guarantee anything of the kind. But he was fairly certain Vince wouldn't go after Minal's benefactor over this, and in for a penny, in for a pound. 'Now, I understand you were involved a couple years ago with Long on a, uh, professional basis.'

'That's right,' she said, so softly he had to lean forward to hear.

'And you haven't had contact with him since?'

'There's no such thing as being finished with Puff, Mr. Herriman.' The bitter anger in her voice surprised him. When he first brought up Long she acted like prey. Now it was the rabbit showing long fangs. 'I'm scared of him, Mr. Herriman. More scared than you can possibly imagine.'

You have no idea, he thought. He said nothing. The first skill of interviewing clients or witnesses, Dr. Pretorius had insisted, was let the person *talk.*

'Let me show you something.' She started to pull up her sweatshirt.

'No! Wait! Please.' A part of his mind yammered. *What are you doing? Check out that rack!*

Her breasts were impressive, although confined in a gray sports bra. By the time they came into view he'd forgotten all about them. Minal's torso was covered with what his rapidly overheating mind could only describe as a shag carpet of long, flesh-colored nipples that moved gently, like wheat in a breeze.

'Um,' he said.

He realized they were actually small tentacles. 'They're my stock in trade,' Minal said. 'I can make them do whatever I want. My clients were willing to pay highly for the experience. And . . . they're *very* sensitive. Like normal nipples.'

For the first time in several days, a racing pulse and the sweat absolutely *pouring* down inside Charlie's shirt had nothing to do with fear.

'See this?' Minal pointed under her left armpit.

Feeling nine kinds of self-conscious, Charlie leaned forward. He wasn't sure at first what he was looking for; this was unfamiliar territory, at least in first person. Then he saw the ugly patch, like scars and shriveled skin tags.

'You know Puff's flaming spit trick? He hocked a hot drop on me. Just to *brand* me, he said. Not damage the goods.' She let the shirt fall. Charlie felt a brief and shameful disappointment. 'That's why I know Lu Long is capable of *anything*, Mr. Herriman. That and things I've heard and seen during the course of our … relationship. And that's why, knowing the risks, I'm willing to tell you all about them.'

He fumbled the small oblong stick of his digital voice recorder out of a coat pocket. 'You mind if I tape this, Ms. Patel?'

She smiled. 'I insist.'

He clicked on the recorder. 'What makes you sure the killing of Joe Twitch wasn't just the righteous shoot the police claim it was?'

'You doubt it?' she said in surprise.

'No, Ms. Patel,' Charlie said, pointing at the tape recorder. 'But I need to hear your reasons.'

'Joe died just a few hours after he left my place. When he was there, he didn't have a gun or any dope on him. I'd never seen Joe carry a gun, ever. His ace was super speed. He carried a knife and said he could cut a man's trigger finger off before they could fire a shot.' She glanced down, her face pained. 'At least that's what he claimed. Joe talked a lot.'

'He could have picked up a gun and the drugs in the hours after he left you,' said Charlie. 'You don't know where he went after that, do you?'

She shook her head. 'No. But before he left, Joe told me he was up to something big. Something that he thought was going to be a big payday, but also scared him. It wasn't drugs, though. I think he was blackmailing someone. Someone powerful. He said something about someone paying for "burning" something. Paying Joe, I mean. I don't know how to explain it; he wasn't very coherent. Sometimes he talked so fast he left words out. But it wasn't a drug deal like the cops say. Joe was a hustler, not a dealer. I think Joe went to go meet whoever he was putting the squeeze on, and those two cops shot him.'

Charlie glanced at his watch, started to ask about Joe's history of hustling, then did a double take and said, 'Shit! I have to go. But thank you so much for your help with this.'

Minal grabbed his upper arm as he started to turn. She grabbed high enough that her fingers were holding his upper flipper and not the prosthetic. Charlie felt an electric tingle shoot through him, and froze.

'If someone paid Puff to kill Joe, he'll still have the money. That man considered actually paying for anything a moral failing. He'll still have it.'

'We can look at his bank accounts,' Charlie said, doubtfully, 'but ...'

'He's smarter than that. But not much.' Minal laughed again, this time with humor. 'Puff has no imagination. He used to have an account under the name Peter Long, because he said it made him sound like a porn star. Look for dick related names. That'll be Puffy.'

'Thank you, Ms. Patel.' Charlie started to turn toward the door.

'Anytime, Mr. Herriman,' she said with a wink and a smile.

Pulling his flipper out of her grasp was the hardest thing he'd ever done in his life.

Charlie flipped open his cell phone and dialed Ratboy as soon as he was outside of Minal's apartment. 'Vince, I've got a recording you need to listen to.'

'Give me the gist,' Vince said. Charlie could hear the rumble and clack-clack of a subway train in the background.

'Where are you?'

'Just on my way to Fort Freak, someone there I need to chat

with. But I've got time for a quick meet. Cup of coffee somewhere?'

Charlie told him to meet at Squisher's Basement in half an hour. On the way there, he listened to the recording several more times, almost afraid that Minal's voice would fade away if he didn't.

He ran down the steps into the below street level bar, and found a dark corner. Squisher's old fish tank cast an eerie green glow across the faces at the bar, making even the jokers look ethereal and alien. Charlie had only just sat down when a well-built black man with prominent ears walked in and scanned the room. As he passed the glowing tank, Charlie could see the angry set of his features. When he got to Charlie's booth, he slammed his hand down on the table. 'You better be goddamned glad I know who you are, Flipper,' he said. 'If you weren't a damned cripple I'd drag you out of this place and kick the shit out of you.'

Charlie's throat closed up, and his stomach went liquid. It was his usually panicked reaction to violent confrontation; that didn't make it any less humiliating.

'Why don't you pick on someone your own size, Detective?'

Vince! If being terrified was humiliating, being relieved that someone had come to fight your battle for you was on some other dimension of self-loathing, but Charlie found himself incapable of resisting. 'Vince, thank God. I don't—'

Marinelli cut him off. 'Detective Stevens,' he said as he pulled out a chair. 'Why don't we all just sit the fuck down, and I'll try to figure out some way not to just arrest you right now for assault. How's that sound?'

Detective Michael Stevens stood silently for a moment, clenching his fists. Finally he nodded and sat down.

Vince waved at a passing waitress and made coffee pouring motions to her. 'So I ask myself,' he said. 'Why a guy with a nice clean jacket and a recent promotion to detective wants to throw his career away by threatening, of all things, a lawyer with the public defender's office.'

'I—' Michael started.

'No, let me tell you why. Some hooker you used to bang gets herself in hot with the Demon Princes. She goes on the run and comes to you for help. You take her in, keeping her off the radar. I don't know why. Maybe she's scared a dirty cop will sell her out. Maybe she doesn't want Puff to find out where she's hiding, though that raises more questions than it answers.'

'Maybe she was scared, and I wanted to make sure she stayed safe,' Michael said. He seemed to have traded his righteous fury in favor of a resigned weariness.

Charlie butted in. 'She was with Joe Twitch right before he died.'

Vince's whiskers twitched, but otherwise he didn't react to this revelation. Charlie pulled out the little recorder and pushed it across the table. Ratboy made it vanish.

Charlie turned to Stevens, feeling bolder now that Vince had his back. 'I have a hard time believing she didn't tell you that, Detective.'

'Yeah,' Vince said. 'So your old squeeze was with Twitch, then Joe gets himself offed by another cop who used to do the horizontal bop with that same former squeeze. Why would you keep that to yourself, Mikey?'

Stevens shook his head slowly. 'It isn't like that. She came to us beat half to death by the Princes. We took her in to keep her safe. Yeah, she told me about Twitch, and yeah, I told her that going up against Puff and Angel on that was not a smart idea. I didn't have to convince very hard. Puff's hurt her bad in the past.'

'I saw,' Charlie said. 'And I believe she was frightened. But she was brave enough to give me some information that might help get Puff out of her life for good. She's . . . special. I understand why you want to protect her.'

Stevens gave him a smile and a nod, then said, 'What now, Marinelli? Am I going to take a rip for this?'

'Well,' Vince replied, absently scratching one large testicle with his paw. 'I don't see any reason to make a stink about this right now. But if we need your new roomie to come in, I don't want to get the runaround.'

Michael nodded again, and stood up. 'Minal told Flipper here everything she knows. Leave her out of it.'

'If I can,' said Vince, 'but if I were you, Stevens, I'd have been doing some poking around of my own, on the quiet. Fort Freak's a small place, don't want to ruffle up the dragon's scales. Just remember our numbers, if you turn up anything. We're all friends now. And friends share. Otherwise we'll have this talk again, *capisce*?'

SNAKE IN THE HOLE

by David Anthony Durham

Marcus eased one corner of the manhole cover up, pressed his cheek against it, and scanned the narrow sliver of the alley. Quiet. Still. A bit brighter than he liked because of one glaring spotlight, but he chose the spot because it was hidden from the street. And for its proximity to Bippee's Bagels.

Keep it quick, man, Marcus told himself.

He shoved the cover to the side as quietly as he could and thrust himself up into the chill night. The moving air prickled his skin, so different from the stale, rank air of the sewers. He tried to work the kinks out of his tail as he slid forward, wishing he was warmer and knowing the October chill would make him more and more sluggish the longer he was out.

Keep it quick.

The bagel shop backed on to the alley. There was a Dumpster a few strides from the door, but more often than not there were day-olds just tossed on the steps, as there were this evening. Marcus jammed a sesame in his mouth and grabbed up several more, clutching them to his chest. The dry bagel immediately felt like cardboard in his mouth. He needed a drink even more than food. But it had to be something clean. He'd already been a week wrapped around his roiling stomach after drinking sewer water. Felt like he was gonna die. He'd probably lost fifteen pounds and was still a bit light-headed because of it. Being a fugitive sucked. No doubt about it.

He decided to try the diner at the other end of the block. They put out their recycling daily. He didn't much care what he'd find in them, or whose backwash he'd be sucking down. He knew the thought should sicken him, but he couldn't help it. He craved liquid, sugar, syrup on his tongue and lips.

He had to slide through a narrow corridor beside the diner, just beneath the window and a little too near the street. He planned to only be in sight for a moment. Might've managed it too, except that his eyes darted up through the window and caught sight of a face on the late news, on a television hung from the ceiling of a diner.

His father? It couldn't be! But there was his name, right there in yellow letters. Marcus pressed against the grubby glass to watch, thirst forgotten, bagels spilling onto the ground. He couldn't hear their words, but he could read them crawling along the bottom of the screen.

> ANCHOR: Our affiliate in Baltimore caught up with re-spected surgeon Jerome Morgan at his North Baltimore home.
> REPORTER: Dr. Morgan, how does it feel to learn your son is wanted for murder and assault? He only left your home a few months ago, and now he's a gang associate, a murder suspect, linked with prostitution and …
> MORGAN: I am not taking questions. I have a statement to …
> REPORTER: Are you surprised by your son's actions?

The surgeon was trying to position the note to read, but couldn't seem to find the right angle among the press of microphones thrust at him.

> MORGAN: This … uh … has nothing to do with us.
> REPORTER: You don't dispute that the Infamous Black Tongue is your son, surely?
> MORGAN: My son was Marcus Morgan. He died to me months ago. Now …

REPORTER: Have you had any contact with him? Has Infamous Black Tongue reached out to you? Some have speculated that he's fled New York, perhaps with family aid.

The father met the woman's gaze, his unease replaced by something more derisive.

MORGAN: Infamous Black Tongue? You people with your names ... Look, he knows better than to contact us. Like I said, he's dead to us. That's what I came here to say. Please, leave us in peace.

He turned and moved away, waving the note at the reporters in dismissal.

Marcus slid down the wall and stayed huddled a long time on the filthy concrete there, amazed that after all he'd been through he still half hoped that his father would say he loved him, was proud of him, still believed in him. He had dreamed just the night before about returning to him, weaving all the way south to Baltimore. But that was stupid. It would never happen. 'I'm dead to him,' he said.

'Maybe to him,' a voice said, 'but not to us.'

Marcus snapped his head around. A big, muscled Chinese cop stood a few feet away, baton in hand.

'Don't do anything stupid, kid,' the cop said. 'We got the drop on you. Both of us.'

Another cop cleared his throat, this one standing in the alley that Marcus had just come out of. Slim white guy, with the latch on his holster up, his hand resting on his handgun.

'We already called it in,' the first cop said. 'Take it easy and this'll be no worse than it has to be.'

Marcus's eyes darted around, checking the alley, gauging the space, looking for a way out. 'Screw that. I'm not going to jail.'

'You gotta get this behind you, kid. One way or another. You've been, what, hiding in the sewers? You look like shit. You're eating left bagels? Man …' He reached around and unclipped his hand-cuffs. 'Come on. Man up and deal with what you've done.'

'I didn't do anything!' Marcus looked up. The lowest platform of the fire escape looked a little too high to reach, but his coils flexed instinctively.

The Chinese cop said, 'No you don't!' He pointed his baton at Marcus and sang in a high-pitched, girly voice. It was the weirdest thing. Until a pink, sparkly light bloomed around Marcus; then *that* became the weirdest thing. It freaked him out. He shot up and grabbed a gutter he thought had been out of his reach. He hauled himself away, expecting the other cop to open fire on him at any moment.

He didn't, but once on the rooftop Marcus realized why. He hadn't escaped anything. He shone like a half-snake lightning bug stuck in the glow mode, which made him a beacon, announcing himself to the police helicopters that came skimming toward him over the cityscape.

Marcus took off, slithering across the rooftops at whip-fast speed. He shot over the openings between buildings without look-ing down, rose and fell as the buildings did. But it didn't do him any good. The helicopters closed in, each movement of his clearer than if they had him spotlighted. In fact, they didn't even use their spotlights. They just followed his shimmering progress.

He gave up on the roof. He careened down a fire escape at free-fall speed and hit the ground hard enough that he had to lie there breathless for a moment. But not long. The helicopters hovered above and squad cars screeched in to one end of the alley, sirens screaming. He hurtled the opposite direction, frantic now, not really thinking, just squirming as fast as he could, nothing matter-ing but escape.

He didn't plan to end up on the Williamsburg Bridge. He just did. Halfway out he realized how bad a choice it was. Squad cars followed him. The bridge traffic slowed them, but squirming through the cars and pushing past panicked pedestrians didn't help him either. He heard sirens coming from the far side of the bridge. Above him the helicopters circled – not just cop ones anymore either, the press had joined the pursuit. A voice from a loudspeaker shouted that he was trapped. They ordered him to surrender. To lie down face on the ground, arms out to either side, tail straight out along the concrete.

He looked over the edge. The East River stretched below him. Black as the night and yet shimmering with the city's lights also. Would the fall kill him? Maybe, but what did it matter? He dove, his tail snapping out behind him as he fell. He heard an audible gasp from the crowd. At least he gave them a show. At least his father would know exactly how he went out, on the evening news, even.

Instead of death, though, the impact with the surface only hurt like fuck. Then he figured the water would kill him, but his tail swam better than his two legs ever had. Squirming, he dove deep and stayed down as long as his breath held, getting as far away as he could, only coming up once he was under the docks and hidden.

Father Squid set a steaming teacup down on the table gently. The suction cups on his fingers made light popping sounds as they released the porcelain. Marcus might not even have heard the sound if he hadn't been watching the motion of the man's hands, so large and powerful, in contrast to the delicate china.

'Do you take milk?' the priest asked.

'Milk?' Marcus asked.

'Yes,' Father Squid said, 'in your tea? Would you like milk mixed in?'

'Oh, no.' Marcus picked the cup up by its dainty handle. 'No thanks.' He slurped the brown liquid, felt the sudden heat of it fill his mouth and had to force himself not to spit it out. He swallowed. 'I never really drank tea much.'

The priest of Our Lady of Perpetual Misery took a seat across from him, the two them alone in the quiet church office. He tented his hands on the table and studied Marcus. Father Squid had always been a solid, broad joker. The years had not diminished him much. Enclosed within his priestly cassock, he was still a formidable bulk of a man. With his gray-skinned face, large eyes, and the cluster of tentacles that hung down over his mouth, twitching, he could easily have been frightening. Marcus had almost bolted on first sight of him, before the man's gentle gestures and kindly voice won him over.

'I don't suppose you get much opportunity to drink tea these days,' the priest said. 'I can see by looking at you life as a fugitive has been hard. Hard. You may not believe me, but I've been following your story very carefully.'

Marcus smirked. 'Yeah, you and everybody else in the city.'

'The people like a story. You've given them that.'

'Infamous Black Tongue,' Marcus said. 'How stupid is that?'

The priest shrugged his massive shoulders noncommittally.

'You know the weird thing is that yesterday I picked up a copy of the *Cry*,' Marcus said. 'I sat there reading about Infamous Black Tongue, and it was like ... like I'd forgotten that they were talking about me. Like I was reading about some other guy. It was almost ... fun. And then I remembered.' Marcus set his cup down, and then picked it up. And then set it down again. 'And then I felt sick all over again.'

'I'm sorry, son,' Father Squid said. 'Yours is a difficult situation. A fugitive. Murder pinned on you. Injured cops. Police mug shots blazing across the newspapers and television screens. Oddity bent on destroying you. They know not what they do, Marcus. Please understand that.'

Marcus didn't want to talk about Oddity. 'The cops know what they're doing. They're all crooked.'

'No, not all.'

'And the newspapers too!' Marcus couldn't help raising his voice. 'That editor is always writing about me. Lies. All lies! It's like he hates me.'

'No, Marcus, no. Lucas Tate is a good man. You must see things from his perspective ...'

'Why? They're not seeing things from mine!'

'No, they're not,' Father Squid agreed. He blinked, nictitating membranes sliding back and forth across his eyes slowly. 'But you are the one in trouble, Marcus. Not they. You are the one that must be careful. Thoughtful. Sage in how you act.'

'Tell me you'll help me. Keep me hidden.'

'I cannot do that, son.'

'What? I thought that's what your church was all about – protecting jokers!'

'Our Lady of Perpetual Misery is a place of refuge, yes. And I believe there is more to your story than the police have admitted. I even believe you've been wronged. But hiding and running will not solve this for you. You cannot possibly hope to hide forever, not in the sewers of Jokertown, not elsewhere, either. No, the only way through this is to face it.'

Marcus suddenly felt like crying. To keep from giving in to that, he said, 'Don't tell me you want me to turn myself in.'

'That is an option to pray on. You could tell …'

'Bullshit!' Marcus tossed his teacup down, too hard. The bottom chipped as it skittered across the tray and tipped onto its side. It rolled in a sharp crescent before the handle caught and stilled it. 'Forget I even came here,' he said, rising up on his coils, preparing to depart.

The priest rose, surprisingly fast, and set a hand on Marcus's shoulder. The motion brought with it a salt tinge, a scent like the sea. Marcus found it strangely calming.

'Marcus,' the joker said, 'if you won't go to the police, go to Lucas Tate. You may think he's your enemy, but in many ways he's been a champion for jokers and an enemy to corrupt cops. He may well listen to you. If he writes your side of the story the police will have to deal fairly with you. You must promise me you will do him no harm, though. If you can promise that, I can tell you where to find him.'

Marcus crossed his arms. 'I don't know,' he said grudgingly. 'Maybe. I'm not promising anything.' And then, aware of how ungrateful he sounded, he added, 'Sorry about the teacup.'

◆

Marcus returned to his subterranean world. It wasn't easy scrounging food and clean water, but the subway lines helped him move around under the city in ways he couldn't above it. He learned to hear oncoming trains from far off, to recognize when they were on his line or not. He learned to anticipate the distance between side tunnels and maintenance areas. He could usually bypass station stops, and the work crews were easy to avoid. He felt signs of other things living down here, even sensed the movements of giants at times. He kept well clear of them. At some instinctual level he understood that he'd staked out a section of the underworld and marked it with his scent, like an animal communicating with other animals. Maybe that's what he was becoming. An animal.

Unlike an animal, though, he knew music when he heard it. It was music that drew him to the theater. He'd never heard anything like it. From a distance he found it discordant, like it had too many notes and too many of them worked against each other, but he couldn't help wanting to hear more, perhaps just to be near whoever was creating it. The notes came to him muffled by distance, echoing in the subterranean chambers. As he worked his way nearer, he found a sensuous rhythm in the way the plucked notes of the string instrument entwined with the beating hearts of several drums and tinkling of bell-like instruments.

He squirmed up close to the gap in the wall and poked his head through. The music was louder here, clearer. He slipped through the opening, pushed through the stage machinery that hid it, and crept closer. The music grew louder still.

A theater! He was in a theater, beneath the seating. He felt the heat and hum of the audience just above him. There were openings through which he could see the backs of people's legs. He hung back for a time, but before long he needed to see whatever it was they were seeing. Finding a clear area, he peered through. That's how he saw her.

God, she's beautiful.

In the center of the stage a single figure swayed at the hips, her feet stepping delicately and her arms like serpents as they twisted in time with the music. Slim and dark brown, with large eyes elongated with black pen, her cheeks powered with gold flecks, lips full and sensuous: she was indeed beautiful. Her black hair trailed down her back in one hawser-heavy braid. It moved and flexed like another muscled appendage. Around her torso ribbons of light writhed like the coils of a serpent.

Marcus leaned forward, transfixed.

Energy rippled in the air around her, filling the chamber as if with an extension of herself that was somehow physical and auditory and seismic. The serpent coils slipped around her hips, gaining tangible form, sliding over themselves. Marcus felt parts low in his tail stir to life, throb and press against his scales. There was lust in the feeling, but that was just part of it. It was pure excitement also, a feeling of joy that seemed to pass from the dancing woman right into his deepest regions.

The feeling grew as the serpent shapes became ribbons that stretched out into larger orbits above her. The woman climbed up on to the ribbons and danced atop them, leaping from one to another. At times she stepped right off into empty air, only to be caught as she began to fall. For a while the shimmering energy fields became ghostly human forms, a troop of dancers mimicking her moves like stylized light-energy versions of herself.

At the conclusion, the music and visuals faded and the woman stood alone on the stage as the audience erupted in applause. 'Thank you. Thank you,' she said. She spoke for a moment in a language Marcus didn't understand, and then said, 'I am Natya.' She entwined her hands, wrapping them around each other like two snakes in a mating dance. A moment later she stilled, the fingers of both hands stretching out like the delicate flower that bloomed above her.

Natya. Marcus never saw her leave the stage. He just realized she had as the flower faded and the energy fields dissolved and the stage lights dimmed. He sat there for a long time after the theater cleared out above him, stunned, thinking, *I've found a reason to live.*

If he was going to live he had to clear his name. That's why he slipped inside an unlocked window of an apartment late the next night. He had to test a few, stretched up as far as he could reach, but he found one. He'd staked out the place enough to know that Tate was alone, no spouse, no kids, no dog. He hoped Father Squid was right. He wasn't at all sure, but he had to do something.

Once inside, Marcus stood coiled, listening, taking in the place. Even in the dim light he could feel the expense of the decor. He could almost smell it. Antique furniture, an intricate Asian rug, a piano the size of a tank, lined with slim-limbed statuettes. *African,* Marcus guessed. Masks of all shapes and sizes hung displayed on one long wall, a United Nations of masks. Some looked menacing, with monstrous, elongated features, wide-mouthed grimaces. Others were intricately beautiful, delicate and finely crafted. Still others appeared to be plastic or cheap cloth, like costumes kids would wear at Halloween.

A fucking mask museum, Marcus thought as he slid beneath them. *Everybody needs a hobby.* He moved down the hallway toward the snoring in the master bedroom.

The guy lay on his back. For a moment Marcus thought a sheet covered him, but then he realized it was a black hood. *People are getting weirder and weirder,* he thought. He moved quickly to the bed and clamped a hand down at the base of where he thought the man's throat should be. His other hand he cocked into a fist, and he brought his coils flowing up onto the bed to press the man down. The hood's eyeholes showed the man's eyes snap open. Marcus wanted to yank the cloth off, but something held him back.

'Are you Tate? Lucas Tate?'

The man nodded.

'I'm not here to hurt you. I just need someone to listen. The cops won't.' Marcus stared at the formless black satin a moment. He'd expected a bit of groggy protest. Instead, the eyes just barely visible through the fabric stared at him. 'What are you hiding behind the mask?'

The answering voice was unnervingly calm. 'I'm not hiding anything. I'm at home in bed, easily found, obviously. I've nothing to explain. You, however … you think laws don't apply to you or something?'

Releasing him and drawing back a little, Marcus asked, 'You know who I am?'

Tate gathered himself up, tugging his pajamas in order to solidify his dignity. 'If you're not Infamous Black Tongue I'll step down as the *Cry*'s editor.' He let his eyes drift over Marcus's coils. 'I trust my job is secure. What do you want?'

'I want you to stop writing lies about me.'

'I get at the truth as best I can and put it out there. Always have.' Tate scooted away slightly. He pressed his back against the elaborate metal headrest. 'So you're here to bully me? Good luck, but you're not the first thug to try.'

'I'm not bullying anyone,' Marcus said. 'Just listen. I didn't kill anyone! I tried to stop Twitch from being killed. The cops did it. Those cops are dirty, man! Every word out of Lu Long's mouth is a lie. You can see that, right? You know about police corruption and all that, don't you? I heard … I mean, someone told me that you used to fight corruption.'

The hooded eyes seemed to be considering, sizing him up. At least he was listening; that was an improvement. Marcus kept talking. Tate, as far as he could tell, kept listening. When he'd talked himself silent, Tate said, 'Sounds like a difficult situation.'

'Seriously screwed up.'

The fabric of the mask billowed near the nose as Tate exhaled a laugh. 'No matter what else it is – it's that. Best you can do may be to play by the rules. Turn yourself in. Get your lawyer in the loop. Talk it through with the police. They're not all—'

'No way. Why's everyone keep saying that? I'll never trust a cop again! They'd say they caught me. They'd shoot me dead and say I was trying to escape or something and everyone would believe them. Think like a reporter, man! You know things go down that way.'

Tate was silent for a moment. 'You've got a point there,' he finally said, his voice softening. 'Listen, I'm not saying I buy your entire story, but it deserves looking into.'

'Yeah? You'll look into it?'

'Sure. I'm a reporter at heart.' He kicked his legs over the edge of the bed and reached down for his slippers. 'Let me get a pad and pen. I'll make some notes. I'll ask some questions. We'll get to the bottom of this. Don't you worry. Hey, you hungry? I've got some leftovers from a dinner party last night. I make a mean *bigoli* con salsa, you know.'

Marcus had no idea what that was, but still he felt the tension drain out of him, right down the long length of his tail. 'Yeah, I could do with a bite to eat.'

THE RAT RACE

PART 9.

Michael's eyes glittered in the light of the votives on the altar. He looked at them like he wanted to touch them, to run his fingers through the flames in a quick, warm pass that would leave them sooty. But he didn't. He asked Father Squid, 'So the Infamous Black Tongue came here, and you told him what?'

'I told him that this is a safe place,' replied the priest carefully. 'And I thought perhaps he'd rest here a bit. But he changed his mind – I don't know why. He's terribly afraid.'

Leo snorted. 'Yeah, well. He ought to be.'

Father Squid shook his head slowly. 'The whole city wants him. His jitters are understandable.'

'Is he injured?' Leo thought to ask, knowing that would be too easy.

'I don't believe so. He was exhausted from running, but I don't think he was hurt. And he's quite young. He recovered quickly.'

Michael's cell phone rang, but he didn't want to take the call in the sanctuary. He said, 'Excuse me,' and left through the nearest side door.

'Hey, Father,' Leo said in a tone that implied a change of subject. 'I wanted to ask you something. Something you said the other night. You said you knew Lizzie Wallace, the counter girl who died at the Rathole.'

Father Squid turned to tend to the candles, or to stall. 'I knew her, yes. Lovely woman.'

'Were you a regular there, back then?'

His back still turned, his body cast in shadows from the brightness before him at the front of the church, Squid said, 'I suppose.'

'Do you know anything about her boyfriend?'

The priest turned, just enough to show his profile, backlit by the small flames. 'I beg your pardon?'

'She had a boyfriend. Some slimeball, is all I know. Gangbanger. No one wants to give me a name on him, but that only makes me think he was actually dangerous.' Leo pulled out his notepad and clicked open a pen, just in case he was about to hear something worth writing down.

'Ah,' Squid said, and he faced Leo once more, leaning back on his hands against the table. 'It's been a long time, but I knew of him, yes. He became rather notorious; it doesn't surprise me that no one wants to talk about him, even now.'

'But you will?'

'His name was Peter, but I believe you may know of him as Warlock. He was in the Werewolves, years ago. Ran the club, eventually. I think.'

Leo's pen froze, leaving a wet blue daub on the notebook's thin-lined page. 'Wait a minute. Warlock?'

'Oh, yes.'

'Warlock,' Leo repeated under his breath, and once again the pen nub moved in a swift scribble. Behind him, the side aisle door opened and Michael came back inside, slipping his cell phone back into a pocket.

Father Squid continued. 'I don't know where he is these days. I'm not sure how you'd go about finding him.'

'I do.' Leo quit scribbling and slapped the notepad shut. 'He's in lockup on Governor's Island. Got himself convicted of manslaughter a couple years ago.'

'But he might not want to talk.'

Leo grunted. 'He likes to talk. He's his own worst enemy.'

Michael waited out the tail end of this conversation and said,

'Leo, I've got something waiting for me back at the station. We done here?'

'I think so.'

'Then thanks for your time, Father,' Michael said, and after a round of handshakes, the two cops were on their way. As they walked the return blocks, they tightened their coats and shivered, adjusting hands into pockets and stomping feet to keep them full of feeling.

'Hey, Leo,' Michael said with a little reluctance.

'Hey what?'

'You were doing it again, just now. Weren't you?'

'Doing what?' Leo asked.

'Digging around in the Rathole stuff. While I was on the phone.'

Leo said, 'So what? What shit do you give if I ask a couple extra questions?'

'I don't,' he said, too fast. 'I really don't, but other people, you know. And we've got all these open cases, waiting around, stinking up the place. Maybe you should—'

'Maybe I should what?' Leo interrupted.

Michael backed down. 'Maybe you should be more careful, is all I'm saying. You don't have much time left with the badge, and there's no sense in screwing it all up at the last minute. Hey,' he said suddenly, brightly. 'Maybe after New Year's you could go get your private license, and do some detecting that way. That way nobody would yell at you about it.'

'Mind your own business,' he groused. And then his own phone rang. He answered it, and without any preamble or pleasantry, he was treated to the shouted declaration, 'Leo, I've been robbed!'

'Tate, is that you?'

'Of *course* it's me. Same as the rest of the thefts in the papers – just like that, gone! This is getting ridiculous – I won't stand for it!'

Leo wanted to tell him to 'get in line' if he wanted to register a complaint with the department's handling of the burglaries, but he didn't. He asked, 'Did you file a report?'

'Of course I filed a report. But no one there would tell me a goddamned thing, so—'

'What makes you think I'll tell you any different?'

'I'd like to think we're friends.'

'Sure, we're friends. But the force ain't holding out on you, Lucas. We're stumped, and we're working on it. I swear to God, that's all I've got. That's all anybody's got over here.' He folded his notebook shut and stuck the pen to its cover. 'What'd you lose?'

Lucas swore softly, and said something to someone else. It was muffled, like his hand was over the receiver. Then he said to Leo, 'A few things that aren't worth a damn, and a few things that are irreplaceable. Mostly, I'm upset about the masks.'

'Ah.' Those precious, ridiculous, ubiquitous masks of Tate's. 'I see.'

'Some of them were vintage pieces – absolutely irreplaceable. I lost a genuine Venetian carnival mask, a painted leather Jetboy mask that I practically *stole* at an estate sale, a vintage owl mask, a Holbrook's limited edition … and never mind the Monroe mask signed by Marilyn herself! If you don't recover it, I'll never be able to replace it. Never!'

'Masks. Okay. I'll …' He wasn't sure what to promise, so he said, 'I'll keep my eyes open for them. I assume you gave a more precise description when you filed your report.'

'Yes, I did.' He sounded impatient and none too pleasant, but Leo let it slide.

'All right then. Anything else I can do for you?'

'Doesn't sound like it.'

'Then I'll let you know if we learn anything.'

'Thank you. I appreciate it,' Lucas Tate said before hanging up.

Leo sighed, glanced at the time on his phone, and said, 'Fuck it.'

'Fuck what?' Michael asked. 'Lucas got his stuff lifted?'

'Yeah. I'm going to go talk him off a ledge,' he lied. 'I'll catch you back at the station.'

FAITH

PART 2.

October, 2010

Father Squid wasn't much of a drinker even in his wild days, and now, he thought, it was too late to turn for solace in that direction.

He sat alone in the small, comfortably furnished living room of his rectory, the only light in the room the soft glow of his television set, tuned to a Knicks game with the sound off. He watched the patterns made by the players as they ran back and forth, up and down the court, without comprehension. His mind was still occupied with the conversation he'd had with Storgman who was, unwittingly perhaps, dogging the ghosts of his past with the determination of a bloodhound on the scent.

December, 1978

Dorian Wilde leaped to his feet, threw his hands up in the air, and let out an exasperated cry that sounded something like 'Hnnngghhh!' He clutched at his flowing, greasy hair with his right hand. The tentacles that made up his left just twitched animatedly and dripped a foul-smelling goo over the sleeve of his Edwardian jacket.

'No! No! NO!' he yelled up at the actors on the makeshift stage. He wasn't happy. 'I know,' he said to the batrachian joker playing Balthasar, 'that you're a simple *bouncer* in a common *bar,* but you are *supposed* to be one of the *Wise Men,* not a *wise guy.* If you cannot speak the lines I have written with eloquence and passion, at least *try* to remove those atrocious Brooklyn accents from your voice. Again!'

The joker cleared his throat and said, 'Hark! We gotta follo yonda star to da manager—'

Dorian tore at his hair again and groaned, 'Manger! Manger! Manger!' He glared at Father Squid. 'George Bernard Shaw never had to put up with this!'

'I'm sure he had his problems too,' Father Squid said mildly.

'You simply must get me better quality actors – for the important roles, anyway,' Wilde complained. 'These hacks simply *are not* believable as Wise Men.'

Father Squid sighed. Never in a million years would he have believed when he'd decided to take the cloth that one of his duties would be that of casting director. But there it was.

'It's hopeless,' a pessimistic Wilde commented.

'Nonsense,' Father Squid said. 'It's going splendidly. They just need a little more practice.'

Wilde grunted gloomily.

'It's late and I could use some coffee, and a bite to eat,' Father Squid said. 'What say we break for the night? Tomorrow will be a better day.'

'What makes you think that?' Wilde said.

'Faith, my son,' Father Squid asserted. 'We must have faith.'

'I put my faith in drink,' Wilde said, 'and I could use a strong one. How about that new place – the Crystal Palace. I hear that it's quite the venue – and the proprietress is supposed to be something to see.'

'Hmm, yes,' Father Squid said. Wilde was right about Chrysalis, the owner of the Palace. But it was Lizzie whom the priest really wanted to see. 'The Rathole is near at hand. Their portions are certainly bigger and their prices cheaper.'

'Ah, yes,' Wilde said with a puckered mouth. 'My favorite. Cheap, abundant slop.' He waved his tentacles at the stage. 'Dismissed. Go home, and for God's sake, *rehearse.*'

The Rathole was quiet when the priest and the poet walked in. A few drowsy patrons sat nursing mugs of coffee, one plainly asleep, his heads on the table and snoring in unmelodic counterpoint. The dive looked just about what a place in Jokertown called the Rathole would look like. Mismatched tables and chairs. A cracked linoleum floor. An old-fashioned counter with torn and scarred Naugahyde seats. Dim lighting – which was probably for the best. Although it was surprisingly clean and potted plants were scattered around the countertop and tables and in window boxes, providing an element of surprising color in an otherwise dull and lackluster setting. *Lizzie's doing,* Father Squid thought. She was unrelentingly cheerful no matter her surroundings.

She was working the night shift alone again, except for Hash, the short-order cook. Father Squid worried about that, but Lizzie laughed off his concerns, telling him that the Rathole was safe as anywhere in Jokertown … besides, Hash kept a sawed-off shotgun in case a customer got squirrelly. That did little to ease Father Squid's mind. He knew that Hash dealt drugs out the back door as a sideline, and mixing drugs, cash, and guns was always a recipe for disaster.

Father Squid and Wilde took seats at the counter behind which Lizzie floated a few inches off the floor. It was a minor power, but useful for a waitress who worked long shifts. She was a small girl, plump and smiling, with large dark eyes and short dark curly hair. She was on the cute side of plain though to Father Squid her smile was one of the most beautiful he'd ever seen. Her jokerhood was as minor as her power. Her skin glowed an iridescent green, which to Father Squid's eyes was rather pleasing. But it was her smile that had taken his heart.

'Glad you could come by,' she said to them. 'How was your day?'

'Fabulous,' Wilde said. 'I always enjoy—' He stopped when he realized that Lizzie was paying him no attention whatsoever.

'Excellent,' Father Squid said. 'The pageant rehearsals go well.'

'Wonderful!' Lizzie leaned closer to Father Squid. 'I'm making something for you, for the pageant. I'll show it to you – later.'

Dorian Wilde coughed discreetly. 'Can I trouble you for some coffee? If I'm not interrupting, that is?'

'Of course not,' Lizzie said, turning her smile on him. 'The Pie Lady was just here,' she added, 'and she dropped off some yummies. Apple. Key lime. Chocolate—'

The Pie Lady was a fixture around Jokertown. She hawked her homemade comestibles on the street and to eateries like the Rathole. As opposed to Hash, she could actually cook.

'Apple,' Father Squid said.

'That sounds good,' Wilde said.

'You got it, boys.' She floated off into the back and soon returned balancing a tray loaded with a slice of apple pie on a plate, the rest of the pie on a bigger plate, a pot of coffee, two large mugs, spoons, and forks. She slid the single piece in front of Wilde and the rest of the pie in front of Father Squid.

'Hey,' Wilde said, 'how come he gets the whole ...' But his voice trailed off as he saw the expression on Lizzie's face as a new customer entered the diner. His features were hidden by a cheap plastic Marilyn Monroe mask, a poor match with his tall, strongly built frame and his black leather jacket with silver chains dangling from his shoulders. 'Who's the rough trade?' the poet asked.

From the look on Lizzie's face, Father Squid thought he knew who he was.

'I told you not to come around here, Peter,' Lizzie said in a voice that tried to be brave.

'Since when do I listen to crap from women?' The mask muffled his voice only a little. 'Especially my woman.'

'I don't belong to you, Peter.'

The mask jiggled as he frowned underneath it. 'You belong to me until I say you don't. And don't you ever forget it, bitch.'

'See here—' Wilde began.

Peter glanced in his direction. 'Shut up, faggot.' He turned his gaze at Father Squid, who was rising ponderously from his stool. 'And you sit your fat ass down.'

Father Squid rose, somewhat resembling an island emerging from the sea.

'Bob—' Lizzie began in a warning voice.

'It's all right, Lizzie,' Father Squid said pleasantly.

The man she called Peter looked past Father Squid. 'This lard-ass the new boyfriend? A priest? Jesus, he's one ugly motherfucker. I always knew you was kind of simple, Lizzie, but I never knew you were stupid enough to leave me for an ass-face like this.'

'I didn't—'

'That's right,' Peter said. 'You didn't leave me. You went on a little vacation. Sure. I understand. You just get your shit together and come on back.' Father Squid could hear anger behind his deceptively mild words. 'It'll be just like before. It'll be good times, baby. Things are coming together. You'll see.'

Lizzie shook her head, her lips compressed in a thin line.

'She doesn't want to go back to you,' Father Squid said reasonably. 'Why don't you—'

Peter turned on him. 'Why don't you shut the fuck up, lard-ass?'

Any second now, Father Squid thought. 'Son—'

He knew that word would do it.

Peter hurled himself at the priest, reaching for a length of chain that dangled off his shoulder. He was taller than Father Squid, though the priest was broader by far. He probably also believed himself faster and meaner.

But in another life, under another name, Father Squid had killed from close at hand and from far away, and once you've done that you never forget how. His body moved ponderously, but his curious-looking hands were fast and strong. His long, attenuated fingers caught Peter's right wrist, stopping him from swinging the chain, and his throat. Father Squid squeezed and Peter's cry of rage turned into a gasp for breath.

'Let's be reasonable,' Father Squid suggested. 'All right?'

Peter's head bobbed up and down, and Father Squid released him. Peter put his hands to his throat, gasping for breath.

Father Squid counted slowly to himself. *One ... two ... three ...*

Peter hurled himself at the priest again, this time with a raspy scream of rage. Father Squid slapped him once, hard enough to send him spinning to the floor and knock the mask off his face. He crouched there for a moment, blood spraying from his nose and running over the hands covering his face. If he was a joker, his abnormality wasn't apparent. His face, what the priest could see of it, was plain, with undistinguished features. Except for his eyes. They were crazy.

'My mask! You took off my mask!' Peter pushed to his feet, but Father Squid, the veteran of countless fights, knew that he was finished. 'I'll get you for that, you fat fuck!' He looked straight at Lizzie. 'And don't think I'll forget you either, bitch.' He lurched to the door and out into the night. Most of the Rathole's scattered patrons didn't even seem to notice.

Wilde looked at the priest speculatively. 'What was your rank?'

'You're very clever,' Father Squid said.

'I am,' Wilde said. 'But it doesn't take a high degree of perspicacity to figure out who's the punk and who's the soldier.'

'Sergeant,' Father Squid said ruefully. 'Four times.'

'Vietnam?'

'"Last to go,"' Father Squid quoted, '"first to die."'

'Motto of the Joker Brigade.' Wilde looked at Father Squid's impassive face. 'We'll get drunk some night and you'll tell me all about it. I could get a sonnet cycle out of it.'

Father Squid shook his head. 'Some things I have no wish to relive.'

October, 2010

If I hadn't humiliated him so thoroughly, the priest thought again, as he had thought so many, many times over the years. *If I had shown some grace, instead—*

Another hand had pulled the trigger, Father Squid knew, Warlock's or Deedle's or someone else, but deep inside he was still convinced that his own actions had made the killer pick up the gun. He couldn't think of that without wanting to die himself.

Leo Storgman was peeling away the layers one by one. But there was still so much that Ramshead did not know. About Lizzie, about Deedle, about Father Squid himself. *All my sins return to haunt me.* Father Squid wondered how long it would take the detective to uncover all the rest of it. And what he would do when that day came ...

THE RAT RACE

PART 10.

A uniformed guard led the prisoner into the row where all the little orange phones were lined up in the narrow, privacy-free booths. Leo wasn't sure what he'd been expecting, but he was surprised anyway.

Much like Lucas Tate and any number of other jokers of a certain age, Warlock had lived a lifetime without appearing in public unmasked. His devil's mask had once been a symbol of intimidation on the streets – a fierce warning and a mean reminder that the gangs ruled and everyone else could play along or die.

But as the big man in the blue jumpsuit settled onto the stool and picked up the orange phone, Leo racked his brain trying to recall having ever set eyes on the convict's face before. It must've been made public at some point. During a trial, or during booking. But he couldn't place it.

He gazed at the face of a large white man now well into his fifties. There was nothing remarkable about it, except it was flat – like it'd been pushed into a wall one time too many. His nose was crushed down until it pointed at his upper lip. His eyes were small and dark, and squinted like maybe he was nearsighted and didn't want to wear glasses.

He said, 'What do you want?' into the phone as if he wanted to strangle it.

'I want to talk about Elizabeth Wallace.'

For a split second, a puzzled frown bloomed on the joker's face – then it faded into realization. 'I remember her. But that was a long time ago. What do you care, anyway? And who are you?' He eyed the detective hard, looking to infer something useful. 'Some old cop from Fort Freak.'

'Yeah, that's me. The boys call me Ramshead.' Leo pointed at his horns, using the joker name on the off chance it might give him something in common with the convict. Something to remind Nance that kind of, in a certain way, they were the same breed.

The sneer on Warlock's face didn't tighten, but it didn't ease. 'Good for them, or good for you – whatever. So you want to talk about Lizzie, huh?'

'Her, and the Rathole. What happened there, back in '78?'

'Bunch of people died.'

Leo nodded. 'Including Lizzie. You have anything to do with it?'

The dark, deep-set eyes went even narrower. 'What's it matter now? Nothing you can do about it. Nothing you can do to *me*.'

'That's true,' Leo let him think it. 'But rumor had it, she was stepping out on you. Any truth to that?'

Warlock leaned back, forgetting he was on a stool and there was nothing to support him. He came forward again, toying with the receiver. 'Might've been. Might not've been. But I didn't like hearing about it, either way.'

'You do something about it?' Leo asked.

Whatever Warlock had been weighing, he made a decision and said, 'Sure I did. Not that you could prove it.' Warlock was talking about his 'death curse.' 'I cursed her,' the convict said, as if he were afraid he hadn't spelled it out clearly enough.

But Leo had never believed in death curses – from aces, jokers, or anybody else. 'That curse thing. It always works?'

'*Always.*' The sneer was smug now, and even less pretty than before. 'And I didn't like what I heard about Lizzie, so I put her on the list. You know how it was, back then. Me on top. Couldn't have that kind of thing floating around.'

'Sure. So when she turned up pregnant with some other guy's kid—'

Warlock jerked – a little spasm of honest surprise.

The detective said, 'You didn't know.'

Nance sniffed. 'Wouldn't have changed anything. And if she was pregnant, it was mine. You can bet the farm on *that*.'

This gave Leo an idea. 'You want to put your DNA where your mouth is? I bet I can chase up some tissue samples to prove for sure.'

'Yeah, I don't care. I know what I know,' he said, but the sneer was slipping.

'Okay. I'll hold you to that,' Leo vowed. 'Anyway, you killed her. That's what you're telling me. With your death curse. How's that work?'

'I curse people and they die.'

'That's not what I'm asking. I know your record. Last I heard you'd been batting a thousand since the sixties. That's one hell of a success rate. You ever decide a curse is taking too long, or that karma needs a helping hand? Or a helping .45?'

'No! I don't! Because I don't *have* to. When I curse somebody, that's *it*,' he asserted with a chop of his hand, left to right. 'I just sit back and wait. And I never wait long.'

'That's a big claim.'

'I've got a big power.'

'I hear you've got a big phobia too, just like a little kid,' Leo said, fishing for something in his pocket. He found it.

Warlock said, 'I'm not afraid of anything. I'm sure as hell not afraid of some stubby old cop with curly little horns that aren't even pointy or nothing. Some useless little old joker cop. That's all you are. And you ain't got nothing.'

'I got a mirror,' Leo said. He lifted it up – a small compact, the kind that goes in a lady's purse. In fact, one that had come from Wanda's purse. She'd left it at his house, and he'd tossed it into a pocket, intending to return it.

The mirror was no bigger than two inches square. But it elicited a high squeak from Warlock, who threw himself off the stool in an effort to look away. The receiver fell from his hand and dangled from its cord, slapping back and forth against the reinforced glass and the wall. 'That's not fair! Put it away!'

'Oh, I'll put it away. As soon as you tell me—'

'I'm not telling you *dick*. Guard!' he called. 'Hey, guard! Get me away from this fucking lunatic! Get me away from him!' he demanded. He begged. And he never once looked back toward the tiny reflective square that Leo pressed up against the window, right at face level.

The guard opened the door and Warlock would've fallen through it if another guard hadn't caught him.

Leo hung up the receiver and stuffed the mirror back into his pocket.

He made a mental note to hit up the lab for a swab kit; and when he got home that evening, he added 'Peter Nance' to his list of suspects on the white board.

THE STRAIGHT MAN

by Kevin Andrew Murphy

The apartment looked like it had once been a basement laundry room that had at some point been converted into an illegal bath-house. A discolored hot tub stood empty in one corner, and Jim had no idea how it had been fit down the stairs. Teleportation? Shrinking? Maybe someone had turned it two-dimensional then rolled it up like a large rug?

That's how Jim would have managed it, assuming he could do something as big as a hot tub, but the thought made him wince. It had been hard enough just working up to his clothes. And it still didn't explain why the place reeked of rancid fondue. But given Jokertown, there were a dozen explanations, each equally improbable but equally possible.

The wild card virus had shattered Occam's Razor over sixty years ago.

'So what's that smell?' asked one of the other prospective tenants. He appeared to be an ordinary college student, at least if you overlooked the thin green-lipped mouths that puckered his skin like scars. But this was hard when they all moved in unison when he talked. 'The guy who lived here before or what he ate?'

'A little bit of both.' The landlady was dressed in an orange-and-black pinafore printed with pumpkins and candy corn. It looked like something you'd see on a small child or very large doll, but in this case was appropriate: she looked like a five-foot Kewpie doll, with an oversized head, tiny body, vestigial wings, and wobbly little legs. 'Mr. Cheesy was very fond of cheese ...' She'd left her scooter at the top of the stairs and had come down clutching the handrail.

The last prospective tenant, a pygmy hippopotamus dressed like a bank clerk, glanced in the hot tub. 'Did he die here?' Only the neat gray pantsuit gave a clue as to her gender. That and the dangly light-up jack-o'-lantern earrings she was also wearing in honor of the day.

'No, he died at the clinic.' The landlady shrugged her stunted wings and handed the applications to both of them, and a significant moment later to Jim, who the wild card had just made beanpole tall and rail thin. He knew he wouldn't be getting this apartment either, even if he wanted a basement that smelled like dead cheese joker. Which at this point he did.

The department's temporary housing expired today, and tomorrow, he would have to grovel to Inspector Maseryk or, worse, to Captain Mendelberg. Anything was preferable.

Jim glanced over the application. Two months of hunting had got him over sticker shock. While ruinous compared to Phoenix, the price was reasonable for Manhattan, if a bit steep for Jokertown. He printed his name, along with the name of his employer – New York's 5th precinct, aka Fort Freak, the scarlet letter that confirmed him as a joker for all the apartments he'd tried to rent outside of Jokertown, rather than just an unusually tall, absurdly slim nat. Discrimination was illegal, of course, not that that stopped anything except coming out and admitting it.

The landlady looked at the form. 'Oh, you're with the precinct ...'

Jim felt his cell phone vibrate in his pocket, the tug of the department's leash. 'Just transferred last August.'

'Well, thank you, Detective McTate. I'll be giving this my careful consideration.'

The look in the huge Kewpie-doll eyes said it all. She went off to chat with the other two applicants as Jim checked his phone. The text from Tenry, his new partner, was succinct: POSSIBLE MAGPIE THEFT AT DIME MUSEUM: CAN YOU CHECK?

Jim glanced at the back of the landlady's enormous head and

texted back: SURE. The hippo would probably get the place anyway, due to actually needing the hot tub, even if it did smell like cheese. That was the way things worked in Jokertown: if you could pass as a nat, then you were treated as a nat. And if you were an ace …

Jim ducked out of the apartment, literally. The department psychologist back in Phoenix had suggested the transfer: in Manhattan, he might find acceptance, maybe even salvage his career, rather than being treated as the department's token joker-ace freak. Fat lot she knew.

There was a lot to get used to with his new body. For one, ducking for doorways. For another, looking down at the top of everyone's head. In Phoenix, while freaky enough, this had just consisted of getting an aerial view of hairstyles, noticing bald spots, and suddenly being unable to make eye contact with anyone wearing a hat. In Jokertown? Horns were as common as bald spots, cloaks were more common than hats, and eye contact with short people and hats were suddenly no longer mutually exclusive when someone's yarmulke winked.

Jim looked away from the giant eyeball that made up the crown of the joker's skull, walked faster, and shivered. Halloween in New York was also a heck of a lot colder than it was in Phoenix, and Jim now had no body fat and a hell of a lot more surface area relative to his mass index. He loped past an obvious pink wig, pink hair that was obviously not a wig, and a long rubbery green nose poking out of the hood of a black velvet cloak. The individual with the witch nose was pulling a collapsible shopping cart with a box with three bright-eyed kittens perched on top. Jim stole a glance back once he passed: the witch nose belonged to a green-faced witch mask. He hoped the kittens were just pets and costume accessories, but when a good portion of Jokertown's residents viewed the neighborhood pet shop and grooming salon as a combination beauty parlor and sushi bar, he knew he couldn't take that for granted.

Jim was glad the wild card had not given him a taste for kittens.

He was also glad that New Yorkers heated their lobbies, since while the Famous Jokertown Dime Museum was not yet open for viewing, it was open for ticket sales. Admission was now thirty-five dollars. But to be fair, the exhibits had gone more upscale as well. In place of the infamous 'hideous joker babies' in formaldehyde (now rumored to be relegated to some embarrassing back corner), the Dime Museum now showcased historic curios and waxworks. A particularly attractive example was mounted on a rotating platform: international supermodel and heroine, Michelle Pond, who was indestructible and could go from fat to thin in an instant. With her hands upraised, the improbably gorgeous platinum blonde looked like she was conjuring the bubbles coming out of a discreetly placed bubble machine.

Despite the fact that Bubbles was out of his league in the ace scale of things, known to be in at least one relationship, moreover lesbian, and had recently been the size and density of a lead zeppelin crashed into New Orlean's Jackson Square, Jim would still rather look at her than the joker behind the counter. He looked like another waxwork, but one that a thousand chain smokers had stubbed out their cigarettes in, flesh dripping from his face in frozen rivulets.

Instead of making eye contact, Jim read the joker's name tag: JASON. He leaned down and flashed his badge. 'You reported a theft?'

The joker nodded, then put out a BACK IN 15 MINUTES sign. 'Let me show you.' He led Jim through an archway labeled Hall of Villains. 'We caught it on the Turtle's cameras.'

Jim wondered since when the Great and Powerful Turtle, the world's most powerful telekinetic, was classed as a villain, but once they had passed waxworks of a blond hunchback kissing a severed head, an old man embedded in a section of brick wall, the horrible doughy bulk of an alien swarmling, and the even more horrible, more doughy, and more bulky immensity of the monstrous Bloat, chief villain of the Rox War, he saw the diorama and it was self-explanatory.

A car hung suspended from wires just below the skylight, the make and model obscured by a battleship plate and the spot where a license plate would go replaced with a battery of cameras. It was one of the Turtle's shells and it was pointed at a section of the original Brooklyn Bridge, infamously shattered by the Turtle in the Rox War. Beside one of the Victorian lampposts stood the reason the mysterious ace had broken it and an even greater villain: Herne the Huntsman.

The antlered porn star turned international terrorist held a battle spear upraised, sitting astride a rearing and anatomically correct black stallion. Whether Herne matched or exceeded the stallion was unanswered due to the angle and position of the terrorist's stag haunches and the artfully styled mane. There was a button on the explanatory plaque below the figures and Jim pressed it. Herne raised a great golden horn and an eerie call filled the vault, the echo of a primeval hunting cry as his and the horse's eyes glowed green. The Turtle's shell blazed alight in response and a quadrophonic version of the Mighty Mouse theme song thundered out of the speakers placed in the wheel wells.

Jim looked to Jason who simply pointed mutely to the next diorama, suspended in the vault at the same level as the Turtle and now spotlighted by one of the Turtle's floodlamps. Standing in an exposed portion of the gondola of a blimp that appeared patched together from weather balloons was a snarling man in an old-fashioned diving suit missing the helmet along with half his face. Not a joker but a scarred nat, the left half of his face replaced by a featureless metal prosthetic. The rest was a mask of rage and he had a .45 in one hand, the other on a swirled glass sphere glowing with its own light, a Chihuly sculpture from hell. It was a replica of the Takisian canister that had first brought xenovirus Takis-A to Earth and the disfigured nat could be none other than Dr. Tod, the career criminal who'd found it. He'd created the first black queens in his lab, along with the first jokers – if you believed in conspiracy theories, maybe even the first ace – then tried to black-mail Manhattan with an alien plague. He was the man who'd killed Jetboy, the first and greatest villain of the wild cards era.

Jim had an urge to shiv the waxwork with a two-dimensional hand, but it was at least fifteen feet up, and tall as he was now, his jump shot was not that good.

'Don't you see?' said Jason. 'We put it up there because we were having vandalism problems, but now somebody took the helmet. And it's authentic!'

'Authentic?' Jim said incredulously. 'Are you saying Dr. Tod survived the explosion? He's the first ace? Maybe he's been sharing a condo in Buenos Aires with Hitler's brain?'

'We're a history museum.' Jason rolled his eyes. 'Dr. Tod blew up with the blimp. But that suit didn't. It's from one of his henchmen, Smooth Eddy Shiloh. He jumped just before.'

Jim thought back to his elementary school history reports. 'The last man to see Jetboy alive. But no one pays to see a second-rate criminal, so you used the suit for Dr. Tod.'

Jason nodded. 'It's physically identical. Or at least it was until the helmet vanished.' He went over to a display under the Turtle's shell. There were a number of old televisions, a bucket seat from a car, and the words SEE WHAT THE TURTLE SEES! 'I got the feed hooked up so people can check it out from the website. Someone e-mailed and told me it was gone. Look.'

He punched a few buttons and Jim watched as the view in the TV screens changed. One moment, Dr. Tod's waxwork wore a copper diving helmet like you saw in old movies and cartoons. Then the camera panned dramatically to the glowing swirled menace of the virus canister and evil spiky letters Jim assumed were Takisian hazmat warnings. When it panned back, the helmet was gone. The time stamps read between 8:48 and 8:49.

'We open at ten,' Jason explained. 'I'm the only person here right now. Mr. Dutton's going to flip when he finds out.'

'Does that skylight open? Could someone have rappelled down?'

'Not unless they could phase through glass. That's been there since they cut a hole for the Turtle's shells.'

'So how do you get up to the exhibit? Have someone on staff who levitates?'

'We use a ladder,' Jason said. 'It's in the back.'

Jim had him get it so he could take direct photos of the crime scene. It was more a mobile staircase, but wasn't something that could have dodged the Turtle's other camera angles. He had to admit it was an ingenious way to hide security cameras. It was also going to make extra paperwork, but Jason was able to e-mail him a copy of the relevant footage, which would help.

'We'll be on it,' Jim promised, leaving Jason to contend with the horde of tourists now lined up with discount coupons in their hands and claws and assorted other appendages ready to pay thirty-five dollars or somewhat less to see the Dime Museum as a Halloween tradition.

Jim crossed Elizabeth Street, dodging the twelve-foot-tall guy with stilt legs who pulled a rickshaw around Jokertown. Jim looked, considering. Stilt Guy or whatever he called himself could have reached the diving helmet, but he'd also need to be able to walk through walls and turn invisible to get it, and while not impossible, it was unlikely. Jim shrugged it off.

Mostly, he was just glad the wild card had not made him that tall. Tall as he was, he was still in the nat realm of possibility, and not even the tallest guy on the force. That place was currently held by Beastie, aka Officer Bester, one of the rookies, who was the size of a grizzly and with his horns and snout looked like one of Sendak's Wild Things.

He was in the break room and Jim did a double take: Beastie's red fur now had large purple patches. But this looked not so much a case of a renewed wild card affliction as a case of Manic Panic hair dye. Bester was also wearing a huge purple tie-dyed T-shirt that he proudly displayed, silk-screened with a fin de siècle silhouette of a horrified nat, a prancing googly-eyed cow with its tail tied in an elaborate knot, and a verse Jim should have seen coming:

> I never saw a purple cow
> I hope to never see one
> But I can tell you anyhow
> I'd rather see than be one
>   – Gelett Burgess

Jim gave a weak smile. After all, if the wild card had turned you into an eight-foot-tall horned monstrosity, *what else* were you supposed to go as for Halloween?

Beastie was sitting in front of his chessboard, as usual, opposite Franny, the department's newest rookie, who was just wearing a paper crown. Except Francis Black was a nat, middling height, darker haired than Jim, but otherwise looking somewhat like what Jim remembered his body being last year. Last year before he'd eaten one too many donuts cramming for his detective exam, passed, and then stressed out trying to lose enough weight to pass his yearly physical.

The wild card had helped. It had stretched him out and slimmed him down till he was almost seven feet tall without an ounce of fat. Then, like a senile genie, it took it farther, letting him compress his molecules side to side until the phrase 'thinner than a razor' literally applied.

'Hey, Slim Jim!' Razor Joan called from over by the coffeemaker. 'Dr. Dildo brought dim sum. Come and get some before they're all gone!'

Razor Joan, aka Detective Lonnegan, was one of the department's other nats. She was First Grade Detective-Investigator to his Third Grade, and the one who'd hung him with an ace nickname that made people think of lock picks and jerky sticks. She had already reserved the name Razor for herself. But since she'd taken it off a joker serial killer with a Sweeney Todd fetish, she'd also saved Jim from possibly the greatest faux pas an ace could make in New York. He might as well move to London, call himself The Ripper, and expect that to go over well.

But just as there were worse jokers than just being extremely tall and thin, there were far more embarrassing ace names than Slim Jim. Case in point: Dr. Dildo, aka Officer Tranh, the vibrating ace. The dim sum he'd brought didn't look like any that Jim had ever seen. 'Is it ... Vietnamese?'

Dr. Dildo shook his head, making the chartreuse ostrich plume on his cavalier hat quiver. 'No, it's Takisian.' He picked up some strange thing wrapped in translucent pastry and popped it in his mouth, chewing delightedly.

Was it made with real Takisians? No one had seen Dr. Tachyon in years, so that was a distinct possibility. But given what Jim had seen on Asian menus around the city – jellyfish, sea cucumber, stuffed pig uterus – he had even less urge to sample exotic Takisian delicacies.

He sidled over to the next potluck table and looked for something safer. In the back was a brushed steel crock pot with a neatly printed label taped to the front: OTTO'S SECRET RECIPE CHILI. Jim didn't know 'Otto,' but he lifted the lid and sighed in relief. It was a meat chili, not some abomination with beans. He dished up a bowl, then looked for an eating utensil. 'Hand me a spork, could you?' he asked, spying a cup the other side of some guy with a flat top.

'Of course …' said a deep voice from below the retro haircut, 'but the … implement … is more properly termed a *runcible spoon*.' Jim accepted one from a hand almost as long and nearly as thin as his own, if far paler. 'They are not part of the standard surgical kit, but I find them uniquely suited for removing eyeballs …' Jim found himself looking down into a pair of these, hugely magnified but not by the wild card. Rather, this was accomplished by the thick Coke-bottle-bottom lenses of Dr. Gordon, the precinct pathologist. Gordon was tall, if still shorter than Jim's ludicrous height, and almost as thin, but dressed far more expensively. Usually. Today he'd traded the Armani for a lab coat marked MAD SCIENTISTS UNION #901H. He was also a hunchback, and this, combined with a habit of oversharing clinical details and talking as if he were narrating some personal melodrama, led to him being known as Gordon the Ghoul. But since the wild card had stretched both of them out in a similar fashion, for Jim's first couple weeks at the precinct – before Razor Joan's 'Slim Jim' moniker had thankfully taken hold – people had been describing him as Gordon the Ghoul's tall, tanned cousin Spike.

Jim could have lived with being called Spike. Not so much with being related to Gordon.

'Uh, thanks …' Jim grabbed a random soda and, as often happened when he became nervous, uncomfortable, or just plain creeped out, started to thin. He let it go all the way and ducked out of the break room, literally again, but also two-dimensionally, narrow enough to step through the crack between the door hinges. He didn't go 3-D again until he had safely slotted himself through the crack to his office.

Tenry Fong, Jim's partner, was fifty-four – twice Jim's age – and like Razor Joan, also a nat. He jumped, causing an avalanche of papers to spill off his desk. 'Would you not *do* that?'

'Do what?' Jim asked, three-dimensional again, or at least as three-dimensional as he got. 'I had my hands full, and Maseryk told me he wanted me to practice ...' He held up the drink and the chili, again 3-D. 'Didn't spill a drop.'

'Well, I suppose it is an improvement over last month's soda geyser.' Tenry scooped up the spilled files and proceeded to straighten them. 'Mendelberg wants to see some progress on the Magpie Burglaries, but all I'm seeing is a bunch of random thefts and no fingerprints.' He shuffled through a few files. 'If we don't have anything solid to investigate, she has suggested that we might assist with parade security this evening.' Jim's partner had an excellent poker face, but Jim could tell how little he relished that option – Mendelberg's 'suggestions' were legendary. She had 'suggested' that Tenry's previous partner take early retirement, and while that had freed up a desk and detective shield for Jim, his own status was still very much probationary. The Magpie Burglaries were now technically their case, insomuch as he and Tenry were the lowest-ranking detective team and Mendelberg had 'suggested' they look into them.

Tenry closed the top file and sighed. 'Any luck at the Dime Museum?'

Jim shrugged. 'Sort of. Mostly another Magpie theft. But there was security footage.'

'Oh?' Tenry asked.

Jim handed him his phone, letting the loop replay and briefing his partner.

Tenry handed the phone back and sighed. 'Did the apartment hunt go better?'

Jim shook his head and leaned against the wall.

'Apartments in New York can be difficult. I moved in with

my grandparents in the seventies, and after they passed on, their apartment belonged to myself and my wife – with the same rent,' Tenry added significantly and smiled. 'My two eldest daughters are in college now, and they've moved in with my parents, who are fortunately in good health, but …'

Jim popped the soda and began to tune out as Tenry waxed rhapsodic about his family's wonderful cheap rent-controlled apartments and the legal ways to game the system. Jim was from suburban Scottsdale and was probably the first in his family in generations to set foot in New York. He took a sip. The soda was berry-flavored, some store brand from a chain Jim had never heard of, but inoffensive enough. He then used the runcible spork to sample the chili. Not bad. A little wimpy on the peppers, but what was he supposed to expect from New Yorkers? But overall, not bad. He tried to place the meat. Beef? Chicken? Maybe venison?

It didn't matter. He was going to have to grovel to Maseryk or Mendelberg, and if he was going to do that, he'd need to solve a bigger mystery than what meats went into Otto's chili.

Jim picked up the phone and dialed the precinct clerk. 'Apsara? Anything new? Gang stuff with the Werewolves and Demon Princes? Burglaries? Theft? Anything need handling?'

'Hi Jim. Tony's Pets called. Special on kittens today. Someone's been eating them.'

'What, again?' Jim was really starting to hate Jokertown. 'Same guy?'

'Maybe,' Apsara said, 'but this time it's eating without paying.'

Jim remembered that case. Lupo the Wolf-Headed Wino, supposedly once a well-regarded Jokertown bartender but now just a sad middle-aged alcoholic who was so drunk he started to eat the kittens he bought before he left the shop. 'Could you get Beastie to handle that? He's better on these neighborhood cases.'

'Sure thing,' Apsara said. 'I was meaning to call him anyway.'

'Thanks.' Jim sighed. 'Any case that doesn't involve kittens?'

'What about cats?' Apsara laughed lightly. 'There's some crank on line three who keeps calling back. Says a giant black cat stole her Halloween candy. Want to deal with that?'

Jim put the soda can against his forehead to cool it. 'Sure, what-ever.'

'Thanks, Jim. You're a sweetheart.'

Part of being in any precinct was dealing with crank calls and other frequent fliers. Half were paranoid delusionals and the other half were lonely senior citizens. But since there was some overlap with both groups, there was a small percentage that were actual crimes. And given that this was Jokertown, even the ridiculous calls often bore investigation, since that was the only way to separate the delusions from bona fide reports of wild card powers at work.

Apsara patched the call through. 'Fifth precinct, Detective James McTate. I understand you've had a theft?' Jim listened as a hysterical woman (or at least a feminine voice) described what Apsara had said: the theft of a bowl of candy, magically stolen by a giant black cat.

In Phoenix, Jim would have dismissed the call as a crank, since the suspect appeared to be Mr. Mistoffelees, the Original Conjuring Cat. But in Jokertown? Since Jim himself could now creep through tiny cracks and walk on narrow railings, as per the song from *Cats*, he'd be a poor detective were he to dismiss the possibility that someone had turned their card in the middle of a production and was currently conjuring candy. The person on the line was also ranting about it being worth hundreds of dollars – which seemed a little pricey for chocolate, even in Manhattan – but even if the caller were certifiably insane, it at least warranted a welfare check.

And this could be a break. With the Magpie thefts, the items taken ranged from the costly to the lame, and a bowl of candy certainly went on the lame side. But unlike the others, here there was a witness. And while the *Jokertown Cry* had dubbed them the Magpie Burglaries, it would be ironic – though hardly impossible, given Jokertown – if instead of a metaphorical magpie, their cat burglar were an actual cat. Certainly it would explain the lack of prints.

'A lead?' Tenry asked, looking up from his desk.

Jim held out a hand, thinned it down to credit-card thickness, and waffled it. 'Maybe. Keep looking for patterns. I'll tell you if it pans out.' He went 2-D and ducked back through the door crack. It was only a couple blocks, and Jim had long legs now anyway.

Despite the Jokertown address straight across from the Dime Museum, a nat woman cracked the door, one blue eye peering out past the chain. The slice of her Jim could see was blondish and pretty if a bit on the chubby side, and not quite fitting the cheap pirate wench costume she was wearing. Jim flashed his badge. 'This the place with the missing candy?'

'My, you're tall ...' The woman stared up at him. 'Do you play basketball?'

'In college.' Jim didn't mention that was just with friends, when he was a foot shorter. But as most college teams didn't allow jokers, the subtext was that he was just an amazingly skinny nat.

She seemed to relax a bit. 'Please, come inside.' She fumbled with the chain, then held the door open. Jim ducked inside and took the place in. The apartment was neatly furnished, with white walls, brown bookcases, and a thick layer of dust on top of all of them. It was gross, but a sight Jim was getting used to and useful for gauging length of occupancy.

He took out a notepad and pen. 'Could I get your name again?'

'Shirley,' the woman said. 'Shirley Litt. Litt with a double T.'

'This your apartment?'

'No,' Shirley said. 'It belongs to my fiancé's brother. We're subletting.' She bit her lip. 'Oh, this is going to sound terribly shallow of me, but I was afraid you were going to be a joker. Not that there's anything wrong with that, mind you. I just have a little phobia ...'

Jim raised an eyebrow, glancing to the window and the neighborhood below.

Shirley nodded. 'I know. When Ted asked me to come to New York, I never thought ... He never told me his brother was a joker. Then last week, he told me he used to be one too ...'

This case was becoming uglier but more interesting by the moment. 'Used to be?'

'He grew up here,' she explained. 'He was born a joker. He showed me his childhood photos, and he looked hideous, but he said he was happy. But then that awful virus started killing him, and he said the doctors said the only way to save him was to give him the trump. So they did. And he turned into this absolutely gorgeous man who was always tripping over his own feet.' Her lower lip quavered as she wrung her pudgy hands around a huge diamond engagement ring. 'He used to have tentacles ...'

Part of being a detective was letting people talk when they were in a mood to, and Jim saw no reason to make her stop.

'But now we're here, and I'd never even seen a live joker before college – I mean, I'm from Pocatello! And I just want to go home. But Ted said this apartment has the best view of the Halloween parade, and if we stayed for that, I'd get over my phobia and see jokers as people just like everyone else. And while I think I can get used to jokers – I mean, Jesus was okay with lepers, and it's pretty much the same thing, isn't it? They're just diseased cripples, and Ted was cured anyway ... But how can I cope with those satanic aces and their awful alien powers!?'

Jim stifled an urge to turn two-dimensional, since, gratifying as it might be, horrified screams weren't useful when taking a witness statement. 'About that. You said there was an ace used in the robbery? So where was the candy taken? And how? And you said something about it being worth hundreds of dollars? What sort of candies are we talking here?'

'Not the candy. The bowl. It was Tiffany. Tiffany crystal.' Shirley fluttered her hands in agitation. 'Oh, Ted's going to kill me! He said it was a family heirloom!'

If Ted did kill her, it might be justifiable homicide, but Jim didn't think the marriage would get that far. 'Could you just give me the events of today, as they happened?'

Shirley bit her lip, but nodded. 'Okay. The bowl was here, on the table by the window. I'd filled it up, but I'd eaten a few Snickers, so I went to the kitchen to get another bag. Then I came back *and I saw* it!'

Jim raised his pen. 'It?'

'The giant black cat! It was there, hissing at me!' She pointed to the window.

Jim went over and looked down. It was a picture window, recently cleaned, and there was a small ledge outside with no obvious paw prints or claw marks, just a bunch of pigeon droppings and a five-story drop to the ground. He could even look across the way to the Dime Museum and see the tops of the Turtle's shells through the skylights. Jim raised an eyebrow and turned back to Shirley. 'Okay, when you're saying "giant," what do you mean? My height? Taller than me? Smaller than me but bigger than a regular black cat? How tall are we talking?'

Shirley looked perturbed, her indescribable horror now being put into quantifiable units. 'Um, it was maybe a little bit shorter than me, but then it got taller. You know, how cats puff themselves up when they hiss?'

'But still shorter than me?'

She craned her neck up. 'Yes, shorter than you.'

'And how did it get the candy?'

'It was there on the table, then it vanished and suddenly it appeared in the cat's paws.'

Jim jotted that down. 'So we're talking bipedal cat joker? One that stands on two legs?'

Shirley nodded.

'And how did it leave? Did it teleport? Jump?'

'I, uh, didn't see. I screamed and turned away, and when I looked back, it was gone.'

Jim nodded. 'And the time on this?'

'Uh, about a couple hours ago? Just before I called the station.'

Jim nodded. He could get the time of the first call from Apsara, but already had a suspicion of when it would be. 'Anything else?'

Shirley shook her head.

Jim handed her his card. 'If you think of anything else, or see the cat again, just call. Or you can stop by at the precinct. Ask for Slim Jim.'

'Slim Jim?'

'Ace nickname,' Jim explained, then winked. He went 2-D and

stepped out through the door crack. There was a scream from the other side. 'Happy Halloween!' Jim called.

He knew he should not have done that, but Tenry could handle all further questioning of Shirley Litt. The important thing was, they finally had a lead on the Magpie Burglaries.

Tenry was not in their office, but was in the break room, along with Gordon the Ghoul, Rikki, Tabby Driscoll, K-10, and the rat from Internal Affairs.

Rikki ran over to him, wearing a pair of pink gauze fairy wings with her uniform. It made her look a little more odd than usual. Miranda Michaelson was the only officer on the force with a smaller waist than Jim's, which was saying something, but she made up for that in chest capacity with a rib cage the wild card had redesigned for running. Add in tiny fangs and she looked a bit like a humanoid whippet. Now with pink fairy wings.

She followed Jim's glance and explained, 'Tinkerbill gave them to me. People kept giving them to him, but there's no way he's going to wear them.' Jim understood: Bill Chen was almost as tall as Jim, but massed at least three times as much, most of that muscle. Unfortunately, along with a deuce that let him surround people with a sparkly pink glow, the wild card had also cursed him with a voice that sounded like Betty Boop. Rikki clutched Jim's arm but he had to bend down before she could whisper, *'Tell me you did not eat the chili.'*

'What's wrong with the chili?' Jim asked, looking over to the crock pot.

'Nothing … is wrong … with the chili …' said Gordon the Ghoul. 'Did … you like it?'

'It could have used some chipotles …' Jim said, realizing that everyone was looking at him. 'What's in the chili?'

'That is … for me – *to know* – and you to … find out!' cackled Gordon the Ghoul, aka Dr. Gordon, aka Dr. *Otto* Gordon as Jim remembered from an old pathology report.

'I'll tell you what's in the chili,' said the rat from Internal Affairs.

Detective Vincent Marinelli, aka Ratboy, was so named not so much for his position as the fact that the wild card had turned him into a four-foot-tall giant rat. 'He made the chili out of rats!'

'Rats?' echoed K-10, aka Officer Dina Quattore. She was Jim's age and exactly his type, at least before he'd spontaneously grown a foot taller: small, buxom, with curly black hair and curves in all the right places. She was also a telepath, but thankfully not the creepy sort; she only read the minds of dogs. 'You made the chili out of rats?'

'Well in that case I'll definitely have to try some,' said Tabby Driscoll, the department's undercover officer, a shapeshifting ace who could change from a large battle-scarred ginger-haired Irishman to a large battle-scarred ginger tomcat. 'I like a good rat every now and again.'

'It also has cat in it,' Marinelli declared, tapping a humanoid finger to the side of his long pointed muzzle. 'Trust the nose.'

Tabby turned green, and he hadn't even eaten the chili.

'A little dog too,' Marinelli said, causing K-10's olive complexion to turn sallow as she looked at Otto Gordon with even more horror. Ratboy's rat nose sniffed the air, whiskers twitching. 'And something else ...'

'Yes! Yes ...' Gordon the Ghoul cackled with delight. 'Something ... else? I scraped it – out of – a wheel well! But I could not ... identify it ... either ...'

Half of Jim wanted to throw up and the other half wanted to call up his old department's psychologist and give her a piece of his mind. Or maybe combine the two, but his ace unfortunately did not include cross-country projectile vomiting. Instead he just sat down.

Tenry came over next to him. 'If it's any consolation, they eat stranger things in China.'

'It is *so* not a consolation,' Rikki said for Jim, patting him on the shoulder.

Jim glanced to Tabby, who with Ratboy and K-10 were converging on Gordon the Ghoul, then looked to Tenry and swallowed. 'We've got a definite lead on the Magpie Burglaries. Do you know any jokers who look like large *black* cats or aces who can turn into them?'

Tenry paused, then nodded.

'Good. Then excuse me for a moment while I go vomit.'

The sign read THE LAND WHERE THE BONG-TREE GROWS and the façade was painted with a mural of nautical charts and an islet with an anthropomorphic owl, an anthropomorphic cat, and an anthropomorphic pig joker wearing nothing but a loincloth and an amazing collection of tattoos and piercings, including the requisite ring on the end of his nose.

The fantastical geography theme was picked up on the walls inside the shop. Jim spotted *Nowhereland, Wonderland, The Rox*, and *The Torrible Torriby Zone* being almost overcome by a mixture of mint and patchouli oil and the realization that he'd just stepped into Jokertown's head shop. Bongs and hookahs lined one wall, arrayed in order of size like pipes in an extremely fanciful calliope. Psychedelic posters were displayed on another, illuminated with black light, showing a range of rock idols from Joker Plague's six-armed Drummer Boy all the way back to the Lizard King from Destiny. And there were cases and racks filled with patches, stickers, rolling papers and drug paraphernalia, books, CDs, *chachkas* of all description, and tie-died T-shirts silk-screened with classic illustrations and literary quotations. A three-headed mannequin modeled one with the image of a clown doing a headstand and a verse:

'My lady fair,
Why do you stare
At poor old Mr. Joker?
You're quite as stiff
And prim as if
You'd eaten up a poker!'
           – L. Frank Baum

The next had Alice and the Cheshire Cat, with the following:

'But I don't want to go among mad people,' Alice remarked.
'Oh, you can't help that,' said the Cat.
'We're all mad here. I'm mad. You're mad.'
'How do you know I'm mad?' said Alice.
'You must be,' said the Cat, 'or you wouldn't have come here.'
— Lewis Carroll

Again, Jim had the urge to call the psychologist back in Phoenix and bitch her out.

'Hoo hoo hoo!' cried a voice that sounded like nothing half so much as an owl. 'Have I got the shirt for you!' A chunky young woman in a gypsy skirt and peasant blouse fluttered over, figuratively at least, and began going through the rack of T-shirts. She had the head of a black cat, but Jim realized a second later it was just a flat paper mask. Behind that was the actual head of a barn owl. 'Ta-da!' she announced, holding up a shirt that was long and thin and sized for Jim. It had a cartoon of a nineteenth-century joker coiled up like a cinnamon roll along with a limerick:

There was an old person of Pinner,
As thin as a lath, if not thinner;
They dressed him in white, and roll'd him up tight,
That elastic old person of Pinner.
— Edward Lear

What was even more troubling was that it looked like it would fit Jim perfectly, without needing to be taken in or altered in any way.

'We've got a changing room in the back,' said the owl-headed joker.

'Actually, I'm here on a case.' Jim looked for Tenry, and fortunately with his height it was easy to see over the racks to where his partner was talking with the shop's other proprietor.

The Pussycat was a three-foot-tall black cat joker, dressed like a

Rastafarian Puss in Boots, except that he had a flat paper owl mask pushed up atop his knit Rasta beanie so he could talk more easily. 'Man, you can't bust me for anything,' he told Tenry. He had a bong in one paw and his green cat eyes were slightly bloodshot. 'Catnip's totally legal!' He waved to a hydroponic garden display filled with some lush member of the mint family.

'We're not here about the catnip,' Tenry said. 'This is my new partner, Detective McTate. Jim, I see you've already met Olivia. This is Javier.'

'Call me Javi,' said the cat. 'Or Pussycat.' He grinned like the cat that ate the canary, or something else, and leered in the direction of the Owl's skirts.

She hooted coquettishly and hung the long Jim-size T-shirt back on a rack.

'We've had some reports of thefts.' Jim went down on one knee so he could look at the Pussycat at something closer to eye level. 'Do you by any chance have Cheshire Cat powers? Appearing, disappearing? Maybe conjuring stuff, like, say, bowls of candy?'

'That would be totally sweet!' The Pussycat lost his grin. 'But no. Wish I could.'

'Can you make yourself bigger?'

His hackles went up slightly. 'Are you making fun of me, man?'

'No, no, just trying to solve a case,' Jim said, realizing the Pussycat's paws holding the bong did look pretty catlike, and he could see the tips of claws sticking out.

'Man, the only perk the wild card gave me is the ability to get totally baked on catnip. But like I was telling your partner, it's completely legal. So unless the feds just made catnip a controlled substance, you can't bust me for anything.'

'No trouble. Just checking reports.' Jim thought a stoned cat joker with the munchies would more than adequately explain the missing candy bowl, but suspicion was not the same thing as proof. 'Do you have an alibi for where you were between eight and nine this morning?'

'Sure, man, I was here the whole time. Olivia can vouch for that.'

The Owl nodded, making her paper cat mask bob.

Jim stood back up and rubbed his neck. It looked like this was a dead end.

The Owl cocked her head behind the cat mask. 'So this is about those thefts in the paper?' She turned to the Pussycat. 'Javi, did you sell the fancy water pipe in the front window? Because I didn't see it in the receipts and it's gone.'

The Pussycat looked up at her. 'Oh, crap. The Magpie hit us too?'

Jim raised an eyebrow. 'You're missing a bong?'

The Owl shook her head and pointed to a sign: *The items you see for sale here are pipes and water pipes and are only meant for use with tobacco, catnip, and other legal substances. If you refer to them by any other name, we must ask you to leave the premises.*

'So The Land Where the Bong-Tree Grows only sells water pipes?'

The Owl nodded her paper cat mask. 'We consulted with Dr. Pretorius before choosing the name. If you check our Yellow Page listing, you'll see we're a bookstore that specializes in nineteenth and early twentieth-century children's literature with a special appeal to the Jokertown population, along with related novelty items.' She gestured to a display under an American Library Association READ poster with Drummer Boy smoking a hookah facing some blonde in a blue gothic Lolita number. Jim realized a moment later DB had been posed as the Caterpillar, and the particularly mature Alice was Pop Tart from *American Hero* sans her black wig. There were several editions of *Alice* on the shelves below along with various *Oz* books, *Old Possum's Book of Practical Cats, The Walrus and The Carpenter,* and other assorted books of nonsense verse. Jim picked one up and opened it to something called 'The Mad Gardener's Song.'

> He thought he saw a Banker's Clerk
> Descending from the bus:
> He looked again, and found it was
> A Hippopotamus.
> 'If this should stay to dine,' he said,
> 'There won't be much for us!'

Jim shut the book and put it back on the shelf. He'd seen that just this morning, and it didn't do his sanity much good to find that his current life could be summarized by the demented ramblings of Victorian children's poets. Finding that hookahs had been shoe-horned in under 'related novelty items' for children's literature by the notorious Dr. Pretorius was less surprising, given the stories he'd heard around the station of Jokertown's answer to Melvin Belli.

He thought back then to confusion about hippos and bank clerks, yarmulkes and eyeballs, and then looked at Olivia's cat-shaped mask covering her owl-shaped face.

Jim turned to Tenry. 'Wasn't one of the other Magpie thefts a cat mask? And the owner a "Mr. Dutton"?'

Tenry met Jim's gaze and nodded. 'From Holbrooks. I'll set up an appointment.'

Gilded Victorian capitals in the window proudly and genteelly proclaimed HOLBROOKS, with smaller script below that reading *since 1954*. Jim had heard laments from older Jokertown residents that the neighborhood was becoming gentrified, but judging by the shop inside, this had been the case for quite some time.

With the gleaming brass and polished mahogany, Holbrooks had the appearance of a high-class milliners or haberdashery, but instead of hats displayed on the mannequin heads and metal stands, there were masks. Very expensive masks, with hand-tooled leather and feathers or fur.

It being Halloween, it was also busy. 'One moment,' a joker with a crane head told two customers, then came over to Jim and Tenry, and Jim realized what he'd taken for a crane-faced joker was in fact an individual of uncertain wild card status wearing a mask with an oversized beak. Mixed with round smoked spectacles, it gave the appearance of a gas mask. Worn beneath a flat-brimmed black hat, along with a long black oilcloth robe and gloves, it completely concealed the wearer, like a medieval hazmat suit. The whole thing made Jim a little nervous.

'The Plague Doctor's costume,' explained the individual in a lilting voice of indeterminate age, gender, and sexual preference, gesturing with a stick in one hand, like a headmaster's pointer. 'Our wands of misery are turned in Williamsburg, but the masks are fashioned in Venice from the traditional molds. But I believe you are here to see Mr. Dutton.'

It nodded to another clerk, garbed in a silvery moon mask, and ushered them into the back room. Some podgy paleolithic goddess recast in sequins and rhinestones sat at a table busily adding same to a number of masks, but before Jim could figure out whether she was a joker, a costume, or something else, their guide tapped on a door and they were let into Dutton's office.

Like the shop outside, it was all lavish mahogany and brass elegance, with masks displayed in lawyer-style glass-fronted bookcases and a gleaming tantalus off to one side of the desk, the liquor bottles mostly full, but a cigar box distinctly absent. Dutton rose, a wiry old man in a yellowed, skull-faced mask with ruby eyes. 'Thank you, Shelley,' he told the clerk in the Plague Doctor's costume as it shut the door, and Jim realized that the yellow skull with the red eyes was not in fact Dutton's mask but his face. It turned to Tenry, then looked up at Jim. 'Ah, you would be the new detective. My employee Jason described your visit to the Dime Museum this morning. Welcome to Jokertown. Would that this were under better circumstances. Have you recovered my diving helmet?'

'Uh, no,' Jim said.

'Pity,' said the skull, turning. 'But Detective Fong, I'm to understand that you may have located another piece of my property? A valuable cat mask?'

'May have,' stressed Tenry. 'It may have been used in the commission of a crime.'

'Or crimes,' Jim added. 'One of which might be the theft of your diving helmet this morning. And that's an odd coincidence, so we were wondering if you might have any enemies, or information about who the Magpie might be.'

The talking skeleton placed one liver-spotted yellow hand to his chest. 'Young man, one does not become a personage of stature in any community without making a good number of friends, a greater number of acquaintances, and, I'm sad to say, inevitably a few enemies, if just by association. I am no different. But I have no insights as to the Magpie's identity.'

Jim's partner had an excellent poker face, but Jim could tell Tenry's bullshit detector was going off the scale, and that he'd had many past dealings with Charles Dutton over the years, some of which he might enlighten Jim about later. But he only said, 'Well, about the cat mask. The photo in the original report was a bit grainy. We were hoping you might have a better one.'

Dutton dimpled, or at least that's what Jim took the wrinkling of the sallow skin around the perpetual death rictus to be. 'I can do one better,' said the talking skull. He was more skin and bones than Jim would ever be – he hoped – but moved spryly enough, unlocking a case. He reached to the back, taking out a black silk box that he opened to reveal a mask, stitched with thousands of iridescent black glass beads, stylized but unmistakably a hissing black cat.

'The report said the mask was the only one of its kind,' Tenry said.

'For sale,' Dutton qualified. 'This is my personal copy.' He lifted it from the box and placed it over his skull. 'A *Gatto*, one of the traditional masks of *Carnevale*, honoring the cats who protected Venice from the rats of the plague. Though as you can see, Erté also drew inspiration from the fierce witch's grimalkin of our American Halloween,' the angry black cat lectured mildly. 'He made a series often, some larger, some smaller, but the majority in this medium size. Aside from numbering, this mask is twin to the one taken from my window.'

Jim took out his cell phone and snapped a few pictures as Dutton modeled. 'And you value it at fifteen thousand dollars?' Jim asked, a little incredulous.

'It's an Erté original, young man.' The black cat snarled up at Jim, Dutton's red eyes looking out of its beaded sockets. 'Hardly the most valuable Holbrooks has for sale, but one of our finer pieces.' Dutton looked Jim up and up. 'I take it you're rather new to being a joker.'

Jim kept himself from thinning by an act of will. 'What makes you think I'm a joker?'

'A certain … bearing.' An emaciated yellow hand made an elegant gesture. 'As a shopkeeper, it's something you learn to spot. Also, those born as jokers, or who have had time to grow accustomed to their new skin, are generally more familiar with the virtues of masks.' Dutton removed his and the yellow skull grinned at Jim. 'A mask can make others more comfortable. But more than that, it allows one to be someone else for a time. A joker may be a nat, a nat may be an ace, and even an ace may relax into the anonymity of a joker.' He placed the black cat's visage back in its silken sepulcher and replaced it on the shelf. 'Masking is older than the wild card, but not older than disease. The Plague Doctor was born of the Black Death, and his attendant Zannis and Scaramouches, Columbines and Harlequins, followed soon after.' He gestured about the room, from a pair of masks with grotesquely exaggerated noses to a feminine half mask to a simple oval of exquisite natlike perfection, a single black teardrop stark against the white cheek. 'The beauty marks of the court of the Sun King were first devised to cover the sores of syphilis,' Dutton remarked conversationally. 'It was only later that the charms of the patch box were discovered by the unafflicted.'

Jim was more used to seeing teardrops tattooed on the faces of Mexican-American gangbangers. There was a certain irony to find they had originated with syphilitic French courtiers.

Dutton pointed to a ghost-white mask with normal enough eyes and nose, but no mouth, and a chin pointed like a locomotive's cow-catcher. 'Even the monstrous babau, the bad-bogey of the nursery tales, was pressed into service, creating the blank-faced *Bauta,* the mask of anonymity from the time of Casanova.' He took the *Bauta* from its case and placed it over his skull, adding a black tricorne hat with a matching head drape in the back, hiding him completely. The cultured voice continued beyond the mouthless face. 'And even without disease, a mask has other virtues: the old may be viewed as young, and the young may gain the respect of age. With a mask, all one can judge you by are your words and deeds.'

Jim was fairly certain Dutton had used variations of this speech many times before, just before closing the deal on an overpriced mask.

It continued: 'You should really consider getting a mask, officer. Every joker should own at least one, and a Holbrooks mask is a thing to be treasured for generations. Each and every mask we sell comes with a lifetime warranty, with complimentary service for minor repairs or alterations, and free inscription for all those special occasions in a joker's life: graduations, weddings, anniversaries. And we keep impeccable sales records, so if a mask is lost or stolen ...'

'About that,' Jim said. 'The report said yours disappeared from a locked shop window?'

'Indeed' – the *Bauta* nodded in assent – 'and I have the sole key.'

'And that window would be on the ground floor?'

'Holbrooks has only one floor. The ones above us are apartments.'

Jim nodded slowly, glancing to Tenry. 'Could we see this case?'

'Of course,' said Dutton. Jim inspected it. There were no obvious signs of forced entry, and the lock was something reasonably secure, difficult to pick, and only used during regular business hours, same as a jewelry shop. He took some photos anyway while Tenry asked if some long-dead business associate of Dutton's had left any files and Dutton repeated ritual denials that he had them or, indeed, had any idea where they might be.

Jim didn't believe that for a minute, since one rule of the detective business was that people always lie, and you didn't get to be as old or as wealthy as Dutton without having an awful lot to lie about. But one of the benefits of having an older partner was having someone who could explain things to you later.

'We'll let you know as soon as we learn anything more, Mr. Dutton,' Tenry finished.

♣

Tenry went back to the precinct to check another lead, but Jim had a hunch, and not the type your back got from the wild card. The cat face appeared to be a mask, and since that pointed away from a cat joker physically scaling the building, Occam's razor might not be completely broken, just severely bent. While there were world-class aces with multiple powers, most aces were like Jim: one power, possibly useful but still limited in scope. Meaning most aces used mundane means for everything else.

For example, the window-washing rig outside Shirley Litt's building.

Jim waited for it to touch down, then hailed the operator by flashing his badge. 'Yeah, officer?' The man cringed.

'Just wanted to ask you a few questions.'

The man continued to cringe as Jim looked him over. 'I didn't do nothin'. Honest.'

He appeared to be a perfectly ordinary young African-American man except he already had his hands in the air. If they could be called hands: his forearms were elongated and broomstick thin while the palms and fingers were warped and splayed out, the nails fused into long cartilaginous ridges. They looked like nothing half so much as two giant squeejees.

'Have any ID?'

The joker nodded. ''Round my neck.'

Jim looked and yes indeed, he was wearing a chain that bore a city window washer's permit and a New York State identification card for one Purcell Aloysius Jones, age twenty-three.

'You don't by any chance own a cat mask, do you, Mr. Jones?'

'You think I'd cover up the only human thing I got left?'

Jim didn't think that he would, and Shirley Litt had described the cat as having 'paws' as opposed to 'giant squeegees.'

'Don't bust me, man. Please.' The joker cowered. 'It weren't my fault.'

As always, letting people talk when they were inclined to was part of the detective's job. 'So what happened?'

'It's Halloween, man. I went to take a leak, and when I got back, some damn punk had grabbed my rig and was joyridin'. I yelled, and when he came down, I chased 'im off.'

'Did you make a report?'

'Fuck no! I could lose my job. I'm not allowed to let anyone unlicensed up.'

'And this individual was wearing a cat mask?'

'Yeah, damn Halloween cat and was playin' it up. Laughed like an old lady then was all "meow-meow-meow-meow" like a bunch of kittens from a damn cat food commercial!'

Jim looked at the window-washing rig. Come to think of it, he'd always wanted to go up in one himself. 'Tell you what, I'll give you a break on one condition ...'

The view from a window washer's perspective was a lot like what a detective usually saw: a messy apartment, a clean apartment, a cluttered apartment, a tasteful apartment with a number of paintings and objets d'art, an apartment with numerous bookcases as well as Shirley Litt and a handsome man in a cheap pirate costume who Jim presumed was her formerly tentacled fiancé Ted. Jim used his cell phone to snap a few pics of the first four, waved hello and snapped a picture of Shirley and the presumed Ted as well, then turned and had Purcell Jones take them down slowly. From just outside the third-floor apartment there was a perfect view across the street of Dr. Tod's head, now missing one diving helmet, but clearly visible through the Dime Museum's skylight. Jim snapped a few pictures, then went to the first four apartments from the inside. There was no answer at any, so he turned a hand 2-D and slipped in his card with notes to call if the occupants had witnessed anything or noticed something missing.

Relatively pleased with himself, Jim went back to the precinct where he found Tenry in their office even more self-satisfied. 'Guess what I have here.'

'It looks like an antiquated VCR.'

'Right. But that's exactly what we need for what Midtown just sent.' Tenry pulled an old videocassette tape out of an interdepartmental mailer and popped it in the VCR. A bit of rewinding later, Jim was watching a surveillance tape of a jewelry store window with a prominent display of bling including what looked like a Fabergé egg. A minute in, someone in an Easter bunny costume hopped up, basket of eggs and all. A second later, the Fabergé egg vanished from the case, reappearing in the Easter bunny's fluffy white mittens. The bunny then deposited it in the basket, placed a stuffed toy goose atop it, and hopped off, jaunty as you please.

Jim turned to Tenry. 'So our Magpie Burglar is also the Easter Bunny Bandit?'

'They called him Peter Cottontail, but yes.' Tenry grinned. 'This is from 1988.'

Jim nodded, then rewatched the tape, then handed his phone to Tenry, showing him the pictures and outlining his own findings. The profile was coming together. Someone with a fondness for masks, short to middling height, at least late thirties by this point and likely older, and judging by the mittens and the movement, Jim was leaning toward female rather than male.

There was a cursory knock, then the door opened. 'We found her,' Tabby said.

'Who?' asked Tenry.

Tabby grinned like a ginger-haired Cheshire Cat. 'Your Magpie.'

'Ahem,' said K-10, pushing past the department's other under-cover specialist and her chief rival. 'I found her. Tabby was just along for the ride.' Dina held a sheet of paper close to her ample chest. 'I looked into the minds of the puppies in the window at Tony's Pets.'

'No one's eating kittens on my watch,' Tabby declared fiercely.

'But here's the kicker,' Dina added. 'They weren't eaten. Guess what happened?'

'They were teleported,' Jim supplied.

Dina looked slightly crestfallen, but then Tenry rewound the tape and showed them the footage of Peter Cottontail and the Fabergé egg. 'Okay,' Dina said. 'That's good. But I had Eddy do a sketch, and look, I got her without her mask.'

She showed off Eddie's sketch. It was black-and-white but showed an old woman with warts and an extremely long nose. Either a very mild joker or a very ugly nat. Or something else.

'What color was this woman's skin?' Jim asked.

Dina gave him one of those looks. 'I don't know. Dogs are color-blind.'

Jim took the sketch, clipped it up to the top of the white board, then popped a dry-erase marker. 'Hey!' Dina protested as he scribbled across it quickly.

Jim handed her the sketch, now green. 'I saw Witchiepoo this morning. It's another mask. But the black velvet cloak is the same. And the red shopping basket.'

'The puppies didn't see "red" but did it have two wheels?'

Jim nodded. 'And a box with three kittens on top.'

'That's enough to make the perp,' said Tabby. 'I'm on it. No one's kidnapping kittens on my watch either.' He started shrinking then, going from a big beefy Irishman to a short hairy Irishman to a fat furry orange-faced joker midget sprouting a tail until finally there was nothing except a large orange tabby tomcat crawling out of a pile of clothes. '*Meowwww!!!*' he stated declaratively then stalked out of the office.

'Don't look at me,' Dina said. 'I don't speak cat.'

'Didn't say you did,' Jim said.

There was an awkward silence, then Dina asked conversationally, 'So, any luck with the apartment hunt? I know the deadline's ...'

'Don't ask.'

She sighed. 'That's rough. I'd offer my couch, but my apartment's upstairs from my parents and their pizzeria, and they're kind of traditional Catholic and ...'

'Yeah,' Jim said. 'Even if we were dating ...'

They exchanged glances, then Dina looked to Tenry, but Tenry said, 'I'm afraid my wife is very particular. Traditional Chinese family, you understand.' He nodded sympathetically to Jim. 'I'm afraid you will really just have to speak with Captain Mendelberg ...'

It was a speak of the devil moment. After three more beats of awkward silence, a figure appeared in the doorway and a pair of small evil red eyes looked down at the pile of clothes, lingering for a moment on a distinct set of hash marks. 'I see I just missed Officer Driscoll,' Captain Mendelberg remarked, then smiled up at Jim. 'But at least you're here, Detective McTate.' It was not a nice smile, and it made the veins in her strangely vaned ears dilate. 'I just had a most interesting phone conversation with a Ms. Litt, and while I must commend you on finding a lead in your Magpie investigation, it would make my job far easier if you didn't flaunt your ace in front of those with professed phobias. Would that be a problem?'

Jim felt himself thinning and clenched his jaw to make it stop. 'No, Captain.'

'Excellent.' She glanced to Tenry and Dina. 'I wanted to let you know that I'll be needing everyone on the street tonight, even and especially our detectives and undercover officers. So even if you're about to break a case, we need extra security for the parade. Any worries with this?'

'No, Captain,' said Tenry. 'We have a physical description of the Magpie, but we can look for her on the parade route as well as anywhere else. Tabby's already on it.'

'Mazel tov. And word to the wise, unlike last Halloween where they wore Playboy bunny ears, this year the Werewolves are being classy and wearing those white carnival masks – *Bautas*. Don't ask how we found out, but they are.'

'There are going to be a lot of people wearing *Bautas* who aren't Werewolves,' Tenry pointed out.

'And?' said Captain Mendelberg. 'There are going to be people in heavy-metal T-shirts and satanic jewelry who aren't Demon Princes. Use your common sense. Now, if you could tidy up Officer Driscoll's *schmatta*.' She glanced to Jim and gestured to the soiled underwear. 'I have someone I would like you to meet. Let me introduce the Grand Marshal for this year's Halloween parade.'

Jim was glad he had not been tasked with worse shit duties than just picking up Tabby's cat-fuzz infested clothes when he saw who it was. He'd first seen her ten years ago when he was sixteen, she was sixteen, and she was his favorite swimsuit model to spank off to. Before he was an ace, she was an ace, and she was the waxwork figure he'd seen that morning in the Dime Museum lobby. But now she was wearing this impossible gown of pink taffeta and a matching crown, like something a fairy princess would wear to the Oscars. Any lesser woman could not have pulled it off, but being who she was, she did. It was Michelle Pond, aka Bubbles, famous Committee ace, hero of New Orleans and Africa, and star of his teenage wet dreams.

His body wanted to thin, but he instead channeled the nervous energy into wadding Tabby's clothes up two-dimensionally and shoving them through the crack of the filing cabinet. There was a brief bang of a drawer derailing once he pulled his hands out and put them behind his back, acting as if nothing had happened.

Michelle Pond was slightly more zaftig than her waxwork, but that only made her more beautiful, more out of his league, and didn't change the fact that she was still a lesbian, which made her even hotter in the fantasizing-about-unobtainable-women way. He was also glad that she was not a telepath, because she might have killed him for his thoughts. She was also looking at him and the filing cabinet as if she were trying to figure out what was going on.

'Ms. Pond,' said Captain Mendelberg, 'let me introduce Detective McTate, our *newest* addition to the force, his partner Detective Fong, and one of our undercover officers and aces, Officer Dina Quattore.' She paused then added, 'You just missed Officer Driscoll.'

'You can call me K-10,' said Dina. 'It's like K-9 but better.'

'You can call me Bubbles.' She smiled radiantly. 'But let me introduce Adesina. Come on out, honey. It's all right.' She leaned down, moving aside the extremely full skirts of her gown, revealing the frightened face of a young girl hiding behind them. The girl was African, with large eyes and classic features, her hair done into two braids tied with blue ribbons, but her head was too close to the ground. Jim thought for a second she was crouching or crawling until he saw that the girl's head was attached to the body of an insect the size of a small dog. It had wings and was holding a basket in one set of chitinous legs. There had been an attempt to dress the insect body in a child's blue gingham dress, but it wasn't working, and the sequined red shoes that went with the outfit were just tied on to one of the apron strings as an afterthought.

The girl gazed up at him wide-eyed, and Jim hated the wild card, not just for the awful thing it had done to her, but for the fact that it made him loom and frightening children was about the last thing he wanted. He crouched down. 'Hey, honey,' he said. 'You're Dorothy, right?'

She beamed, and one insectlike claw reached up and caught Bubbles's hand. 'Yes,' she said in oddly accented English, then a worried expression came over her face. 'Are you a joker?'

Jim paused, uncertain. 'I'm more of a straight man,' he said and grinned weakly.

She look confused, so he held out one hand. 'Here. Watch. Magic trick.' He thinned his hand down to paper thickness and tilted it back and forth. 'Now you see it, now you don't.'

She smiled then and laughed, squeezing Bubbles's hand. 'Mama gets fat.'

Michelle Pond smiled at him, and Jim realized that she was coutured as an extremely glamorous Glinda and there were few things that could make her wear that dress apart from money or making a child happy. He also realized that Adesina had to be one of the African children who had been deliberately infected with the wild card, then used as soldiers when they weren't just killed or left for dead. She had to be one of the latter and had probably seen worse horrors in her short life than he had in his time as a cop.

Jim popped his hand back three-dimensional and straightened back up. 'I think Tenry keeps some candy in his desk.'

The joker girl beamed, then scuttled forward with her basket. 'Trick or Treat!'

Tenry may have been a nat, but he was also a father and he opened the drawer.

Michelle Pond touched Jim's forearm. 'Thank you,' she breathed sotto voce, then looked worriedly after the joker girl.

'Don't mention it.' Jim touched his arm where she'd touched him. 'You can call me Jim. Or Slim Jim.'

She glanced at him. 'Okay.'

'Well,' said Captain Mendelberg, 'there are a few more people to meet before the parade, and we should leave these officers to their business.'

Michelle Pond gave him a wry smile and beckoned to Adesina. The insect girl actually flew after her as she left with Captain Mendelberg.

Jim exchanged looks with Tenry and K-10. 'Well, then I guess it's the parade route. Together or separately?'

'Separately,' said Tenry with the decisiveness of a senior partner. 'You two get started and I'll brief the rest of the force so we'll have some more eyes on the lookout.'

'Sounds good,' said K-10.

◆

The crowds were already starting up on Bowery, though thankfully as a detective Jim could just patrol, rather than be responsible for the barricades. He also got to go plainclothes, or at least as plainclothes as his height and weight made him.

Though it was uncomfortable to admit, Dutton's suggestion of a mask did have some merit. He passed Plague Doctors and Scaramouches, Zannis and *Bautas,* even one Columbine wearing a Utilikilt to better display her three green-scaled chicken legs, before realizing he was violating another unwritten rule of Jokertown: Halloween was not Wild Card Day.

Wild Card Day was the day to wave your freak flag and for jokers to hassle nats or even other jokers who didn't or couldn't wave that flag hard enough. Jim had found the best way to get around the neighborhood on Wild Card Day was to stay two-dimensional. But it seemed Jokertown's Halloween festivities were more egalitarian: nats could dress as jokers, jokers could dress as nats, and everyone could dress as aces, even if they possibly shouldn't. On one corner, posing for pictures, was a nat transvestite in a long brown wig, blue sequined gown, and brown feathered angel wings posing alongside an apelike joker in a blond wig and Dodgers cap along with a baseball glove and jersey that read *Curveball.*

Wearing either of those outfits on Wild Card Day could get you stabbed: the first for impersonating a joker, the second for idolizing an ace.

Jim snapped a pic with his cell, forwarding to his former psychologist without comment, then noticed the looks he was getting and realized exactly what he was doing wrong: it wasn't a case of *could* but *should*. It was Halloween and he did not have a costume.

He paused at a newsstand where the walrus joker who ran it had accessorized his usual Hawaiian shirt with a red wig and Takisian plumed hat. It looked equal parts ridiculous and festive, but that was the point. When in Wonderland ...

Jim tossed a few quarters on the counter, picked up a copy of the *Jokertown Cry,* and proceeded to fold a hat. Fine. He was the Man in White Paper. It was an extremely minor character from *Through the Looking Glass,* but worked as well as anything, and let him have the headline MAGPIE STRIKES AGAIN! along one brim for extra irony points.

'Detective McTate?' asked a voice at his shoulder once he'd put it on.

Jim looked down, seeing a black tricorne over another creepy mouthless white *Bauta* mask, a rather old and expensive-looking one. About the only other distinguishing feature apart from a height of about six feet was a few tangles of matted flesh that fell out the drape at the back like scab-encrusted dreadlocks. 'Yes?'

'How goes the investigation?' When Jim didn't answer, the figure raised a gloved hand to his chest and made a polite little half bow, made awkward by wearing a hat while looking up at someone almost a foot taller. 'Lucas Tate, editor of the paper you're wearing on your head.'

Jim had an urge to take it off and read what that was but instead just glanced over at the stack on the newsstand. 'Ah, the *Cry.*' He was fairly certain, despite Tate's current choice in masks, that the editor of the paper was not a member of the Werewolves, the same as he was pretty certain Charles Dutton was not one either. But he was also from the southwest and believed in handshakes. 'A pleasure,' he said, catching Tate's. It was firm and human, but also strong. Jim's was less so on all counts, thinning on instinct until Tate's glove was wrapped in an exceptionally robust paper sculpture.

'I can see where you get your ace name.' Tate released it. 'So, any progress?'

'On what?'

'The Magpie investigation.' When Jim didn't respond, Tate continued. 'I'm not just the person who coined the name, I'm also one of the Magpie's victims. Seven rather valuable masks were recently stolen from my apartment. Ramshead was looking into it for me.'

Jim translated: Ramshead was Leo Storgman, the oldest detective at the precinct, and another joker. 'Why aren't you asking Ramshead?'

'Because he's not available at the moment, and when I asked, Apsara told me that you and Detective Fong had taken lead on this case. And you are more physically distinctive.'

Translation: even in Jokertown, he stuck out in a crowd.

'So,' Tate asked conversationally, 'do you think the Magpie is currently in the area?'

Keeping the cards close to the vest was standard operating procedure, but making nice to the press was also sometimes useful. 'There've been a few thefts today, so she may be.'

'"She"?' Tate asked interestedly. 'You're suspecting a woman?'

Jim kicked himself mentally. 'I can't give official comment on an ongoing investigation, but we've worked out a profile and we have our suspicions. Have you heard anything?'

'Nothing today,' Tate said slowly, 'but a reporter does have his sources.'

Making nice with the press was one thing, but involving civilians in an investigation was another. Then again, Tate knew the neighborhood, and another pair of eyes was always useful. Tate's were brown and natlike enough. 'Okay, this needs to stay out of the paper for the moment, but there've been quite a few more thefts.' Jim skipped over the bit about teleporting and simply sketched out the list of items the perp was likely to have with her today.

'Dr. Tod's diving helmet, a bong, and the three little kittens?'

Tate repeated incredulously. 'What, is she on a scavenger hunt?'

'You tell me. But like I was saying, this needs to stay out of the paper for the moment.'

'My lips are sealed,' Tate voice said from behind the *Bauta*'s mouthless visage.

Jim nodded, looking away to another face without a mouth, but this wasn't a mask. The owner made up for this lack via interpretive dance and six breasts without a bra.

He turned away again, but Tate had stepped away. He was standing by himself, his pallid mask cocked at an angle that made Jim suspect he had a Bluetooth headset underneath.

Jim sighed and set off, shivering slightly. The reporter could catch up, but the crowds were neatly lined up, easy to search from his vantage point as the parade started.

The Jokertown High School marching band was first, relatively normal compared to what he was expecting. A lot of the high school kids had not turned their card yet, or were fortunate enough to have a nat parent, or had simply drawn jokers that were adequately disguised by green and gold marching band uniforms vaguely reminiscent of the green-whiskered gatekeeper from the Emerald City. They were also playing the triumphal march from *The Wizard of Oz*, probably a conscious choice, since in the middle of the band was a fuchsia-colored stallion. The joker kid switched his tail, swinging up a drumstick attached with green and gold athletic tape, and hit a bass drum on his back with the legend MIGHTY CHIMERAS. A girl with a flügelhorn for a head danced past, waving a drum majorette's baton, and the rest of the band followed, mostly marching, but also hopping, or flopping, or skittering along in motorized wheelchairs.

Jim had still not seen a joker who had been turned into a purple cow, but he had now seen one who had been changed into a fuchsia stallion. He would still rather see than be either.

Jim didn't bother taking a picture for his former psychologist. He just kept taking stock of the crowd and keeping an eye on the parade. The Jokertown Players float was next, with cavorting jokers singing '*Willkommen,*' promoting a remarkably staid revival of *Cabaret*.

Captain Mendelberg and Sergeant Tienyu followed. At least Jim took it to be Sergeant Tienyu. It looked like a 1931 Duesenberg convertible with Mendelberg waving cheerily from the passenger seat. But since there was no one behind the wheel and yet the car was still driving, Jim was fairly certain it was animated by Vivian Choy, one of the desk sergeants who had some ace that let her possess cars and other devices she tinkered with in the precinct garage.

They passed, and then came the main event, Michelle Pond the Grand Marshal as Glinda the Good with her ace providing her very own giant bubble to stand in. The theme of her float was 'Somewhere Over the Rainbow,' complete with rainbows and blue-birds, and while no one was singing, an instrumental version was playing over the speakers. Adesina fluttered around Bubbles inside the bubble, a joker bluebird Dorothy, but actually seemed happy, if just for the moment.

The float's banners declared the sponsor to be the United Nations Children's Fund, which made sense since 'Trick-or-Treat for UNICEF' was a long-standing charity and Michelle Pond was their new spokesperson, just returned from her work in Africa for a press junket. As frivolous as a parade float might be, the point was to raise awareness for the plight of war orphans and child soldiers in Africa, especially forced victims of the wild card like Adesina. And as the float stopped, Michelle Pond raised her wand-shaped microphone and started to talk about just that.

The crowd hushed in response but that was when Jim spotted her: the Magpie.

She wasn't dressed as a magpie, of course, but still had the same black velvet cloak he'd spotted with the witch mask that morning. That was now in her shopping cart, along with a beaded black cat mask, a crystal bowl, a bong, a diving helmet, and a box of kittens still perched up at the top. The mask she was wearing now was that of an owl, a barn owl like Olivia's face, but made of painstakingly glued feathers with an enameled beak. She was standing on the corner, up against one of the barricades and lamppost with her cart on the other side of her, walling her in but also keeping her from being too crowded. And Jim noted that like him, she was also not giving full attention to Bubbles's speech. He thinned out on reflex so he'd not only be virtually invisible from the Magpie's vantage point but also so he could slip through the crowd.

Like any good pickpocket, the Magpie waited until her marks were well and truly distracted by something – in this case Bubbles's horrific but true tales of the plight of African child soldiers – and then made her move. Unlike regular pickpockets, she had an ace, and Jim watched as she looked across the street to the opposite corner where a scaled joker perched on a milk crate wore a belt of inverted crucifixes along with a red jacket emblazoned with inverted pentacles to underscore that he was a Demon Prince. Under the milk crate was a small box.

The next moment, there wasn't. The Magpie didn't bother to check her prize, just quickly stashed it in her cart underneath the kittens.

That was more than enough for Jim. He moved in for the collar.

Unfortunately, it was also enough for someone else: a shambling mass of multifaceted red eyes and thorny green tendrils, looking like nothing half so much as a possessed raspberry bush sporting a cheap *Bauta*. Unlike Tate's and Dutton's, Jim was certain this *Bauta* belonged to a Werewolf. The joker got in the way, then next moment, shoved the Magpie to the ground. She cried out as her cart was knocked over, kittens spilling into the crowd along with a crystal bowl that shattered. A mass of brambles snaked out, securing the Demon Prince's sample case, then for good measure, another reached out and ripped off the Magpie's mask. She screamed, covering her face with her black velvet gloves.

That was enough for Jim as well. 'Freeze! Police!' He pulled his Colt, aiming it at the center of the mass of tendrils and what was hopefully a vital organ.

Thorny tendrils whipped inhumanly fast, knocking the revolver from his hands as another mass wrapped around his throat. 'I'll snap your scrawny neck, narc …' hissed a chorus of dulcet feminine voices from unseen orifices amid the brambles and glittering raspberry eyes.

It was instinct. It was fear. And while it was one thing to snap a scrawny neck, it was another to snap a scrawny double-edged razor blade. The chorus of voices shrieked as blood and ichor fountained from severed tendrils along with an aroma like fruity children's breakfast cereal.

Bautas filed out of the crowd then, at least a dozen of them, squaring off against a gang of jokers dressed in heavy-metal T-shirts and assorted spiky accoutrements from Hot Topic. The Werewolves and the Demon Princes had chosen this street corner and this moment for their gang war and were brandishing chains and claws and even a couple pitchforks that did not look like props when there came the blast of a loud explosion followed by a voice on the microphone. *'Are you people fucking nuts!?!?!?'*

Bubbles's bubble had burst. She stood there on the float, 'Somewhere Over the Rainbow' still playing in the background, protecting a terrified Adesina with one arm while holding her sparkly wand microphone in a hand that trembled with rage. *'There are children dying in Africa in real wars with real armies and you assholes are going to fight over a few square blocks of Manhattan? How dare you! I'll take you all on! I'll take you all on right now!'*

The Werewolves and the Demon Princes stared. There were probably a few minor joker-aces among them, but they were facing one of the world's most powerful aces, looking like Glinda the Good at her most bad-ass, ready to level the Wicked Witch of the West.

The crunchberry triffid joker fainted either from terror or ichor-loss or some combination thereof. The Demon Prince's sample case vanished from her brambles along with the owl mask.

Then chaos erupted, or to be more precise, a whole lot of people out to watch the parade decided there were many places they would rather be than audience to a three-way confrontation between two rival gangs of jokers and a pissed-off ace protecting a small child.

The crowd overturned the barricades, running down side streets in both directions. Someone also thought to smash a window, because what was a crazed Jokertown riot without some looting? Besides which, it was Holbrooks and it had good loot.

Jim stepped up, but being plainclothes meant being ignored,

and he was unwilling to slice and dice the mob with his ace. Fortunately Franny and Tinkerbill were already there, in uniform, and Tinkerbill at least was more imposing and his deuce was less lethal. He snatched up one of the wands of misery from the window display and starting poking looters with it, who immediately fluoresced pink and sparkling as he scolded in his Betty Boop voice, 'You put that crap back, you asswipes, or I'll haul you in right now!'

Jim looked at him and then picked up a wand of misery himself. He didn't want to pull his backup pistol just yet, and could still turn the wand into a razor if necessary. He took a Plague Doctor's mask from a glowing pink looter, then, on impulse, tossed off the newspaper hat and put the mask on instead. The Magpie had already seen his face, and if he was going to track her, it would be better to be yet another Plague Doctor.

He then called Tenry. 'Damn it. I had her.'

'The Magpie?' Tenry was smart but it was always good to ask for confirmation.

'The same.' Jim briefed him on the rest. By standard procedure he should look for his piece, but this was Jokertown, and he was certain it was now in someone's plastic pumpkin bucket. The Werewolf would end up in the hospital. Hard to miss a possessed raspberry bush.

Finding someone in a black velvet cloak with a folding shopping cart? More difficult.

The three-way Mexican standoff between Bubbles and the Werewolves and Demon Princes continued. Jim saw Captain Mendelberg get out of Sergeant Tienyu's haunted Duesenberg, marching forward purposefully with a megaphone in one hand.

He had every confidence in the captain's negotiation skills so opted to hunt for the Magpie instead. The barricades lay scattered and the main portion of the crowd had fled down the west side of Broome Street. Jim followed, loping down, searching, until a block later he spotted her again. She was no longer wearing the owl mask, but still the same black cloak, the same cart, a cabbie helping both into the back, and Jim did not think there were that many Halloween revelers currently wearing 1940s diving helmets.

Jim was not Rikki but at the moment didn't need to be. He spotted an unoccupied vintage Duesenberg puttering down Broome Street and vaulted in. 'Tienyu! Follow that car!'

'Slim Jim?' Vivian Choy's voice crackled from the nonvintage police radio.

'Yeah.' Jim didn't know how she sensed things, but assumed she did, and the Plague Doctor's wand of misery made a great pointer. 'That cab right there.'

'Got it.' The Duesenberg revved up and Jim relayed the particulars, and a moment later Vivian's voice was on the radio, doing the same. It was a low-profile thing. They'd spooked the Magpie once before and there was no sense in spooking her now.

There were obviously more subtle ways to tail someone than a Plague Doctor riding in a possessed roadster, but it was Halloween in New York City, and the Magpie didn't know who they were. Tienyu kept a reasonable distance, tailing the cab up Lafayette and across the city, and once they'd entered the Gramercy Park district, it stopped in front of an old brownstone on Eighteenth Street. The cabbie helped his fare out, and Tienyu drove a little farther down to where there was a bar on the other side of the street, classier than anything there was in Jokertown.

The lettering on the edge of the awnings read PETE'S BAR – NEW YORK'S OLDEST ORIGINAL BAR – EST. 1884 and the party was in full swing. There was also valet parking.

Jim got out, watching as the Magpie went up the steps of the brownstone, opened a door, and disappeared inside. Jim pointed the wand of misery. 'What's that building over there?'

The parking valet was young, white, nat, and chosen to exude class. 'That's Stuyvesant's Folly,' he said with the pride of a native. 'Oldest apartments in the city.'

Jim raised an eyebrow but knew it didn't show with the mask. 'Thanks. Get the car whatever she wants.'

Jim felt a twinge of jealousy. Here he was, new to the city, looking at basement apartments that smelled of dead cheese joker. Meanwhile, an ace pickpocket was living in one of the city's most desirable old addresses. What he got for walking the straight and narrow.

142 East Eighteenth Street was undeniably old, but Jim had seen which door the Magpie had gone in, and with his ace, he didn't need to ring a bell. Straight and narrow were the operative words. A door crack was easily navigated, as were flights of stairs leading up and up.

It was a loft apartment, with the emphasis on loft, the vault of the place going up almost two stories into the mansard roof and the skylights. A life-size Styrofoam peregrine figure was suspended in the middle, an advertising figure from the eighties, dusty but still impressive. That seemed to be the theme of the place. A forest of curio cabinets and mirror-backed vitrines were set about the floor, illuminated by discreet track lighting and not-so-discreet chandeliers.

Jim glanced in the first one. It appeared to be a collection of Four Aces memorabilia, focusing on Golden Weenie, everything from a vintage action figure of him as Tarzan to a more recent Happy Meal toy from his turn as one of the villains on *American Hero* to a couple rather risqué black-and-white boudoir photographs of him and some attractive young brunette Jim did not recognize. Atop the vitrine there was even a Golden Boy snow globe, the Judas Ace posed with a tank over his head and drifts of gold glitter around his feet.

The next vitrine was topped with a Dr. Tachyon snow globe. In fact, several of them, and a couple of his sentient spaceship *Baby* for good measure. Inside was an ostrich-plumed hat the good doctor could have worn and, Jim suspected, had, a *Captain Cathode* lunch pail featuring a character obviously based on Dr. Tachyon and the infamous scene where he decides to 'borrow' the Hope Diamond (supposedly based on an actual incident with the Prince of Takis, but denied in the press), and next to that, the actual Hope Diamond.

Jim did a double take. It looked like the one he'd seen when he was twelve on the class field trip to the Smithsonian. They'd said it was the real one, but Jim had had his doubts.

The next curio held a jar that was purported to hold John Dillinger's penis. Jim didn't think that was a fake either.

Jim glanced in a few more. Mixed with Depression glass, Venetian glass, Takisian Barbie and Madame Alexander dolls, bobblehead jokers, yet more snow globes, and unbelievable collections of oddments and collectible grot were Ming vases, Meissen porcelain, the Voynich Manuscript that had been missing for thirty years, priceless jewels and antiquities. It was like the contents of eBay and the Victoria and Albert had all been vomited into one room.

He then came to a gun case with an amazing display of historic firearms. They were all dusty except one off to one side, a Colt .44 Magnum revolver. Jim recognized it. It was his.

Jim picked it up and checked it. Still loaded. Then it vanished.

He heard the sound of the hammer being cocked.

Jim turned and looked. The Magpie was there, his gun in her hands. The diving helmet was off, revealing a very old woman with a shock of white curls. She would have looked like someone's sweet old great-grandmother if she hadn't been holding a gun.

'So, who are you?' she asked, and a moment later Jim realized this was a rhetorical question as she raised one hand away from the gun. The Plague Doctor's mask vanished from his face, reappearing in her free hand. Jim was slightly dazzled then suddenly saw what he'd been missing – the vitrines were angled like a hall of mirrors. She'd been tracking him the whole time. 'Oh, it's you, sweetshanks! Don't know what was up with that nasty Werewolf ...'

She took the mask over to one wall where there was a series of hooks and cubbies, adding it at the end, alongside a devil, an owl, a pussycat, a pea-green witch, and a copper diving helmet. She looked to Jim and gestured. His wand of misery appeared in her hand, and she pointed it a ways away where there was an antique settee. 'Have a seat on the davenport. Don't mind the kitties.' She paused. 'You're not one of those horrible kitten-eating jokers, are you?'

'Uh, no,' Jim said, trying not to remember the incident earlier with Otto's chili.

'Good. I can't abide those. Awful monsters wanting to eat my poor pussies ...'

It was like being at his great-grandmother's house, if his great-grandmother were an ace.

Jim took a seat, amid a number of cats and a couple of kittens who looked familiar. They blinked at him blandly, the way only cats can. An old ginger tom deigned to sit in his lap.

The Magpie took his Magnum over to the gun rack and put it back in its place, and Jim came to a realization. 'You're the one in the photographs with Golden Weenie.'

She beamed. 'I was a hottie back then.' She came over to the couch and sat on the other end. The bong was on the coffee table along with the Demon Prince's sample case. 'Let's see what we got for trick-or-treats.' She opened it delightedly. 'Do you partake?'

'Uh, no.'

'Well then, no sense in filling up a whole hookah.' She took a meerschaum pipe out of a drawer and tamped it full of hashish, lighting it and puffing on it expertly. 'For my rheumatism,' she explained. 'So,' she said, looking Jim up and down. 'How did you get in?'

'I'm an ace.'

'Everyone's an ace now. Throw a rock at a game show and you'll hit twenty of them.' She rolled her eyes. 'I meant, what's your ace? Do you teleport?'

'No.'

'Good. Then you won't be leaving immediately.' She looked at him slyly. 'I used to teleport, a little, but it made me sick. Now I just teleport things. What do you do?'

'I, uh, get thin.' Jim held up a hand as demonstration.

'You're wasting your talents,' she said with grandmotherly disapproval. 'Look at everything I have here.' She waved the meerschaum at the room. 'You could have the same.'

'You stole all this?'

'In a manner of speaking.' She exhaled hash smoke contentedly. 'The skylights were open the first Wild Card Day. The owners melted and the place was just filthy with spores, so I got it for a song. Furnishings too. So many lovely things.' Dust rose as she patted the antique sofa. 'Anything people thought was contaminated they were just throwing out on the street!'

'Weren't you scared?'

'Not then,' she said. 'I was already an ace. Even before the Four Aces.'

'There were no aces before the Four Aces.'

She looked at him as if he were deeply stupid and took a toke. 'I worked for Dr. Tod.'

It hit him like an elementary school history report: the test that had gone wrong at Dr. Tod's lab. There were rumors of one other person there, someone who'd simply vanished. And while the conspiracy theories said that was Tod ...

'You're the first ace ...'

She nodded proudly and set down her pipe. 'I mostly got coffee, but I was there.'

'So that's why you took Dr. Tod's helmet?'

'That wasn't Dr. Tod's helmet. That was Edward's.' She pursed her lips. 'Poor man. Did you know he lost a foot? But he was always sweet to me and I wanted something to remember him by. And it's terribly disrespectful to put his helmet on Dr. Tod and say it was his.' She smiled then. 'If they wanted something that belonged to Dr. Tod, they should have just asked me. He taught me how to fire a gun, you know.' Two .38 specials appeared in her hands. 'I don't know where I put the one he gave me, but these were Bonnie and Clyde's.'

Jim thinned to nothingness, but angled on a couch, this was awkward. The tom leaped off his lap with a squall, giving just enough of a kick that 150 pounds of razor-thin joker-ace cut through the cushions. Then the guns went off, one then the other, multiple times. Snow globes exploded. Pussycats screamed and hissed, hiding under coffee tables and vitrines, and a bullet whizzed by where Jim's ear would have been if he were still 3-D. The Magpie fell back, partly from the recoil, partly from the large orange tomcat sitting on her chest, his claws pulling her hood over her eyes, the whole of him getting larger and fatter, losing hair, until a fat naked red-haired Irishman was sitting on her, bawling, 'Get the guns! Get the fuckin' guns!'

Jim struggled to free his ass. Another round went off and there was a crash. Glass rained down and the next moment the Styrofoam peregrine swung through the air to decapitate herself on the wall. At last Jim freed himself, willing his hands 3-D enough that he didn't lacerate the Magpie too badly as he pried the revolver from her right hand while Tabby sat on her left arm and chest and covered her face.

'Leghwoavme! Leghwoavme!' the Magpie protested through the velvet as Jim disarmed her other hand. He still had his cuffs, but they were taking no chances with a known teleporter.

Thankfully, it being Halloween in New York City, a fat naked Irishman hugging a black velvet ghost in the backseat of a 1931 Duesenberg convertible raised no eyebrows.

With the ponytail, pegleg, and nineteenth-century knee breeches, the notorious Dr. Pretorius looked the very image of a pirate, far better than Shirley and Ted ever would. He'd taken off the tricorne hat and stuffed parrot, but Jim saw them on a chair in the corner of the briefing room behind the strange joker woman who looked like she was made out of blue ice. She had no nipples, no genitalia, and no clothes, but judging by her posture and the way she turned toward Dr. Pretorius, Jim guessed she was some sort of legal secretary.

Captain Mendelberg's eyes looked redder than usual. Jim didn't dare to ask what had happened with the parade. She spoke: 'She would also need to wear a monitoring bracelet.'

'I'm certain that given my client's advanced age and delicate condition, that will not be necessary.' Dr. Pretorius stroked his silvery goatee sagaciously.

'I'm certain that given Trudy Pirandello's crimes and past associations, it will,' said Charles Habersham III, the new assistant D.A., who had strawberry-blond hair, a southern twang, and the attitude of the newest generation of old money.

'I object to those characterizations,' said Dr. Pretorius.

The judge's face was a mass of wrinkles with no eyes, but apparently excellent hearing. 'Objection sustained, but I must agree with the prosecution and the police: a monitoring bracelet is standard.' The judge looked like a man-sized gray worm wrapped in a Snuggie with a judicial robe over that. Jim was fairly certain the Snuggie was due to the hour.

'Thank you, Judge Burkhardt,' said the D.A.

Mendelberg nodded. 'As I was saying, the department would also require a probation officer to aid Ms. Pirandello in cataloging her various "acquisitions" over the years.'

'Again, I must stress, most of my client's items were acquired via legitimate channels, and those few that may not have been are beyond the statute of limitations and only of interest to the insurers. And given the biohazard potential of a historically documented spore cache—'

'Historically documented?' the judge repeated.

'My client has told me—'

'She told me the same thing, Your Honor,' Jim put in. 'Before the arrest.'

Judge Burkhardt's wrinkles wrinkled. 'Well, let's just say "alleged" spore cache. No one's going to want to mess with that either, and testing will need to be done in any case.'

Mendelberg pursed her lips. 'I'm certain at least the Hope Diamond can be sterilized.'

'Yes, yes, we have already agreed to that,' Dr. Pretorius continued, 'but—'

'But I have a number of wild cards on staff,' Captain Mendelberg pointed out. 'Officer Driscoll and Detective McTate have already been on the premises' – she gestured to Tabby, once again a cat, and Jim – 'and I myself will be making an inspection.'

'Moving along,' said Judge Burkhardt. 'I believe we were talking about having a probation officer in residence as part of the terms of Ms. Pirandello's parole.'

Dr. Pretorius stroked his beard. 'Now I do not believe that is strictly—'

'Let's not mince words, Henk,' the judge snapped. 'We've both known each other too long and it's too late for this beating around the bush. Either your client is suffering from age and diminished capacity such that she warrants assistance, or else she's competent enough to not need it in which case she's competent enough to go to jail. Which is it?'

'Age and diminished capacity, Your Honor.'

The worm turned. 'Is this acceptable to the prosecution?'

'Well, given the suspect's recent activities and varied acquisitions—'

'A simple "yes" or "no" will do.'

'Yes, Your Honor.'

'Good,' said Judge Burkhardt. 'From the description of the place, I doubt housing will be a problem. Do you have a parole officer in mind, Captain?'

Mendelberg smiled. 'The department's housing for Detective McTate expired about an hour ago – and from what I've heard, you haven't found an apartment yet?'

Jim shook his head, then when he remembered the judge couldn't see, added, 'No.'

'Then it's agreed,' said Captain Mendelberg. 'Detective McTate gets a room or adjoining apartment or whatever seems most feasible, as a condition of Ms. Pirandello's parole.' Her red currant eyes looked to Jim. 'And you, tomorrow, will begin to help her catalogue her possessions.' She paused, then added, 'Detective Fong has had an eventful night as well. But he is very good with paperwork, and he will be at no risk from spores from digital photographs.'

Captain Mendelberg was a master at understatement, but Jim was certain that Tenry would fill him in on what exactly his own 'eventful night' had entailed.

'I believe I have a draft of a preliminary agreement that should be acceptable to all parties concerned,' said Dr. Pretorius.

'Good, Henk,' said Judge Burkhardt. 'Please allow opposing counsel to examine it.'

The strange blue joker woman produced a sheet from a legal

folder and handed it to the strawberry-blond D.A. He gave it studious attention as the blue woman handed a copy to Captain Mendelberg as well.

There was a long silence punctuated only by the tick of the wall clock. The judge was the first to break it: 'Does everything appear to be in order, Mr. Habersham?'

'Yes …' the D.A. drawled slowly, 'but if I could—'

'By all means, *take your time*' – Captain Mendelberg laid the document on the table – 'but this is *fine* with the department.'

The clock ticked by as her red currant eyes attempted to bore a hole through the D.A.'s forehead, but either Mendelberg lacked an ace or else Habersham had one too. Either way, he eventually lowered the document and turned to the judge. 'No objections, Your Honor.'

'Excellent,' said the worm. 'Now, if we can get all the appropriate signatures …'

There was a light knock on the door, then Apsara came in. She was young, Asian, pretty, and worried-looking. 'Captain, I hate to interrupt, but I've got Lucas Tate on the line. He's heard that we caught the Magpie, is wondering how he gets his property back, and is also asking for an exclusive on the story. What do I tell him?'

Captain Mendelberg said something in Yiddish that Jim didn't catch but caused Dr. Pretorius to suspend his pen and raise his eyebrows. 'You can tell him that he may visit me during normal business hours, that I assume he's already filed all the necessary paperwork with Detective Storgman, and that if he's going to continue living in Manhattan for any length of time, that he should get renter's insurance.' Her red eyes glittered. 'You can also tell him that the department makes it a policy to not comment on ongoing investigations, and when we do talk to the press, we never give exclusives.'

Apsara nodded. 'Of course, Captain.' She shut the door.

Captain Mendelberg looked to Jim and sighed. 'Mazel tov, Detective McTate, on cracking your first case for the department. You were instrumental.' She smiled a small-toothed grin. 'I'm looking forward to your full report.'

Jim nodded, steeling his fingers on the table and keeping himself from thinning. 'Thank you, Captain Mendelberg.'

'*Meowww,*' added Officer Driscoll.

Jim didn't speak cat, but he thought he knew the meaning: *We're all mad here. I'm mad. You're mad.*

'Meow,' Jim agreed.

NOVEMBER

THE RAT RACE

PART 11.

Leo was standing before the snack machine debating the merits of a bag of chips versus a packet of cookies when Tabby Driscoll slunk up to him, smelling of something strong enough to power a lawn mower. 'Hey Tabs,' Leo said without meeting the undercover cop's eyes; he settled on the cookies and riffled around in his pocket for some change.

'Ramshead.' He coughed into the back of his hand, then again into the crook of his elbow. 'Been asking around. Been looking around,' he said quietly, and leaned against the wall beside the machine.

Leo spied a bottle neck poking like a turtle head out of Tabby's lowest right jacket pocket, but he didn't call attention to it. 'Learn anything good?' He pressed the buttons, watched the snack spiral curl and drop the cookies into the tray. Retrieving them, he opened the package and took a sniff.

'Sleeper's crashing on the west end of the neighborhood. Holing up with that limey. Had to follow her forever to find him.'

'You got an address for me?'

'Trade you for a cookie.'

'You got it.' Leo passed one over, and took the folded up piece of paper. 'Thanks.'

'You owe me,' Tabby said restlessly.

'Close your pocket, Tabs. Your habits are showing.'

After work it was dark and cold, same as just about always these weeks; but Leo didn't go home. He followed the address instead, tracking it down the streets and around the corners, past the alleys and off through the blocks of Jokertown until he found the building he needed.

He showed his badge to the doorman and slipped upstairs without incident, tracking down an elevator and finally, on the eighth floor, apartment number 833. It wasn't a real nice building but it wasn't bad, either. Leo knew the kind – a newer structure, with units that were clean but blank and smaller than the usual small. The door didn't have as many locks as it ought to have.

He knocked. No one answered. He knocked again, to the same response.

A few minutes later he returned with the building manager, explaining that there'd been a call from a concerned family member, asking the police to do a quick check-in to make sure everything was okay. The manager let him inside, muttering about dead bodies and how they didn't happen in his establishment.

Leo sent him away and started poking around.

The unit was furnished by Ikea. A queen-sized bed without a headboard was pushed against one wall, and a futon-style seater was pushed against the next. A large television faced the seater. Empty soda cans, take-out containers, and foil corn chip bags were shoved into corners.

The leftover sauce at the bottom of the nearest lo mein was still damp. The trash needed to be taken out, so the place smelled a little manky. But it didn't smell stale.

The place was basically one big room, with a narrow kitchen offset to the right and a bathroom immediately inside the front door. But there was a closet. A big one, if he judged the layout right. One of those walk-ins that are advertised as a potential bedroom or office, but not for anybody over four feet tall.

He turned the knob and the door opened to darkness. A pull chain dangled above his head; he pulled it, and a yellow lightbulb clicked on revealing clothing – some men's, some women's; some on hangers, some in piles by the shoes – and a few boxes. He poked at the boxes and saw nothing to get excited about.

But in a corner there was a big old bathrobe slung over a suspicious shape. Leo watched it hard, waiting for it to breathe, sniffle, or gasp. It didn't. Whatever was under there, it wasn't alive. Leo gave the robe a yank and then leaped back from confusion and a touch of fright.

She – for it was definitely a 'she' – glittered warmly in the low yellow light. A statue or, the detective thought as he recovered himself and reached forward to touch her head ... something stranger. Life-sized and frozen, crystallized into absolute immobility. His fingernail tapped against her as if she were made of glass.

Unsure of what to do or how to feel about his discovery, Leo replaced the robe and retreated from the closet.

He then tried to make himself comfortable on the hard-packed futon. He thought about turning on the television, but he didn't see the remote and he figured he didn't need the extra noise. It was a good call. He heard them approach, outside in the hall through the door that wasn't thick enough and didn't have enough locks.

'Calm down, dear.' A woman. The blonde, he assumed.

'I need more pills.' Croyd.

'We're almost home. You can take whatever you need,' she told him. She had an accent. British, but Leo couldn't place it any closer than that.

Someone's keys wiggled in the lock, and the door flung open with a snap as Croyd went banging through it. He moved like he was a little drunk or delirious, and the blonde came in behind him – then crashed into him when he stopped abruptly.

Seeing Leo. Sitting on the couch.

'What the ...' the Sleeper began.

Leo stood up and flashed his badge. 'Hey there, Croyd.'

The girl made a sharp gasp, but Croyd waved a hand behind himself. He said, 'Stay back.'

'But—'

'Just stay back.' He was trying to hold steady and look strong, but Leo knew the signs. The Sleeper had been awake for a long time, sucking down pills like candy to stay awake – anything to stave off the terror of the next nap. His eyes were bloodshot and rimmed with bags, and the edge of his mouth quivered. When he held his hand out at Leo, as though he could hold the cop in place, his fingers shook too.

Croyd said, 'What do you want? What are you doing here?'

'I only want to talk.'

'You could've called.'

'I tried an ad in the paper. Didn't work,' Leo griped.

'I don't read the paper much. Get all my news on the Internet like civilized people,' Croyd replied, but Leo hadn't seen a computer anywhere in the shoe-box efficiency. 'You going to arrest me?'

'Depends on how this plays. You want to sit down like a civilized person and have a talk, or does this get messy? It's your call.'

Croyd slowly reached his far hand back, as if to comfort the blonde. He moved with caution, like Leo was pointing a gun at him – even though he wasn't. But instead of telling the girl to shut the door and come inside, he touched Leo's hand and barked, 'Abigail, go!' He spun on his heel and began to chase her toward the door.

Leo started after him but a sharp, loud noise behind him nearly stopped his heart. He whirled to meet whatever was there and stared into his own eyes. His own face. Standing nose to nose with him. It would've taken his breath away except that he remembered what Tabby had said about duplicates. Of people. Of anyone.

The double matched him inch for inch. Same from the newsboy cap to the snow-damp loafers. It shocked him, spying his own whitened, blotchy skin and knobby-horned head. But it was only a duplicate, and it didn't do anything but stare.

So Leo followed his instincts, turned, and ran away from it. He dashed to the door where Croyd and the blonde – Abigail – had escaped only seconds before.

'Stop it, Croyd! You're making this a bigger mess than it needs to be!' he hollered, spying them in front of the elevator banks, waiting for divine providence in the form of a ping and an open pair of doors.

They didn't get it.

Abigail stepped in front of Croyd. 'No,' she begged. 'Please, don't. He's only tired, he's not – we're not—'

But whatever else she meant to say was cut short when the Sleeper nudged her aside and said, 'Just leave her out of this, you hear me?'

Leo'd had no plans to involve her, but he was too busy running to explain himself. He barreled down on them and Croyd misread it as an attack – when Leo was only catching up.

'Stop, God damn it!' the detective commanded.

Croyd took up a defensive stance, and as Leo approached, he took a swing. Leo ducked past it, and Abigail fumbled into the middle of things again, saying, 'Please, just leave us alone!'

But Croyd pushed her now, trying to keep her back, and he readied himself to take another strike. He was off balance, though – that much was obvious. The exhaustion oozed out of his pores; it made him sweaty and too impulsive. It made him slow.

The old cop lowered his head and his hat slid to the side, and then to the ground. He braced himself, lining up his back and shoulders to give his frame the support he needed to take the hit, and to give one back. Just like his joker name, and just like his broad forehead and thick, curled horns implied he might, he backed himself to the nearest table. His arms crooked in a pugilist's ready stance, but held low, over his chest. He took three steps forward.

Storgman's head caught Croyd in the solar plexus and the bigger man bounced back, breathless. He ricocheted against a potted plant, slapping his arm against a decorative stone column. He rolled, and he clattered to the ground.

Leo stood up straight. Left to right he bent his neck and it cracked. He went to the place where his hat was lying on the floor; he picked it up and with a jamming motion he smashed it back over his bald spot.

Croyd's head was lolling back and forth.

Abigail was pale, but Leo pointed at her boyfriend hard and ordered, 'Don't let him fall asleep. He stays awake until I get a chance to talk to him.'

The Sleeper mumbled, 'That's what I'm *trying* to do.'

Leo pushed his arms under Croyd's pits and hauled him upright, but Croyd fell and drooped. 'Help me here,' the detective told Abigail. 'Let's get him back.'

'Back ... back where? Are you arresting him?'

'Back to your apartment. And no. Not if he's feeling cooperative.' Together they hauled the staggering Croyd back to the apartment, and dropped him down on the bed. 'He must have coffee around here,' Leo said to Abigail. 'See about making him some, will you?'

She gazed fretfully at her stunned partner before dashing over to the kitchen area and turning on the faucet.

Leo sat down on the edge of the bed and used one of its pillows to prop the Sleeper up. 'Croyd,' he said. 'I don't think we've ever met. Not official-like.'

Croyd said, 'I don't know.' And he didn't look up.

'I'm Detective Storgman. And before you conk out on me, I want to ask you some questions.'

'Where's Abigail?' the Sleeper asked. 'She okay?'

'She's making coffee. She's not in any trouble,' Leo added, since that's what Croyd was really asking.

'Good. She's a good kid.'

'Little young for you,' the detective said, but looking at Croyd now, up close, it was hard as hell to tell how old he really was. His abnormally young face was framed with dark curls; only his eyes gave anything away. They looked like the eyes of a man in his seventies – a man who'd seen too much, stayed awake too long, and changed too often. God only knew how long he'd lived like that, bouncing from power to power, joker to ace and back again. He could live to be a thousand. Or he could live until tomorrow. Every new draw risked a black queen, and no one knew it better than Croyd did.

The Sleeper said, 'Yeah.' And he brought those old eyes up, and they were exhausted, but they made a game effort to stay focused on Leo. 'So what is it? What do you want? I was there looking for something to stay awake, that's all. Old story.'

'I want to talk about another old story,' the detective said.

'How old?'

'Nineteen seventy-eight.' Leo pushed. 'There was a diner called the Rathole. An all-night joint. Bunch of people died there, maybe you heard about it.'

Those dark old eyes went sharp. His shoulders sharpened too. He was awake now. Real awake, if only for an instant. He pushed himself up on his elbows. 'I heard about it.'

'Here it is, Crenson: I know you were there, and I'm not accusing you of anything. I don't think you had anything to do with the killing, but I think you're the guy who called in the tip. I think you're the only surviving witness.'

Croyd was tense now, and wary. Leo didn't like that look on him. 'Why now?'

'Because thirty years ago I didn't solve it, and I don't have much more time.'

The Sleeper might've been sleep-deprived, but he wasn't stupid. 'Retiring?'

'It's not up to me.'

He sighed, and the last half came out in a yawn. 'I'd like to help you,' he said.

'Then give me something. *Anything.*' In the kitchen, the bubbling of the pot said Abigail had successfully navigated the coffee-maker, and caffeine was in the works.

Croyd leaned up, so their faces were only a foot apart. In a fierce whisper he told the cop, 'Everything I ever knew about the Rathole I said into a pay phone down the street in '78. There was ... there was a *guy*. Some dude. He was wearing an owl mask—'

'An owl mask? I thought it was a ...' Leo wished he had his notes handy, something to reference. 'I thought it was a hawk, or an eagle, or something.'

'It was an owl, I think. It was kind of stylized, you know? And he comes in, and he's freaking out – totally strung out – and he's got a gun.'

'Keep talking.'

'He starts shouting about this car—'

'What car?' Leo demanded.

'I don't know – a *car,* in the parking lot outside. A big black Mercedes, that's what he kept shouting. Kept asking who it belonged to.'

'*That* car,' Leo said. The one with Don Reynolds's stuff in it.

'Yeah. He just – he throws this shit-fit about the car. And the melty-looking guy at the bar, he pisses himself when the counter girl points him out. Then Hash came out from the kitchen, and he had that sawed-off, and then both of those assholes opened fire.'

'What about you?'

'Me? I hid.'

'Where?'

He said, 'Back then, my skin and whatever I was wearing – I could change it. Practically made me invisible.'

'You had some kind of chameleon power?'

'Yeah, like that. Chameleon. I ducked down under the counter and did my best match of the background. Nobody saw me, I don't think.'

'I guess not, since you're still alive.'

'That's one way to look at it. But I swear to God, that's all I know. That's all I've got, and I'm so ... son of a bitch, I'm so tired. I need my pills!' He said the last part loudly, plaintively.

From the kitchen Abigail said, 'Coffee's coming, I promise! And I'll get your pills.'

'All right. I'll take your word for it, for now. And I appreciate it,' the cop said as he found the door to let himself out. 'But don't leave town, okay?'

The car. The black Mercedes. Had to be the one Deedle'd been driving when he was caught.

The shooter had wanted to know who it belonged to.

Now Leo did too.

... AND ALL THE SINNERS SAINTS

PART 3.

Charlie was in Maria's bodega picking out vegetables for dinner after a particularly hard day in court. Clyde, aka Nergal, had decided that threatening the judge and the D.A. was a good way to win acquittal. Now he was not only facing his murder charge, but the D.A. had tacked on the assault charge for attacking Jimbo. Clyde seemed determined to spend the rest of eternity in prison, but only after making his attorney look like the biggest idiot in New York City, or at least Jokertown.

'Fuck my life,' Charlie muttered.

He was judging the comparative merits of two different bell peppers, and weighing whether or not this was the kind of day where you felt justified buying a six-pack of Rheingold to go with them, when Maria called out. 'Charlie, somebody came in with a message for you. Little kid with three eyes. He's not from the neighborhood. Said a black guy in a Dumpster gave him five bucks to come find you here. But he had to go, so I told him I'd pass the message along.'

'A black guy in a – what was the message?'

'He said all good Christians go to church on Sunday,' Maria said, then shrugged. 'You don't go to church, Charlie?'

'Uh ... not as often as I should, Mamma Maria.' Charlie took his purchases to the counter to pay for them. On his way to the counter, he felt the trapdoor beneath his increasingly normal life pop open and drop him straight back into the shit.

Good Christians go to church on Sunday. Fuck my life twice.

They'd met at Father Squid's church last time, so that's probably what the message meant. Marcus would only meet at night when he could move around more freely. He probably meant Saturday night at midnight, when the day becomes Sunday. If he didn't show up, Charlie could try again Sunday night. But something told him that the Infamous Black Tongue would be there the first night.

Saturday was still a couple days away. It would give Charlie plenty of time to work up a really good worry.

He briefly considered calling Vince and asking him to come along to the meet, but dropped that idea quickly. Vince might feel obligated to try and arrest the fugitive, and Marcus would almost certainly fight back. Plus, once Charlie had gotten Vince his information for him, the rat squad detective had acted like he'd forgotten all about him.

Maria took his money and made change. Charlie was trying to juggle his bags and put his money away when he turned around and ran right into a tall man with a wiry but solid build. His bags tumbled to the floor, spilling green peppers and cherry tomatoes across the tile. He was already apologizing as he bent down to pick up the mess.

Before he could pick anything up, the man he'd run into said, 'Forget that shit,' then very deliberately stomped on one of the cherry tomatoes, crushing it and squirting juice across the floor.

Charlie's head snapped up in anger, but it quickly switched to fear when he recognized the face. Sam Napperson. One of the cops at the 5th precinct. Vince had told him that Snap, as the other officers called him, had been Lu Long's partner before Angel Grady. Snap had a smirk that told Charlie he'd enjoyed stomping on the tomato, and would like to move on to something a little bigger. Like maybe Charlie's face.

'Why don't we step outside,' Napperson said. 'Let someone else clean up that mess.' Without waiting for Charlie's answer, he turned and stomped out to the street. Charlie followed, whispering apologies to Maria as he went, telling her he'd be back to pick up the mess. Maria shook her head, a frightened look on her face, and came around the counter to do it herself.

Outside, Snap lit a cigarette, then spit on the sidewalk. He smiled at Charlie while blowing a cloud of smoke at him.

'Can I help you, officer?' Charlie said, trying to keep his nervous twitching to a minimum.

Snap didn't answer right away, just kept smoking his cigarette. When he'd smoked it to the filter, he flicked the butt out into the street. With the least genuine smile Charlie had ever seen, he pointed around him, then up at the apartment building above the bodega. 'This ain't a great neighborhood, counselor.'

'It's okay. I like the people here.'

'Lotta crime, neighborhood like this,' Snap said.

'I guess.' *Where is this going?*

'Guy in a neighborhood like this, people find out he's a lawyer, think that means he has money. Maybe they might try to mug him. Maybe break into his place and steal stuff. Sometimes they're hopped up on drugs and the victim gets hurt. That shit can happen, place like this.'

Charlie had no idea what reaction Napperson was looking for. He felt like he was in a play, and no one had bothered to give him his lines. So he just nodded and said, 'I guess,' again.

'So I think to myself, why a guy.' Snap looked Charlie up and down, slowly. 'A *vulnerable* guy. *Crippled* guy. Would try so hard to piss off the police that protect him from that unfortunate fate.'

Wow, thought Charlie. *I'm actually being strong-armed.* 'I appreciate your concern, officer.'

'What I would do, if I were a guy like that,' Snap continued, as though Charlie had not spoken, 'is I'd get myself some goodwill with the local police. Maybe let them know where my fugitive client was so he could be brought in. Turning in a guy who tried to kill a cop, that'd go a long way.'

Charlie didn't say anything this time. Napperson was going through his script, and Charlie's participation wasn't necessary.

'So,' Snap said. 'Maybe you know where a fugitive from justice might be hiding? Or if not now, where such a fugitive might be later. Say, on Sunday.'

Oh, shit. Charlie hadn't heard Snap come into the bodega. How long had he been there? The whole time? Had he heard everything Maria had said? Most cops knew a little Spanish, at least enough to get by on the street. How much of Maria's message to him had he understood?

'Officer Napperson, I'm afraid I can't help you. But I appreciate your concern for my safety. I'll make sure to let your lieutenant know about our conversation, and your worry about me getting mugged or robbed. That's the kind of personal touch that seems to be missing in community police work.' Charlie smiled his own version of a fake smile, trying very hard not to let the pounding in his chest give him away.

Napperson nodded once, as though acknowledging the threat. He started to speak again, but before whatever threat he was planning to level got out of his mouth, Charlie's cell phone started ringing. 'Oh, sorry, officer, I need to take this,' he said, holding up one finger. While Napperson gaped at him, he ducked back into his building and closed the door. The caller offered him a great discount on satellite television if he chose to sign up for their exciting service. He kept the woman on the line until he got to his apartment and locked the door behind him.

'Fuck my life,' Charlie muttered.

He walked head down along a run-down back street heading toward Our Lady of Perpetual Misery, pushing his way through driving sleet whose chill cut right through the woolen scarf wound around his neck and the gray houndstooth coat his dad had bought him ... because, even if he lowered himself to the status of mere public defender, likely future New York Attorney General Eric Herriman's son was by-God going to look *like* a lawyer. Charlie wore the coat because it was hip in an ironic-retro way. And also warm. Only not now.

Sparse streetlights cast funnels of lusterless flicker. The

wet-pavement smell crowded out everything but the eternal inner-city diesel stink and a waterfront whiff of marine decay from the East River nearby. *I'll insist Marcus turn himself in this time,* he told himself. *I've done my duty. I've done more than any normal attorney would do for his client. I've gone above and beyond.* His client needed to trust in the system.

But Puff and Angel are part of the system too, said the part of his mind in charge of making him uncomfortable. If his body got as much exercise as his insecurities did he could just throw over law and become a cage-fighter.

'Okay. Fuck. Okay. I'll get Marcus's statement for him.' He had a compact digital video camera in his pocket for just that purpose. 'I'll give it to Vince. And that'll be that. With that and the Minal tape, plenty to go on. No, wait . . . I'll tell Marcus I'll go in with him. Make sure everything's done by the book.'

And what a great idea that *is,* his bad brain jeered. *What if Marcus and Minal and Ratboy are all right? What if it was a bad shoot? Puff and Angel can't be the only ones involved. Somebody else at Fort Freak has to know. Any number of somebodies. Michael told Minal not to come forward. Napperson tried to threaten me. Who knows who else is in on this?* Fort Freak had a bad reputation going back decades. He'd heard it said that Maseryk had cleaned the precinct up, but maybe that was just talk. *What kind of target will you be painting on your forehead if you go in with the kid?* 'Fuck. Fuck, fuck, fuck.' And fuck Marcus for picking the church for their rendezvous. *We might as well meet in front of Jetboy's Tomb.*

At least not many tourists were going to be abroad on a night like this. Or anybody else who didn't have to be. That was the good thing about shitty weather. But who wanted to find good things about shitty weather?

Anyway, it was all bullshit evasion and denial. If those were recognized athletic events Charlie'd be in contention for the championship. He had never thought of himself as possessing *innocence.* Virtue, blighted and doomed to go tragically unrecognized due to the turn of the wild card, sure. Not innocence.

He wasn't sure how he was even walking. He felt as if all the cotter pins had been yanked from his joints. As if he should simply fall down right now into a pink bag of loose bones and gurgling mush. Some force he didn't recognize was all that held him together. Habit, probably.

Three blocks from the church he saw something poke out of an alley half a block ahead. Some instinct, possibly a remnant of a childhood spent dodging bullies eager to torment a kid whose flipper arms rendered him near helpless to defend himself, made him slide aside into the recessed doorway of a long-shuttered milliner's shop. It was a head, turned away from him. He saw a silhouette in the glow of a streetlight not yet shot out by the gangs.

The head vanished. A moment later Charlie saw it start to emerge again. This time it looked toward him. He had good reflexes, if not coordination; he managed to duck back before he was spotted. He pressed his back against chill glass, scared to breathe. *It's him,* he thought. *It's Lu Long. The dragon. Oh, Christ.* That meant that Napperson had heard everything Maria said, and had passed it along to his old pal.

Charlie risked another quick look. A dark figure with horns and a thick tail now ghosted along the sidewalk away from him. Toward the place where he was supposed to meet Marcus Morgan.

Thinking, *This is a BAD idea,* he followed.

Long didn't look back. That surprised him. Puff was a veteran street cop. Shouldn't they be more alert? Maybe he was that focused. Or just that arrogant. Ratboy had said everyone thought Lu Long was a prick.

Keeping to the shadows, which wasn't hard, he followed. Lu Long was intent on *something.* Something that pinned all his attention straight ahead. Charlie dared edge away from the comfort of the building fronts into the gutter. Half a block beyond the figure he took for Lu Long, a vertical sliver of deeper shadow indicated an alcove cut in a brick wall. Suddenly he knew.

Without thinking he found himself picking up the pace. As he was asking himself, *What the fuck am I doing?* he saw the right shoulder of the shadowed figure ahead of him dip and the left elbow raise. As the right elbow began to pull out to the side he broke into a balls-out sprint.

He glimpsed the joker's scaly dragon face in profile, expression set like concrete, and a handgun being thrust two-handed toward the alcove as Lu Long turned. Before he had time to think better of it, Charlie put his right shoulder down and slammed into Long from behind.

He didn't have much experience with contact sports. He certainly didn't have any experience with street fighting. But running into Lu Long from behind felt very much like running into a member of the New York Giants offensive line. Or a brick wall.

He bounced, and went down painfully on his knees. Long staggered away in front of him, then fell face-forward onto his elbows. He managed to hold on to his gun.

Charlie caught a flash of Marcus Morgan's face, looking very startled beneath a watch cap pulled down over his ears. Then Marcus was out of the alcove and twining up a dead light pole beside it as if he had a rocket up his ass. *Son of a bitch, he's running off and leaving me!* Despite the pain shooting out of his knees, Charlie jumped straight to his feet, turned, and ran back the way he'd come. *He didn't see my face,* pounded in his head to the time of his frantic steps. *He couldn't see my face. He mustn't see my face, he –* oh, shit!

The last came in response to a yellow flash reflecting on the wet pavement in front of him, and the loudest crack he had ever heard. Current Internet wisdom held that gunshots aren't really that loud. Which Charlie knew to be true – he lived and worked in Jokertown, after all. *If* you heard the shots from one block over.

The people who made that claim clearly hadn't heard a gun fired directly at them from less than fifty feet away.

A new surge of adrenaline gave Charlie more speed than his slick lawyer shoes and the wet pavement could handle. He went down in a spinning crash that seemed to happen all at once, and came to a stop with all new pains in his knees and chin. The straps to his left arm had come loose, and the prosthetic dangled like a failed amputation from the end of his flipper. He rolled to his knees and looked back down the street, visualizing Lu Long lining him up in his gun sights.

Which was exactly what Lu Long was doing.

Charlie squeezed his eyes shut, which was a scared four-year-old's reaction. *I'm going to die on my knees, whimpering, with my eyes closed.* Some part of his brain that hadn't given over completely to panic wondered if he'd actually hear the shot that killed him. When the shot finally came Charlie flinched, but no pain accompanied it. Instead, there was a loud crash and a series of curses from Lu Long.

Charlie finally found the nerve to open his eyes, and saw Lu Long locked in mortal combat with a twenty-foot snake.

Marcus!

Charlie lurched to his feet, planning to rush over and help his client, but he was only able to remain upright for a few seconds before the pain in his legs knocked him back down. And, on second look, it didn't look like the Infamous Black Tongue needed much help. The young joker was twisting his body like a giant anaconda, throwing loop after loop around the struggling cop, squeezing hard enough that Charlie could hear Lu Long's joints popping.

Puff seemed to have lost his gun in the struggle. That didn't mean, however, that he was unarmed. He hocked up a flaming spitball onto the snake that sizzled and burned like hot grease. Marcus screeched in pain and surprise and loosened his coils. Long pushed his way out of the loops and slammed his thick tail into Marcus's chest, hurtling the young joker against a nearby building hard enough to shatter bricks.

The Tongue recovered quickly though. He ducked under Long's second tail swipe and slithered out of range with a pit viper's speed. Puff let him go, and began searching the ground for his gun. Marcus shot out his long black tongue, coated with its deadly venom, clearly hoping to end the fight with one quick strike. Lu Long snatched the lid off a nearby trash can and used it like a shield, deflecting the tongue. Then he slammed the lid against a wall, pinning Marcus's tongue between them. 'Not me, motherfucker,' the dragon said with a wicked grin, then spit another flaming loogie onto Marcus's tongue.

Marcus screamed again, and his long serpentine body writhed in pain. He yanked his tongue back, scraping it badly on the brick wall and the garbage-can lid. When it had retracted, he turned to Charlie and yelled, 'Run!'

Charlie didn't need to be told twice. He grabbed his loosely dangling prosthetic arm to keep it from falling off, and ran down the alley as though all the hounds of hell were at his heels.

Or maybe just one dragon.

Charlie rolled and rocked in restless dreams. Masked men in bulky black uniforms kept kicking down his door and rushing into his bedroom, yelling and bristling with machine guns.

Once he'd reckoned he'd gotten clear of Lu Long, who didn't seem to be chasing him, Charlie had sagged to his already raw knees and puked up whatever remained of everything he'd eaten in his entire life into a storm drain. He was every bit as terrified by the fact he'd bodychecked a cop as the fact he'd been fucking *shot* at.

Once home, he took a long hot shower. And then the adrenaline shock ebbed so suddenly he was barely able to pull on his usual T-shirt and boxers and shrug off his arms onto their handy rack before falling face-forward into darkness that swallowed him before he felt the sheets.

The latest dream door-bang was followed by a bright light that blasted through his eyelids as if they were flesh-tinted windows. He was just wondering whether he was dreaming about being killed and seeing the tunnel of white light when hard hands yanked him out of bed and upright. Before his sore and unprepared knees could buckle he was slammed sternum-first into a chest of drawers. Another hard hand between bony shoulder blades pinned him there.

Dark figures moved around him like demons tempting a cloistered saint. 'Fuck,' said a voice muffled by a lower-face mask. 'He's got no fucking arms to cuff.'

'What am I being arrested for?' Charlie asked. He had a good idea. He also had presence of mind enough to play dumb.

A face leaned close to his ear, and a high-pitched voice said, 'Just stay calm and don't make a fuss. I'll make sure you get to the station in one piece.'

The big Chinese guy. Bill Chen. Charlie forced himself to relax. 'I'm cooperating,' was all he could squeak out before another body pushed into him, not so kind. 'I'm not resisting. Not even a little bit.'

'Shut the fuck up,' this second person said. Napperson. Charlie hoped Bill Chen was as good as his word. He doubted Snap would make the same guarantees.

'Use the barrel,' a third voice said. Police departments these days carried special harnesses, basically quick-latching plastic sleeves, to shackle unconventionally shaped suspects. One of these was quickly clamped on him and yanked constrictor-tight with sizing straps.

Before his brain cleared he was hustled out into chill dark-thirty air, smelling of early-morning delivery and the grease of the all-night diner down the block. Someone he assumed was Bill Chen, only because the hands didn't go out of their way to hurt him, pushed him into the back of a squad car.

They didn't bring his prosthetic arms. Nor did they bring his inhaler. When they marched him, shivering in an orange denim jumpsuit, down the corridor to lockup, breathing was like trying to pull open a deflated balloon with your fingers.

The cage door clanged open. 'Fresh meat, boys,' called the nat night-duty cop.

The hard, mean faces that turned toward Charlie didn't look altogether human. Whether they belonged to jokers or not.

'Eat up, baby!' Mamma said, beaming. 'I made you your own special. I know how you love tofu lasagna.'

I fucking hate tofu lasagna, Vince thought, *with a purple fucking passion. But when you're lactose intolerant* and *Italian, what you gonna do?*

'The boy hates tofu,' said his father, Big Pete. He weighed three hundred pounds and had a mustache like a nineteenth-century Black Hand crime boss. His name tag on his blue shirt even said Big Pete. Though not as big as on the back, where it said, BIG PETE EXTERMINATORS.

Yes, the universe hated Vincent Marinelli. He'd learned to put up with it. If never accept it.

'He eats the tofu because he doesn't want to disappoint you, Mamma,' said Vince's younger brother Leo, who was named for some pope or another and somehow wound up in his mid-twenties without having to get a job.

'Don't be ridiculous,' said his mother, who worked in denial like Michelangelo in oils. 'Now, Vinnie.'

'Ma, please. You know I hate being called that.'

'Vincent. Please chew with your mouth closed.'

'Ma, I got incisors the size of fence pickets. I can't chew with my mouth closed!'

She had lovingly polished those very teeth with Pepsodent when he was a chubby rat baby, to combat their regrettable tendency to turn orange. It made no impression. In the movie of his life, Vince was played by DeNiro. In his mother's movie, he was always Macaulay Culkin. At seven.

His phone rang. He took it from his belt and flipped it open.

'Vincent,' his father said, 'it's not respectful to your mother to talk on the phone at the dinner table.'

'Dad, it's official. I got to take this.' Holding up a paw to fend off the usual familial debate that accompanied – well, anything – he said, 'Yeah? Marinelli.'

Then he said, 'He did what? Fuck *me.*'

He closed the phone to find himself the focus of an oblong of horrified faces.

'What?'

'You got visitors, Flipper,' Sergeant Squinch said.

Sitting on a hard bench dozing, Charlie snapped his head up and his eyes open. He was immediately reminded of the old *Far Side* cartoon where one dude tells another to wake up because he's having a nightmare: 'Of course, we *are* still in hell.'

Charlie jumped up. 'Dr. Pretorius!'

'Well, hell,' said the outsized brown rat who stood at Pretorius's side. 'Here I expected they'd have you bent over a bench, taking turns having their way with you.'

Charlie felt his cheeks flush hot. 'No, nothing like that, Vin – Detective. Half these guys in here have been my clients at one time or another.'

'Evidently you're doing a decent job,' Dr. Pretorius said, 'notwithstanding the fact they're here.' His deep barranca-running tan contrasted with his trademark white ponytail and beard. He wore a pin-striped lawyer suit and a prosthetic that looked like a normal foot in shoe and sock.

'What are you doing here?' Charlie said. 'I mean, I'm glad to see you, but—'

'Springing your tender and fortuitously unviolated butt,' Ratboy said as a visibly disgruntled Sergeant Squinch swiped the key in the reader.

'Dad paid my bail?' *Oh, holy shit,* Charlie thought.

'No,' Pretorius said. 'I did.'

'I can pay—' Charlie started.

Pretorius stopped him with a quick wave of one hand. 'Young man, that is the very least of your problems,' he said, walking Charlie toward the clerk who would return his possessions. 'You assaulted a police officer, aided and abetted a criminal fugitive, and probably committed a dozen other crimes the D.A. will charge you with, once he thinks of them.'

'But—' Charlie started to protest, and was summarily cut off again.

'Not here,' is all Dr. Pretorius would say.

'They had a couple problems with Puff's story upstairs,' Vince said as they exited the precinct. 'Starting with, an officer discharged his weapon repeatedly without actually hitting a suspect. But don't believe for a second that means they'll drop the charges.'

A slim translucent blue figure stood at the bottom of the steps waiting, looking like an art deco sculpture of a woman carved in blue ice. When they reached her, she tipped her head slightly in Charlie's direction.

'Hi, Sibyl. Thanks for coming by to spring me from the big house,' Charlie said with a grin he didn't really feel. Sibyl didn't reply. Her lips were, as they say, sealed.

They walked through a morning chill sharp as glass, down Elizabeth Street away from the white building with the powder-blue entryway, 1881 inscribed above it and old-time carriage lamps to either side, toward the Jokertown Ice Cream Factory and around the corner on Bayard near Mulberry.

It took Charlie a moment to respond to Vince. He was having trouble hearing, for how loudly he was saying, *I'm alive. I'm free. I'm alive. I'm free,* in his head. He didn't take either of those things as so safe and guaranteed as he had twenty-four hours ago. 'So what do I do now?' he said.

'Now,' Pretorius replied, sliding his arm through Ice Blue Sibyl's and guiding her down the street, 'we get some food in you and come up with a plan.'

◆

Dr. Pretorius's tastefully decorated apartment smelled like a cheap diner. He had made good on his promise of food, and seconds after they'd arrived he began cooking using enough pans for four meals. The air was filled with the competing smells of butter, frying meat, and hot grease. To Charlie, it smelled like heaven, and when the food finally arrived, tasted even better. He was on his second plate of ham, two eggs over medium, and hash browns when he finally came up for air.

'You pack that in like somebody who puked his guts up last night and hasn't eaten since,' Ratboy observed.

'Detective,' Pretorius said. He'd piled his own plate high with pancakes, over which he liberally poured real maple syrup. When you routinely ran fifty miles at a shot you didn't have to count calories.

'Huh? Sorry. Rats suck at small talk. Let's figure out what to do with our boy, here.'

'Let's say, hypothetically,' Charlie said, 'that I actually attacked Officer Long. Wouldn't your zero-tolerance sense of law enforcement mean you want to see me hang for assaulting a police officer?'

'First off, "zero tolerance" has bad connotations. Sending SWAT to bust kids having a food fight isn't just prime dickery, it's a fuck-stupid waste of resources. Anyway, if you hypothetically did something as butt-headed as knocking down Lu Long the fucking dragon with his SIG in his hand, I'm sure it was to prevent him committing a thoroughly illegal act. Such as murder of a witness. That's a meritorious act of civic duty, not a crime. Hypothetically.'

'Well ...' Charlie saw Pretorius nod encouragingly at his brief hesitation. He recalled his old law professor's frequent words: *Never wholly trust a cop.* And Pretorius had examples of how fanatical true believers – like, say, Detective Vincent Marinelli – could be worse to deal with than the crooks. 'Let's say, *hypothetically,* I was supposed to meet a certain client. In order to urge him once more to turn himself in. And purely by accident I happened on Officer Long in the act of drawing his piece and pointing it at my client. And who sure didn't look like he was about to order my client to surrender. Hypothetically.'

'That's one fuck-storm of a hypothetical, Charlie.' Vince mopped runny egg from his plate with his last scrap of bread and popped it in his big, toothy mouth. 'You got any witnesses?'

'Just Marcus. My client. He saw the whole thing. Sadly, he's more of a fugitive than I am. Even if there were other witnesses, who's to say they'd talk? Everyone's scared of Puff and most of them think Angel walks on water. And now that Puff has shot at him, who knows how deep a hole Marcus will crawl into.' He turned to Ratboy. 'I haven't heard two words from you since I gave you Minal's tape.'

'Hey, when I have something to tell you, I will,' Vince replied. 'I helped get your ungrateful ass out of jail, remember.'

'What sort of information did this Minal have?' Pretorius asked.

'She told me about Joe Twitch not carrying a gun or drugs the night he was killed, and about some other stuff possibly involving blackmail. Oh, and she told me what alias Lu Long likes to use when hiding his money. She only blew the whole case wide open. That's all. Which, by the way, was corroborated by one of my clients, a Demon Prince enforcer who said pretty much the same thing about Twitch.'

'Yeah,' Vince said, 'I admit it was solid stuff. But these things proceed slowly. You have any idea how many banks there are in New York? Not to mention the Jersey, Connecticut, the fucking Cayman Islands. And "look for dick names" doesn't exactly narrow it down. Puff gets even a whiff we're looking for his ill-gotten goods, they'll disappear forever, and maybe him along with them.'

Charlie had had enough. 'I quit.'

'What?' The other two said it simultaneously. Then Vince ceremoniously said, 'Shakespeare, kick in the rear.'

Charlie and Pretorius looked at him. 'Sorry. Brooklyn.'

'What do you mean, Charles?' Dr. Pretorius asked. 'You've been passionate about fighting police injustice in the past.'

'That was before it started kicking in my door. Also before somebody shot at me. A dragon man *shot* at me. Jesus! I can't believe I've been shot at.'

'Don't forget he missed,' Vince said. 'Hypothetically.'

'What if he hypothetically *hit* me?' Charlie shook his head. As usual it made his bangs flop in his eyes. 'I'm not cut out for this. I'm no fighter. I lost every fight I ever had in my life. And those were only the ones I couldn't run from or weasel out of. Face it: I'm a total coward.'

'Taking down a three-hundred-pound dragon man with fiery spit and rage issues,' said Ratboy, 'that's the kinda shit they give medals for.'

'I'd thought about it for a nanosecond I never would've done it! They're *on* to us. Watching us.'

'No shit,' Vince said. 'They got that *stugats* Tabby ghosting me.'
'Who?'

'Officer Thomas Driscoll,' Pretorius said. He knew the Fort Freak roster as well as Captain Maseryk did. Maybe better, given the CO's notoriously reclusive nature.

'It's not bad enough I got to deal with a giant-ass snake,' Vince said, gulping black coffee. He'd been visibly annoyed when Pretorius didn't have any nondairy creamer. Something to do with lactose intolerance. 'But the assholes set a fucking cat to spy on me. I could run his furry orange ass in for obstruction, but he'd be out quicker than a Republican senator in a public pisser.'

Charlie was confused. 'What's your problem with Marcus? You're both jokers.'

'Take a look at my face,' Vince said, leaning forward. 'I'm a *fucking rat*. He's a *snake*.' He reached out to rap Charlie's forehead. 'He*llo*. Anybody in there?'

'Oh.' Charlie shook his head. 'This is getting off-topic. I just can't take this stress. I'm pretty sure Napperson told Puff about my meeting with Marcus. I can't fight the whole precinct. Oh, and I'm just about to be disbarred and thrown in prison. Just in case it needed to be worse. I got you the information from Minal. You have the tape. But I'm done. People calling me names and laughing at me is one thing. That's happened my whole life. It's going to prison I can't handle. Or death.'

'Kid, kid. You're really gonna do this?' Vince asked, barely disguised disgust in his voice. 'Fuck your client in his ass? If coral snakes have asses?'

'There's nothing I can do for him, except tell him to turn himself in. Which I've done before. He won't.' Charlie held up his artificial hands. 'I can't. You don't know what it's like to be me. It's hard enough always being the outcast. The wimp. The dirty joker. I'm just – I'm just beat down. I can't fight this.'

'Poor poor you, huh,' Vince snorted, causing his long whiskers to vibrate. 'They oughta make a parable out of you, Charlie. "I wept because I had no hands. Then I met a man who was a *fucking giant rat*."'

Blinking furiously, Charlie sat back. 'Sorry, I didn't mean to be—'

'Put a sock in it! I don't want your pity, either.' Ratboy stood up suddenly. 'Next time you go in your pockets, see if you find anything down there but change. You do, you know my number.' He nodded to Sibyl, who was sitting in the living room with a number of cats draped across her lap. Her face was, as always, enigmatic. 'Ma'am,' he said, then stalked to the door and slammed it shut behind him.

'Perhaps,' said Dr. Pretorius, 'it is time for you to go as well, Charles. Give some thought to what you want to do next. I'll talk to some people about getting you a good defense attorney.'

THE RAT RACE

PART 12.

Wanda Moretti leaned against a file cabinet and said, 'I think I've got it. Look, honey. Over here.' She handed him a clipping from a folder with the date 'December 4, 1978.'

He took it from her and said, 'Nice job.' At first he didn't see it, the tiny mention down at the bottom of the page, but there it was. He skimmed, and summarized aloud. 'Ramona Holt struck by a black car. Late-model Mercedes,' he said with a grim smile of satisfaction. 'A partial plate was reported; I dug it out of the archives at the station, but it's not mentioned here.'

'You said it belonged to the archdiocese.'

'No, I said it'd been *stolen* from the archdiocese, or that's what the old case file said when I finally scared it up. The Mercedes we found in front of the Rathole was reported stolen' – he held up the folder and pointed at it – 'on the fourth. That morning. Middle of the night, anyway. A week and a half before the killings.'

'By whom?'

'I don't know. The church didn't supply any particulars.' He leaned his backside against the table, sitting on its edge while he processed this new information.

Wanda left the filing cabinet to sit beside him. She took the folder from him, flipped through its contents a little, and said, 'Who reported the partial plate?'

Leo made a frown that turned into a gleam of possibility. 'I don't know, but I bet we can find out.'

Wanda took a deep, measured breath and closed the folder again. 'I guess you've got some work to do, then.'

'I guess I do. And I need to find my way back to the precinct, anyway. It's already been a long lunch break.'

'But worth it.'

'Definitely worth it,' he said, and he kissed her.

When she was finished kissing back, she said, 'Go on then. Get out of here, and I'll see you tonight.'

On the way back, something was bugging him but he couldn't put his finger on it. While he dug through the old records looking for info on Ramona Holt, something kept on bugging him; and when he double-checked to make sure that no, no one at the archdiocese was interested in talking about the car, that same unknown thing continued to bug him. It itched under his cap, two pieces of one thought that couldn't find their way to a meeting place.

And then he saw the signature closing the file.

The two pieces met. They clicked together like magnets.

He went to the hospital with the folder under his arm and Ralph Pleasant's room number at the front of his mind. The door was ajar and the machines were beeping, and Ralph was lying back, not asleep.

But he said, 'What, no flowers? No booze this time?'

And Leo said, 'Hey.'

'What are you doing back here?'

The detective pulled out a different folder, one with police paperwork and not newspaper paperwork, and he opened it. Silently, he read a few lines as he stepped to the path between Ralph's bed and the window. 'It'd been driving me nuts, Ralph. I couldn't figure out what you were doing here—'

He interrupted with a cough. 'Dying.'

'I was wondering how you could afford it. I know *my* insurance wouldn't cover a suite like this. I know the church hospitals take charity cases, but they don't put 'em up in style.' Leo glanced to the large window with the bright, clean curtains and the phone on the freshly dusted nightstand.

'What are you getting at?'

'At first I thought it was ridiculous, spending this kind of hush money to keep an old man comfortable; but then I figured it wouldn't be such a big thing, not for a big church with big pockets. You've only been here, what – a year? Less than that?'

Ralph glared in response, but otherwise didn't answer.

'Then I thought about the money the church spends keeping kiddie-diddling priests out of the news, and I wasn't so sure. Bad press is bad press, ain't it?'

In the folds of his bedding, Ralph burrowed down like an angry grub. He opened his mouth to reply, but hacked up a glob of something nasty instead.

Leo continued. 'Nobody likes bad press. It must've been pretty bad, if you sat on it all this time and they still let you cash it in.'

Ralph didn't make any objections, or swear ignorance, or lie outright. He only said, 'Bad enough.'

'The hit-and-run,' Leo prompted. Matter-of-fact. Not even asking, anymore. 'The black Mercedes parked at the Rathole that night in 1978, it belonged to the archdiocese.'

Ralph gave a nod so slight that he might've only been swallowing another gob.

'And somebody reported it stolen, conveniently enough, right after a hit-and-run that killed a girl down in the Bowery.'

'Sounds about right.'

'Who was driving it that night, when the girl was killed? And don't give me some line about how nobody knows, since it was stolen. That's the oldest trick in the book. Someone from the church killed that girl and ditched that car.' He looked down into the folder again, as if it were a crystal ball and could tell him something new. It wasn't, and it couldn't. 'Don Reynolds had been driving the car for a week. His ex-wife said she had no idea where he got it from – he told her he'd found it. We thought he stole it, but maybe we were wrong.'

'Maybe *he* hit the girl.'

'And maybe I'm your mother,' Leo countered. 'Who was the man behind the wheel? Who ditched that car, and got away with murder?'

'Vehicular homicide?' Ralph asked, his mouth moving around more of the thick slime that came up with every clearing of his throat. 'Leaving the scene of an accident?'

'Oh, don't dick me around about this,' Leo grumbled. 'I just want to know who was driving.'

Ralph thought about this. He gazed briefly past Leo's head, to the window and its lovely view. Then he said, 'He's been dead for years.'

'If it doesn't matter, just spill it. I'll keep it to myself, I promise you that.'

'You promise, eh?'

'You heard me.'

He gagged again, a garbled noise of gumdrops and oil. He said, 'His name was Contarini. He was just a little collared shit, back then, but ended up being a bigwig in the church.'

'Never heard of him. What was he doing here?'

Ralph shifted his shoulders, a horizontal shrug. 'Visiting from Rome. He was Italian.'

'But he killed a kid, and you let it go. You didn't even look into it.'

Ralph looked like he wanted to sit up and fight, but there wasn't enough fight left in him for that. He blustered weakly, 'Course I looked into it. That's how I knew he did it. But what was I supposed to do? The guy had diplomatic immunity.'

Leo had to admit, the situation would've been tricky. 'But you just signed off on it.'

Ralph didn't respond and Leo didn't know what else to say.

Of course Ralph had just let it go. Back then, especially – you didn't fight the church, not in those days before the public knew about the pedophile priests, and the lawsuits. You didn't fight the church, and you sure as hell didn't fight with anybody's embassy, and if the two doubled up, well. Even if Ralph hadn't been Ralph

… even if he hadn't been an essentially lazy son of a bitch with an opportunistic streak a mile wide … it shouldn't have surprised Leo to see it swept under the rug.

Ralph watched him, looking up, examining his old partner's face. 'I don't think he even knew he'd hit her. Not at first.'

'What makes you say that?'

Ralph hacked more goop and followed it up with, 'That's how I heard it. He was all wound up about something, running away from something. Driving like a bat out of hell, in case that's funny.'

'Yeah, Ralph. Real funny.'

'I'm just sayin'. When he figured out he hadn't clipped a dog or a trash can, he panicked. Dropped the car, filed a report. Caught the next flight home.'

'Got away with it.'

'Sometimes, they do.'

Leo agreed with a nod, and the wheels were turning again, dredging up questions Ralph probably couldn't answer. But he tried a few anyway. 'What about the girl who got killed? Who gave a damn about her?'

'She ran with the Demon Princes. Gang might've cared. Like they do, sometimes.'

Ralph had a point. Leo gave it to him. 'Maybe. And that just brings me back around to the gangs. But shit, Ralph. It never looked like a gang hit. You thought it was Deedle, you said so yourself. You let the neighborhood kill him for it, just to close it down.'

'I been wrong before.'

A new thought occurred to Leo. He asked, 'Hey, you ever hear of a button man called Raul Esposito? He was in town, back then.'

Ralph's eyes clouded over with thought. He said, 'Sure. Worked for Don Gambione … yeah. I heard about him. Big ol' nat who liked doing business in Jokertown. Gave him an excuse to wear a mask.'

Leo's ears pricked, and the back of his neck went warm. 'He used to work in Jokertown? And wear masks?'

'Yeah. You ought to talk to him. He knew Hash. He knew the Princes.'

'He knew more than he was saying,' Leo said under his breath.

'I heard he was slicker than whale shit through an ice floe.'

Leo thought about the tall, elderly man with the very nice clothes and the teenage whatever-she-was. So things changed. Sometimes things changed a lot. 'I'll have a word with him.'

Ralph looked like he wanted to say more, but he was seized with a fit of gagging convulsions, as if the drainage had finally won out. He waved at Leo, and Leo took that as his cue to leave – before any doctors or nurses accused him of upsetting the old cancer patient.

He bailed out the door, leaving it ajar as he'd found it, and was nearly to the stairs when he heard an alarm go out – calling doctors and crash carts and crying ominous codes to a room. He didn't catch the number but he was afraid it might've been Ralph's.

Leo turned on his heel, and dashed back the way he'd come.

Around the corner he collided headfirst with a girl who had thin arms and legs, and a blue streak in her hair, and lots of black spandex under a fake leather jacket. Rattled, they bounced back away from each other – Leo's nose smarting and starting to bleed from the way it'd connected with her skull.

Speak of the devil. Or think of her, anyway.

Leo held a hand up to his face and he looked at her, somehow knowing who she was before his eyes quit watering enough to see her clearly. 'You,' he said.

She froze, and looked both ways – desperately casting for an out.

He blocked his end of the hallway and tried to tune out the frantic beeping and flustered conversation down the corner, in the next corridor. 'You've been following me,' he said. He asked, 'It's Maggie, isn't it? Why are you chasing me around?'

But she was silent, and her wild eyes did calculations, measuring how fast she could move and how old the cop in her way was.

She bolted, fast as a deer dodging out of traffic.

The medical call went out over the intercom again, and this time Leo heard the room number. Not Ralph's, which was a relief, he guessed.

Released of that particular concern, he lashed out and caught her by the upper arm, pulling her back and drawing her up under his face. She was almost as tall as him, but not quite. And not half so heavy. 'Did Esposito send you?'

She whipped off her glove and grasped him in return. Suddenly the room was moving, fogging. Dimming.

Tiny and strong as nails, the bones in her hand dug into his as she grasped it.

Suddenly he understood. Not everything, but something.

He understood that she was hurting him – just by touching him. He could feel his body constricting against her, surging to get away from her; and some primal instinct overrode his cop inclination to hold her in place.

He let her go. She let him go.

She ran.

He staggered, and put his hands on top of his knees, and waited for the room to stop spinning.

HOPE WE DIE BEFORE WE GET OLD

PART 2.

Today, Oddity's hands were mostly Evan's. When that happened, they always went to Dutton's Dime Museum.

Some time ago, Dutton had asked Evan to create figures for a committee diorama: Drummer Boy, Curveball, John Fortune, Rustbelt, Lohengrin, Bubbles, Earth Witch, the Righteous Djinn ... Over the last year and a half, Evan had worked on them as often as he could. Evan had set up his sculpture bench in the space where the diorama would eventually be set, curtained off from the rest of the Dime Museum during operating hours ... but now, with no customers wandering through the museum, they'd moved the heavy curtains back. He was working on Drummer Boy's head, inking the rock star's tattoos into the waxen, bare skull, copying them from a set of publicity stills that Dutton had acquired for him. It was slow, tedious work, and Evan was already exhausted. The other figures crowded around them in various stages of assembly. He'd spent a lot of time here in the last few months, working the wax over the head forms into their proper shape, trying to get the details so perfect that someone viewing the sculpture would feel as if they were looking into the person's own face. His fingers were slick with the wax, the sharp scent of it filled his nostrils, and he was having trouble keeping their eyes focused on the work. Both eyes seemed to be Patty's, and her vision wasn't as good as his own.

[Hang in there,] he heard Patty say. [We're both tired. Work while you can and I'll take Dominant when you're finished.]

[Are we doing the right thing, keeping John in Passive all the time?] he asked.

[Do we have a choice?]

Oddity shook their head. No, John couldn't be trusted with the body. Not anymore. Since Wild Card Day, his symptoms had only accelerated.

[… you don't know me you're both keeping me prisoner here let me out I can handle it I can …]

Beyond the diorama, the main hall of the Dime Museum loomed. The bright multicolored gleam of the Fresnel spotlights was gone, replaced by the distant, dull glow of the after-hour fluorescents high against the black-painted ceiling. In the pale bluish light, they could see one of the Turtle's old shells hanging on wires from the ceiling, or across the hall the Rox diorama, with the massive figure of Bloat dominating the scene, his immense body seeming to be cut off by the very walls. To the right there was Carnifex in his white fighting suit; to the left the Four Aces.

Ancient history, most of it. Evan remembered it all too well, but he wondered how many of those who wandered through the museum did.

[I do,] Patty whispered above the constant muttering of John. Oddity's body shivered and twisted as she spoke, as if John were shaking Oddity's rib cage like the bars of a cell. [I remember …]

Evan sighed. He set down the tools, groaning as he lifted Oddity's body from the stool on which they'd been sitting for too long. He walked out into the hall, glancing around at the various display pieces, many of which he'd made himself – those that Dutton hadn't bought or acquired in other ways.

Oddity's body twisted under the cloak. The pain stabbed at them like a sword's slash, and Evan half moaned, half shrieked in response. The pain was white-hot and it blinded them; he felt Oddity sink to their knees. Something tore loose inside and seemed to rip through their mingled organs, their knotted and snarled muscles and tendons. Oddity doubled over, forehead to the floor. Patty and Evan both howled in pain.

Evan couldn't hold against the agony. The pain flung him from the summit of Dominant, sent him hurtling down through their mingled consciousness. He felt Patty try to take control of the body, but John pushed upward at the same moment. Protected from Oddity's eternal pain by the mental distance of being Passive, well rested for having been there for so long, he was stronger than either of them. They felt him tear loose of the prison of Passive and rise, rise, hurtling past Patty's presence and clawing at Evan, casting him down, down, down ...

It felt momentarily wonderful to be in control of Oddity's body again.

Momentarily.

Then the pain hit John, and he could also feel Patty clawing at him inside, trying to toss him back down and take Dominant, and he/Oddity roared in mingled agony and defiance, their hands fisted so tightly that the nails dug bloody crescent moons in their palms and dripped blood on the tiles of the museum. John glanced around through the fencing mask; he saw Bloat with several young people gathered around him, and he recoiled. 'Jumpers!' He remembered them, the jumpers. They'd taken Patty away to the Rox and Bloat was playing judge and jury with the bastards and Patty, and he couldn't allow that.

John bellowed in fury, rising from the crouch in which he found Oddity's body. 'No!' he shouted to Bloat. 'Don't you dare hurt her!' Bloat didn't move, didn't even react as Oddity slammed into him, as they tore at the sewage pipes that impaled the joker's horrid sluglike body and ripped them out. There was a shriek of metal, and plaster was falling around them in a solid, white rain. One of the pipes groaned and slammed into Oddity's head, denting the fencing mask and thrusting the steel mesh back into their face. They screamed, lashing out blindly with their fists. 'No!' John screamed. He saw a flash of white cloth, and realized that Carnifex must have arrived. John struck out at the ace before Carnifex could respond, knocking over the man. It seemed like many of the aces had come, and John was confused, not certain who was there and why they were helping Bloat.

None of it made sense. But they were there, and they had attacked him. He knew only one response to that.

[John! Calm down. I'm here.] It sounded like Patty's voice but it couldn't be her; she wasn't here, wasn't inside with them. It was that bastard jumper David trying to fool him, and he knew it.

[John!]

[... I'm sorry Patty I couldn't hold him I couldn't stay in control too weak too tired sorry ...] Evan's voice was an exhausted whisper, but John couldn't figure out why he was talking to Patty.

None of the aces were there to help Oddity. None of them ever were. The aces were always out for themselves. Oddity was alone against those who threatened the residents of Jokertown. The lone vigilante dispensing true justice – sometimes final justice, if it must be. Oddity roared and wailed, spinning and lashing out at those around him. Alarms were shrilling now, and he thought he smelled acrid smoke. He didn't know how long he'd been fighting, but there was blood in their eyes and everywhere he looked, he saw people. He gathered Oddity's strength and continued to fight, using anything he could find, ripping down pipes to use as weapons, tossing any wreckage he could find ...

[John, please! You have to stop! You're destroying everything ...]

There was movement to his right: he saw that new ace with the rusted metallic body – what was his name? John couldn't remember – but John charged at him with both arms wide, growling and bearing him down. His powerful fists pounded at the ace. Like the others, he crumpled, and Oddity laughed. They were so much weaker than he was.

'Oddity! John!'

Oddity whirled around. John squinted through the dented mask and the blood smears toward a cadaverous figure. He looked vaguely familiar, but John couldn't remember the name. Patty was screaming a name over and over – [It's Charles, John. Charles Dutton ...] – but the words meant nothing to John and he shut out her voice, refusing to listen to it. It wasn't Patty, couldn't be Patty.

He blinked; there were other figures gathering around the thin, skeletal old man wearing a mask: cops. He saw uniforms, badges, the guns they held. He roared again in defiance and pain and rage, grabbing the corpse of the rusted metal ace and hurling it toward them. He saw the skeleton man go down, saw the cops duck, and he began to throw anything he could grab. The skinny guy tried to get up again, and Oddity lifted a fist, beating him back down; the mask slipped off, exposing a face like a dead skull.

He saw a metallic sphere drifting in the air. Something hit them in the side, sending a searing jolt of electricity through their body; John heard the chatter of the current, smelled the ozone, and he reached to pluck out the electrode darts, tossing them back toward the cluster of officers. 'Shit, that just made it mad,' he heard someone say. 'Hit him again, Sarge.'

The flying machine dipped in the dark air under the fluorescents and another pair of silver darts flew toward Oddity, trailing coiled wires. This time they struck him directly in the chest, and John roared with the pain. Oddity's body shuddered with the voltage, but again he yanked them out, still screaming, and pulled hard – the flying machine struck one of the supporting pillars and fell.

A monster yelled, and a huge, furry form leaped at Oddity. He roared and met it. They collided, and John – the rage now a red mist that overlay everything in his sight – used Oddity's strength to power them backward. They slammed into a display of large glass bottles, which toppled and shattered around them. The smell of formaldehyde rose around them, and they were covered with grotesque and deformed bodies. 'Fuck!' John heard the furry cop say. He pushed again, and the beast's hands fell away from him. Oddity staggered through the broken glass and bodies back toward the knot of blue-clad attackers, roaring.

John saw one of the cops pointing his nightstick at him as if it were a gun. He grabbed the nearest uniform and tossed it toward the cop as the man whistled; a pink aura bloomed around the officer in the air as his body slammed into the group.

[Get out! Gotta get out!]

Oddity ran, plowing through a wall into an open space. He heard people yelling behind him, and he continued to grab whatever he could and throw it behind him as he moved, moving quickly through the dark space with their powerful legs. He saw a door, went through it, and found himself outside. There were blue and red lights flaring from down the street. Oddity grabbed a trash can, crumpled it, and jammed the door shut by closing it on the can. He heard someone pounding on the other side and shouting.

Then John turned their body and ran away from the sirens and the lights and the commotion, sliding quickly into the darkness of Jokertown, wondering how he got here and snarling at any movement he saw.

It was perhaps an hour or two later when Patty managed to wrest control from an exhausted, raving, and manic John. She tore him from Dominant and took Oddity's body herself, and Evan – despite his exhaustion – threw John all the way down back to Passive.

[… don't you see they were attacking us I did it to save Patty I had to they were going to kill her …]

They were near the docks of the East River, at the very edge of Jokertown – John had been waiting for Charon to ferry them across to the Rox, only no one had seen Charon in decades and the Rox had gone to wherever Bloat had taken it. The oily water slid past them, heading toward the tip of Manhattan and the sea on the tidal flow. A tourist boat passed, a spotlight flickering over them for a moment before Patty had Oddity slide back behind a stack of packing crates. 'I think that might have been the Oddity, folks,' a distant, tinny voice said. 'A rare glimpse …'

[… see they're still hunting us still want to hurt us …]

[I'm so sorry,] Evan said to Patty. [The pain came so fast and hard. I couldn't hold on, couldn't keep John down.]

[It's okay,] she told him. [I couldn't hold him either. It's no one's fault. But my God, Evan, what he – we – did. I think we hurt Charles pretty badly, and who knows what we did to Beastie, Tinkerbill, Black, and the others.]

[You want to find out?]

They both felt Oddity nod their head. The tourist boat, the running lights on it a wave of shimmering red and white reflections, had continued upriver, diesel engines thrumming. Oddity turned and faced west. They moved back into the city.

Half an hour later, they entered the emergency room of the Jokertown Clinic through a side door, stopping the first nurse they saw, a joker whose left arm branched at the elbow into a quartet of forearms. She was smoking a cigarette, which she dropped as she noticed them. 'Charles Dutton,' they grated out, their voice a ruined baritone. 'Where is he?'

The nurse stared. 'You're not allowed to be here. I can't tell you.'

'We're not here to hurt him. We want to apologize. Or do you want us to just open up all the rooms and find him ourselves? That would be far more disruptive.'

All five hands pointed. 'Third room down,' the nurse said. 'But I'm calling security. You understand?'

Oddity nodded. 'Do whatever you need to do.'

The nurse ran inside, stopping at the first desk and speaking frantically into a microphone. 'Security, Code Red Emergency. Code Red,' they heard the PA announce. Oddity walked down the hall, uncaring.

Troll's huge form came rushing toward them from around a corner, two burly attendants behind him. 'Hey,' Troll boomed. 'You can't be here.'

'It's Patty, Troll,' she said, holding up a hand – it was mostly hers, with Evan's thumb. 'John's in Passive. It's okay.'

Troll looked uncertain. 'You need to leave,' he repeated, frowning.

Oddity's head shook. 'I gotta know,' she told him. 'Dutton is our friend, and I've hurt him.' She could hear their voice breaking; Troll heard it also. She saw him take a long breath.

'I'm calling the precinct,' Troll said. 'And I'm staying with you. If you do *anything* . . .' He let the warning trail off.

'We'll behave,' she said. 'I promise.'

Troll grunted. One of the attendants rushed away – to call the cops, she figured – while the other stayed with Troll.

Oddity pulled aside the plastic curtain screening off the third room and slid into the wash of light there. Dutton lay on the bed: his right arm was casted, and both legs. An IV dripped saline and painkillers into his left arm. His skeletal face looked even more white than usual and his eyes were closed. Father Squid was there also, a chair pulled up next to the bed. Leaning against one wall was a joker wearing a simple black full-face mask with the mouth set in an eternal frown, but the fleshy dreadlocks pulled back and held in a bright blue scrunchy behind the mask told Oddity that it was Lucas Tate, the editor for the *Cry*; as Oddity entered, Tate pushed off from the wall, the eyes behind the mask glinting as if suddenly eager.

'Oddity,' the joker breathed; yes, that was Tate's voice.

Dutton's eyes opened, and it hurt Patty to see the open fear there. 'Charles,' she said. 'I'm so sorry, so sorry ...'

'Patty?' Dutton's voice was a pained whisper.

Oddity nodded. 'John ... John managed to take over, and he was terribly confused. He thought we were back in the Rox, that all the wax figures were people attacking us ...' Oddity gave a great heave and a moan as their body shifted under the cloak. Troll growled low under his breath and moved closer to them, putting a hand on their arm. Patty ignored it. 'I'm so, so sorry,' she repeated to Charles. 'I don't know how we can make it up to you. Evan says to tell you that as soon as he can, he'll get the figures back together.'

Dutton nodded, but his eyes went quickly unfocused and closed again. Father Squid patted the man's left hand on the bedsheet. 'Patty,' he said, the tentacles that served him for facial hair wriggling, 'this wasn't your fault, or Evan's. Charles knows that, and you must know it too. God has sent you a burden I can only imagine. It's getting worse, then?'

Oddity nodded solemnly.

'I'll keep all of you in my prayers, and if there's anything I can do, please let me know. You should pray too, Patty – for forgiveness. For this, and for ...'

'I know,' Patty told him. 'And I do pray. Believe me.'

Father Squid looked uncertain, but a smile lifted a corner of his lips under the tentacles. 'Good,' he said. 'Maybe, if you would come to confession, Patty. You're a member of the faith.'

'I was once, long ago,' she told him.

[If we need to pray for forgiveness, it's mostly thanks to John,] Evan said inside. [We've beat down lots of good-for-nothings. Let's confess how we beat Deedle to death right in back of his church. I'm sure the good Father remembers how that asshole looked after John was through with him.]

Father Squid was still smiling his gentle smile. 'I know that you don't come to church very often, but if you, Patty, or Evan or John need to talk ...' He stopped. Down in Passive, John railed: [... he knows, he knows what we did to Deedle and we can't let him tell, can't let him ...] They felt John rising from Passive, trying to take Sub-Dominant, but Evan pushed him back down again. Patty shivered – if Father Squid had been telepathic, she might have worried. But his smile was genuine and unforced. [He doesn't know, John,] she said. [Be quiet, and don't worry.]

[... are you sure Patty he may know and he could tell Captain Black or Chrysalis or Hartmann ...]

[John ...] Her sigh matched that of Evan. [They're all long gone or dead. That was decades ago.] He wasn't listening; he still raved on, and she realized that the priest was waiting for her to speak. 'Thanks, Father,' she said. 'I appreciate it.'

Father Squid patted Dutton's hand again, shifting in his seat. 'You've talked to Dr. Finn? There's nothing he can do for you medically?'

Oddity shrugged, though under the cloak it looked as if three shoulders lifted, and bone scraped against bone, making them moan again. 'He suggested some drugs. We tried a few, but they affect the wrong one of us more often than they affect John, or we all feel the effects, and usually not in good ways. We couldn't control John at all then.'

'I'm sorry,' Father Squid said, shaking his head so that the tentacles moved sluggishly again. They heard Tate take a step forward into the room, close to their right side, though he stayed a careful few steps away.

'Finn has the trump,' Tate said. 'Did he suggest that?'

Oddity turned toward the masked joker. 'Yeah,' Patty said flatly. 'He did.'

Tate nodded. 'I hate to say this so bluntly, but it really might be your best option,' he continued. 'John's not going to get better. I had an uncle with Alzheimer's, and I watched what happened to him. Your situation *will* deteriorate. John's going to be less and less coherent, living more in the past than in the present. He's going to get increasingly angry, confused, and—'

'We know what's happening to him, believe me,' Patty said abruptly, cutting off the man. 'Finn's given us the lecture and as much literature as we could carry. We know.'

If Tate was irritated by their interruption, his eyes didn't show it and the mask hid the rest. 'Then the trump ...'

'Lucas,' Father Squid interrupted, 'that's not a decision you or I can make for them. I'm not sure it's a good solution at all.'

This time, they did see the eyes narrow behind the mask's eye-holes. 'Maybe not,' he said. 'But John running amok in Oddity's body isn't something anyone in Jokertown wants, either. Next time, he may kill innocent people.' He gestured toward the bed and Dutton. 'Ask Charles when he wakes up. Or ask the cops a few rooms down.'

'Still,' Father Squid began, but the curtain to the room parted suddenly to reveal what looked like a red-haired and plush Sesame Street monster crammed into a police vest and pants, more than seven feet tall and *still* hunched over; if he stood up, his wolf-snouted and horned head would have gone through the drop-in tiles of the ceiling. Behind him, Oddity could see an Asian woman in police uniform, her gun drawn and pointed directly at Oddity's chest: Officer Chey Moleka. [Beastie ... Good, we didn't hurt him badly.] The furry creature spoke in a gravelly bass voice; Patty thought that he still smelled of formaldehyde. 'Oddity, you're under arrest for assault and resisting arrest. Put your hands on your head and turn around. Slowly ...'

Oddity paused. They could have pushed the massive joker back into his nat partner and maybe have reached the turn in the corridor before they had a chance to recover, but Moleka might have fired off a few rounds and hit someone. John would have done it. Maybe even Evan. But not Patty. They'd hurt too many people already this night. She turned Oddity's body, put their massive, tricolored hands on top of the cloak's hood and the fencing mask underneath. Father Squid, Tate, and Troll were staring at them; in the bed, Charles opened his eyes momentarily and then closed them again. She heard the jingle of metal and let the joker cop pull their hands behind their back and handcuff them.

'Tell Charles, Father,' Patty said. 'Please tell him how sorry we are, that we *all* are sorry.' Father Squid nodded.

A furry, meaty hand clapped their shoulder. 'This way,' Beastie's deep voice said, and they allowed themselves to be directed out of the hospital toward the waiting police wagon.

Sergeant Jessica 'Squinch' Penniman's special talent was the ability to shrink living animals. 'Do it,' Patty had told the sergeant. 'Shrink us and put us in your dungeon.' She waved toward the fairy-tale castle of iron sitting on a long table in the cell. On the turrets, tiny flags sagged in the windless air of Fort Freak's lockup.

'Pretorius will just have you out tomorrow,' Squinch protested, tousling her short blond hair into Patty's burgeoning protest, her blue eyes wide. 'The captain said to put you in normal lockup.'

'Make us little,' she told Squinch. 'I'll tell Pretorius that it was my request. We can't hurt anyone if we're a few inches tall.'

'It takes time to wear off,' Squinch continued to protest. 'It'll be weeks before you're back to your regular size.'

'We don't care. Do it.'

Sergeant Squinch had shrugged. She'd touched Oddity's shoulder and for a moment the world went strange around them, like a video lens zooming in on reality. Squinch's face looming over them was huge, with pores the size of saucers (though Patty thought it best not to mention that) and hair strands like bridge cables. She put her hand on the floor. 'Step on and hold on to my thumb,' she told them, then lifted them up to the table where the wooden castle sat. She opened the ornate building – the entire side was hinged, so it swung open like the two halves of a book – and gestured to one of the open doors on the table level. She locked it behind them with a key that was massive to Oddity, but only a tiny sliver in her gigantic hand. Then she swung the castle shut again; they heard the sound of the clasps being locked – the sound reverberated, shaking the entire structure.

In the darkness, they could hear the sound of tiny, shrill voices, calling to them from the other cells in the fortress. They ignored them, focusing on their own interior conversation. Oddity moaned as their body shifted again, the pain lancing from abdomen to chest, making their breath catch. Patty fisted their hands against the torment until it passed.

[… why are we here why did Squinch do that to us we need to talk to Snap or to Pretorius we don't need to be here I'm fine I'm fine and I'm sorry …]

[He almost sounds lucid,] Evan said to Patty. [He knows where we are, knows the names.]

[And an hour from now, he'll be lost in the past again and angry,] Patty said. In the past few months, they more and more spoke of John as if he wasn't actually there, as if he couldn't hear their voices. [God, I'm so tired. Let's just rest and try to get some sleep.] They both knew the fallacy of that; Oddity had to sleep as did any person, and if they didn't then the person in Dominant would become exhausted from the pain of holding the body and fall away into Passive. But their dreams – there was no true rest even in sleep, not when their dreams were as fused as their bodies, nor when John's increasing paranoia and fury dredged up horrible images that plagued them all.

[… no no I'm fine and I'm so sorry I won't do it again I won't …]

[Did we kill an innocent man?] Evan persisted. [Maybe they're right. Maybe Deedle didn't kill Lizzie? He kept denying it, all the way to the end, but we were so sure …]

They remembered that night all too well.

John had been in Dominant, but it didn't matter – Lizzie Wallace had been a good friend, and the killings at the Rathole had shocked all of them. They'd waited in the alley that night ... they'd been told to go there ...

Not long after they'd settled in, they saw Deedle hurrying up the street and ducking away along the side of the church toward the rear. Oddity sniffed in satisfaction and moved after him. Toward the rear of the building, they paused again, glancing around the corner. Deedle knelt down in front of the tiny flower garden at the base of a statue's pedestal.

'Deedle,' they'd said as they stepped from the deep shadow in which they were hidden, and the ugly joker nearly jumped a foot in the air, the coarse red hair covering his body lifting visibly.

'Shit!' he said. 'You damn near scared the piss out of me, Oddity.' His gaze darted past Oddity toward the freedom of the side yard and the street. He rubbed his good hand over the bandaged one missing its thumb. The handcuffs were gone; he must have found a hacksaw somewhere. 'Look, man, I gotta—'

'You killed Lizzie and the others,' Oddity said.

'No, man. It wasn't me. Honest.'

'They found you with their things, Deedle. There was blood on your clothes.'

Deedle started to try to dash around Oddity, but one huge hand threw him back against the stone wall of the alcove. The joker crumpled there. 'Yeah, I stole some wallets and stuff,' Deedle said, 'but they were already dead when I got there. I swear, man. That's the truth.'

'Right. And you bit off your own thumb to escape, because that's what any innocent man would do.' Oddity moaned and laughed at the same time. Their fist drew back and Deedle shielded his face from it, but it did him no good. The first blow broke Deedle's hand as well as his nose and shattered bones in his face. The next drove his teeth down his throat. The one that followed sent blood spattering over the statue of Our Lady. She didn't flinch, but only stared sadly down at the beating as it continued, and at the broken husk of a corpse they eventually left behind.

It was the first time they'd actually killed someone. They'd administered dozens of beatings before, but had always stopped short of taking a life. They felt as they'd done something good, as though they'd avenged Lizzie and the others, who could rest easily now ...

[Maybe he wasn't lying,] Evan said again.

[... who cares who cares he stole from them he was the one he had to be the one we would do it again if we had to ...]

[Like we nearly killed Charles?] Patty sent down to Passive, but John didn't respond, though he went silent for a few moments. [We'll kill more innocents if we're not careful,] she said: to herself, to all of them. [We won't be able to avoid it.]

Oddity moaned, slumped against the wall of the fortress. They lifted the fencing mask from their face, and the cold air of Fort Freak bit at their mingled, distorted features like frozen knives. They drew in a searing, frigid breath, and they tried not to think at all.

THE RAT RACE

PART 13.

'Goddamn, Charlie,' Lucas Tate said to Dutton, bound like a mummy on the hospital bed. Then to Father Squid he added, 'Begging your pardon, Father. But I mean, Jesus, look at him!' he pointed.

Father Squid patted Dutton's hand. It was one of the only parts that wasn't bruised, busted, or bandaged. He said, 'Oh, come on now. It's not that bad.'

'The hell you say,' muttered Dutton through a split lip and a cracked tooth. The ass-beating he'd taken would've been hard enough on a young man; on a guy his age, it had laid him flat.

Leo contrived a chuckle and said, 'You *do* look like death warmed over. But then again, you always have.'

'Very funny,' said the injured party, but his swollen mouth drew tight in a grin. 'At least some of you Velvets thought to come and see me.' He wasn't quite slurring but his words were thick on his tongue. Might've been the swelling. Might've been the painkillers.

'What's this about the Velvets?' Dr. Pretorius leaned into the room. He waved jauntily with one hand and held out some flowers with the other, then followed them both inside.

Sibyl trailed behind him, so silently she didn't even leave footsteps on the cold, pristine floor. Father Squid nodded at her, and she nodded back, then went to Dutton's side. She put out a hand and touched his forehead, but did not smile or offer sympathy, or make any other emotional gesture. Her lovely, unreadable face remained just so. And having paid her respects or shared her concern, she retreated to a corner by the window. There, and out of the way, she watched the men chatter and fuss – doing their level best to cheer up their old friend.

Before long, visiting hours were up. Lucas Tate, Dr. Pretorius, and Sibyl took their leave before the nurse could usher them on their way; Father Squid and Leo were the last to go, and when they left, they left together.

Leo had planned it that way. He had more questions, but he wanted to keep them quiet and private. 'Hey, Squid,' he said as they walked together. The hall was not crowded but it was occupied with nurses, assistants, and the occasional gurney awaiting a patient to tote. No one paid the two jokers any attention. So he went on. 'I want to talk to you about the Rathole. I'm not finished with it yet.'

The priest didn't express any surprise. If anything, his posture settled into resignation, as if the weight of the conversation was expected. He fidgeted with a paper cup of hospital coffee; it steamed itself cool while he didn't drink it. 'You're nearly out of time.'

'I've still got another month before they give me the boot. And I still want to know what happened. I've got a new name, and I want to run it by you. What can you tell me about Romulus Contarini?'

'Contarini? He was a high-ranking Vatican representative. He hated jokers above few other things in this world. He's dead now, though. Has been for years.'

Leo had looked up that much, after he'd gotten the name out of Ralph. 'But before that. He was here in town, wasn't he? December third, 1978. He was visiting from Rome.'

'Yes, Father Contarini came to me. I believe he called it a "fact-finding mission."'

'If he hated jokers so much, I can guess how he felt about the facts he found.'

'Yes, you can.' Father Squid sighed heavily. 'I realize that he had not found what he *expected* – and I expected philosophical differences. But, you must understand—' He took his eyes off the cup and turned to Leo. 'He was horrified – by the church, by *us*. By what we became, and who we were.' He was noodling with the rim of the paper cup – rolling and unrolling its edge between his fingers. 'Contarini went home to Italy and declared us heretical. He excommunicated me.'

'But while he was here,' Leo stressed, bringing it back around to 1978. 'What happened in the church, between you two?'

'He … he became violent. He broke things. He picked up candles and threw them, trying to burn the place down. So I threw him out. I had no choice.'

Leo Storgman looked at the slope of the priest's big shoulders, and the meaty cut of his back. Squid was not a small man, and not a weak one. Even now, old enough to claim a senior discount at the coffee shop, he was not the kind of fellow who often got mugged or harassed – collar and cassock aside. 'When you say you threw him out …' he said.

'We were both young then, but I was stronger.'

'Jesus, Squid. What did you do for a living before you … before you did *this*?' Leo gestured at the cassock, the collar.

Father Squid did not immediately reply. He glanced to the emergency exit, as if he wouldn't mind running for it, but he only kept walking slowly down the hall at Leo's side. 'I was a soldier,' he said.

But Leo guessed that it wasn't as simple as that. 'What kind?'

'Did you know that there was a joker brigade in Vietnam?'

'I knew. Were you in it?'

'I was a sergeant. Four times over. And four times over, busted back down.'

'Problems with authority?' the detective guessed.

'With authority. With my temper. Take your pick. I left it, anyway. Years ago. Years before the Rathole, even, and years before Contarini paid me that visit in '78. And the last I saw of him, he was driving off in that shiny black car. I'll never forget it, or forget the sound of the tires as he fled, as fast as that car would take him.'

A moment of silence fell between them, pocked only by the paging of a doctor over a tinny intercom.

Leo said, 'That car.' Because he couldn't think of anything else. He couldn't say it – that Contarini, in all his fear and dread and hatred, had fled the scene and run over a girl, killing her. He couldn't add that to the pile of whatever Squid was carrying. So he asked instead, 'Did you ever know a girl named Ramona Holt?'

Squid frowned and looked Leo in the eye. 'I don't recognize the name.'

'She died a long time ago. I just wondered if she'd ever been a parishioner here. She was a teenager, ran with the Demon Princes. She didn't see too good, and she didn't get around too good either. I thought you might have known her, coming or going, looking for charity.'

'I'm sorry. I don't remember her. That's not to say she was never here, but … did she have something to do with what happened at the Rathole?'

'She might have,' Leo conceded.

Father Squid sighed, and slowed. He stopped in an eddy of the hallway's flow and set the coffee cup on top of the trash can he found there. 'I still think it *must've* had something to do with the gangs.'

'Warlock?'

He nodded. 'It had to be him. He had motive, means, opportunity—'

'Well, he had the means,' Leo said. 'And I could assume an opportunity, but what I don't have is a motive for him. And anyway, he never killed with bullets, he killed with his curses.' *Though Sergeant Squid was surely handy with bullets.* Leo pushed that thought out of his mind. Then he changed his approach. 'What about Deedle?'

To the priest's credit, he didn't ask, 'Who?' He only said, 'Ah.'

'Well?'

'Well, what about him?' Father Squid asked.

Leo knew a dodge when he heard it, so he pressed harder. 'Kid's real name was Bernard Augustus. He might've been a member of your congregation; or even if he wasn't, I think he did the same as the Infamous Black Tongue – he came to you for help. What'd you tell him? What'd you give him?'

'Now we're getting into tricky territory, Leo,' Father Squid said firmly.

'How's that?'

'Confidence between a priest and a—'

'Damn it, I'm not asking you to tell me about his confession. I'm asking you why he was found dead behind your church!'

A shift in the priest's shoulders betrayed a small stiffening, as if he'd made a decision and was steeling himself to hold it up. 'I can't talk about Deedle. I can't talk about the Rathole anymore, Leo.'

'Can't, or won't?'

'It's up to you. But my promises to God outweigh your professional curiosity. Go home, Leo. Let the dead rest, and don't ask me to compromise my vows.'

'Squid—'

'We're done here,' he said, and he walked away.

Leo watched him go, and when the priest had rounded the corner and proceeded out of sight, the detective picked up the paper coffee cup off the trash can lid. He didn't throw it away. He took it with him.

And that night he added Father Squid's name to the white board's list of suspects.

He wiped it out with the back of his hand. He looked at the smudge left behind, capped the marker, and walked away.

FAITH

PART 3.

November, 2010

Beneath the catacombs, there was a lower level, a dank subbasement devoted to storage of less sacrosanct items. The rooms down here had not even been electrified yet. There was so little money and so many things that had to be done. Sometime, soon maybe, Father Squid told himself, as he pulled up the trapdoor and went slowly down another metal-runged ladder.

It would not be long now, he sensed. Leo knew about Contarini. He was a good detective, old Ramshead. Soon enough he would learn the rest. *All my sins will be uncovered.*

This second level smelled more earthy than the one above. Old furniture was tossed about in all sorts of disorder along with battered church vessels, outworn habiliments, and useless artifacts of every sort that Father Squid really should have gotten rid of. He sneezed once explosively as the dust he stirred up tickled his tentacles, then went right to a battered footlocker on an old wooden table by one wall.

Fortunately, he didn't have to bend over it. His knees were getting creaky too. The priest selected a key from the ring he kept in a cassock pocket and unlocked the chest. He lifted the lid and it fell back with a hollow *thooom,* stirring up more dust. Father Squid caught his breath and looked inside, overwhelmed as he was every time he came.

374

He was overwhelmed by memories that were three decades old, but felt as fresh as yesterday. That brought back old griefs and joys that never, he knew, never would fade no matter how many times he opened the locker. Never. Never. Never.

December, 1978

A pack of mothers with their babies in tow descended on the store-front community center on the day they held auditions for baby Jesus. Father Squid knew it would be bad. He didn't know that it would be *this* bad.

'Steady,' he said in an aside to Dorian Wilde, who was nervously clutching at his flowing, greasy hair with his normal right hand. He looked about ready to bolt. The collection of twitching tentacles that was his left hand simply wiggled with more verve than usual, a stream of ichor dripping from them onto the stained lace cuff of his dubiously laundered white silk shirt.

'I'm not getting paid enough to put up with this,' Wilde muttered.

'You're not getting paid anything for this,' Father Squid reminded him.

'Remind me, then, why I'm doing this.'

'Out of the goodness of your heart?' Father Squid suggested.

'Right.' Wilde was going to say more, but Father Squid put a long-fingered hand on his sleeve – the clean one – stopping him.

'Forgive me, Dorian,' the priest said, 'but it looks as if something has arisen that I must deal with. You organize the mothers and pick out a Jesus.'

'I'll get you for this,' Wilde said as Father Squid hustled over to a newcomer who was standing just inside the community center's front door, a frozen expression on his handsomely patrician features. Father Squid couldn't say exactly what his expression conveyed, but it seemed to be caught somewhere between suspicious and outright hostile.

Father Squid had never seen him around the neighborhood before; he was much too elegant for Jokertown. He seemed to be in his mid-thirties, but his thick wavy hair had already gone silver at his temples. Although he wore a clerical collar, his suit was not off the rack. Even Father Squid, not exactly a fashionista, could see that. It was cut from rich, smooth cloth that draped his lean form with an almost imperial elegance. It was probably worth more than the community center's quarterly operating budget.

The man, who had been dividing his attention between the mothers and infants whom Wilde was attempting to chivvy into some semblance of order and Gary Giamatto, a joker artist who was sketching out some murals for the community center's walls, turned to look at him, frowning. 'I am Monsignor Contarini,' he said, 'of the Vatican's Office of Theological Purity.' He spoke excellent English with a slight Italian accent. His voice was deep, powerful, and completely disapproving. 'Are you in charge of this …' His voice dwindled as he gestured vaguely at the church and surrounding grounds.

Father Squid cleared his throat. 'Actually, Father Coughlan—'

'Yes, yes,' Contarini interrupted with the wave of an elegantly manicured hand. 'I know all about *him*. He sent me here. It's you whom I've come to see. If you're Father … Squid.'

'I am,' Father Squid said mildly. Only the twitching of his facial tentacles betrayed the sudden tension running through him.

Contarini's lips twitched. 'Yes. Of course. Who else would you be.'

Giamatto had turned and was frowning at Contarini. The joker artist was small but brawny. He had four arms. His four hands had six fingers each. His two left hands were holding sticks of colored chalk. 'And who is this?' Contarini asked.

'Ah, yes,' Father Squid said. 'This is Gary Giamatto. A very talented artist. He is preparing a decorative mural for the community center. Gary, show the monsignor your sketches.'

Giamatto silently handed Contarini a well-used drawing pad. Contarini's eyes grew wide as he thumbed through the pages. 'What … is … this?'

'Roughs for a wall mural. Some iconic images that our parishioners can relate to. That' – he struggled to find the proper words for a moment – 'that have some relevance to their lives, their situation as jokers.'

Contarini had stopped on a page depicting a slight figure with burnished red hair who was dressed like a Renaissance fop and was two-faced like the Roman god Janus. His right face was angelically serene, the other leered like a bestial demon. He held an unburning sun in his right hand, a bolt of lightning in his left. 'That is the creator,' Father Squid explained, 'who blesses with one hand and damns with the other.' Silently, Contarini turned a page. A handsome, golden-skinned man whose face had a look of sorrow and shame was juggling an arc of thirty silver coins. 'Ah,' Father Squid observed, 'the handsome betrayer who regrets his sin.' Contarini turned another page to reveal a smiling Madonna with beautiful brown and white wings cuddling a two-headed babe at her breasts. 'Of course,' Father Squid said, 'this is—'

Contarini closed the pad and handed it back to Giamatto. 'You don't have to tell me what it is,' he said, frowning. He looked around the center. 'And what's going on here?' the monsignor said, focusing on a desperate-looking Wilde, who had been surrounded by a knot of impassioned mothers who were all holding their infants up for him to see.

Father Squid smiled. 'Casting for our Christmas pageant.'

'Good to know that you celebrate the day of Our Lord's birth.'

'Of course,' the priest observed mildly.

'All right,' Wilde said suddenly, loudly. 'All right.' He glanced around himself with the look of a trapped animal. 'You!' He pointed with his ichor-dripping tentacular hand. 'You, madame, what's your name.'

'Dockstedder. Mimi Dockstedder.'

'Your child will be the baby Jesus!'

A dissatisfied cry arose from the dozen disappointed mothers as Mimi Dockstedder held her child up in triumph over her head. Both heads wailed like lost souls. Father Squid smiled indulgently. He turned to look at Contarini and was startled at the look of black rage on the monsignor's face. 'You dare to engage in such revolting blasphemy!'

Father Squid shrugged his massive shoulders. 'We are simply utilizing a strategy the Church has used over the centuries, over the millennia, to relate to indigenous communities around the world. The Virgin of Guadalupe. The legend of Noah and the Ark. Why the very placement of important events of the liturgical calendar as Christmas and Easter on commemorative days sacred to the prior pagan beliefs of the people—'

'You dare!' Contarini shouted.

Suddenly the mothers stopped complaining and turned to stare at them. Wilde took the opportunity to scurry for the back door as the mothers looked on, their expressions divided between curiosity and anger that they readily turned from one target to another.

'What's the matter, mister?' Mrs. Dockstedder asked. 'My Rick and Mick ain't good enough to be baby Jesus?'

Contarini sputtered in incoherent rage. He shouted in Italian, which, perhaps fortunately, no one understood. He grabbed a nearby bank of votive candles and, to assuage his fury, swung in the direction of the knot of women. They gave a collective gasp compounded by fear and their own outrage. 'Watchit, mister,' Mrs. Dockstedder warned, clutching Rick and Mick to her bosom. 'We got kids here!'

'They're not children,' Contarini spat, 'they're demon spawn! Devils! Vermin—'

Father Squid had had enough. He grabbed Contarini by one well-tailored sleeve and spun him about. 'They *are* children,' he said, 'formed in the shape of Our Savior, Jesus Christ—'

'You dare,' Contarini hissed between his teeth, 'to spout liturgy at me!'

'I dare to demand recognition as a human being. For myself, and my people.'

'You are nothing more than heretics,' Contarini said severely. 'And will be dealt with as such. I will report back to Rome. I will see this parish closed. I will see you, personally, excommunicated—'

'And I will see you removed from my parish.' Father Squid turned to Giamatto, who was observing the proceedings with a jaw slack with astonishment. 'Gary – open the door.'

As the artist sprang into action, so did Father Squid. His hands closed on Contarini's collar. The monsignor flinched as the vastly heavier joker gave him the bum's rush through the open door and onto the street beyond, where Contarini slammed up against a big black Mercedes.

'You will pay,' Contarini said in a shaking voice. 'You will pay for your heresy and blasphemy, for laying your disgusting hands on me, you, you—' Words failed him then, so he yanked open the car door, slid behind the wheel, and sped off into traffic without even bothering to glance around, leaving a bevy of honking horns and indignant cries in his wake.

Father Squid sighed, rubbing his eyes wearily. The anger had drained out of him as quickly as it had come.

They cheered him when he came back into the center, crowding him happily and congratulating him. 'That's showing the bas – I mean, bum,' Mrs. Dockstedder said.

Father Squid shook his head. 'I'm afraid that I showed very poor judgment,' the priest said. He held up his hands at the chorus of 'no's.' 'And I'm afraid also that that's enough excitement for now. I – I have to go meditate upon my actions.'

'Sure, Father,' Mrs. Dockstedder said. 'You do that.'

'You take it easy and don't worry,' another mother called out. 'We're with you. We got your back.'

Father Squid nodded and left the community center, grasping Giamatto's hand and exchanging nods as he went out the door. He was tired. He was pushing himself too hard. There was so much to be done. There always would be. And now he had Rome to worry about. He desperately wanted to continue in his position in Jokertown. He genuinely loved his people. He felt, finally, as if he'd found a home, a place in the world, a mission to perform, a people to help. If he had to battle Rome to do so, so be it. He'd worry about that later. Time enough for that, he thought, in the future. He had more immediate things to worry about.

He turned off Orchard Street and went down a shortcut through an alley that took him to the side entrance of an apartment building, a six-story walk-up. He shuffled his way up the stairs to apartment 2-C, took the key ring from his cassock's ample pocket, and opened the door. The apartment was tiny. Though furnished with second- and thirdhand furniture, it was as neat as a dollhouse that was home to especially tidy dolls. The small living room was colorful and comfortable with brightly hued throws and rugs abounding. Though he had warned Lizzie a thousand times, the window leading out to the fire escape was slightly open, leaving it chilly even by Father Squid's thick-skinned standards. He crossed the small room and closed and locked the window, reaching over the plant box filled to bursting with still-blooming pansies to do so.

He bypassed the tiny kitchen that shared a hallway with an equally tiny bathroom. The bedroom door was ajar. Lizzie was at work in the small niche in the corner of the bedroom that was her sewing nook. She looked up as Father Squid stood in the doorway, a momentary frown quirking her normally smiling features. 'Darn it, Bobby, you caught me. I wasn't finished yet.'

'You should still be sleeping—'

'Couldn't,' she informed him. 'Too much on my mind. Plus, I wanted to finish this before the pageant.'

Her mouth curved in her usual smile. To Father Squid she was magic. She was one of the sweetest, kindest people he'd ever met during a hard life fraught with violence. And despite his hideous looks, despite the blood that stained his hands and haunted his dreams, she loved him. She was a miracle.

'What is it?' he asked, mystified. All he could see was that it was red.

'Oh,' she said, quickly stashing it aside, 'you'll see it when I'm done.'

'Can't be a wedding dress,' he said, coming into the room and sitting facing her on the edge of their bed. 'It's the wrong color.'

'Yes.' For a moment her smile faltered. 'We have to talk.'

'About a wedding?' he asked. 'I know that you're just out of a bad relationship. I know you're still feeling, well, concerned about, about things—'

'Bobby, I'm—'

'Just a second,' he said quickly. 'Let me say this. Of course, I'm a priest. I feel, well, not guilty, exactly. I've broken my vow of celibacy for our Church, but, really, I wouldn't call it living in sin because what we have—'

'Bobby, I—'

'Just a second. You know that I love you. That I regret nothing we've done. A priest must experience all aspects of life if he's to properly guide his flock—'

'Bobby, will you just shut up for one second,' Lizzie said, exasperation showing in her tone.

'All right,' Father Squid said in a small voice, suddenly nervous beyond all reason.

'Bobby, I'm pregnant.'

For a moment the words lay between them like an unexploded bomb. The fear and nervousness only expanded in Father Squid's mind.

'But we used birth control,' he said in that same small voice.

'Well, it didn't work,' Lizzie said. 'The question we have to face now is what do we do.'

She didn't have to spell it out for them. His initial thought was of awful, incoherent fear. Had a vengeful God taken action against him because of all the sins of his life? But that was nonsense. His faith wouldn't allow him to believe it for even a moment. He had sinned, certainly, and God may indeed be a vengeful deity, but why would he take a man's sins out on an innocent babe?

Both he and Lizzie carried the wild card. It was one hundred percent certain that their child would as well. The only question was the nature of the card their child would draw. An impossibly rare ace? The somewhat more probable joker? Perhaps, most horrible of all, the fatal black queen? Virtually everyone who carried the mark of the wild card knew the odds, though they were too terrible to contemplate. One to nine to ninety.

His guilt was his own. His child had no part in it. But whether the fate of their child rested on cold, rational science or the will of a possibly vengeful God, it was something they had to deal with, consider carefully, and plan for.

'Well,' Father Squid said. It was a statement rather than a question. He looked into her eyes. They were hooded with concern that trembled on her lips and quirked her mouth in a twist that threatened to break into tears. 'What do you want to do?' he finally asked.

'Oh, Bobby!' Her expression shattered like glass and she started to cry, hurling her into his arms. He caught her, absorbing her tiny form into his great, thick body as she wept aloud. 'Oh, Bobby,' she said again, 'thank you, thank you for asking me. Thank you. You don't know what it means to me.'

I guess I don't, Father Squid thought, but he was smart enough not to say that.

'All my life,' she said through her sobs, 'someone has always told me what I should do, what I think, how I had to live. No one has ever *asked* me what I wanted, what I thought was right, what I should do.'

'What,' Father Squid said, 'should we do?'

She pulled away from him a little, no longer sobbing, and looked seriously into his eyes. 'I think we should keep the baby,' she said. 'I mean, I know the odds are against us. I know, I know it could be terrible. But look, Bobby, the odds were *already* against us, but here we are. The both of us. We *survived* the wild card. We *survived* life as jokers and we met and we fell in love. Maybe it's too much to ask for another miracle, but what have our lives been other than a series of miracles, leading up to this?'

Father Squid nodded ponderously. 'Yes,' he said. 'You're right. We must have faith. Down through the centuries people have faced lives as hard, harder even than ours. They faced cold, privation, starvation, rampaging armies, and disease. Locusts and storm and drought and famine. They stood together, brought their children into the world, and fought to keep them alive against impossible odds. Can we do any less? Is our love any less? Our faith?'

Lizzie shook her head. 'No, Bobby. We can face anything, together.'

'Together,' he said, and they held each other as if they'd never let go.

November, 2010

Of course, fate had stepped in ... using Warlock and Deedle as its dread instruments ... and resolved the problem of their child's genetic heritage for them.

Father Squid had been a hollow man afterward. He went about his daily business with a brusqueness bordering on coldness that was not like him. He had no one to talk to, no one to unburden himself to. There was nothing that anyone could do, anyway. At night he dreamed of Lizzie, and the poor souls who had died with her in the Rathole, slain for his pride. He found himself wishing that he had been there too. If only he had set out half an hour earlier ...

The horror of the Rathole had tested his faith severely. Even his very belief in God had wavered. How could the loving God he believed in have let such monstrous things happen? he had asked himself. Had his sins been so terrible as to bring down such savage wrath?

Perhaps it had. *There is blood on my hands,* he reminded himself when he knelt to pray. *The blood of innocents.*

And Contarini had been as good as his word. He had seen Father Squid excommunicated from the Church, the Jokertown parish closed, the faithful abandoned. But that had just opened another path that had proved better suited for all the needs of his parishioners. From that dark time Our Lady of Perpetual Misery had arisen.

I have tried to atone, O Lord, he prayed. *For Lizzie and our unborn child, for Deedle, for the innocents. I have ministered to my people, I have done good works, I have done penance and begged for your forgiveness.*

Yet the sins endured. And soon the truth must out.

THE RAT RACE

PART 14.

'Well, old man, what do you think?' Dr. Pretorius asked with a sweep of his arm, indicating the dining area of the High Hand. 'Plenty of room, excellent food and service ... and best of all, you won't have to pay for it. It was Michael's idea, but me and Tate pulled a few strings, and Dutton's offered to open his wallet.'

Sibyl stood beside him, taking in the scenery too. She padded over to the nearest table and ran her glassy blue fingers over the silverware, as if she approved. Not that Leo could tell. He never had any idea what she was thinking, but that didn't set him apart from very many people. Probably just Dr. Pretorius.

Leo told him, 'It's amazing, and I can't believe you're going to pull it off. It'll beat the hell out of the New Big Wang, where Ralph had his racket.'

'Excellent!' The lawyer slapped him on the back. 'We've got the date pinned down and everything; I give the go-ahead, and the night's all yours.'

'Thanks,' Leo said, shaking his hand. 'You're all right, Pretorius. I don't care what everyone else says about you.'

'Nor I you.' He winked back.

It was early yet, but the restaurant would be opening in a few minutes and the staff members were coming and going, moving place settings and arranging pitchers of water on tables, and sorting out centerpieces, lighting candles despite the hour. The lawyer said, 'I've got to get going. Have some notes to sort through before a hearing tomorrow, and I have a feeling I'll be up half the night with it. Sibyl?' he said without looking for her, knowing she'd find his side easily enough.

'Thanks again,' Leo said, and they saw themselves out.

The detective stood there a few minutes longer, in the near quiet before the patrons arrived and things began to hum. He liked the venue – it'd be hard not to. The place was gorgeous, spacious, and generally outside his price range but hey, like the song says, 'With a little help from my friends,' he mumbled with a smile.

It was good of them, real good. Above and beyond.

His smile dimmed. Of course, they were mostly work friends, weren't they? Michael, obviously – and even the lawyer with his sleek cerulean assistant. All the cops, all the courthouse guys … almost everyone he knew. And work was going away.

'Detective Storgman, wasn't it?'

Startled out of his brief, glum reverie, Leo turned to see Raul Esposito standing beside the kitchen doors with their fogged round portals; he was likewise watching the first-gear windup of the extravagant restaurant.

'Esposito.' Leo met the mobster's eyes. Actually, Esposito didn't look much like a mobster, not today. He was dressed up sharp, and all his accent points – buttons, cuff links, shoe tips – were shining. He looked like someone's rich old uncle. 'What are you doing here?'

'Oh,' he made a little gesture with his hand that said, 'nothing important.' But then he replied, 'Making some deliveries. For whatever you may think of me and my past, I'm in a new business now.'

'Out of the guns, and into the gumbo, eh?'

'Something like that.'

'Hey listen, since you're here, can I ask you something?' He approached Raul and stood to the side, lest he get smacked when the next door opened and the next server or cook exited the food prep area.

'By all means.'

'Your little friend. Your ward, you called her.'

'Maggie.' He nodded.

'She's been following me around,' Leo said.

Esposito looked honestly surprised, but long years of working with crooks told the detective that it didn't really mean anything. 'Whatever for?' he asked.

'I was hoping you could tell me. Ever since I first came up to your place, I keep seeing her everywhere. She's hard to miss, and she's a terrible sneak.'

'Detective,' he said with his earnest frown and buckled eyebrows, 'I can assure you I haven't sent her on any such mission to tail you.'

Leo didn't figure he had, and he said so. 'I didn't really see you sending a teenager after me.'

'Thank you for the vote of confidence,' he said, but the pensive frown didn't quite leave. 'But I'll absolutely have a word with her, when I see her this evening. The poor dear, she's had such a difficult time of things. Sometimes her behavior is a bit ... erratic.'

'How so?'

'Oh, you know. Joker, card turned, ran away. It's an old story and a common one, but nonetheless painful for those who live it,' he said vaguely.

Leo wanted to say that if the girl was a joker, she was a lucky one; at least she looked normal enough. But that wasn't always true, and he'd felt the world turn and flop when she'd touched him. So he went ahead and asked, 'What does she do? Now that her card's turned?'

'She ...' He considered his wording. '... ages things. Rapidly.'

'Things?'

'Anything organic,' he clarified. 'Poor dear can't even wear all-natural fibers. Cotton and leather just rot and fall off her within half an hour or so.'

'Can she kill people?' Leo followed up.

'I assume so,' Esposito responded carefully. 'But I can assure you she never has. She's very careful not to touch anyone, except perhaps in self-defense. She has no control over the ability at all. It's a lonely way to live.'

'Good thing she has you, then.'

'I ... I found her,' he said, again with great vagueness. 'And we work well together. But given her condition, you may safely revise your previous notions about our relationship. I know what it looks like, and I know what people think. I look out for her, that's all. Though sometimes I think I ought to adopt your first polite guess, and tell people she's my granddaughter.'

Leo gave a nodding shrug. 'Might be a good idea. But what do you mean you work well together?' After all, it sounded a little sinister – immediately after confessing that the girl was capable of accidental murder.

Raul's frown evaporated entirely. With a twinkle in his eye, he asked, 'Now it's my turn to ask you a question, Detective. Have you ever eaten here before?'

'Once or twice.'

'Have you ever tried the steaks? Aged to perfection, if you will?'

Leo said, '*Oh,*' in one long breath. 'Gotcha. But wait, what's *your* contribution?'

'Hmm. That's a trickier question, and one you might find less palatable.'

'Very funny.'

'No, I mean literally,' he insisted. 'Though if you really must know, I'd ask you to step with me around the corner.'

Something in the back of Leo's head didn't think it was wise to step around a blind corner with an old hit man, but they were in such a marvelous public place, and anyway, he was curious. So he followed Raul Esposito around the nearest wall, which put them past the main dining area, and behind a long red curtain that had been drawn aside.

'You must understand, Detective, this is not something I broadcast. I've spent years building a reputation as a reliable broker of specialty steaks and mushrooms; and although Maggie's involvement would likely not distress anyone, mine ... *might.*'

'Why's that?' Leo wanted to know.

'Because I don't import the mushrooms. I make them.'

'You make them? Out of thin air?'

'No, Detective.' His right hand reached for his left wrist, and rolled up the sleeve cuff there. The skin beneath it was mottled and lumpy; and when Leo looked closely he could see that the bumps looked rather remarkably like tiny round buttons or caps – even though they'd been pressed by his clothing. 'I'm a joker too.'

Leo struggled to recall if he'd had anything with mushrooms in it, and tried not to go green in the process. 'That's … that's …'

'I know,' Raul Esposito said as he rolled up his sleeve. 'And for obvious reasons, I would appreciate your discretion. Likewise, I promise I'll have a word with my ward. I'll see what she's up to, and ask her to restrain herself.'

'Thanks,' Leo said, turning away before he gave too much of his own revulsion away. He excused himself, since it was time for him to return to the precinct; he left saying, 'And I'll keep your secret to myself. Believe me.'

Back at the station, all the talk between cases was of the holidays. Thanksgiving was right around the corner and people were making plans. Michael was on the phone with his girlfriend, talking about who was coming over for supper; Slim Jim was sitting on the edge of his desk, arguing with Tenry Fong over whose relatives were more trouble; and over by her office door, the captain was telling Puff that she planned to eat a whole table's worth of turkey.

The season's first premature Christmas tinsel was sparkling on the corners of desks, and over by the coffeemaker someone had already stuck a small plastic tree – which had almost immediately become decorated with empty sweetener packets and plastic creamer cups. Someone had even gone to the trouble of fashioning a skinny red star topper from a pair of chewed-up coffee stirrers.

Ah, such festivity.

Leo wasn't feeling it. His earlier warmth was effectively gone, even as he looked around and liked most of the people he saw. The fact was, he wouldn't be seeing them much longer. Not every day like this. And everyone said, 'We'll stay in touch!' but in the real world, everyone knew it didn't play that way.

Thanksgiving was looking lonely enough. No plans, except maybe some Chinese takeout and football in front of the television.

His wife had been dead going on thirteen years. Wanda was spending the holiday with her kids and grandkids. His daughter had a new boyfriend, and she was spending this first holiday with his parents – doing the whole 'meeting the family' thing with someone else's family.

And who else did he know, anyway? Nobody who didn't have plans with children, in-laws, spouses, or soup kitchen volunteering.

When his shift was over he went home alone to the empty apartment, and he thought about calling Wanda just to have someone to talk to; but then again, he didn't want to sound all maudlin, and he didn't want her to feel guilty about leaving him alone for Thanksgiving. Not after he'd already gone to all the trouble to insist that it was fine, and he hoped she had a great time.

So he didn't.

Instead he called a pizza place and ordered himself a little something special for delivery. And he stood in front of the white board while he waited, staring at the connections, the names, the circles, the suspicions.

He picked up the blue marker and crossed out the Sleeper.

He added a question mark after Raul Esposito.

SANCTUARY

PART 2.

Kavitha was having a hard time concentrating at the studio – her body was an assortment of random aches. She wasn't sure she could even count all the bruises she'd accumulated in the past weeks. The three of them had done a pretty good job wrecking the living room that first night, even though they'd been trying to not wake the kid. It was a good thing Isai was a sound sleeper. And two months later, the sex was still just as much fun, just as crazy. There was something about Minal that made every inhibition drop away – even thinking about her now was enough to start a flush of heat racing through Kavitha's body, from cheeks to thighs to toes. She shook her head, trying to clear it. Minal was watching the kid, giving Kavitha a gift of a few precious hours to work; she needed to take advantage of that. Life didn't stop just because you met an incredibly hot girl and got her to join you and your boyfriend in bed. On the couch and the floor, to be accurate, but eventually the bed too. Over and over and over again. But now it was work time – she had to work, damn it. Kavitha had a show coming up in two days! She couldn't keep thinking about sex – or if she was going to, then she had to channel it into her work.

Kavitha stared at the posters for the next show, wondering if she should have changed the design. Her stage name, *Natya*, stretched across the top in a funky South Asian-style font – she was a little tired of playing up the ethnic angle in the promotion for her shows.

Although it *was* appropriate, given the content of the work. This whole next set of shows was focused on the ongoing war in Sri Lanka, the misery of so many of her distant relatives. So maybe it wasn't so bad to emphasize that connection; it might help draw in people who already had an interest in the problems of her tiny home island. And even if it just brought in white guys who had a thing for exotic brown girls – well, they could be educated too. She wasn't above using her body and art to sell her agenda. Not after the horrors she'd seen, long ago and far away.

Lately, the war had been more and more on her mind. Kavitha was having the nightmares again, waking up in a cold sweat with the memories of men stumbling across the street, screaming, with tires around their necks, wreathed in flames. Women thrown up against the sides of buildings, their saris torn. She kept seeing the same little girl, walking through rubble and smoke, her forehead trickling blood. Too much blood. When they'd first come to America as refugees, Kavitha had had the nightmares every night. They'd eventually faded away, but the last few days they'd come back, with a vengeance. Maybe it was Minal's presence in their home, the fading cuts and bruises on her face a reminder. The marks were almost gone now, but sudden noises still made her look startled, terrified. It made Kavitha want to find the men who had hurt her. But what would she do if she did find them?

Sometimes Kavitha wished she could go back home, do something to stop the war. There had been peace for years, but recently the fighting had broken out again, tearing her poor country apart. A new guerrilla group proclaiming the righteousness of the Tamil cause, a new prime minister, eager to win votes with a hard-line stance against the rebels. She'd even written out a letter to her uncle, who was prominent in the government there, offering to help – but she'd never sent it. Even with her powers, what could one ace do against an entire guerrilla force out in the jungle – or against an entire government-supported army? Hell, not only did she not know *how* to fight, she wasn't even sure which side she'd be fighting on. Better to stay here, keep her powers directed toward the dance. Michael kept saying that she should at least try to learn how to use the power to defend herself, but the thought of deliberately injuring someone else was abhorrent to her. She'd wanted to be a doctor, damn it – she'd only given that up because dance called her too strongly. And now, Kavitha thought she was doing good work here. Raising awareness, helping to build a peace movement.

Every once in a while, though, she just wanted to hit someone, especially when she heard some of the stories Minal told. In the middle of the night, when hours of sex had made them all exhausted and drowsy, barriers came down and they shared old stories. Minal told them some of the things she'd gone through, her voice remarkably calm and matter-of-fact. Kavitha couldn't take them so calmly; she wanted to cradle Minal in her arms, protect her from all the bad things that had happened to her – but it was too late for that. If she couldn't save Minal, sometimes Kavitha wished that she could visit a little righteous retribution on the people who had hurt her. Maybe hitting someone would make the nightmares go away.

But there was no one to hit. She took a deep, deliberate breath and settled into working instead.

'Son, do you seriously think that you aren't going to be at our dinner table for Thanksgiving?'

Michael bit back a sharp retort, reminding himself to be patient with the old man across the desk. His father leaned heavily on a mop, a bucket of dirty water at his feet. Wisps of white hair fluttered in the breeze from the creaking station fan, the last remnants of a once-glorious 'fro. Joe Stevens had been a janitor at the station for forty years, and he wasn't about to start calling his son 'Detective,' even if he was secretly proud of how far his only child had come. Michael had asked him to call him by his title in front of the men more than once, and his father just laughed. It didn't help that his partner had known Joe since before Michael was born, and laughed right along with his dad.

Leo chimed in now, 'Yeah, Michael. What are you thinking, not going to your parents' for Thanksgiving dinner? If I had a mom who cooked braised short ribs like yours, I'd be there every night.'

'Stay out of it, Leo.'

His partner shrugged, and bent his horned head back over the pile of papers on his desk, pretending not to listen. The truth was, with Leo so close to retirement, there wasn't much else for him to do but eavesdrop, especially with the station so dead; nothing was happening around here this week. Everybody was gearing up for the holidays, even the bad guys.

He tried again. 'Dad, I promised Kavitha that we could have Thanksgiving at our place this year. She really wants to try making a turkey. Don't you think it'd be nice for Isai to have Thanksgiving at home with her parents? You know how difficult it is to manage her at your place.' His parents' apartment was tiny and full of stuff – every time Isai shifted, she knocked something over.

The old man shook his head. 'The child should spend time with her grandparents; you hide her away too much, as if you're ashamed of her. Michael, you know damn well that this is one fight that you are going to lose. Your mother has been cooking for *days*.'

'Dad, she isn't going to make us eat two Thanksgiving dinners again, is she?' Michael had thought he'd complained enough last time to get them off that hook – for all the years he was growing up, his mom had insisted on making a full American Thanksgiving for them to eat at midday – turkey, stuffing, sweet potatoes, the works. And then, about six hours later, a Korean feast – *ba bim bop,* barbecued pork, kimchi, and more. Even with Kavitha joining them for the meal, it was way too much food for four people, but his mom looked so hurt if he didn't eat some of everything that he couldn't bear to let her down. He got a wicked stomachache, every time. Yet another reason not to celebrate at his parents' place this year. Besides, it would be so crowded in his parents' tiny apartment, four adults with an active toddler who sometimes became a *flying* active toddler.

His father shook his head. 'No, I talked her out of the double dinner; it'll be just the one meal. But she's making southern food for me, Korean food for her, American for you, and something Sri Lankan for your … *girlfriend*.' His dad hesitated before that last word – his parents still weren't pleased that Michael hadn't married Kavitha, especially now that they had a kid. His mom prayed about it in church every Sunday morning. That was one reason why he didn't want to bring Kavitha to their apartment; Kavitha didn't need to deal with the pointed comments. He was sure she'd like to get married, and Michael wanted to marry her, he did. At least he thought he did, most of the time. He just wasn't sure. The thought of being tied down to just one woman, for the rest of his life – that wasn't an easy thing to wrap your mind around. Especially with Minal in their house. *Especially* that.

Back to the problem at hand. 'Dad, that's crazy.' Four different cuisines – there would be enough food to feed an army. Tasty, delectable food – even the Sri Lankan food that his mother had never made before was sure to be delicious. But still.

'Bring me back a doggy bag,' Leo interjected.

'Shut *up*, Leo.' Michael ran his fingers over his shaved-bald head, almost wishing he had grown out his hair into a big old 'fro like his dad's, just so he could tear it out.

His father shrugged. 'Crazy or not, that's what she's doing, and the meal is half cooked already, so you had better just adjust your mind to the facts, boy. Unless you *want* to break your mother's heart.'

Michael sputtered, 'I've been *telling* her that we're not coming this year. I've told her and told her.' Admittedly, not to her face. But he'd left messages on the home phone, when he knew his mom would be working at the laundromat. Messages he knew she'd heard, but apparently heard wasn't the same as accepted or agreed.

'So?' His father gazed at him expectantly.

'Damn it.' Michael sighed, giving in.

'I knew you'd come around, son.' His father beamed, flashing two straight rows of white teeth. He straightened up, picking up the mop and dunking it back in the bucket. 'If you're worried about managing the kid at our house, why don't you bring along that nanny of yours too? Your mother will be happy to have another person eating her food. And tell Kavitha to bring a few pies for dessert, okay? If she buys them at the store, I won't be the one to tell your mother. Why you'd pick a girl who can't cook, I will never know ...' His father trailed off, muttering, as he pushed the bucket down the dank hallway. No matter how much time his father spent scrubbing, somehow the place never looked clean.

Michael bit his lip and pulled out his cell to call Kavitha, heading toward one of the conference rooms as he dialed. This wasn't going to go well. The only consolation he had was that family drama might help distract him from what a mess things were at work. The Joe Twitch case was never far from his thoughts. If only Michael knew exactly *what* to say, and *who* it was safe to say it to. He trusted his partner with his life – but could he trust Leo with what Minal knew? Bad enough that Ratboy and the kid lawyer knew. Michael would have sworn that Angel Grady, one of the two cops involved in the Twitch incident, was a straight shooter. So maybe Minal was just wrong about the gun and the drugs? If not, if she was right about Joe ... well, if Puff and Angel were dirty, how could he be certain *anyone* was clean?

Last night, after Minal had fallen asleep, Michael had heard Kavitha whisper, 'I love you.' She could have been speaking to him, but he was pretty sure the words had been for Minal. Which made everything complicated; he knew his girlfriend well enough to know that she wouldn't take love lightly. She couldn't. Michael wasn't sure exactly what *he* felt for Minal – he didn't really want to think about it. Mostly, he'd been enjoying the hell out of the sex and just hoping the women kept on thinking this was a good idea. He didn't want that to end, and he also didn't want Minal to get hurt. The thought of Minal getting hurt made his throat tighten and his stomach churn. Was that love? He had no idea.

For now, Michael was keeping his mouth shut and his eyes open. He had enough to worry about; he didn't need to go looking for more trouble.

Just as she finished her warm-ups and was about to settle seriously into working, her cell rang. Kavitha bit back a curse and reached for the phone, checking to see who it was. Michael. Damn it. She answered, hoping at least this would be something quick.

His voice on the phone, 'Hey, sweetheart.'

That wasn't good. Michael wasn't the endearment type. 'What's wrong?' If he messed up this day any further ...

Luckily, he knew her well enough not to screw around with her. 'We're going to my parents' for Thanksgiving.'

'Michael, you *promised* me.' Kavitha's head was already throbbing and they weren't two minutes into this conversation.

'I couldn't do it to my mother. I just couldn't.' He paused and then offered weakly, 'My dad said I could invite the nanny too.'

Kavitha felt irritation flare up in her. 'You are *kidding* me. Do you seriously expect Minal to pretend to just be the nanny for an entire Thanksgiving dinner? And you expect me to pretend it too? With your parents sitting there in their holiday best, asking me when we're going to finally get married?'

Michael protested weakly, 'They wouldn't—'

She cut him off. 'Of course they will. They ask every damn time they see us. What are you going to tell them this time?'

'I'll tell them we're not ready ...'

'And do you have a plan for what you're going to tell them when their granddaughter calls the nanny *mommy*?' Mostly Isai called Minal *aunty,* but every once in a while in the last few days, she was *mommy* instead. Kavitha was always *mama* – Isai hadn't forgotten her, but she was adapting to her new family structure. At first, Kavitha had felt a little twinge, seeing how close Isai and Minal were – but really, it was to be expected, since Minal was the one at home with her most days. Mostly, it was a relief having Minal there, mommying. She was more patient and better suited to full-time mothering than Kavitha ever had been. Their lives had all gotten so much better since Minal had moved in that Kavitha had started fantasizing about what their life would look like if Minal just stayed. It looked really good to her – if Michael didn't fuck it up. 'Michael, tell me you're not going to do this.'

Silence on the other end of the phone, silence that lingered and grew until it was hanging, a dark cloud between them. She could almost see it, hovering in the air like one of her fields.

Kavitha sighed, and tried to soften her tone. 'Michael, love. Why don't you tell them? I told *my* parents that we were seeing someone else.' Admittedly, that had been maybe a little premature – Kavitha hadn't even told Minal that she loved her yet. But she was going to; she was just waiting for the right moment. She'd been wanting to say it for weeks. And in the meantime, Kavitha didn't want her parents hearing mangled rumors from somebody else. It was amazing how quickly the Sri Lankan gossip network could spread news, and all it would take would be some relative or acquaintance seeing Kavitha and Minal holding hands as they walked in the park. 'Tell them and get it over with. Just talk to them.'

Michael laughed, bitterness clear down the phone line. '*You* told your brother, who then sent an e-mail to your parents. It's not the same.'

She snapped, 'I'd talk to my parents if they were willing to talk to *me*.' Kavitha knew what she was asking him to risk, after all. Her parents hadn't spoken to her in two years – not since Isai was born, and they realized Michael wasn't just going to go away. Kavitha had hoped that a grandchild would improve the situation, but somehow Isai's birth had just hardened her parents' position. They'd refused to even see their granddaughter. '*Your* parents won't cut you off. You're their only child, and they aren't as ... old-fashioned as mine.' *Racist* was perhaps the more accurate word.

Her parents had already been pretty mad at her about all the med school money she'd wasted by dropping out. She'd promised to pay them back, but realistically, that was going to take a while. And then they'd almost had heart attacks when Kavitha had told them that she was moving in with a half-black, half-Korean man. Worse, one who pretty much looked black. You'd think that all the men and women Kavitha had slept with up till then would have broken them down, but apparently black was still the final color barrier. It hadn't helped that Michael was a cop. Adding Minal to the situation couldn't make the situation with her parents any worse, she was pretty sure. And if it did – oh, well. Might as well be hanged for a sheep as a lamb, right? Kavitha would pick love over filial duty any day. 'Didn't your folks defy their families to pick each other? They'll be fine with this.'

Michael snapped, 'That's easy for you to say!'

Easy? Did he really think this was easy on her? Sometimes she wondered why she even wanted to marry Michael anyway – did he know her at all? Her head was pounding and her heart ached. This had to end; it would tear them apart otherwise. Kavitha took a deep breath and then said, her voice shaking, 'Look, I'll go to your parents' on Thursday if you want. But I'm not going to lie to them, not if Minal is sitting right there in the room. And I'm not going to leave her sitting at home alone on Thanksgiving. So you have two options. We can cancel and stay home, or we can all go and you can tell them the truth.'

'Kavitha—'

She shook her head. 'I have to work, Michael. And you have a decision to make.' Kavitha hung up the phone and closed her eyes.

Time to channel this anger into the dance. Kavitha stretched her slender body in her black dancer's leotard. She arched her back, leaning right, forward, left, back. Up to *relevé,* down to plié. Her neck: forward, left, back, side, letting her long braid swing freely down her back. Her rib cage shifted, following the same pattern. And reverse. She linked the fingers of her two hands together, stretched them out in front of her. Then Kavitha allowed her right hand to form an *abhinaya* in the shape of a flower, and called on her powers to awaken. She could feel the kundalini, the coiled and sleeping serpent energies lying at the base of her spine, arouse and ascend her body, flowing from back to arm to wrist to hand. As the energies reached the tip of her fingers, the power flowed out, creating a great, glowing, golden flower in the air. Beautiful.

Kavitha still couldn't believe how lucky she'd been when her card turned. She'd been a starving dancer for years, and then a slightly better fed one once she'd moved in with Michael. She was a good dancer – but New York was full of good dancers, desperate for their big break, or even for a small one. It was her power that made her dance special, and since she'd started incorporating the kundalini fields into her work, that power had finally started to get her a little bit of fame. Kavitha still performed in tiny venues that seated a few hundred at most. But now many of her shows were sold out, and if her audience continued to grow … well, Isai wouldn't have to go to community college. If Kavitha managed to send her daughter to Harvard, well, *that* would show her parents, wouldn't it? And that wasn't going to happen unless she focused on her work.

She snapped her fingers, and the flower exploded into a rainbow of tiny fragments, scattering across the stage and then fading away. If Kavitha wanted them to last longer, she'd need to build up the power with her dance, feeding more charge into the fields. She'd warmed up enough now – she was ready. She could feel the energy built up inside her, aching to get out. She'd been channeling it into sex for days, but she couldn't afford that indulgence anymore. Now, she needed to dance, needed to pound the floor with her feet – if she didn't get some of this power out, she felt like she was going to explode. She flung her arms out, and the energy poured out in a bright shimmering blaze, surrounding her. Surrounding *Natya* – that's who she was now, the living embodiment of an ancient dance. Thousands of years of art, funneling down to this one moment. With one sharp hand movement after another, Natya built a series of glittering crimson bridges across the stage, arching higher and higher. Then, taking a deep breath, she flung her body across them and began to dance.

'Isai, come down from there!' Minal reached up, but Isai was just out of her reach – the child had shifted to Garuda form, flown to the top of the cabinets, and then shifted back. It was her newest trick, and was not easy to deal with. So far, Minal had been able to handle everything the kid threw at her, and she was already ridiculously fond of the little monster, but this was just unacceptable.

'Isai, if you don't come down right now, Aunty Minal will get very mad!'

'Aunty get mad?'

'That's right, Aunty will get mad!'

'Aunty Minal not mad. Aunty happy!' The child chortled, safe from retribution on her perch, *knowing* that she was causing trouble. Isai put her hands up in front of her face and then peeked out, a game she'd been playing for years, her parents said, but one she never seemed to get tired of. 'I see you, Aunty! I see you!'

Minal tried to keep a stern look on her face, but she couldn't help grinning a little – the kid was just so cute. 'I see you too, little monkey.' More of a bird than a monkey, of course – in Garuda form, Isai's wings were stunning. The eagle beak was pretty sharp too. Kavitha and Michael were lucky that Isai loved her parents enough that she'd never tried pecking them or beating her wings at them. When shifted into her largest form, Garuda-Isai had a twelve-foot wingspan; barely big enough to fit into their apartment, and plenty big enough to knock her parents down.

Michael kept muttering that he ought to start commuting to work on his daughter's back, but Minal was pretty sure he wasn't serious. Isai would love to give her dad a ride, of course, but who could trust a two-year-old to fly them anywhere? It'd just take a single bright shiny distraction, and Isai would shift back into her own form, possibly high up in the air, which would be no fun for anyone. Her parents didn't *think* she'd stay human if she were plummeting to her death – but they couldn't know for certain, which was why she was strictly forbidden to shift without close supervision, and *never* outside. Which forbidding normally did, oh, so much good when it came to things like not drawing on the walls in pen, and not digging the soil out of all the plants' pots. Still, they had to try, and as a good babysitter, Minal had to try too. And now it was time to shift tactics and try begging. 'Come down, baby, please?'

Isai giggled again, shifted for just long enough to coast down, and then shifted back, landing, a warm, naked bundle, in Minal's arms. The child's clothes always dropped away with the shift, and then she was naked until they got her dressed again. Undiapered too, which was risky, but right at this moment, Minal was willing to take a small risk. The warmth of the toddler snuggled against her was soothing. Isai wrapped her arms around Minal's neck and whispered, 'I love you, aunty.' Minal whispered back, 'I love you too, baby.' A dangerous thing to say out loud, but it was true. She was dangerously close to being in love with the child's parents too, though she hadn't had the nerve to say so. What would she do when Michael and Kavitha got tired of her invading their nuclear family? Even if it were safe to go back to work, her old life seemed empty by comparison.

Minal stroked Isai's hair as she walked her over to the changing table. Practiced hands fastened a diaper, and then struggled to slide wriggling arms and legs into a T-shirt and pants. 'Hold still, baby, please. Aunty's arm is still ouchie.' The doctor Kavitha had dragged her to had said that given the extent of the damage, a nat would probably have needed a year before the arm was fully healed. Minal was way ahead of that schedule, but it was definitely still mending. Still, she managed pretty well. Isai settled down long enough for Minal to get that last leg into her pants. Hmm ... they were almost out of diapers. Michael was the one coming home first – Minal pulled out her cell and punched in his number. He answered on the second ring.

'Hey, Michael. You need to stop at the drugstore on your way home.' But before he could say anything, there was a knock at the door. 'Wait – hang on. Kavitha must have forgotten her keys again ...' Isai was squirming in her arms, getting ready to shift again. Minal tried to juggle the phone, the child, and the doorknob all at once, distracted by a stab of pain as Isai's flailing leg jabbed at her bad arm. 'Hold on ...' Her hand was on the knob, turning it.

'No, Minal, don't—' But someone was already shoving the door open with enough force to break the safety chain right off the wood frame, and suddenly there were men inside, one man she knew, a man she had hoped to never see again. He grabbed her, and the other man pulled Isai from her, the child screaming. Minal only had time to shout, 'Nicor, no!' before he casually swatted the side of her head with something hard. And the world went dark.

'Leo!' Michael had been hiding out in one of the back rooms for his phone call, an automatic move to protect his privacy. Now he was cursing the length of the hallway as he raced back down it, calling to his partner. He'd tried calling Minal back, but no one had answered. It just rang and rang and rang. What the fuck was going on? 'Leo!!!'

His partner came around the desk and grabbed his shoulder. 'Calm the fuck down. What's wrong with you?'

Michael's voice broke. 'Something's wrong with my kid. Someone broke into our place. I heard her screaming.' *Oh God, oh God, oh God.* He couldn't think straight. There was a procedure for this, wasn't there? *Fuck procedure* – he just wanted someone to tell him what to do. Before he ripped someone's throat out with his bare hands.

'Come on.' Leo was checking his gun, grabbing his coat. 'Let's go.'

Go. Yes. That's what he needed to do. Maybe if he got home fast enough, he could do something. Figure out what had happened. He was a detective, wasn't he? He knew how to figure these things out. If he could just think. If he could think loud enough to drown out the sound of his little girl's screams, which echoed in his ears, getting louder with every step.

Leo grabbed his arm and dragged him out, ignoring the queries from others in the station. They slammed through the front door, out into the blistering cold and the dark and the snow. His daughter was out there in that. And he didn't even know if she had her coat.

Minal came to with the sound of Isai sobbing in her ears, the child curled hard against her chest. Her head was throbbing and she had to swallow to keep from hurling. She blinked her eyes, wincing. It took her a second to realize that they were in the backseat of a car, some beat-up old thing. There were no handles on the insides of the doors. No way out.

'Hey, she's awake,' the thug sitting next to her said to the man up front. The thug looked mostly normal, except for the sharp bird's beak he had instead of a nose. He wore the black-and-silver leather of the Demon Princes.

'Get her to shut the kid up, then,' Nicor snapped back, without turning his head. Water was dripping down his hair as usual, drenching his clothes and the seat of the car beneath him. It'd be running down his face too, a constant, cold stream, as if he were standing under a rain shower. Water sliding over his abnormally wide nose, and the flared gills along his neck. But she couldn't actually see Nicor's face – he was keeping his eyes on the road. They were hurtling through the city much faster than was safe, weaving in and out of traffic. Where the hell was he taking them?

'Shhh, shhh, baby.' Minal had already been trying to calm Isai down, but when Nicor said that, she almost stopped, she was so pissed off. What the hell was he thinking? But with Isai to protect, she couldn't afford to piss off a Demon Prince, especially a scary dangerous ace. Minal bit her lips and kept stroking the child's hair.

These idiots hadn't even gotten her shoes on before leaving – Isai was just wearing a T-shirt and pants. Didn't they notice that it was fucking freezing outside? There was snow on the ground, damn it. Who brought a kid outside like this?

Minal's clothes were even worse; she'd been feeling sick enough she hadn't bothered dressing today, so she was just in a battered white T-shirt and a pair of red silk pajama shorts. No pants, no sweater, no coat, no shoes. Her arms and legs exposed to the cold, and to the eyes of the goon a few inches away. Her nipples were hidden under the T-shirt, but just barely. And from the way he was staring at her torso, this guy knew exactly what was under her shirt. Minal hugged Isai closer, feeling her heart jackhammering in her chest. 'Shhh, baby, shh. Everything's going to be fine,' she whispered.

'Hey, Nicor,' the bird-beak asked, never taking his eyes off her, 'is it true what they say about this one?'

Nicor laughed – a low, bitter laugh with no actual humor in it. 'Raum, everything you've heard is true, and more.'

Raum started reaching out a hand toward Minal, and she cringed away, back against the cold metal of the car door. The sensation was almost too much to bear, the cold icing through the tendrils on her back, through the thin material of her shirt. Still, it was better than his hands on her, his hands that were sharply pointed at the fingertips, like claws. Before he could touch her, Nicor snapped out, 'Hands off!'

'But, Nicor …' Raum started whining.

'Forget it. He said no touching. Not yet.'

Raum slumped back in his seat, glaring sullenly at her. He muttered, 'I don't answer to you, you know. I'm not going to answer to anyone for long. I am the fucking Lord of Crows, and I am going to be moving *up* in this organization.'

Nicor shook his head and said, 'You ain't moved up yet.'

Raum looked even angrier, but he kept his claws to himself, thank the gods.

Minal finally got up the nerve to say something then. If they weren't supposed to touch her, maybe they wouldn't hurt her or Isai. Not yet. She had no faith that they'd stay safe once they got wherever they were going, so she had to ask while they were still in this car under Nicor's control, had to use this chance as best as she could.

She softened her voice, asked as nicely as she could. 'Nicor? What's going on? I thought you and I, we'd left things okay between us.' Nicor had been a regular client. He'd always left a decent tip when he could afford it, and he'd never roughed her up. It wasn't exactly fun fucking him most of the time – all that cold water sort of killed the mood, even if she turned the heat up high in the room. Not to mention its tending to wash away any lubrication. But it wasn't all bad – when he felt like it, Nicor could use his power over water to give her pleasure, send the ocean surging through her, which he'd had no obligation to do. He'd been one of the nice ones, and she'd liked him.

Nicor shook his head, eyes still on the road. 'I can't talk about it, babe. I got orders.'

Minal swallowed. 'Nicor. She's just a kid. If they want me, why don't you have someone take her home. Her parents will be home soon, and her dad's a cop. You don't want to grab a cop's kid.' Kavitha and Michael would never forgive her if she let Isai get hurt. She'd never forgive herself.

'No dice, *chica*. They said to bring you, and anyone with you. The kid was with you, so she's along for the ride.'

Nicor glanced at her then in the rearview mirror, finally meeting her eyes for a brief second. Minal shivered when she saw what was in his eyes. Pity.

She opened her mouth to ask him to let them go, one more time, but he cut her off. 'No more talking. We're almost there.'

The apartment door was wide open, but aside from that, nothing was missing – nothing was even disturbed. It might be hard for a stranger to tell, given the toddler toys and books scattered across the apartment, but that was just the normal chaos; Michael was used to editing that out of his view. He couldn't figure out what the hell was going on. Who would break in here and not even steal anything?

'Why would someone take her? She's just a baby! If they had just taken Minal …' Michael ground out the words, pacing frenziedly back and forth across the small living room. If he could just think.

'They destroyed your door,' Leo said. He stood erect in the doorway, more alert than Michael had seen him in months. Much good it was doing them. 'Minal's the sitter?' Leo asked.

Michael hesitated – but he had to tell the truth. He had to trust Leo – he needed him. 'She's – more than a sitter.'

'Oh?' Leo asked, an eyebrow lifted.

'We're involved,' he admitted.

Leo shook his head. 'Sleeping with the nanny, huh? Better not let Kavitha find out. If I had a hot girlfriend, I don't think I'd risk it for some fun on the side with the nanny.'

Michael didn't know what to say, how to explain. 'It's more complicated than that. Look, I'll explain it all later. That's not important now.' He couldn't think about Minal right now, couldn't picture last night, the three of them in their big bed. They'd all been tired, but they'd managed a quickie, a tangle of arms and legs and soft whimpers, with Minal whispering periodically, 'Don't wake the baby!' Eventually they'd settled down to sleep, with Kavitha in the middle – she was always cold at night. And Minal got too sensitized sometimes; she needed to be able to roll away, to get a little space to let her extra nipples settle down after lovemaking ... 'What's important is that the Demon Princes are after her. She said a name on the phone. Nicor.'

Leo frowned. 'Hell.'

'Exactly.' Michael started pacing now, planning. 'They're probably at McGurk's. We should call it in, get a squad out there ... We have to move, Leo. We might not have much time.'

Leo was already heading out the door. 'Let's go.'

Natya was resting when the phone rang, two hours into her practice. If she'd been in the middle of a dance, she would have let it ring, but she didn't have that excuse now. She sighed and walked over to pick up the phone.

'Yes, Michael?'

His voice on the phone was rough and low. 'I have bad news. Isai and Minal have been kidnapped.'

'What?' He couldn't be serious.

'They were taken from our apartment. But we think we know who took them, the Demon Princes: We're going to get a squad and go get them from McGurk's.'

Her chest was pounding. All she could see was the little girl from her dreams, with blood running down her face – but now her face was Isai's. 'McGurk's Suicide Hall? Why there?'

'That's the gang headquarters. They'll be holding them there.'

'You can't go in there with guns blazing. What if someone shoots one of them by mistake?' She'd seen too much gunfire in the war. Terrible, random.

Michael said, 'We know how to handle this. We're trained for it. Just sit tight. Or better yet – come to the station. I can't be sure someone won't come after you too.'

She was on her feet, shaking, feeling the power starting to build again, just with that small motion. 'If you think I'm going to just sit there while someone's hurting my little girl – and I'm half a city closer than you are. I can be there in five minutes.'

He was shouting now. 'Don't be an idiot! You don't know any-thing about fighting.'

'I know a hell of a lot more than you do, Michael.' She'd never told him what she'd seen in the war, what she'd *done*. He thought she was an innocent, but there was already blood on her hands. 'And I'm going to go get my girl and make sure she's safe. Now.'

'Kavitha, no. Do you hear me? I said no!'

'It's *Natya*. And I'm going. Get there as soon as you can.'

Minal stumbled as Nicor shoved her into the hall, still clutching Isai to her chest with both arms. Her injured arm was aching, but she didn't dare let the little girl go; Isai was sobbing quietly, gasping between her tears. If Minal put her down, she didn't know what Isai would do.

There were maybe a dozen men in the main lobby, nobody she recognized, a sea of black leather and grotesque appearances. One particularly freaky guy had three heads. No sign of the one with the crown of horns, the one who'd dislocated her shoulder. Nicor walked up to one of them and asked, 'Is he here?' The man jerked his head toward the hallway. 'In back. He's meeting someone right now, so just keep her here. Keep her quiet.'

Nicor came back to her side, water streaming down his face faster than she'd ever seen it – maybe that meant something? Maybe he was scared, or sad. He said quietly, 'Look, just sit down, okay? With any luck, it'll all be over soon.' He didn't say *how* it would be over, but Minal could see it in his eyes. At this point, the best she could hope for was that it would be quick. And that they wouldn't hurt the kid.

Minal bit her tongue and slid into a chair. It was a gorgeous vel-vet, very plush, but dirty. Typical. She'd seen way too many rooms like this, back in the day. Part of why she took so much pleasure in cleaning Michael and Kavitha's apartment, even knowing that Isai would make it a disaster area half an hour later. Her skin crawled as she sat down, and Isai didn't seem to like it either.

'Aunty Minal? Want to go home!'

'I know, baby. Shh ...'

'Want Mama! Want Daddy!' Her voice was rising, and the men were glancing over at them now.

'Quiet, Isai. Quiet down, little girl.' The poor child was shaking in her arms; she was probably freezing. Minal was on the verge of demanding Nicor's coat, at least, when she realized, terror rising in her throat, that Isai wasn't just shaking. She was shifting, growing. Changing.

'No, baby. No, no, no ...'

But it was too late. Isai was just too panicked, and with a loud cry, the child exploded out of her arms, blazing into her largest Garuda shape, larger than Minal had ever seen her. Wings at least a dozen feet wide, a naked girl-child body and an eagle's head above, tipped back, shrieking its fear and rage. Isai pushed off for the ceiling, her talons raking bloody furrows in Minal's body as she went. And Minal howled herself, clutching after the child, seeing the panicked men raising their guns to take aim.

Michael turned to Leo, his face ashen as he put away his phone. 'Natya's heading to McGurk's. I couldn't talk her out of it.'

Leo kept driving with one hand, hanging up his own phone with the other. 'K-10 confirms that your kid's at McGurk's – some dogs saw her dragged inside. A short human female was carrying her, which I'm guessing is Minal. The dogs said the pup smelled scared, but they didn't smell any blood. Captain Chawah says we can pull whomever we need for this. Dr. Dildo and Rodriguez, Beastie and Chey will all beat us there. Dildo and Beastie will take down some walls if they have to. Puff and Angel are coming in too, ditto Wingman, but they're ten minutes away. We'll be there in five.'

'*Natya's* going to beat us there. Gods, Leo. She's a goddamned pacifist – what the hell is she doing running into the middle of a firefight?'

'She's not exactly powerless, from what I saw at her last show. Natya ought to be able to take care of herself.'

'She doesn't know how to fight. She can't even watch action movies or fucking hospital TV shows – she gets too upset when she sees the blood. She's a fucking *civilian*.'

Leo shook his head. 'Michael, they've got her kid. She's going to fight faster and harder than *anyone* else. I've seen moms do some crazy shit, protecting their kids.'

Michael tried to swallow down the panic in his throat. He'd known he loved her – he just hadn't known how much. And now there was Minal too … He was so furious and scared that he couldn't think straight. He ground out the words, 'Just drive faster.' He knew Leo was going as fast as the battered patrol car could manage, but Michael leaned forward anyway, as if he could make the car beat Natya there by sheer force of will.

Natya had a plan. She had a whole, calm, sensible plan that she'd carefully worked out as she raced the several blocks to McGurk's, the power building in her with every step that pounded into the pavement. She would throw a field around Minal and Isai first, something to protect them. Then another, around each of the men. However many men there were. She could do it; she'd built dozens of kundalini spheres in her performances. Usually she didn't bother to make them solid, but she was pretty sure she could do it, if she built up enough power first. And the power was there, plenty of it, fueled by the movement of her body running through the city streets.

She just had to keep going, keep it up. She could do this. She could go in, build the spheres, contain them all until the cops came. It was a perfect, peaceful solution, and no one would get hurt. It was a great plan, and it went right out the window the moment she burst into McGurk's and saw the guns lifting up, raising to the ceiling, taking aim at her little girl.

Her peaceful intentions shattered. She flung one arm out, and a blazing crimson wave of force sprang out with it, throwing three men against a wall, knocking them out. Maybe she hurt some of them, maybe killed them. Natya couldn't care less. She couldn't do the same on the other side of the room, not with Minal in the center of that group. Natya took two quick steps toward them instead, as the guns swiveled down toward her, and then she *leaped* into the middle of the crowd, grabbing Minal and pulling her close.

Natya spun into a pirouette, dragging Minal with her. A gold cyclone rose around them, the force of the winds sending the two men left staggering away, their guns falling. Minal pulled away, long enough to hold her arms up to the ceiling, where Isai flew, directly above. Before Natya could do anything more, Isai was shifting back and falling into them, a small naked bundle, screaming, 'Mama Mama Mama!!!' She ignored Minal's outstretched arms and slammed into Natya, the force of the fall knocking them both to the floor.

As soon as Natya stopped moving, all of her fields died, leaving them, for a moment, defenseless.

Minal shouted, 'No, Nicor!' He was raising his arms, and she knew what came next – and here it was, a tide of water rising out of nowhere, knocking her off her feet, sending Natya and Isai under. 'Nicor, please!' He could drown them all, she knew – he'd chosen his Demon name for his ace ability, named for a demon of old who could raise the waters and call down tempests. It would exhaust him quickly, and the more water he raised, the sicker he'd be afterward, his own body drowning as well. The last time he'd raised a wall of water for the Princes, he'd been out for weeks with pneumonia; he'd nearly died. And maybe Nicor was remembering that now, or maybe he was remembering the nights they'd shared. Maybe he wasn't quite as indifferent to her fate as he'd acted in the car, because the waters were already receding, dropping down, down, until Natya and Isai were coughing on a sodden red carpet – but alive, alive.

But now it was Raum's turn. Raum, a man who had ambitions. Raum, Lord of Crows. Raum threw his head back, shrieking a loud *caw, caw* into the night. And the crows answered, first a few, then dozens of them, hurtling in through the inner doors. How long had his crows been nesting in McGurk's? Just as Natya started struggling to her feet, a wall of crows hurled into her, beating their wings and pecking, pecking, surrounding her. She flung her arms up to protect her eyes, her face, but that left the rest of her body vulnerable, protected only by a thin layer of clothing, soon shredded. She was bleeding. And little Isai was shrieking, swinging her arms wildly at the crows, but they ignored her, all of them under Raum's direction concentrating their attack on Natya. And Raum was rising up into the air – what Minal had thought was a black trench coat turned out to be black feathered wings folded against his back. Now they were open, raising him up, and he was swooping up high, directing the battle from above.

Minal had never felt so helpless in her life. What the hell could she do against crows? She could hear sirens blaring now, the megaphone of cops demanding that those inside surrender, that they come out with their hands up. Nicor was on her, grabbing her uninjured arm and trying to drag her away. To what she didn't know – maybe he was trying to get her to safety, or maybe he was just going to deliver her to his boss. He was stronger than she was, but she was a hell of a lot angrier than him, and with a quick jerk Minal yanked her arm out of his grip. Then she grabbed a massive metal pot from a nearby column with *both* her hands, ignoring the scream of pain from her still-healing shoulder, and slammed it into his head, knocking him to the ground. *That* felt good.

Kavitha was bleeding, bleeding – covered in blood from a thousand tiny cuts, and it was her nightmare all over again. She was a child, covered in blood. Blood dripping down her face from a thrown stone that had cut her forehead. Blood on her body from a stranger who had staggered into her in the rioting crowd. Blood on her parents, struggling to pull her through the chaos, to get her and her siblings to some kind of safety. And she had seen the man raising a gun to point it at her mother. She had bent down, grabbed a stone, and with the strength and surety trained into her from childhood cricket games with her brothers, Kavitha had hurled the stone straight at the man's head. And he'd cried out, and stepped back, lost his footing, and fell down in the crowd. Maybe he'd gotten up again – it was possible. Her parents had pulled her away, into the safety of a neighbor's house. Maybe the man had gotten up, walked away. Or maybe he'd stayed down, been trampled by the crowd. In that crowd, on that day, either was equally possible.

And here she was again – but of course, she wasn't. Kavitha shook her head, trying to clear it. Just that motion sent a bit of the kundalini energy pulsing through her, and that cleared her thoughts even more. She wasn't in the chaos of a civil war, with thousands of civilians and soldiers rioting on the streets – she was in a fight with a few overgrown bullies, greedy men who were just in it for the money. And she wasn't a terrified child anymore – she was a grown woman, and more than that, a mother. A mother with her own child in danger, and that thought was enough to set her feet to thumping, her arms to moving in the precise motions of the dance. The snake dance, to combat birds.

Heedless of the beaks and wings that still tore at her, Natya steadily called the power, raising it from her core, pulsing it up and up until finally it spilled out in a cascade of coruscating fields of light. Pushing out, out, until the birds were forced away, until they fled, cawing wildly, to their master who flew high above. Now her eyes were open again, and there was the front door, splintering into dust. There was a massive creature – a bear? – running into the room, followed by a good handful of cops, and yes, there was Michael among them, relief and fury mixed equally on his face. Most importantly, now she could see Isai, transformed again into Garuda form, and as far as Natya could tell, unharmed – but just as Natya reached out to gather her daughter into her arms, Isai shrieked her rage and hurled herself up into the sky. Chasing the birds that had hurt her mommy.

Michael stormed in to find the fight almost over. Four men were down already, and Minal and Kavitha were still standing, although Minal's face was crumpled in pain, and Kavitha's clothes were bloody rags. No more men on the ground, but the last of the battle was taking place up in the air. His eyes went up and his gun followed, tracking the flight of the crow-man who swooped above, surrounded by a crowd of birds. And there – there was his little girl, screaming her toddler rage louder than he'd ever heard before, her eagle head snapping at the crows that buffeted her body. There was nothing to shoot – the crow-man was half hidden behind Isai's body, and the crows were too small to aim at. He'd never regretted being normal before, but now he would have suffered the agonies of the virus a thousand times over if it would have just left him with one power, something that he could use.

The other cops were equally helpless – there was nothing left for Dr. Dildo to vibrate, and Beastie wasn't nearly tall enough to reach the action. Michael was reduced to shouting to his daughter, 'Isai! Isai, come down here right this minute!' But she wasn't normally inclined to listen, and she paid even less attention now. 'Isai!!'

And then Natya was beside him, flinging her arms out, building a great gold staircase out of thin air. She was dancing furiously, whipping her body around like a serpent, and he knew that she couldn't keep that up for much longer. But he didn't need long. Gods bless them, the other cops followed as he raced up the staircase, up and up and up the steps built of dance and dreams. Trusting his judgment, as he trusted Natya to keep him safe, keep them all safe. Up two stories through a crowd of crows and then he was at Isai, he was grabbing her, heedless of wings and talons, pulling her into his arms, and then she was shifting back, clinging to him naked and weeping. 'Daddy Daddy Daddy! The bad birds hurt Mommy!'

'I know, sweetie, I know,' he whispered. 'It's going to be okay.' And around him the others stood on the final upper landing, their guns out, pointed steadily at the crow-man. Leo was the one who got him cuffed and herded him down the steps – which was just as well, since if it had been up to Michael in that moment, he would have blown the bastard's brains out right there. Instead, he held his daughter close until she was safely down on the ground. When the last cop made it to the floor, Natya stopped dancing and collapsed into his arms. Somehow, he managed to hold them both. And then Minal walked over, and not caring what the other guys thought, he pulled her into the embrace too. His girls were safe, all of them. He would never let them get hurt again.

◆

'So that's it? It's over?' Minal couldn't quite believe it, even though it had been a full twenty-four hours since that hellish time at McGurk's, and they were all feeling better. It turned out that when she slept with someone for a long time, holding them close, some of her healing powers extended to them as well. She'd never cuddled someone for long enough to find that out before – it was a nice bonus to her powers. It made up for some of the downsides. They'd all stayed in bed together until hunger finally drove them out – Minal had made towering piles of pancakes and eggs, and Isai had devoured so many that she'd collapsed, falling asleep on the dining-room floor. Michael had carried her to bed, and then come back to curl up with them on the love seat. Minal was snuggled into Kavitha's arms, but managed to shift back a few inches – enough for Michael to squeeze into the little space, though he had to wrap his arms around them to manage it. Oh, the tragedy.

Michael shook his head. 'We can't know for certain, of course. All of the upper-level Demon Princes had cleared out by the time we showed up. But word at the station and on the street is that they're not interested in you anymore – they seem to have decided that you're not really a threat to them.'

Minal shrugged. 'Well, they're right about that. Joe didn't tell me anything useful.'

Michael frowned. 'We can't be sure that the kidnapping was even connected to Joe Twitch, although I admit that seems the most likely. I'll keep looking.'

'But they're not after me now?' Minal kept her focus on the important part.

Michael said, 'No. It looks like you're safe. You can even go back home.'

'Oh.' Minal had known this was coming, of course, had known

that her life here was too good to last. 'Sure. Of course.' She started untangling herself, suddenly too unsettled to keep sitting on the little red love seat. 'I can pack up my things. Maybe I can wait and say good-bye to the kid in the morning? Or – no, maybe it's better if I just go tonight. Easier on her, not to have to say good-bye.' Easier on herself too. It was going to hurt, not seeing that kid again.

Kavitha pulled her back down. 'Hey! He said you *can* go back home. Not that you have to.'

Minal froze, and said tentatively, 'It's not like I have any better choices.' Did she? What was Kavitha implying?

Kavitha wrapped her arms around Minal and dropped a kiss on her ear, sending a shiver through her. 'You could stay here. With us.'

'Seriously?' Minal turned her head to Michael – he would be the tough sell, she knew. Kavitha was a softy.

Michael smiled too, lighting up his face. 'Seriously. Move in with us. Please. Kavitha and I talked about it last night while you were sleeping. We like you, Minal. We like you a lot.'

Minal swallowed, fighting back surprising tears. 'I like you too. Both of you. *All* of you.' It was too soon to be saying the word 'love' out loud, she was pretty sure. But that didn't mean she couldn't think it. She was happier with these three than she'd ever been in her life. Even if the quarters were a little cramped … 'Hey, I have an idea. Are you guys terribly attached to this apartment? For sentimental reasons or something?'

'No, not really,' Michael said.

Kavitha said, 'It's just what we could afford.'

Minal hesitated, then offered shyly, 'Why don't you move in with me? I have a three-bedroom condo, and I put a lot down. Everything I'd saved from the first few years of hooking – my dad did teach me how to save, even if he didn't teach me anything else. The mortgage payments shouldn't be any more than what you're paying right now for rent. And it's twice the size of this place. Way more room than I needed, really; I had been thinking about getting a cat.' She smiled. 'But this is better.'

Michael raised an eyebrow. 'If we're paying the mortgage, then does that mean you're going to quit hooking?'

Minal nodded. 'If you guys don't mind me sponging off you for a while. Or at least I'd cut way back on it, just keep a few select clients. *Safe* clients. I could keep babysitting Isai, give Kavitha more time to dance. And—' She paused, feeling stupid even saying it. But then she went on, encouraged by the smiles on their faces. 'Maybe I could go back to school.'

Kavitha grinned. 'That would be great! For what?'

Minal said hesitantly, 'Don't laugh, but I always wanted to become a chef, open my own restaurant. I kept thinking of going back to school, but hooking was easier, and the money was so good.' She shrugged. 'But the life's getting too dangerous. I think I might want to make an investment in my future. Find a career more suited to family life.' Minal stopped, wondering if she'd presumed too much, scared them off.

Michael grinned. 'So you mean your cooking is going to get even more delicious? Excellent.'

'I'd be happy not to share you with anyone else,' Kavitha added. 'For a while, anyway.'

Minal relaxed into the red love seat. It was battered, but she was determined to find a space for it in her condo. It was good luck. 'Then I guess you guys are coming home with me.'

Michael took a deep breath and said, 'And tomorrow, you're coming to Thanksgiving with me. With us. I'd like you to meet my parents.'

'Seriously?' Minal asked. That was an even bigger step than moving in together.

Michael shrugged, smiling. 'What the hell. Maybe I'll invite Leo to join us too. We'll make a real family Thanksgiving this year. If you ladies can take on the Demon Princes – and win! – I think I can manage two aging parents.'

Kavitha grinned, and reached over to drop a kiss on Michael's cheek. 'You're very brave. My hero.'

Minal said quietly, 'Mine too. Both of you. You rescued me.' In so many ways.

Kavitha said lightly, 'We rescued each other, and we're all very brave and noble, but if we keep on thanking each other, we'll be talking all night. I think there are *much* better uses for our mouths, don't you?'

Minal laughed, and couldn't help but agree.

DECEMBER

THE RAT RACE

PART 15.

Leo's retirement racket went down at the High Hand as pre-determined at the insistence of Dr. Pretorius, Charles Dutton, and Lucas Tate. They called it a gift to an old friend; Leo figured they were also calling it a tax write-off, but he didn't mind.

The detective dressed up. Not a penguin suit or anything, but everything was washed and pressed, and he had Wanda on his arm – glittering like a million bucks – so nobody would be looking at him anyway. She was wearing a deep green dress that made her eyes look crazy bright, and her hair smelled faintly of perfume. Her shoes cost more than everything he was wearing put together; and they made her an inch taller than he was.

He didn't care.

But not even the curve of her hip tapping lightly against his could distract him from the strangeness of it – this party to send him off, this event filled with coworkers and pals, and with friends so old they were nearly strangers. They swirled about him, glasses clinking, depositing hors d'oeuvres toothpicks onto doily-covered trays.

Along the far wall of east-facing windows, a table ran the length of the dining area, covered with the things you might expect, and the things Leo had asked for specifically. A pyramid of melon cubes sat next to a crock pot full of chili, and an assortment of cheese and crackers was placed beside a spread of pizza slices shaped like a Chinese fan.

As Wanda pointed out, all the food was disappearing at about the same rate. So people were eating, and that was the measure of a good party, wasn't it? A good, blurry party peppered with back slaps, dirty jokes, congratulations, and questions about what came next.

One arm snaked around Wanda's waist as she lifted a chip to her mouth and chewed with a tight-lipped smile. There was life in him yet. There was also a planned community brochure in his top desk drawer.

There was time to think.

The room was fairly full, and it was populated like an old episode of *This Is Your Life*. Over by the buffet table was Lieutenant Kant, chatting with one of the kitchen staffers – probably asking for another round of something. At one of the large tables, Tenry Fong and Slim Jim were laughing at something Beastie Bester had said. Mitch Moore and Razor Joan were laughing too, and Wingman was looking funny at Rodriguez. Puff was standing by the punch bowl, dipping himself a new drink every couple of minutes and augmenting it with something from the flask tucked into his belt. Angel was beside him, sticking to the alcohol levels that were provided by catering. She looked great – radiant and lovely, if cool. She'd recovered beautifully from her run-in with the Infamous Black Tongue.

The chief was nearby, standing around in her dress uniform and looking slightly less confrontational than usual, but maybe that was the glass of white wine she was holding, since it was mostly empty.

Ralph was the only one missing. He'd been buried the week before.

Leo half expected to glance at an unoccupied corner and spy his pissy white ghost loitering about, sneering at the spread and waiting with a shitty joke about seeing his old partner soon. Leo glanced from vacant corner to vacant corner. He saw nothing. He didn't even feel like he was being watched.

Dr. Pretorius was there too, and Ice Blue Sibyl was with him, wearing an oversized white cloak with a fur-rimmed hood pushed back across her shoulders ... and nothing else. Her glassy blue skin was smooth, poreless, and lacked any visible orifice. Silent and statuesque for something so small, she stood beside her benefactor and if they chatted back and forth, they did it discreetly.

Leo'd already gone out of his way to thank them for coming, even though Sibyl's silent, seamless presence had always unsettled him – he was starting to get used to it. Just in time to quit seeing her so often.

Charles Dutton made it too, though he made it in a wheelchair with a nurse attending him. He camped in the middle of the room and held court there, dressed like a king on a business trip. The nurse looked a little bored by the whole thing.

Tabby Driscoll grabbed Leo's hand and gave it a hearty shake that was made a little heartier by whatever beer the old cop smelled on the younger cop's breath. 'Ramshead, you old bastard. Gonna miss you 'round the Fort.'

'Eh, you'll never know I'm gone,' he replied with a smile that hoped it was lying.

'Of course we will,' interrupted Bill Chen, who spun around to join the conversation. 'You're an *institution*.'

Leo was tipsy enough to laugh, and the party pirouetted onward.

At the edge of Dutton's circle Leo spied Father Squid, quietly nodding at something the wheelchair-bound man was saying. The priest's eyes snagged the detective's, and jerked away. Leo's stomach did a little leap, but he said nothing, and for the purposes of that night, he pretended he suspected nothing.

Pretending only got him so far.

Wanda spied someone's wife. She tugged on Leo's arm and whispered, 'They're looking for a new unit, more downtown than uptown. You didn't hear it from me, but I'm pretty sure she's expecting.' Then she sashayed away from Leo and gave the other woman a predatory, professional greeting.

Otto Gordon was lurking alone near a platter he'd brought and left lying beside the cheese plate, so Leo took the Wanda-less opportunity to visit.

Otto was the morgue's mad – and presumably benevolent – scientist. Everyone called him 'Gordon the Ghoul.' As far as anyone knew, he didn't mind. Gordon was a cartoon of a man, too long and too narrow, and too pointy by half. His sloping forehead, enormous nose, and understated chin conspired to give him the look of an intellectual beanpole in a lab coat.

No one else was eating from his platter, which almost seemed to please him.

Leo sidled up to him and said, 'Hey there, Gordon, got a question for you.'

'Then I hope I have an answer.'

'Yeah. Here's a hypothetical, okay?' He was pretty sure he wasn't going to gross Gordon out, so he ran with it. 'Say I wanted to get some evidence from old tissue. How old can it be, and still give usable DNA samples?'

Gordon dipped a chip in something gray with lumps in it, and stuffed it into his mouth while he considered the question. He chewed slowly before replying. 'It depends, really. Sometimes DNA can be recovered from tissue hundreds of years old – even thousands, though that's less likely. We have to extract it from inside the teeth, drilling down through the enamel into the pulp,' and here he added the appropriate thrust and lift of his elbow, miming a drilling motion. 'But any number of things can cause the DNA to deteriorate. Certain chemicals, humidity, temperatures, and storage considerations could—'

Leo clarified, 'Let's say we're talking thirty-year-old fetal tissue, kept sealed up in evidence.'

The ghoul said, 'Assuming nothing has contaminated it, it's entirely possible. But now we're leaving the hypothetical, aren't we, Detective?'

'Yeah, we're leaving it. And I have a favor to ask you, if that's okay.'

'It's your party,' Gordon pointed out. 'Ask whatever you like.'

Leo reached into his pocket and pulled out a flatted, smashed paper coffee cup in a Ziploc bag. 'Could you take this for me? And swab it for DNA?'

'This is ... not thirty-year-old fetal tissue,' Gordon said as he took the bag. He sounded disappointed.

'No, it isn't. But I'll have that for you on Monday, all right?'

'Very well.'

'Just, um. Stash it, would you? And keep this between us.'

'Absolutely.'

Leaving that encounter, Leo found himself starved for fresh air and – for the first moment in an hour – he was cut loose from the congratulations, vows of enduring friendship, or offers of yet more to drink. The restaurant felt close, and the band where his hat met his pate felt sweaty.

Just a quick breather, that's what he'd take. And no one would miss him. No one stopped him as he found the elevators and let himself down to the lobby, and out into the street in front of the building.

It was colder already than when he'd first come inside to start the festivities. The air was brittle and fogged with ice crystals, and when he breathed his exhalations glittered in the lamplight and the ambient light of the restaurant behind him. He stamped his feet and rubbed his hands together, blowing into them, leaning up against the wall and then changing his mind, wanting to walk.

Just around the block. He'd be back in ten minutes, and the frigid air would clear his head.

He was running out of things to say up there, anyway – there were only so many times he could shake hands and laugh, and glance nervously left to right, and back again. He was troubled by the enigmatic priest with all his secrets; and he was suddenly annoyed with Tate and Dutton for insisting on the venue; and he was horrified by how it might actually be the last time he ever saw some of these people again.

His time left on the force could be counted in hours, if he felt like it. He could tick them off, predicting these last days in the lingo of paycheck stubs and morning coffees shared and spilled with Michael at their desks – jammed together like teenagers in a high school biology lab. Some of those people upstairs at the party worked different shifts, or were about to take vacation time, or would simply be walking different paths in different corridors through Fort Freak; some of them might get injured and knocked out of the game that way – knocked out of his sphere, and out of the familiar course that he'd walked through that station, through this city, for over thirty-five years.

Could he imagine that?

Not really. But awareness of this finality clung to him like cigarette smoke on an old jacket. It wafted around him and made him shudder.

In his jacket pocket he fumbled for his badge and found it, and gripped it, and wiped a bit of chilly mist off the metal with the side of his thumb.

It wasn't fair. He was now more capable than ever – if you wanted his completely unbiased opinion. It was the stupidest goddamn thing in the world, picking a number and calling it the end on a whole career when there were still thefts and rapes and gangs and murders out there, dangling loose threads that might never be tied off.

For the millionth time he thought of the Rathole.

He was almost out of time, and none of the answers he'd found made him feel any better about what had happened there. It made his gut ache, how he found himself wondering so hard about friends and trusted compatriots.

His eyes snapped to the jutting ledge above him, as if he could see through it and back up into the party upstairs. Again, his belly constricted, thinking of the men up there, and wondering about one man and what he might've done decades ago.

Maybe it was just as well he had no proof of anything.

He kicked his toes against the sidewalk to jar some feeling into them. Around the corner he found a narrower road, larger than an alley but nearly as dark. A pair of Dumpsters against a wall smelled like day-old death and last week's vegetables, expired rats and dirty diapers. An old shipping pallet had dried out and cracked in the middle of the way, and it crunched under his foot.

A few seconds behind him, it crunched again.

He stopped.

He knew before he turned around that he wasn't alone. He knew as he stood there, one hand on his useless badge and no gun anywhere on him, that he was being followed again, and he could guess.

He *did* guess.

'You got to leave Raul alone,' she said, and in six words Leo heard bluegrass and hill country. He wondered what had happened to this child, that she'd found her way to New York.

With a pivot on one foot, he faced her then. Hands in his pockets, now. Not wanting to give too much away. He told her, 'Raul has answers.'

'He *doesn't*,' she argued. The billowing wind caught her straggly brown hair, lifting it up and gusting it about – and only her cheap knitted cap kept her mane from becoming an angry cloud of snakes. She was folded in on herself, hands up under her arms and legs jammed together, feet planted heel against heel.

Leo said, 'He didn't send you tonight.'

She was quick to defend him some more. 'Course not. He don't know I'm here, even.'

'Your … your boss, or your guardian, or whatever he is – Raul isn't afraid of me, you know that, don't you?'

'He thinks he's safe.'

'He's probably right,' Leo told her. Though he rather strongly suspected that somehow, someway the mobster was connected to the Rathole, this was one more case where he'd be hard-pressed to prove it. 'I don't have anything on him.'

'But you're *looking*.'

'You think I'll find something?'

She made a puzzled face and tried to hide it. 'No.'

'Then what are you so worried about?'

Leo thought she was going to argue some more, but instead she shouted, 'Don't you get it? He's all I got!' She began to stomp toward him, and it started as a stumble but it brought her up fast. 'There's nobody else on earth gives a shit what happens to me, but *he* does. He looks out for me, and I'm gonna look out for him – even if he thinks he doesn't need me to.'

The detective backed up, just a step. And a second step. Not too far. Not enough to let her think she had the upper hand, but he remembered the disorientation, the nausea, and the draining fear from the time she'd grabbed him at the hospital. So he took a third step, back away from her.

He said, 'Listen, kid, I don't want to hurt you—'

'But you want to hurt Raul.' She kept coming, and he was stopped by a stash of crates that once delivered bottles of something drinkable.

He stopped against them. 'No. I don't.'

'You're going to put him in jail,' she said through chattering teeth that clipped the edge off every word. Her hands came out of her pockets and she reached for him, coming up close enough that the clouds of their breath touched and mingled.

With a swift grasp he caught her by the wrists, grasping her coat-covered arms and holding her naked hands away – at all the distance he could reach. He picked her up almost off her feet and pushed her back, lifting her as she lunged for him, fighting him.

'Kid,' he growled, and she cracked out one long, skinny leg and hooked her foot behind his knee. She pulled.

They both went down, side by side and wrestling. They rolled. He was stronger but heavier, and even though he'd had a couple glasses of scotch upstairs she wasn't tough enough to pin him – but she didn't have to pin him. She only had to get one bit of skin up against his skin, and it'd be all over.

She thrashed and wrestled. He wished for a set of handcuffs.

She tried to hit him. He clamped his fingers around her wrist again, adjusting his grip to keep any bit of flesh from becoming exposed.

'Kid!' he barked. 'I swear to God, if you don't—' and it was a futile thing, the beginning of his threat. It meant nothing and she was thrusting her face down toward his, as if she were trying to bite him or kiss him. Attacking him with her face because she could, and because she had to.

She tried to knee him in the crotch and almost succeeded, but ended up digging into his upper thigh instead. He lifted his own knee, working it between them, preparing to throw her off – all he needed was a little leverage, for God's sake, this was just a child, and he didn't want to hurt her, but he'd be damned if he'd let her touch him.

And then, as immediately as she'd pounced ...

She was gone.

Hoisted off him and out of his sight, as he lay there on the ground – still poised, and hands still held up in a pair of defensive squeezes.

With a scramble that scraped one of his palms he was on his feet again and starting to feel the first dim grumbles of aches in his elbows and knees. Reflexively he reached for the gun that wasn't there. And then he realized he didn't need it.

Sibyl – that blue-glass being with the shimmering, hairless skin – she was there, covered in that long hooded cloak that protected her from the first fluttering chips of the almost-snow that was starting to fall.

In her unyielding arms the teenaged girl raged and cried.

A large cluster of flakes smacked Leo in the eye, leaving him bleary. He wiped at it and watched the two strange women, and he tried to recall if he'd ever seen anyone touch Sibyl before – if she'd ever *let* anyone touch her, even the lawyer whose side she so rarely left.

But now she was holding the girl by the shoulders, and by the hands. The blue fingers entwined with the ghost-white girl's quivering fingers and they were steady, unmoved. Uncompromised by the teenager's awful power.

And Maggie Graves crumpled to her knees, crying harder.

As the detective caught his breath and stared, he wondered if it wasn't very simple, really. Two vulnerable women, no family and no recourse. Both of them taken under the wing of an older man and treated well enough to become protective of those men – protective to the point of murder, if it came to that.

He straightened his jacket and adjusted his hat.

Ice Blue Sibyl's inscrutable eyes peered up from under her hood, telling him nothing.

As he walked around them, back around the corner and back to the front of the building, the girl's tear-choked voice followed him, amazed and moved. Over and over again she was saying the same thing, and it rang in Leo's ears until he was back to the building where the party raged upstairs, and the carousel glass doors had slipped shut behind him.

'You can touch me, can't you? You can touch me, you can *touch* me …'

... AND ALL THE SINNERS SAINTS

PART 4.

Charlie sat planning his legal defense with the attorney Pretorius had recommended to him. Within an hour of their first meeting, he had begun to suspect that he was quite a lot smarter than the man. Now, after several weeks of filed motions and legal wrangling, he realized to his great relief that he was very wrong. His attorney was laying out their strategy for the next round of motions when Charlie's phone rang.

Mother, Charlie thought wearily. Of late she had taken to calling her soon-to-be-jailed son a dozen or more times a day, so he answered without looking. Instead of his mother's worried tone, he heard a loud whooping. 'Uh, who is this?'

'Charlie, my boy, I am about to save your fucking life!' Vincent Marinelli shouted into the phone. 'That was gold you got, Flipper! Absolute *gold.* Richard fucking Long!'

Charlie said, 'Listen, I'm in a meeting with my attorney, and—'

'Jesus Christ on a pogo stick. Fuck your attorney. Richard Long? Dick Long! Look for the dick names, your girl said. We found Puff's secret account, and a big fat payment dropping into it a day before the Joe Twitch murder. We got that motherfucker, Charlie. We got him. *You* got him. I need you to come in and help me plan stage two.'

Charlie slumped in his swivel chair. Relief flooded him. He waved off his attorney's worried glance. 'So we won?' he said. 'This'll nail him?'

'Nope.'

'But – Minal said Twitch didn't have a gun. That he was black-mailing someone important. That the cops shot him at or on his way to the meeting. And she gave us the name on one of the fake accounts he uses to launder his bribes. And you found money in it that arrived just before the murder. Isn't that enough to hang him?'

'Not even close. It's a good start, but the public worships cops. They're well conditioned by all those TV shows. And Angel Grady's a certified war hero. There's flies on her too, but we haven't found the maggots yet. Aside from the fact that she pumped half a dozen rounds into Joe, we also found half the money in Long's account disappeared the day after the shoot. Looks a lot like he paid his accomplice to me.'

Defeat ran Relief's ass out and settled into Charlie as if he were a comfortable pair of slippers. 'So how do we get them if this isn't enough?' He found himself dizzy with the roller coaster of emo-tions Vince's call had already wrung out of him. Now he was back to being excited by the prospect of actually winning. Maybe finally being able to bring Marcus in out of the cold. 'What else do we need?'

'To get an indictment?' Vince said. 'A video of Lu Long kneeling on Jesus Christ's own chest while Angel pounds nails through His palms. And even then the *Cry*'s gonna smear the victim.'

'So we've lost?'

'Oh, fuck to the no, kid,' Ratboy said. 'I told you, you brought the goods. We needed evidence. This is evidence. We can start building a case. And IAB's got forensic accountants who can make this dragon fucker's accounts chatter like seagulls on the pier at Coney Island. But we're gonna need more.'

Charlie didn't even know how to feel at this point. Which left him mostly exhausted. 'Okay. What can we do?'

'I told you I saw maybe some chinks in the blue wall. I been working those. There are some honest cops at Fort Freak. Actually, maybe a whole lot of them.'

'I'm surprised you admit that.'

'If there were no honest cops there'd be no point to doing my job. There's also some maybe not as clear-cut ones who don't care so much for Angel Grady's sexual preferences, or Lu Long's general dickery. And even the bent ones have their limits – until they bend so far they break, like this *gavoon* Puff. If we can prove he's crossed the line to bad-guydom, they'll turn on him. We got to turn one of the fucks. Puff's my choice. He's hotheaded and not terribly bright. Angel is the opposite. Cold as ice, and smart as hell. If he's pulled Angel Grady into a killing for hire, then she's gone full-on supervillian. I'd love to know why, but I don't need to know to nail her. Puff though, Puff's just an asshole. Assholes are candy. Assholes I can work with.'

'They all think they're the good guys,' Charlie said bitterly.

'Kid, here's the deal with cops. Every man, woman, and indeterminate of us believes heart and soul that every crook is fundamentally *broken*. That the act of breaking the law, even once, renders you intrinsically wrong and untrustworthy. Now, what is the one thing Puff and Angel each know beyond any possible doubt? That the other one's a criminal. A murderer. Subconsciously, that's gotta be eating on them.'

Charlie had his doubts. 'Puff seems pretty sociopathic. Hard to see anything bothering his conscience.' He thought of the burn scar marring the odd alien perfection of Minal Patel.

'He's got a sense of self-preservation, right? He's not a genius, but he's not stupid. He knows his partner's not like him. She's a saint to everyone else. The minute that selling him out helps her, she'll do it and walk away clean. We *want* him to be the bad guy. We want her to be righteous. All she has to do is give us a nudge and we burn Puff to the ground. And he has to see that as a bigger threat than anything you or I can do. Because if *she* flips on him, he's toast.'

'So we play them off against each other until one of them really does turn?'

'You got the picture.'

'But – how?'

Charlie could hear Vince's smile right through the phone.

'I got ways,' Ratboy said. '*Trust* me.'

Ernie's Bar and Grill was dark, cozy, and largely empty in early afternoon. It also wasn't a usual cop hangout. Which made it ideal for Vince and his companion to hold their little sit-down.

If Vince Marinelli could be intimidated – and growing up in a tough Brooklyn Italian neighborhood where you were called Ratboy, you'd never make adolescence if you *could* – the uniformed officer who sat hunched in the comfortable cracked-leather booth across from him would've scared pellets out of him. Bill Chen had shown himself to be a decent guy in their own prior meeting, and he had a good rep around the station as a straight shooter. Flipper's former law school chum, Francis Black, had done nothing but sing Bill's praises as a partner.

But now Vince was asking him to turn on a brother cop, and that never went over well. Chen's face was already like a block of granite in its natural state. But his frown line kept getting chiseled deeper and deeper as Minal Patel's recorded voice spoke from Vince's cell phone on the table.

When the MP3 ended, the big cop sat up. 'That's pretty heavy, Detective,' he said in his six-year-old girl voice. 'You think she's straight?'

'Yes, I do, Officer Chen. My girl in the Bureau has identified a second false-name account traceable to Long as well as the one the witness mentions. This account received a large deposit just before the Joe Twitch shooting.'

Bill Chen rubbed his jut of jaw. 'This makes us all look bad.'

'There are straight cops at Fort Freak, Chen. I hear you're one of them.'

Chen grunted. He even did that falsetto. 'I hate it double when a cop of Chinese descent goes wrong,' he said. 'I hate it like poison, but this needs brought into the light. Come what may. What do you want from me?'

'A pair of ears in the precinct house wouldn't hurt. Yeah, I know. You don't want to spy on your brother and sister officers. But think about this – if they committed murder, if they shot Joe

Moritz in cold blood, what does that brotherhood mean to *them*?'

'Okay, I get it.'

'You could maybe drop a hint or two to Grady that if she wants to come back to the straight path, she'd be welcome. If she goes State's evidence she'll never do hard time. I want her badge, but if she comes clean I'm fine if she gets the sweet plea bargain we both know they'll offer. This job's the art of the possible. Long's the real dirtbag. It's his scaly ass I wanna nail to the wall.'

'I wish I could say that was a surprise.'

It bothered Vince to lie to Chen like that when the officer was being open and honest with him, but the truth was he knew that Angel would never cop a plea. She'd throw Long under the bus way before she'd give herself up.

And if she did that, well then that might be enough to get Long to reach out and drag her under the bus with him. And then he'd get them both. At the very least, just the rumor of deals might be enough to drive a wedge between them.

'One more thing,' Vince said. 'If you could put a bug in Sergeant Choy's ear, let her know I'm not looking to bust apple cops here, that'd be a huge favor.'

Chen frowned. 'Why me? Because we're both Chinese?'

'Fuck *me,* officer. Don't let the snout and the lovely brown fur fool you. I'm an Italian cop, right? Someone in the department needs a go-between with me, do they go to a Jewish cop? An Irish cop? A fucking Armenian?'

Chen tittered. 'Yeah. You got me there. And you're right. Choy is one of the good guys. I'm glad you see that. Makes me feel like you're not just head-hunting here.' He looked at his watch. 'Okay, gotta get back to the fort. Franny will be wondering where I am, and I don't want you busting my chops for padding my lunch break.'

'Call me Vince,' Vince said, sticking out a paw. 'And I won't call you Tinkerbill.'

Chen just laughed. 'You'll be the only one, then.'

'I hate to do this, Morgan,' Charlie said. *You don't have any* idea *how much I hate it,* he thought. Marcus had only come out of hiding long enough to leave a message for Charlie a week ago, and already he was being asked to risk his life again. 'We need your help.'

Dry leaves crackled on sidewalks as the wind blew them across the cement and stone. Columbus Park didn't have much cover, but it was pretty empty at this time of night, and Marcus could use trees and light poles as his own personal escape route. It wasn't a bad location for a discreet meet.

And there was your problem with Morgan. He wasn't stupid – far from it. But if he had one-quarter the sense he did ingenuity, they wouldn't be here with Charlie constantly looking over his own shoulder for Doom in many guises.

'I'll do it, Mr. Herriman,' Marcus said. 'I'm tired of hiding in sewers and subway tunnels and eating out of Dumpsters. Even jail has to be better than that.'

I suck, Charlie thought. *FML.* 'This is going to be tricky,' he said. 'If it doesn't work, you might wind up in prison for the rest of your life. But if we want to clear your name and nail two bad cops, it's the only way.'

'You want to use me as bait, don't you?'

Charlie sagged. 'Well, no, we actually need to use you as a threat.'

Ratboy perp-walked the Infamous Black Tongue into the 5th precinct like Eliot Ness bringing in Al Capone … if Ness had been a giant rat instead of just a glory hound, and if Capone had slithered in on fifteen feet of tail with a barrel cinched tight around his arms and upper torso. But still, he made a big show of it.

Charlie followed along behind at a respectful distance, the conscientious civil servant there to make sure his client got adequate representation. Vince did his best to completely ignore him, as befits a scum-sucking defense lawyer.

The show had its desired effect. Cops came from all over the precinct house to watch the fugitive brought in, including both

Angel Grady, only recently returned to active duty and assigned a desk, and her scaly partner Lu Long. Grady played it cool, but Long stared daggers at Marcus, as though he were trying to set him on fire without actually having to spit.

Vince slither-marched Marcus up to Vivian Choy, who was manning the desk that night, and said, 'I'm going to need one of your interrogation rooms for this shithead.'

Choy gestured and Bill Chen and Franny Black came to take custody of Marcus.

'What's IAB doing on a fugitive collar, Detective?' Choy asked, her suspicion palpable. Vince had arranged ahead of time, through Bill Chen, that she be the one to ask the obvious question. Better to get it out in the open from an ally than from an enemy. When he answered her, no one else would ask.

'Well, Sergeant, I happen to be working a case involving this perp. Material witness. And since the officers at this precinct couldn't find their own asses with a map and a flashlight, I went ahead and rounded him up myself.'

Make it about showing the cops at the 5th up, and they'd buy that as motive for a piece of shit from the rat squad. Prejudice and preconception were tools just like anything else.

'His asshole lawyer should be in lockup with him,' Lu Long yelled out. 'We all know he was hiding him.'

'Mr. Herriman is here at Mr. Morgan's request, to protect his God-given civil rights,' Vince replied with a wink.

Bill Chen returned. 'Your guy's getting prepped. We'll move him to three when you're ready.'

'Thank you, Officer Chen,' Vince said. He was playing to the rear seats. Everyone knew he was up to something, but as long as he kept up the act, no one could be sure what. More cops were drifting from the room, moving back to their assignments. Angel gave Lu Long a significant glance and started to head for the staircase. Before she could get out of sight, Vince called out in a loud voice, 'Officer Grady! A moment, before you return to work?'

Angel shared another look with Long, then walked over to him. 'Yes?'

Vince gave her his best rat smile, the one that showed all his sharp teeth at once. It was an obvious attempt to intimidate, which made Grady half roll her eyes and dismiss him as a threat, which is exactly what he wanted.

With Lu Long across the room watching, Vince lowered his voice. 'Puff is done. I've got him. I'd call my union rep right now if I were you. This is going to be a long night for the both of you. Lieutenant Kant has been informed of my intent to arrest you both, and will make sure you don't leave the building. In fact, don't leave this room.'

Grady stared at him. Vince had to give her credit. She was one cool customer. She didn't flinch or start shouting denials. She just waited a moment, then pulled out her phone. Across the room, Long was looking at her, his face a question. She ignored him.

Perfect.

Before Long could come over and ask her anything, Vince crossed the room and got in front of him. 'Officer Long, could you join me in interrogation room three?'

'What for?'

'Mr. Herriman is waiting there. I have a few more questions about the night you claim he attacked you.'

'Yeah, whatever,' Long said, then slouched off toward the interrogation room, his tail dragging across the floor with a sound like high grit sandpaper.

When they reached the room, Charlie was already sitting in it, writing something on a yellow legal pad. He looked up with irritation when they came in. 'Excuse me? I haven't yet had a chance to meet with my client.'

Lu Long snarled and said, 'Your client can suck my balls, shyster.'

'Interesting choice of words, officer,' Vince said with a toothy smile. 'Let's everyone have a seat.' He climbed up into one of the room's uncomfortable plastic chairs. 'Mr. Herriman, what do you run, a buck fifty soaking wet?'

'Around there, Detective.'

'Officer Long, what do you run? Gotta be three bills if you're a pound.'

'What the fuck's that got to do with this asshole attacking me?'

'Well,' Vince said, pulling his feet up onto the chair and rocking on his haunches. 'I grew up in a tough neighborhood. I've been in a lot of scrapes, and I have police training and a gun. And I gotta tell you, Puff, I wouldn't take you on on a dare. I mean, look at you. Built like a brick shithouse, that tail looks like it could break a man off at the knees, and top it off with flaming loogies. You're hell on wheels, big fella.'

Lu Long's expression changed, just starting to realize that he might be being mocked. 'So fucking what?'

'So, what makes a 150-pound joker with flipper arms do a body tackle on Godzilla's baby brother?' Vince turned to Charlie and said, 'So, why did you do it? Must have been something crazy serious.'

'He was about to shoot my client in the back.'

'Fuck you, you fucking ambulance-chasing prick!' Long stood up, knocking his chair over. His tail lashed side to side, slapping against the wall.

'Well, that certainly qualifies as serious enough for a man to do something crazy,' Vince said without missing a beat. 'Officer Long, do you have an alternate theory?'

Long stood for a moment, panting, looking like he was caught between killing Charlie with his bare hands and just running away. 'My theory is that this guy is a shithead, and you assholes are up to something.'

Here we go, Vince thought. *All in.* 'Well, Officer Long, I admit that I told Officer Grady she should call her union rep and her lawyer just before we came in. I'm sure she's doing the same for you.' He charged on before Long could reply. *One way to avoid showing the other side you've got nothing in your hand is to keep pushing chips into the pot.* 'Let me tell you my theory. You and Grady capped Joe Twitch, and Marcus Morgan saw you. Hell, he tried to save poor old Joe. You guys tussle, he gets away, now there's a witness on the loose. But what could Marcus have seen? He saw the shooting, but you guys don't dispute that you shot Joe. Then it occurs to me, Marcus saw that Joe wasn't packing when you capped him, so you had to have used a drop gun afterward. You blasted Joe, then you pulled out that piece of shit .380 and stuck it in his hand. So, sure he can testify that Joe wasn't holding a gun when he was shot, but that's not the part that really fucks you if he gets on a witness stand.'

Puff sneered. 'His word against ours, and he's a fucking black snake that likes to poison women cops. Who will the jury like, asshole? Why the fuck are you wasting my time with this shit?'

'Snakes and rats are mortal enemies,' Vince said, using his best schoolteacher tone. 'I pointed that out to Charles there once. I'm a human trapped in a rat body, and even I get the cold sweats just looking at Marcus. But we do have one important thing in common. Do you know what that is?'

'You're both vermin?' suggested Puff.

'I was thinking of our vomeronasal organs. You know what those are?'

'Tiny dicks?' Lu Long replied.

'No, it's an extrasensory organ both snakes and rats have for smelling. For example, did you know that rats use this organ to smell each other's pheromones? Yeah, they can tell which of the female rats are ready to screw just by the pheromones they give off. And snakes, shit, they're even better at it. They're fucking bloodhounds.'

'So you smell,' said Puff. 'So the fuck what?'

'You and I both know you dropped that gun. We both know Marcus can testify that Joe didn't have a gun at the time of the shooting. But there's no way a jury is just going to buy into his testimony without a real good reason.

'Like ball sweat. I can smell your scaly little balls right now, asshole. And that means Marcus could too. And you had that cheap-ass .380 stuffed down your pants, and no matter how much you wiped it for prints, you couldn't get those pheromones off of it. While you and he were tussling, he kept throwing that tongue of his at you, right? Sure, he can poison you with it, but a snake's tongue does something else too. It grabs scent particles and deposits them on that vomeronasal organ I was telling you about. That's better than a fucking bloodhound. That's like a bloodhound on steroids.'

Lu Long laughed. 'No one is going to believe that shit!'

'Oh, yes they will,' Charlie said over the top of him. 'Vince and I have got it all figured out. We lay out ten identical guns to the one you dropped. Marcus will pick the one you carried every time. We do that over and over again, eventually the jury won't be able to ignore it. Witness testimony can be about all sorts of thing. Things a person saw, or heard ... or in this case, *smelled.*'

Charlie got up and headed toward the interrogation-room door. Vince pointed one finger at Long's face. 'You're cooked, mother-fucker. We got you. I got your account with money going into it the day before the shoot, I got a witness saw you at the shoot, and I got your ball sweat all over the gun you planted on Joe Moritz.'

He stopped when someone knocked at the door. Charlie opened it to admit Sergeant Squinch. She handed Vince a plastic evidence bag with a small automatic in it. The gun they claimed Joe Twitch had when he died.

Vince said, 'Sergeant, is Officer Grady with anyone out there?'

'Yeah, she's been talking to a union rep for a few minutes now. Why?'

'Has this union representative asked to see Officer Long?'

'Nope.'

'Thank you.' Vince turned back to Lu Long. 'I know about the money you paid Grady for her half of the hit. I don't know if you brought her in, or vice versa. And frankly, I don't give a shit. But what I do know is that she took half the money and fired half the bullets, and she's out there right now getting ready to toss you to the wolves.'

'Angel wouldn't—'

'The fuck she wouldn't,' Vince said, raising his voice for the first time. 'I told her that I had you by the balls. I told her she'd better get you a lawyer and a rep fast, because I was about to burn you down. You know what she did? She called her rep. She's out there right now figuring out what kind of deal she can work. And she'll get away with it, because you're a piece of shit who likes hurting people, and she's Angel Grady, war hero and straight arrow. We'll *want* to believe it was all you. We'll eat that shit up as long as she feeds it to us. But what's really sad is that it's a fucking split tail that will send big tough Lu Long to the needle. I got you by your ball sweat, and a fucking woman is going to have the last laugh while you get the hot shot.' *There, push all the chips to the middle of the table and dare the other side to call. When they flip that river card, you go home a millionaire or you go bust.* The adrenaline coursing though Vince's body made time seem to slow to a crawl while Lu Long sat in stunned silence.

'*Fuck no she isn't,*' Lu Long finally growled.

Aces all the way, game over, cash me out.

♦

Sergeant Vivian Choy popped the cork on a fresh bottle of Charles Heidsieck 1995 Blanc des Millénaires champagne. Everyone cheered as white foam frothed out the top and down the sides.

It was a festive early evening at New Big Wang. Dr. Pretorius had sprung for the bubbly and finger food. The lawyer himself cheerfully accepted the first refill.

Though he wasn't much of a drinker Charlie had already put away the better part of a glass. It was *his* party. His license to practice saved from disbarment, his client rescued from a false murder charge. His information let Ratboy nail all the bad guys. Almost in spite of himself, he'd won.

Along with staff and well-wishers roistered representatives of the media and a few Fort Freak cops: Sergeant Choy, passing out the champagne and looking trim and definitely not bad for a woman her age. Franny Black from Columbia, and his partner, that huge Chinese patrol guy everybody called Tinkerbill. Who beneath his permanent frown was grinning and looking to be having a fine old time in his pale yellow polo shirt and tan slacks. Detective Michael Stevens. At the edge of the crowd floated Ice Blue Sibyl, smiling her enigmatic smile. And of course, Detective-Investigator Second-Grade Vincent Marinelli, who was holding court in the midst of an attentive mob. He was running through his line of bullshit about the snake and rat sense of smell again. It was definitely going to become legend.

'So I said, "I got you by the ball sweat, Puff!"' Vince said.

'So you can't really smell people's balls?' Bill Chen asked in his squeaky voice.

'You've got balls, Tink?' someone called out to him. More laughter.

Charlie pushed through the crowd to the front door and stepped outside. The crisp night air grounded him, helped push back the growing surreal feeling he had in the party. A few moments later, the door opened behind him accompanied by a short burst of party noise that faded when the door closed again. Charlie didn't turn around, but he heard the clack of claws on concrete and the raspy sweep of a tail. 'Vince.'

'What's eating you, kid?' Marinelli asked. 'The good guys won. Marcus is cleared. *We're* in the clear. And Puff is merrily spilling his guts about his erstwhile partner, ensuring that both of them will get a nice long vacation courtesy of the Department of Corrections.'

Charlie blinked at him. 'He's going to do hard time, isn't he? They won't plea him down to nothing, will they? He still scares the living shit out of me.'

'He's not getting off with a slap on the wrist, plea bargain or not. He did kill someone for money. They sort of frown on cops doing that. But who knew it was really Angel's show?'

'You believe that? Maybe Puff's just saying that to save his hide.'

Vince nodded. 'Maybe. But it doesn't matter. Someday I'd like to know why Angel went bad too. Did Puff twist her? Some shit she was into? Who can say, and it doesn't change the facts anyway.' He crossed his arms. 'And none of that's why you look like you're about to puke until your asshole gets hung up on your tonsils, is it?'

Charlie shook his head. 'It was such a gamble. I mean, I'm glad you pulled it off, but if you hadn't, Marcus would have done hard time. That's pretty shitty. And I did it because I was scared. Scared of losing my license, of going to jail.'

'You did the right thing. Once the Tongue came in, his odds of getting offed went down about a million percent. And he's off the hook for the real charges. And the community seems to be turning his way. The *Cry* is calling him a hero.'

'But I still put him in harm's way,' Charlie said. 'I talked him into it. How does it excuse what I did, that everything turned out mostly all right?'

'You did the best you could under the circumstances.'

'I thought you were Captain See the World in Black and White,' Charlie said. He meant it ugly. It came out ugly. He regretted it immediately.

Vince didn't seem to notice. 'Kid,' he said, 'if you can't handle moral ambiguity, you're gonna need to find a whole different planet to live on.'

The door opened again, and Sergeant Choy came out. This time, the sounds of a party didn't follow. Sensing something was wrong, Vince said, 'What killed the party? Need to hear my ball sweat story again?'

Choy scowled. 'Puff got away. They were moving him to the courthouse, and he burned a federal marshal's face off along the way. He's in the wind.'

'Fuck me,' Vince said.

It was almost full dark, a couple nights later. His backpack slung over one shoulder, Charlie trotted up the steps of the law library. He and Marcus had a meeting with the D.A.'s office in the morning. He had some research to do first.

The door opened before him. A tall, willowy woman in a skirt and blue-gray sweater emerged. Dark hair hung past her shoulders. She stopped. Her blue eyes went wide. 'You're Charles Herriman!'

'Uh – yeah. Wait. Have I seen you before?'

She laughed. 'I knocked your files everywhere just a few nights ago, in the Diamond,' she said. 'I didn't know I ran into a hero.'

'A – wait, what?'

'I just want you to know,' she said, 'that some of us are really proud of what you did for that poor joker boy. The world needs more lawyers like you.'

And she kissed him on the cheek.

He finally came out of full freeze as she was disappearing down the steps to street level. 'Okay,' he told himself, in a puff of condensation. 'Okay. I *almost* got up the nerve to ask her name. *Next time*. For sure.'

THE RAT RACE

PART 16.

Wanda stood naked by the window, half behind the curtain in some lingering excuse for modesty. No one could see her but Leo, and he looked at her as hard as he could. Light from outside – from the moon, or from some nearby neon, or somebody else's window – cut sharp shadows across her body.

He was still in bed. The quilt was somewhere on the floor, and a tenacious gray striped sheet was pulled up over Leo's waist.

Pillow talk had turned to talk of work, and the end of work. It had turned to the Rathole, and to suspicions, and to conjecture. He'd told her everything he knew, and everything he believed – even the things he probably should've kept to himself. It aggravated him that she wasn't wearing a badge and couldn't join him everywhere. He *wanted* her to join him everywhere, he realized this now. And he didn't think it was some weird compensation for the end of one life, searching for the start of a new one.

Besides, the Rathole was her case too.

'Time's running out,' she murmured, still looking out the window, down at the street and at God knew what.

'No kidding.' He crossed and uncrossed his legs beneath the sheet. 'I'm just not sure what to do next. I've chased every lead, no matter how old and rusty. I've learned things I didn't want to know about my friends.'

'Squid? I saw his name on the white board. You didn't erase it very well.'

'I should've left it up there in the first place. I'd be an idiot if I didn't wonder.'

She chewed softly on her bottom lip. 'What about Esposito?'

'What about him?'

'That awful girl who came after you ... she must believe he knows something.'

'Oh, he knows something,' Leo confirmed. 'He was in it up to his eyeballs back in the day.'

'Are you sure he wasn't the trigger?'

He took a minute. Then he said, 'No, I'm not sure. It *could've* been him. From a certain slant, he even looks good for it. He was in the neighborhood, involved with Hash Maddox, and prone to wearing masks. He was also a bouncer at Freakers, where one of the victims worked. Any way you look at it, he's tied up in it.'

'But your gut tells you no?' she asked.

'My gut tells me he didn't do it. The Sleeper said the shooter was frantic, and demanding to know who owned that goddamned car. I can't see a pro like Raul stumbling into trouble like that.' Leo sighed. 'The case has all the hallmarks of something personal. And his involvement, if he had any, would've been business.'

'You ever try just asking him who the shooter was?'

'Yeah. He says he doesn't know.'

'You believe him?'

'I don't know.'

Wanda turned away from the window, leaning against the wall beside it. 'The car,' she breathed. 'The Mercedes.'

'Don Reynolds either stole it or found it after the hit-and-run a week or two before the Rathole. Contarini had ditched it.'

She strolled forward, crawling onto the foot of the bed and dragging herself toward the spot beside him. The mattress squeaked softly as her knees and elbows and hands pulled her flesh into line beside his. She nabbed a pillow and shoved it behind her shoulders. 'So what about the girl who died in the hit-and-run?'

'What about her?'

'Who *missed* her?' she said, pointing a long fingernail into Leo's side, and tapping an emphatic beat against his skin.

He shrugged his head back and forth, pouting thoughtfully. 'As near as I could tell, Ramona Holt had no family, no partners. No nobody but the Demon Princes, none of whom had any connection to the car.'

'But somebody was really, really *mad* about that car. Mad at either Don Reynolds, or mad at Contarini.'

'My money's on Contarini. And Squid was mad enough to throw him out of church.'

'You don't really believe Squid was the shooter. I know you don't,' she said, but it sounded like she didn't know it. She only hoped it.

Leo said, 'Squid was connected to the car. He was also connected to one of the victims – Lizzie Wallace. He knew her, and he liked her. He's the one point of commonality between them.'

Wanda rolled over to face him. 'If Squid had a friend at the Rathole, why would he go down there and kill her? That doesn't make any sense.'

'I don't know.'

'But the counter girl's boyfriend was in the Werewolves. Right?'

He hemmed and hawed, finally saying, 'Well, yeah. But no one accused the Werewolves of driving the Mercedes.'

Wanda squinted thoughtfully at Leo's face. 'Okay, so maybe it wasn't about Ramona. But you said it looked personal.'

He would've speculated further but her fingers were running gently scratchy, long-nailed circles on the sheet that covered his lap. 'Personal,' he repeated, distracted. Being drawn into a change of subject, now that her nails were picking at the sheet's hem, drawing it back and down, leaving him as naked as she was. 'It's personal at least half the time, with … with …'

She slipped her hand down his thigh and draped one of her legs over his, bringing the soft heat of her crotch to rest against his hip.

'This kind of case,' he muttered, taking her hand in his and kissing it, then using it as leverage to pull her all the way across him, so that her weight was a lovely thing – her breasts compressed irresistibly against his collarbone as her face hovered above his. 'Sex or money,' he concluded.

He craned his neck up to kiss her. She kissed back, and shifted her hips until she fully straddled him. Sitting up, she stretched – giving him one hell of a view. Then she leaned forward again and ran her hand along the side of his face, fiddling with the smooth, bony curl of keratin that spiraled there.

'I can't stay all night,' she said softly. 'Got a big meeting with the housing board in the morning.'

'But one more round?' he asked, already so stiff underneath her that he thought he'd die if she got up and left.

She wiggled her hips to give his erection a little room, rather than keep it cramped down beneath her. 'Again? Already?'

'Oh, you know me. Always horny.' He tapped at the thick growths she'd been toying with earlier, and then added, 'Wocka … wocka?'

She laughed with silly delight and kissed him hard, adjusting herself to better accommodate him between her legs; and as he tensed and grasped her with anticipation, she settled down on him with no small degree of skill, taking him easily inside her. With a gasp he threw his head back but she grabbed his horns and used them to brace herself as she moved – holding them like a steering wheel at three and six o'clock, forcing him to watch – and Leo thanked God he wasn't a younger man because he never could've withstood the sight. Five seconds and it would've been all over.

So age had its privileges after all.

When they were finished, covered in sweat – with nothing left on the bed except the bottom fitted sheet – they lay tangled together. One of her feet hung off the bed. One of his arms was pinned beneath her shoulders, but he wasn't complaining.

Leo turned to her, still panting faintly, and said, 'I want to say this before you take off.'

'Say what?' she whispered back.

'I know I don't talk about it much, but I want you to know. This. You and me. I don't care if it makes me sound soft, but you're the best thing that's happened to me in years.'

'Aw, Leo,' she said, curling up against him, drawing the one distant foot back onto the mattress.

'No, don't say anything. You don't have to say anything back. I just wanted to get that out there. It's meant everything to me, these last few months especially. It's been a tough time. Been a strange time. And the first time me and you came around, all those years ago, the time wasn't right. But this ...' he said, running out of words. 'It feels like a second chance.'

She took his face in her hands and pulled her damp body as close to his as she could. 'So it's a second chance. I don't want this one to get away.'

'I'm not going anywhere.'

'Good, me either.' She grinned, her face so close that her cheek grazed his. 'And you know, you left one out.'

'What?' he asked, afraid of what she might mean.

'What you said before, about motives. Sex and money. Maybe you ought to add a third. Sometimes things happen for love.'

FAITH

PART 4.

December, 2010

Father Squid looked up from the sheaf of forms that Leo Storgman had just handed him. He supposed that the exhumation order was punctiliously correct, but he wouldn't actually know. He'd never seen one before.

He looked past Storgman into the hallway beyond. His office in Our Lady was too small to hold the entourage that the detective had bought with him. They waited in the hallway beyond the entrance, wheeled cart, body bag, and all. He recognized the uniformed cops – the joker named Miranda Michaelson, who looked like nothing more than a human whippet, five feet five, barrel-chested with a tiny waist, long, powerful legs, and vestigial fangs in an otherwise normal face. Rikki, she was called. She looked more odd than ugly. Better-looking, in fact, than her partner Bugeye Bronkowski, who was a nat, but a decidedly unattractive one with large, protruding eyes that were just this side of normal. Father Squid didn't know the two nats caddying the go-to-Jesus cart. Two functionaries, he assumed, from the coroner's office.

'I don't know what you're going to gain from exhuming Lizzie's body,' the priest said.

Leo shrugged. 'Neither do I,' he admitted. 'But that's why we're doing it. Something may turn up.'

'I'd hate to see Lizzie's rest disturbed by a fishing expedition.'

'She's beyond caring, Father.'

Father Squid regretted his lack of eyebrows. It was hard to register skepticism without the ability to lift an eyebrow. He had to make do with a ripple of his nasal tentacles. 'Is she? What about her loved ones?'

'Does she have loved ones?' Storgman asked.

'You'd be surprised,' Father Squid muttered.

December, 1978

Ralph Pleasant dropped by the storefront a few days after the killings. The pageant rehearsal was continuing, but in a lackluster manner. The Rathole murders had shaken the entire Jokertown community down to its very roots.

'What is this crap?' Pleasant said, not even bothering to lower his voice. 'Christ, what a freak show. Joker fags playacting. I hate this fucking precinct.'

Dorian Wilde turned his bleary gaze onto the cop. The whites of his eyes were red, as if he'd been drinking heavily. 'Officer Pleasant, isn't it?'

'*Detective* Pleasant.' Pleasant flashed his badge, started to put it away. His manner gave the lie to his name.

'May I see that?' Wilde asked archly.

Pleasant sighed his put-upon sigh and took out the wallet again, pulling away when he noticed the slime-dripping tentacles that the joker reached out to take it with. 'Fuck, no,' he said, with something of horror in his voice.

'Yes,' Wilde said, 'indubitably, a cop.'

'Mind answering some questions, Padre?' Pleasant asked Father Squid.

'Perhaps we'd better go to my office,' the priest said.

'Perhaps we'd better,' Pleasant agreed.

The office was tiny and ill-furnished and cluttered with cardboard boxes filled with ratty, smelly donated clothing. A small chair for the priest, a small, battered table before it. A single battered, paint-spattered wooden chair on the other side of the table. The detective sat, crossed his legs, and took out a pad and ballpoint pen.

Father Squid had expected to be questioned about Lizzie, but Pleasant never so much as mentioned the Rathole killings. Instead he wanted to know about Monsignor Contarini. When he arrived, when he left, what was discussed. Father Squid answered dutifully. His voice was monotonous, almost zombielike. In truth, he was deadly tired. He hadn't slept at all. He didn't want to sleep, even if he could. Whenever he closed his eyes, he dreamed he was back with the Twisted Fists, gunning down women who looked like Lizzie.

'Had the wop been drinking?' the detective finally asked.

'The monsignor?' said Father Squid. 'No. Of course not. He was … upset.'

Pleasant made a note of that, clicked the pen shut. 'That's all I need.' He got to his feet and put the notepad away.

'What is all this about?' Father Squid asked him.

'Stolen car. Nothing to concern you.'

Father Squid nodded. 'I thought perhaps … perhaps it might concern the Rathole. I go … used to go … there often when my day is done. I … I liked their coffee.'

Pleasant gave him a curious look. 'Coffee? That's it?'

'And their pies. I … I knew Lizzie.' His throat constricted with his words. He had to admit to that. Their affair had been a secret, it had to be, but a lot of people knew that he went to the Rathole and that he often spoke to her. It galled him to cover up their love, to lie about it, even by omission. The guilt it brought him galled him. 'She didn't have an enemy in the world. I don't know anyone who'd want to harm her.'

'Don't sweat it, Padre,' Ralph Pleasant said. 'We got the guy. Joker named Deedle. We found him with the drugs and money he took off the cook.'

Father Squid was stunned. He had been so certain that the killings were the work of Peter Nance. *Drugs? Was that what it was all about?* Deedle was such a silly name, even for a joker. 'Deedle,' he repeated, in a dull monotone. *Deedle killed Lizzie, and our child.* 'Who … who is this Deedle?'

'Just another stupid joker skel,' Pleasant said. 'Thanks for all your help, Padre.' He took a card out of his jacket pocket and laid it carefully on the desk. 'Here's my card. Call me if you remember anything else about the dago.'

Father Squid nodded wearily. *The police have the killer,* he told himself. *Justice will be done.* Perhaps that should have made him feel better, but the hollow feeling inside him still remained. Deedle would pay for his crime, but that would not bring back Lizzie, or their unborn child.

When the day of the pageant arrived, Father Squid sat in the office of the community center, gazing at the Santa suit that Lizzie had made him. At the end of the pageant he was supposed to come forth and distribute gifts to the children in the audience. He didn't know if he could do it. He climbed into the suit and his sensitive olfactory nerves could detect her scent on the fabric—

Someone knocked, rapping hurriedly on his office door. It was probably Wilde. The joker poet had quietly taken complete charge of the pageant. He probably had some last-minute concerns. Father Squid was tempted to tell him to go away, but before he could say anything the door flew open and someone came in, shutting the door after him.

He was tall, skinny, and shaking. He was a joker, covered in coarse reddish hair. He wore a cheap plastic hawk mask and had a rough bandage on one hand that was caked with dried blood. 'Sanctuary!' he cried in a desperate voice. 'Father, I didn't do it! I'm innocent, I tell you! You have to help me, hide me ...'

'Calm down,' the priest said. 'What are you talking about?'

'The killings! The Rathole! I never killed no one. I copped the car and Hash's, uh, stuff, but they was already dead when I got there, Father, I swear it.' He held up his bandaged hand in a grim mockery of a Boy Scout salute.

'Deedle,' Father Squid said.

The joker nodded and took off his mask. His young face was unremarkable, if exceedingly ugly. His pained, grim, hunted expression didn't help. 'I busted out. I had to. They're going to burn me, Father, and I'm innocent. You've gotta help me, please, I'm innocent.'

Father Squid nodded. 'Calm down, my son. Let me think.'

'You have to hide me. Sanctuary, I claim sanctuary ...'

'Sanctuary, yes.' Was Deedle lying? Father Squid knew that he was a career criminal. He had no illusions as to the truthfulness of such. 'Yes,' he repeated. He grabbed Deedle's arm, to stop him from shaking, but it didn't work. 'The church. Go to St. Andrew's – you know it? The door to the back alley is kept unlocked. Go there. Wait for me. I have this ... this pageant to attend to. I'll come by when it's over.'

'Thank you, Father, thank you.'

'Yes.' The priest's mind was still awhirl. 'Go, quickly, before you're spotted.'

'Yes—'

And he was gone.

December, 2010

'You know where she's buried?' Ramshead asked.

Father Squid looked up. The detective was gazing at him with speculation in his eyes. *Does he know?* the priest wondered. *Can he see the guilt in my eyes?*

'You know where Lizzie's tomb is?' Storgman repeated. 'The quicker we find her, the quicker the circus is over.'

'Yes,' he said. 'Yes. Of course. I will take you to her. This way.'

They went down the narrow hall, Father Squid leading the procession like a cowled demon guiding a troop of sinners to hell. The only noise they made were their shuffling footsteps and the squeakily creaking wheels of the corpse cart. Father Squid glanced over his shoulder, his features barely visible in the uncertain light.

'Watch the stairs down to the crypt,' he said, 'they're stone and rather narrow. I'm afraid you'll have to carry the cart, and also down the ladder to the catacombs.'

'Catacombs?' said one of the guys from the coroner's office. 'That means, like, no digging?'

'No digging,' Father Squid agreed.

'I'm cool with that,' the flunky said.

'Here we are,' Father Squid announced after they had made

their descent. 'I'm afraid that our crypt is more of a storage facility than a proper crypt.' It was a large and dark room, its recesses barely illuminated by the light Father Squid had flipped on at the top of the winding staircase that led down into it. 'Careful now,' he warned as they went down the stairs. He gestured about him as they reached the large stone chamber that had various boxes, crates, and chests scattered about seemingly randomly. 'As you see we use it for rather mundane storage rather than as a strongbox for treasure or a vault for bodies. The church has no treasure.' Father Squid paused for a moment as he went to a trapdoor set into the floor and yanked it open. 'And all the bodies are down here.'

The group gathered around the open trapdoor, looking at each other uncertainly and glancing down into the yawning pit that lay at their feet. 'I'll go first,' Father Squid said. 'I'm used to the ladder. Don't start down until I turn the light on.'

'Uh-huh,' Bugeye said, in total agreement with the priest.

Father Squid disappeared into the darkness. A few moments later an uncertain light flickered on, and he called out, 'All right, come on down.'

The cops and coroner's men looked at each other.

'You first,' Bugeye said to the coroner's crew.

'Oh, for Chrissakes,' Leo said. 'What are you afraid of?'

'There could be stuff down there,' one of the coroner's men said. 'You know. Spiders. Rats. Snakes. Alligators.'

'Christ,' Storgman said, and went down the ladder. 'Hurry up,' he called back up.

They all looked at each other, and the joker cop followed him down.

By the time they'd all reached the floor of the catacombs, passing the cart down clumsily, Father Squid had lit a half-dozen votive candles and said a brief prayer.

They looked around at the ossuary. 'Geez,' Bugeye said in a low voice. 'Will you look at all them bones?'

'The ones you want are this way,' Father Squid said, heading off through the catacombs. As they followed him into the darkness Miranda and Bugeye both took out their flashlights and shone them all about. The coroner's crew followed at the rear, their cart trundling over the slightly uneven brick floor, squeaking like a squadron of demon rats.

Father Squid stopped at Lizzie's tomb. 'Here it is.'

They shone their flashlights on the nameplate, illuminating Lizzie's name and dates. *So young,* Father Squid thought, *so young and sweet to die so hard.*

The coroner's team took charge. They put on their plastic gloves and covered their mouths and noses with face masks. 'Been down here a while,' one of them observed. 'Probably won't stink too much. But you never can tell with these oddball burials. Sometimes—'

'Spare us your experiences,' Storgman said, watching Father Squid, who had turned away as they pulled the nameplate from the wall.

There was a small wooden coffin inside the wall niche. The coroner's men levered it out and placed it on the floor. It didn't seem heavy. They used battery-powered drills to unscrew the lid's fasteners, and the coffin's cover came off easily. They peered inside, the uniformed cops glancing over their shoulders with interest.

'Not much left,' one said. 'We'd better take the coffin if we want to make sure to get it all.' He looked at the uniforms. 'Want to give us a hand?'

Michaelson and Bronkowski looked at each other.

Leo Storgman gestured impatiently. 'Sooner we get out of here, the better. Everyone grab a handle. Lift. Slowly. Yeah.' Father Squid watched them put the plain pine box on the cart and zip the body bag up over it. 'Strap it up and let's get the hell out of here.'

'This boneyard gives me the creeps,' said Bugeye.

Father Squid had never thought that of the catacombs. It was sad, yes, but a place of peace and repose. But now, with her gone, it would be a colder, darker place.

HOPE WE DIE BEFORE WE GET OLD

PART 3.

They'd lived in Jokertown for over thirty-five years. They'd moved to J-Town in 1974, perhaps six months after that day in mid-May, 1973, when the three of them had awakened in their bed no longer three individuals, but a single tormented one. Manhattan no longer wanted them after that: didn't want John practicing law in their courts, was no longer dazzled by Evan's art, and the city agency that employed Patty as a social worker decided her services were no longer needed. Their old life had vanished for them, and so they had gone to where all those disfigured by the wild card virus went: to Jokertown, where they were just another sight, where their pain was mirrored by that of the people around them.

And when they'd found their calling as the 'Protector of Joker-town,' as they came to be named, they couldn't even stay in that first apartment they'd taken, nor in Dutton's museum, which had been their next refuge. No, they'd needed to have a private, hidden place: where they could be alone with themselves, where they could be away from the requests and the prying eyes and the world.

They'd found this lost location.

Before Jetboy's spectacular failure, before the world changed forever, this area had been the Bowery, and during the Prohibition era, the mob had run liquor to the various speakeasies through underground tunnels. After liquor was again legal, most of those tunnels had been filled in or forgotten, but portions of them still remained, accessed by locked and innocent-looking doors from various buildings. Oddity had come across the tunnels by the late seventies, around the time of the Rathole murders, and they had become their permanent residence, their hiding place where they could howl their misery and pain and bother no one.

Their 'residence' was a network of tunnels and rooms; they'd barred off the tunnels and erected steel doors so that the joker gangs who sometimes prowled belowground couldn't enter. Those few who did were warned away, sometimes physically. There were signs spray-painted on many of the doors; since no one ever bothered them, Oddity assumed that the marks were warnings by the gangs to steer clear. Inside, there was some comfort: electricity stolen from the buildings above, an old TV from the eighties that still had a beta VCR attached to it (it was tuned to the news: '... attacks on jokers over the last three nights near Bleecker,' an announcer was intoning), bookcases (many filled with John's old law books), carpets on the stone floors, furniture they'd cobbled together from their old apartments. Evan had plumbed them into the city's sewage system.

It was sparse, it was spare, but it was the nearest thing they had to a home. They were, after all, never alone.

After the debacle of the Dime Museum, Pretorius had managed to get them released on their own recognizance, with a hearing delayed (at their request) until after the first of the new year. Charles Dutton had declined to press charges, either for his injuries or for the damage caused to the Dime Museum – now being repaired through donations from Jokertown's citizens – but the D.A. was still charging them with assault on the officers from Fort Freak. They'd stayed in Pretorius's office for almost a week, growing larger each day after Sergeant Squinch's initial shrinking; when they were a few feet high, they'd left without saying anything to Pretorius, coming down here to stay as they continued to grow back to their normal size. Patty and Evan had alternated taking Dominant for the rest of the month, keeping John penned up in Passive. That was becoming increasingly more difficult, and both of them were again at the point of exhaustion.

They couldn't hold John down forever. They knew that his paranoia was growing ever stronger and that the chance of John being as he once had been when he gained Dominant again were small.

[... give Oddity to me I know I can handle it please give it to me there's so much we need to do have to protect those who can't protect themselves ...]

Patty was spiraling into depression. She could feel it. Evan, she suspected, was the same. She looked at the bed – the same bed the three of them had shared in their Upper Manhattan apartment. She imagined the three of them there fondling each other, engaged in long slow lovemaking, laughing and smiling at each other's ecstasy.

That memory was harder and harder to hold on to.

In one corner, next to the television, Patty had placed a small Christmas tree on which were hung a few desultory ornaments and a triple strand of blinking white lights. There was a single gift under the sparse branches: a small wooden box tied with a bow of blue satin ribbon. Patty had put it together. They bent down (groaning as the movement caused something to grate against their rib cage and send waves of momentary agony lancing through them) and picked up the package, tucking it into a pocket of their trademark black, heavy cloak.

[You're sure about this, Patty?] Evan asked. [This is what you want?]

She nodded Oddity's head. [Yes,] she told him, told John. [I think so, anyway.]

[... no no no this is wrong it's wrong we're as strong as we ever were it's our job our task not anyone else's ...]

The fencing mask was sitting on the top of the television set; they switched off the TV and they put on the fencing mask, then lifted the cloak's cowl over that. They looked at themselves in a mirror: Oddity, as the world saw them.

[Let's go,] Evan said to Patty. [It's getting late.] They nodded and left the rooms, walking through the echoing tunnel and sewers and climbing toward the waiting night.

They walked through familiar streets, streets they'd walked a thousand times over the decades, watching for anything that was wrong or suspicious, for any joker in trouble they might help. They considered them *their* streets, *their* people: the poor souls who had been reshaped and reimagined through the wild card virus, those the rest of the world rejected. John had been the first to voice that resolution, decades in the past: *'The wild card has done something horrible to us, yes, but it has also given us a strength we didn't have before, and it's kept us together. Let's use what we have to protect those to whom the virus gave nothing but pain, misery, and mockery.'*

They walked openly through the streets, feeling the stares of the jokers and nats that they passed, responding to the occasional greeting. On the corner of Hester Street and Bowery, they saw Jube's newspaper stand, a set of twinkling Christmas lights outlining the stand. Jube, as ever, was there behind the counter, his porkpie hat askew on his blue-black skull, wearing a short-sleeved Hawaiian shirt in garish blue and gold despite the cold. 'Oddity,' he called out as they approached. His breath smelled of old theaters and buttered popcorn. 'Best of the season to you. Hey, I heard a good one the other day. There's this college professor giving her students a test on Monday after the big weekend game. She tells them that she didn't want to hear any excuses about how they did poorly on the test because they'd been out drinking. One student in the back raises his hand. "What if I've been up all night having sex?" he asks her, grinning. The students all laugh, but the teacher just shrugs. "Then I'd advise you to write your essay with your other hand," she tells him.'

Jube chuckled, his mouth curling around the walrus tusks at the corners. 'Pretty good, huh?'

'You keep trying, Jube,' Patty told him as he laughed. She gestured at the papers on their racks. 'Can we have a copy of the latest *Cry*?'

Jube was still chortling at his own joke as they paid and left. The headline was about the Infamous Black Tongue, cleared of all charges. Below the fold, there was an article about the attacks around Bleecker. They put the *Cry* on a bench at the nearest bus stop. The pages rustled in the wind.

They stopped again at a vacant lot a few blocks away, a dark place like an empty socket in the mouth of Jokertown, made even darker by the holiday lights on the buildings around it. Once, this had been the place to go in Jokertown. [... where is it what happened to it ...?] John fretted, his voice ceaseless. He tried to rise up to Sub-Dominant and Evan cast him back down again, groaning with the effort.

[The Crystal Palace burned down long ago, John,] he said. [Don't you remember?]

[I remember,] Patty answered. [I remember how vibrant the place was, and poor Chrysalis ...] Oddity moaned into the darkness, into the empty space where once the Palace had stood, bright and full of life. They could imagine the laughter floating out, and the music ...

They walked on.

[Where to now?] John asked. [Or is it time?]

[I want to check on Dutton,] Patty said. [Just to make sure he's all right ...]

Outside a nondescript brownstone with a wreath twinkling on the door, they slipped into a side yard and went up to a window shedding yellow light onto the house next door. As they approached the window, they could hear faint voices inside. Peering through the window, they could see Dutton, one arm in a cast and sling, his death's-head face staring down at cards held in his other hand. Three other people were at the table with him; the middle of the table was piled with chips. They saw Dutton toss another chip into the pot as they stepped back.

They continued walking. They didn't move into the side streets and alleyways until they reached Bleecker Street, where they suddenly turned. They heard, from farther down Bleecker, a faint scream, followed by laughter. Those on the sidewalks of the street looked around, clutching packages tightly to them. [Evan? What do you think?]

[Let's check it out.] They limped down Bleecker, groaning quietly, jokers moving aside for them. They heard the commotion coming from an alley near the intersection of Mott Street, and

Oddity smiled momentarily under the mask, but it was not Patty who moved their lips.

[... get the bastards beat the crap out of 'em ...]

Oddity turned into the alley, stopping to let their eyes adjust to the dimness there. They could see movement, could hear someone pleading in a strained and breathy voice with three kids in masks, none of them with any apparent deformities, gathered around someone on the ground, punching and kicking. 'No, please don't ... don't hit me again. Oh, God ... Please ...'

'Hey!' Oddity said.

The kids turned. 'Fuck!' one of them said. He was a nat, wearing a Joker Plague T-shirt, his mask hanging from a cheap elastic string around his neck. 'That's Oddity.'

[... let me have them let me show them ...] Patty could feel John rising, pushing upward. Inside, she heard Evan wail as John clawed at him, tearing him from Sub-Dominant and taking his place. Now his voice was clearer, and she could feel him trying to assert control of Oddity's body. [They're mine. I'll beat the little fuckers so hard they'll never think of coming to Jokertown again.]

Oddity growled in response to John's rage, a low warning that got all the kids' attention. 'We're three against one old asshole,' one of the kids said. 'Let's kick some more joker ass.' He was holding a length of steel pipe. He took a step toward Oddity, pulling the weapon back to swing, but Oddity slid forward and grabbed the hand before it could strike. Patty wasn't sure if it was her or John who had moved Oddity. The *crack* of bone was loud in the alleyway; the sudden scream of the kid was even louder, as was the clatter of the pipe on the ground. Oddity started to reach down to pick up the length of steel – Patty fighting the motion. Their hand closed around it as she and John fought for control of Oddity. [I'll show them! I'll show them what it feels like! Let me go, Patty!] The kids took off as Oddity seemed frozen in position, their leader cradling his broken arm, shepherded away by his masked friends. 'Come on, man, let's get the hell out of here ...'

Patty struggled with John, and now she could feel Evan rising to help her. Together, they managed to throw John back down into the prison of Passive, though it left them both exhausted. [... kill the fuckers next time kill all of them that would hurt jokers ...]

A moan brought their attention back. The joker huddled against the wall wasn't moving. They went over to the battered body; the face was a mask of blood – scaled skin hadn't protected the joker. What might once have been sails of flesh running from arms to the body hung in red-hued tatters around him. One leg was broken, canted out at an impossible angle, and his left arm had a compound fracture of the forearm, bone protruding from the skin. Oddity crouched down alongside the joker.

'They're gone,' they said. 'We'll get you help. Just hang on a little longer ...'

One thing had changed over the years. In the past, they would have gone to find someone. Now they pulled a cell phone from underneath their cloak and hit a stored number.

'Nine-one-one operator. What's your emergency?'

They gave their location to the operator, told her an ambulance was needed. They knelt by the joker and patted him. 'They're coming,' Oddity husked.

[It's time,] Evan whispered. [We can't do this anymore.]

Oddity nodded.

They rose, groaning their eternal pain to the night, and padded away as they heard sirens approaching.

The neon sign had expired a long time ago: UN LE CHOW ERS C AM B R, the unlit remnants proclaimed, and the broken and empty neon tubes hinted at the mollusk with a top hat and cane that had once danced there during the night. To the right of the sign for the ground-floor tavern, a steel railing protected the concrete steps leading down to a basement door, a wooden sign dangling on the unpainted metal by a rusted loop of chain, with a six-fingered hand pointing down and SQUISHER'S BASEMENT painted underneath the hand in crude lettering.

[Looks as good as it ever did,] Patty commented. Evan only

grunted inwardly. Oddity shuffled down the grimy, trash-littered steps and opened the battered steel door there.

The miasma of stale beer, vomit, and decades of cigarette smoke hit them like a physical blow; Oddity sniffed hard behind the fencing mask against the assault. In the dim, smoke-filtered light of the bar, the heads of patrons – all of them jokers – swiveled to look at the door and the roar of conversation over a track from Joker Plague's latest album dropped to a whisper. Oddity saw several of them nod in recognition before turning back to their drinks and conversation.

Squisher's tank sat behind the bar and the rows of grimy and water-spotted bottles. The water in the aquarium roiled as Squisher's head emerged and vented water from a hole in the top of his fish-head face. Squisher nodded. 'Oddity,' he said. 'Been a while. You guys doin' okay?'

'Well enough,' Patty lied.

'Have a drink? On the house?'

Patty shook their head. 'Thanks for the offer but not tonight. Seen Ears?'

The grotesque fish's head jerked toward the rear of the bar; Squisher leered with pointed piranha teeth. 'Back room.'

'Thanks,' Patty told the joker. Squisher vented water again and dropped back into his tank.

In the back room, a shuffleboard game was going on between a woman holding the stick with her prehensile tail and a man with an entirely featureless face who was maneuvering the pucks with his mind, while a knot of jokers were betting on the outcome. In a dark rear corner, a mass of tentacles were wrapped around bodies so tightly that Oddity couldn't tell how many people were there, but from the ecstatic moans, they were enjoying themselves.

Ears was sitting in a booth to one side, alone, though the monstrous elephantine flaps on either side of his head were directed toward the tryst in the corner. Oddity sidled up next to him. 'You always were a voyeur,' Patty said.

Ears tried to jump up and hit his thin legs against the underside of the booth's table. The massive ears fluttered like Dumbo trying to take flight as he rubbed at his shins. 'Shit, Oddity,' he said. 'You nearly scared the piss out of me.' He shivered all over, causing the ears – nearly as long as Ears's entire body – to flap again. 'What brings you here?'

'Thought you might know where someone was,' Oddity said. 'The snake kid,' Patty said. 'The one they're calling IBT now.'

'Thought you didn't much care for him,' the joker said. One ear had opened again, facing the direction of the group having sex in the corner.

'Turns out we were mistaken,' Patty answered.

'Huh,' Ears commented. 'Never known Oddity to be much for apologies.'

[John never was,] Evan said inside. [He was always right, in his own mind.]

[We all have our faults, Evan.] Patty shrugged Oddity's shoulders. 'You gonna tell us or not?' Oddity said. 'Or don't you know?'

Ears shivered again. 'I know. Of course I do. I know everything worth knowing around J-Town. That's why you pay me, right?'

'Yeah. That's why.' Oddity reached under their cloak. A hand that looked to be mostly Evan's placed a twenty-dollar bill on the table.

Ears looked at it but didn't touch it. 'I hear he's staying at those apartments on Mott near Hester,' he said.

Oddity patted Ears on the shoulder. 'Thanks,' Patty said. Oddity glanced again at the corner. The tentacles were writhing frantically and the moans were louder. 'Enjoy yourself,' she said.

'Get the hell out of here,' the kid said when he glanced through the chained crack of the open door. They could see his sinuous, long body trailing back into the room, the scales glistening.

'We'd like to talk to you,' Oddity told him.

The kid regarded them for a long time. Finally, he opened the door, allowing them to slip inside. 'So,' the kid said finally when Oddity said nothing, standing motionlessly on the frayed doormat, 'we taking up where we left off?'

'No,' Patty told him. 'That's not why we're here.'

'Then why?'

'You can't stay here,' they said. 'It's too dangerous.'

'Tell me about it. The place is a shit hole.' He gestured at the room: the gray, peeling wallpaper, the cracks in the walls and across the ceiling, the dingy, worn-out rugs, the ancient and dripping fixtures in the tiny kitchenette. 'Not to mention that I keep getting weird people at the door. But right now, even this is more than I can afford. Why are you *here*, Oddity?'

Oddity laughed. It was a disturbing sound. 'It's almost Christmas. We have a present for you.' Oddity moved a hand and IBT flinched, the tongue flicking out toward them but drawing back. Oddity brought out the wrapped box they'd been carrying all evening. 'Merry Christmas. Here.'

They took a ponderous step forward, holding the box. IBT slithered backward, then stopped. 'What's that?'

Oddity underhanded the box to IBT; metal jingled inside as he caught it. His eyes narrowed suspiciously. 'Keys,' Oddity said. 'And directions to the doors that use them.'

'Keys? You're giving me *keys*? To what?'

Oddity shrugged. 'You'll realize soon enough how much you'll need them,' Patty said. 'Maybe not immediately, but soon if you keep doing what you're doing – if you keep doing what we used to do. You'll need a place to hide, a place where people can't find you and bother you. Those are the keys to what used to be our place.'

'Used to be?'

Oddity nodded ponderously. [… no no you can't do this no …] They moaned as one of their legs threatened to change and buckle under them, the knee nearly giving way as bones shifted. 'We're … retiring,' Patty told him. 'We've been doing this for too long. We figure you can be our replacement.'

The IBT's torso shifted uneasily on his reptilian body. He glanced at the box in his hand. 'You don't know me at all.'

'We don't,' Oddity admitted. 'But from what we've heard … look, someone *has* to do it. Someone has to protect those who can't protect themselves and punish those who go unpunished. Just …'

Oddity's voice broke, and they moaned. When they could catch their breath again, Patty finished. 'Just be certain that those you punish deserve it, because ...'

Again, they went silent.

'I don't get it. Why are you doing this?' the IBT asked.

They didn't answer. Not directly. 'You should retain Pretorius too,' they said. 'A vigilante needs a good lawyer.' Oddity half turned, looking at the filthy, smeared window of the apartment. 'It's a beautiful night for endings, don't you think? We do.'

With that, they nodded to the IBT, shutting the door against his protests and leaving his apartment, moving out onto Mott Street again. They walked back to Bowery, then turned north again. They nodded to all the jokers they passed, as if they were greeting old friends.

[It's time,] Patty told Evan, told John. Oddity lifted their head, and lamps glittered like stars through the grille of their fencing mask.

◆

'You're certain, Patty?' Father Squid asked. 'Truly and absolutely certain? There's no turning back, once ...'

'We're certain,' Patty told him. 'All of us are. Father, we're so tired.'

[Yes,] Evan echoed in Sub-Dominant. From John in Passive, there was only a nearly wordless, angry mumbling.

Father Squid nodded to Dr. Finn – Patty had asked Father Squid to be there if Last Rites needed to be administered. Hooves moved heavily over the tiles as Finn left the room, returning a few minutes later with a syringe and a vial, and Troll in his clinic uniform.

'Patty,' Finn said. 'I'd like you to take off the fencing mask and the cloak. Since we don't know what's going to happen or how your body's going to react, I'm also going to secure you to the bed here; I promise you that we'll release you if we need to. I just don't want, well ...'

'I know,' Patty said. 'It's okay.' Oddity slid the cowl back and took the fencing mask from their misshapen skull, handing it to

Troll, who set it aside. They unclasped the cloak and let it fall. The air in the room was cold and dry. They went to the hospital bed and lay down, letting Finn and Troll strap their muscular arms and legs to the rails. Finn stuck an IV into their arm, taping it down. He filled the syringe from the vial he'd brought in. Father Squid leaned over the bed. He anointed their face with holy water; if he felt any revulsion at what he saw, he showed none of it.

'If there's anything you want to say, Patty, Evan, John, if you want God's forgiveness and blessing ...'

[Yes,] Evan said. [Patty, tell him.]

[... no no it wasn't true never true don't tell him ...]

'Deedle,' Patty said. 'We killed Deedle, Father. We were told that the evidence against him was solid and incontrovertible; we were told where we could find him, we were told we could give him what he deserved for killing poor Lizzie and the others.'

'Patty,' Father Squid whispered, leaning close to them. His tentacles quivered. '*Who* told you?' In his eyes, there was fear. They could see it.

'Ralph Pleasant,' they said. 'He told us. And you, Father, you need to tell Ramshead. Tell Leo we killed Deedle, please. He should know.'

Father Squid's eyes closed. Strangely, to Patty, a tear slid from under one of the lids, and his hand, trembling, went to his mouth. He leaned down toward them again, his lips close to their ear. 'May God forgive all of us,' he said.

He gave a sigh that sounded oddly like a sob as he straightened; Oddity tried to reach to touch him, but their hand only lifted slightly, straining against the straps. 'You can't blame yourself for what *we* did, Father. That was our decision. Ours alone.'

Father Squid gave a small smile at that, wiping at the tears in his eyes. 'There are few decisions that belong to one person alone,' he said.

Dr. Finn approached the bed. 'Are you ready?'

[Evan, do you want to take Dominant, or do you want me to stay here? Maybe it will only affect Dominant.]

[No none knows what it's going to do. It doesn't matter, Patty. I don't care. Stay where you are.]

'Patty? Evan?'

'Go ahead, Doc,' they said. 'We're ready.'

Finn lifted the blue plastic of the IV tip and plunged the needle of the syringe through the rubber membrane. He pressed down, and they felt a coldness in their arm that spread rapidly to their chest and head. [Patty?]

[I love you, Evan. I love you, John. Whatever happens, I love you both ...]

It was her last coherent thought. They had felt pain before, but they had never experienced anything resembling the blinding agony that struck them at that moment. Oddity arched their back, screaming, trying to tear their body loose of the straps. It felt as if giant hands were tearing into their body, grabbing and pulling at whatever they found. They heard Finn shouting orders, but they couldn't see anything. The world was a jumble of bloodred and darkness, shot through with wild pulses of color.

Their scream was a sickly yellow-green, weaving through the inferno of the pain. 'Troll, cut them loose!' Patty heard Finn say from somewhere in the nightmare. 'Now! Help me pull ...' Someone was raking a set of knives down their – her? – body, gouging deep into the flesh. Her – their? – arm was bending at a nearly impossible angle, followed by a *pop* of release. The air was frigid around them. Something was squeezing their calf like a ligature, tightening until she screamed again.

She screamed. It was her voice. Her throat aching and raw. Hers alone.

The pain was receding. She gasped at its memory. Her vision was red and smeared, and she pawed backhanded at her eyes, feeling slick blood. Someone's hands were around her, and she realized she was standing on the clinic floor. She looked down at her body. Streaked with blood, naked, thin: *her* body. She blinked against the blood. [John? Evan?] she thought, but there was no answer.

There was no one there with her.

She felt someone place a white lab coat over her shoulders, over her nakedness. She ignored it.

The bed was a mess of sickeningly bright and thick blood and

Oddity was nearly unrecognizable on it. Their – its – form lay there, the body torn open and parts of it dripping down the sides or strewn sickeningly on the floor. Patty could see white bone among the red, and the bones were still moving disturbingly. Oddity's head turned toward her: it was mostly John's, with some of Evan. There was nothing of her in the body at all. The lips moved.

'Patty?' It was John's voice, as she remembered it from decades ago. The eyes were staring at her: one John's, one Evan's. 'Where are we? I was sleeping, and I felt you get up. I have to get to the office early. Is the coffee ready?' The eyes blinked again. 'Are you okay, Patty? You look awfully strange.'

'Yes, John,' she told him. 'I'm okay.'

'Good,' he husked. 'Just let me rest a few minutes ...' The eyes closed and Oddity groaned. She saw muscles and bone shift in the face, watched darker skin rise to the surface like a continent lifting from a red seabed. Then, with a shuddering gasp, the eyes opened again. They squinted hard, as if they were having difficulty seeing, but she saw their gaze sweep over and past her. 'Patty? I can't ... can't see, but I felt you leave us. Are you ...?'

'I'm here, Evan,' she told him. She took their hand, pressed it. 'I'm outside.'

'Good,' he said. 'I don't think we're going to ...' Oddity moaned again; the whole body shifted. Red fountained in the abdominal cavity, and Finn rushed forward. He plunged his hands into the gaping wound. The front of his lab coat looked like a scarlet Rorschach painting.

'I need a surgical kit!' he barked. 'Packing! Blood! Move!' Troll began to lumber from the room, but Patty shook her head. She went to the front of the bed. She cradled Oddity's head, bending down to kiss the mottled forehead and brush her hand over the strange mixture of hair: the thin gray wisps of John, the tight curls of Evan.

'I love you both,' she whispered into their ear. 'I love you, John. I love you, Evan. I'm going to miss you both so much, so ...' She couldn't say more. Tears stung her eyes and her voice broke. 'I'm sorry,' she managed to say through the sobs. 'I wish it had been one of you who got out.'

She heard Oddity take a rattling, gurgling breath. She thought they were going to say something, but she heard only a sigh. Father Squid was praying audibly behind her. She felt Oddity sag and relax. The body was no longer moving, no longer shifting in its slow internal dance. She glanced over at Finn, shaking her head as if begging him to deny what she knew. Finn lifted hands bloody to the elbows.

'I'm sorry, Patty,' he said. He gestured with his head to Troll. 'We're done here for the moment,' he told Troll. 'Send in one of the female nurses to help Patty get herself cleaned up, and bring in some scrubs for her. I'll come back in to check on you in a few minutes, Patty; there are tests we should run, and I'd like to give you a full examination.' He was staring at her as he'd never stared at Oddity. 'Father, let's give her some privacy ...'

Numb, sobbing, she watched Finn bring a sheet over the body, watched the blood soak through to stain the white. Father Squid patted her shoulder, then followed Finn from the room. She heard the door click shut behind them.

The room was silent except for the hush of the HVAC system and her sob-wracked breathing. Silence. She realized that since the three of them had been merged, she had never really experienced silence. There had always been the ever-present thoughts, the eternal conversation inside.

[John ...? Evan ...?]

There was nothing. Even her own thoughts seemed impossibly quiet and hushed.

With a soft knock on the door, a nurse came in: a joker. Patty looked at her body: her face was ridged with blue lines with white peaks; from a few of the peaks oozed a yellow pus that dripped down the cheeks toward the smeared collar. Her hands were too small, and each had only one finger and a thumb. She had washcloths and towels folded over her arm, and she began running water in the room's sink. The bright splash was incredibly loud in the quiet. She turned, a soap-lathered cloth in her deformed hand.

The woman's body was not like hers – Patty's body was that of a nat. Normal. Yet the nurse smiled gently as she looked first at the sheet-covered body, then at Patty. 'I'm so sorry,' the nurse said. 'Let me help you. Unless you'd prefer to do it alone …'

[What am I going to do now? Please, please tell me.] There was no answer inside. Patty realized that the nurse was still waiting, and she shook her head. 'Alone?' she said. 'No, I don't think I want to be alone.'

THE RAT RACE

PART 17.

Fort Freak was crackling with holiday mayhem. Every nut job, madman, and petty crook was getting into the spirit, so December in the precinct was practically a month of full moons. Perps came and went – loud or sullen, protesting or grumbling – cuffed and ushered along the corridors, back and forth from booking to holding. And under the din of it all, Christmas crept up. The coffee station tree was now bedecked with a garland of origami birds made from tiny square napkins and coffee filters, and small wrapped presents cropped up on desks, accompanied by brightly colored envelopes stuffed with cards. Here and there, Hanukkah blue-and-silver glimmered through the red-and-green, but everyone shared and nibbled from the long line of fruitcakes the captain had brought and left outside her office.

By general consensus, they were actually pretty good.

Leo tried to let the festivity get to him and it did, a little. But the imminence of his departure was getting to him more. Melanie had begun to call so frequently that it was as if she was building some horrible momentum, and when the formal day of his retirement rolled around, he still wasn't sure what he was going to tell her. He loved his daughter, but he wasn't sure how he felt about Florida and the paved, faux-tropical paradise of fellow jokers. And though Melanie had blown him off for Thanksgiving, turnabout was fair play and he was spending Christmas with Wanda and two of her kids, which ought to be a little weird – but anything with Wanda in it couldn't be all bad.

'God damn it,' Slim Jim complained loudly as he struggled to shove a large canvas cart down the narrow precinct walkways. When he reached Leo's desk he bounced off one corner, corrected his course, and swore again. 'Son of a bitch.'

'What've you got there?' Leo asked.

'Property from the Magpie thefts. That old broad had the stickiest fucking fingers ... or ... or whatever. She stole a lot of shit, that's what I'm saying.'

'No kidding.' Leo peered over the rim and saw jewelry, velvet boxes that probably held more expensive baubles, clothes, hats, a couple of power tools, and stacks upon stacks of masks – some of which were probably Tate's. 'Lucas is going to have a merry Christmas,' he muttered. Then he asked, 'You on your way to the property room?'

'Yeah. I'll be typing up catalog descriptions until I retire—' he said flippantly, then caught himself. 'I mean, I'm not trying to say ...'

'I know,' Leo told him. 'Don't worry about it.'

The detective's cell phone began to ring, so Slim Jim took off – continuing his shoving, rolling progress, and trailing epithets behind him.

For a moment Leo didn't answer it; he didn't even acknowledge it, until the persistent chimes finally broke through his thoughts, and he seized it. 'Storgman.'

'Detective,' wheezed an oily voice. 'Gordon here. I've finished that ... ah ... that *task* you assigned me. The results are quite *startling*. I think you'll be astonished.'

Leo glanced across the desk at Michael, who was happily rearranging his filing drawers, and he looked quickly away. 'I bet I won't.'

'Please, when you have a moment. We should speak in person.'

'You'll be down in the dungeon?' He meant the pathology lab.

'Absolutely. At your leisure, Detective,' he said before hanging up.

Leo hung up too, clapping the small phone shut and jamming it into his coat pocket again.

Michael looked up long enough to ask, 'Was that the ghoul?'

'Yeah. I asked him to look into something for me. Don't worry about it. I'll be right back.' As he stood up to walk away from his desk it struck him suddenly that it looked strangely naked, stripped of the stacks of paperwork that usually occupied it – as his cases were either wrapped up or handed off in advance of his departure. It was bare compared to Michael's. It looked like it'd gone out of business.

Down in the dungeon, Gordon the Ghoul greeted Leo without looking up from his clipboard and a table full of jars. 'I hope you know, DNA testing on this scale was … improbable, though the results have proven to be … satisfactory.'

'I knew it was a long shot.'

'Longer than you guessed. The fetal tissues were preserved and available, which was unlikely enough. That successful diagnosis was possible is nothing short of a miracle.' He adjusted his protective eyewear and said, 'A *speedy* miracle.'

'I know you're doing me a favor, and I appreciate it,' Leo said, because it was true. He'd nagged Gordon to give him a DNA report in weeks, when the results often took months – and sometimes longer.

'And should I assume …' He gazed expectantly at the detective, but when Leo didn't respond, the pathologist shrugged the sharp points of his shoulders. 'That this is, ah, shall we say, off the books?'

'Say whatever you want. I'm trying to solve some murders here. And anyway, as everyone reminds me every damn day, I'm on the way out. What are they going to do, write me up?'

The Ghoul gave a snicker like a full body shudder. 'I suppose not,' he agreed. 'But I'm not sure how much help this will be – though it's definitely … interesting. I don't think it *collars* a killer.' He snickered again as if he'd made a great joke.

Leo wasn't in on it. 'What are you getting at?'

'The *fetus.*' He said it slowly. 'I compared its DNA with the samples you gave me both from Warlock's swab and Father

Squid's cup, and we have a match – but I confess, it's not the match I anticipated.'

The pathologist handed Leo a slip of paper.

When the detective didn't speak, Gordon urged, 'Surprising, isn't it? I mean.' He waved his long hands in a gesture of surrender. 'I was of the understanding that there were rules regarding that sort of thing. But it *must* have been a great love affair, for them to have risked so much.'

Leo still hadn't looked up from the paper. Hadn't spoken.

Otto Gordon dropped his surrendering hands and drained some of the gossip from his voice. 'A priest and a waitress? I suppose stranger things have happened. But stranger still if Jokertown's dear Father was ever a killer.'

This time, the detective murmured a response. 'He *was* a killer. Once.'

'Really? Well, he was almost somebody's *actual* father once too. All of it is strange – very strange.'

'So strange,' Leo said, a soft and halfhearted echo. 'And I almost don't believe it. But maybe I have to. Maybe it's so strange it has to be true.'

'Which part?'

Leo swallowed hard.

'All of it.'

SNAKE ON FIRE

by David Anthony Durham

Standing at the bar during the intermission to Natya's increasingly popular show, Marcus felt his chest swell with pride. Flipper and Ratboy had helped clear him. Officer Grady had confessed and cut a deal: Lu Long had fled; the cops had unapologetically dropped their interest in him. Lucas Tate even wrote a couple of articles exonerating him. Oddity had gifted him with a mission, a purpose. Besides all that, he looked good and knew it. He felt eyes lingering on him, on his chiseled chest and arms – and on the sparkling, ringed length of his tail. Why had he ever been ashamed of it? Life was good, and he was hoping it might just get even better.

He'd been at every one of Natya's performances that he could make. No matter how many times he watched her the dance was unique, different enough each time that he caught himself holding his breath on more than one occasion. Near the end of the first half of the show tonight, energy fields had congealed into stylized drops of water that splashed down on the stage in percussive perfection. Last night a pod of dolphins swam around her, splashing through astral waves of blue. Another time her shadow dancers became hulking shapes, threatening her, swiping at her instead of caressing her as they usually did. Marcus almost rushed the stage, sure she was in danger.

She wasn't. She'd ended that evening's performance like she usually did, with a short speech about some political topics Marcus didn't really follow. He'd have to get a library card and read up on South Asian politics. Or maybe he'd get his Mac up and running again and get online. He could do that now, couldn't he? Yeah, once he knew what the hell she was talking about he'd take the next step. Meet her backstage. *Natya, I'm a big fan of your show. Feel like getting a cup of coffee?* Or ... *Hey, Natya, how about them Tamils?*

Just the thought that her finale tonight was called the *bharatanatyam* snake dance made him feel funny inside. He had no idea what to expect, but man, it was a snake dance! Maybe she was trying to tell him something ...

'Well, if it's not Jokertown's newest vigilante hero!' Lucas Tate appeared beside him, patting him on the shoulder. He wore an expensive-looking tux, perfectly tailored. His mask, tonight, had an Asian flare to it, some sort of stylized canine baring a grin of pure devilish joy. 'I didn't know you were a fan of dance, IBT. Man of culture, huh?'

Marcus swirled the ice cubes in his glass. How quickly Infamous Black Tongue had become IBT. Didn't matter. Marcus had begun to like both names. 'I'm Natya's number one fan,' he said. 'Have been for a while.'

'You're full of surprises. But I should know that by now, shouldn't I? IBT, I want you to know how sorry I am. I misjudged you. I can't tell you how bad I feel about that.'

'Don't worry about it,' Marcus said, liking the way the nonchalance felt.

Tate ordered a gin and tonic from the six-armed bartender, specifying that he needed a straw. He also ordered Marcus a refill. 'Listen,' he said, 'I saw you come in earlier. Had to think about it, but now I'm sure. I've got some information you may be interested in.' He leaned in closer and dropped his voice. 'I know where Lu Long is hiding.'

'What?'

'Yep. He's still in the city, if my source is worth anything. Long is in a warehouse on X Street. It wears the number 215B. It's not abandoned, but it looks like it is. Behind the old Penney's building.

The type of place you wouldn't even know was there, unless you know it's there.'

Marcus could feel his pulse in his fingertips. He swirled his glass again, trying to sound calmer than he felt. 'You take this to the cops?'

'It's brand-new info. I just took the call as I was walking here.'

'I'd think you'd call the cops with it.'

Tate slipped the straw inside his grinning mask and sipped. 'I would've, but then I saw you. Got me thinking … This city owes you a break. I owe you. No, I do. I really do. I wrote some hurtful things about you, and I regret it. So here's what I'm offering. You get first crack at Long. Think of the headlines you'll make by bringing him in. Your star will be in full shine, my friend. And, of course, the *Cry* will have the jump on the exclusive. Maybe we'll do an interview. Full photo spread.' Tate indicated the size of the spread with his arms, a gesture that seemed to reach around the world. 'Of course, if you're not up for it …'

Marcus asked, 'What was that number again?'

He found the old warehouse tucked behind several newer structures. Marcus climbed the wall and slipped into an open window a couple stories up. He paused inside, feeling the warm air flow past him into the chill night. Before him stretched rows of desks and tables and sewing machines, lit only by the gray highlights slanting in from outside.

He glided across the room and through an open door. He stood in the stairwell listening. At first he thought the place was silent. The longer he listened the more it seemed to grumble, as if he were in a hungry belly. The furnace in the basement murmured. He slithered carefully up the stairs. His tail still felt a little sluggish with cold, but it was warming. On the third floor some machines hummed in semislumber. On the fourth a clock ticked and rodents scampered through a nearby wall. Below the next landing he paused again. Just across from him a door, cracked ajar, spilled out a yellow glow.

Marcus poked his head through the door. Lu Long stood in the center of the large room, back toward the door as he worked on something laid out on the table before him. Shirtless, the stretch of Long's scaly back was impressive, as was his thick tail, the tip of which plucked out some tune he must've had in his head. A heavy scent floated in the air, like gasoline but different somehow.

Watching the joker, Marcus went through his options. He could back-slither. Call the cops. Let them handle this. He didn't have any doubt that they'd take Long down hard, now that everybody knew how crooked he was. He *could* do that.

But then again he couldn't. That was the old Marcus thinking; IBT had different ideas. He felt as much in his clenched fists, tasted it in the venom seeping like saliva into his mouth. It wasn't just cops who Long had hurt. It wasn't just Twitch. This was for all jokers, for anyone ever exploited by people in power who looked down on them, didn't see or care about their humanity. This was personal. And it was more than personal. It was for justice, delivered fast and sudden as a snakebite.

'Turn around,' Marcus said loudly. 'I want to see your face as you go down.'

Long jerked. His shoulders started to swing around, but then stopped, steadied. 'Who's that talking?'

Marcus slipped closer. His fists tightened into stone mallets. He'd pummel this fucker. *Fist, fist, tongue. Pow. Fight's over.* 'Turn around and see.'

'You know what?' Long asked, his voice growing contemplative. He seemed to be carrying on with whatever he'd been working with on the table. 'I don't have to turn around. I'm thinking you're the squirmer they call Black Tongue.'

'That's *Infamous* Black Tongue.'

'"Infamous"? You even know what that means? Nothing to be proud of, kid.'

'I'll consider it ironic ... Puff.'

The joker grasped some sort of metal container in one hand, a tubelike thing. He bent forward for something else.

'Hey,' Marcus snapped, 'I said turn around!'

'What'd you ever do to become infamous, anyway?' Long asked, ignoring the rising alarm in Marcus's voice. 'Just got yourself in the wrong place at the wrong time. You got a knack for that. Look here, you've done it again. For the last time.'

Long swung around. In addition to the container, he held a monster of a weapon propped on his other arm. Tubes connected the two. The ex-cop hefted the weapon up and pointed it at Marcus. He hit a lever and a tiny flame spurted from the end. Long grinned hideously. 'That's the last time you'll call me Puff. Get ready to burn, motherfucker!'

Marcus suddenly had a very bad feeling about where he was standing. He launched himself upward with all the coiled energy he could, just as a jet of flame roared out of the weapon, toasting his tail as he hauled it up behind him. The room had a high ceiling, with the metal framework exposed. Marcus grabbed the steel girders and surged through them. Long cackled and howled as Marcus stayed just ahead of the jets of fire.

Each time Marcus thought he might leap down, new eruptions chased him on. He kept moving, but he ran out of room quickly. He slammed into a corner, panting, sweating, his lower scales scorched and painful. *Fuck! This wasn't the way it was supposed to go.* Long came on, shoving his way through the desks and other debris.

Marcus leaped. He plummeted downward and hit the joker with all the force of his falling body. He grappled him. They went over twirling, the flamethrower spouting ribbons of fire. A clawed foot caught him in the abdomen and doubled him over. And then another kick, again and again and again. He had a lot of abdomen, and Long was kicking his way down all of it.

Releasing him, Marcus squirmed away through the tables and chairs. He pushed himself upright and twisted around. A spray of flame scorched just above his head, close enough to catch his nappy hair. His Afro combusted. Long began to swing the heavy weapon back around on him to finish the toasting. Hair aflame, Marcus surged forward. His tongue shot out, tagging Long on his forehead with enough force to snap his head back. He grasped the tubing, yanked it free, and ducked as liquid shot into the air, combusting when a lick of flame touched it.

For a few moments, Long leaped and whirled through a twisting, cursing dance of spurting flame. He was no Natya, but it was quite a show. He tossed the canister in one direction, where it rolled into the legs of a jumble of chairs, igniting them. He dropped the flamethrower itself. He kicked it away with his clawed foot, and then stood brushing ash from his scales. He watched Marcus with deep irritation in his stylized reptilian features. Marcus stared back at him, catching his breath, wiping sweat from his forehead. Around them, the warehouse was quickly becoming an inferno. Flame climbed the walls and smoke blackened the rafters, billowing lower and lower with each passing moment.

'All right,' Long said, flexing his neck and moving into his slightly sideways fighting stance, 'let's do this the old-fashioned way.'

The two collided at full force: Long with his sideways attack, Marcus propelled by the sinuous muscles of his tail. Marcus hammered on Long's torso, his fists blistering against his scales. Long swatted at him with his claws. Marcus was quicker; Long had more power. He could also spit fire. He pulled back his head, puckered his lips, and *phoosh*! It was more distracting than damaging, though. The fire extinguished itself as quickly as it appeared, little more than singing Marcus's eyebrows.

They broke apart and for a few frantic moments they exchanged blows with their tails. Marcus tried to trip the dragon up, but Long planted his feet solidly and came on. He connected with a swing that threw Marcus to the side and sent him rolling. Marcus squirmed back. He'd use his tongue instead. He tagged Long on the forehead, on the shoulder, on the chest. Each thwack of impact was wet with venom, but it didn't seem to have any effect. *His fucking scales!* Marcus thought. His venom wasn't getting through them.

'You ain't so tough,' Long said. He spat a quick jet of flame, just for effect. 'Come on, fucker, stop slithering and fight.'

A beam fell from the ceiling, one side of it crashing down and making a diagonal barrier between the two jokers. It landed almost on top of Long, who backpedaled in response. Marcus used the moment.

He shot forward, grabbed the beam as he slid under it, and snapped his tail forward like a whip. He wrapped the tip around Long's neck, pinched it tight. He released the beam and used all his torso strength to draw his upper body forward. Once he was poised above Long, anchored to his neck, he battered him with a quick barrage of jabs. Long pulled his head back to spit, but Marcus was expecting that. He slammed a fist through the joker's puckered lips and into his mouth. He grabbed his tongue and yanked it taut. To the dragon's obvious horror, Marcus leaned in close and licked the length of it. Intimate, yes. Slobbery, indeed. But mostly ... venomous. He released the tongue, which snapped back into Long's mouth, and sprung away.

Long spat and spat again, quick bursts of flame erupting each time, vanishing just as quickly. His eyes stretched wide and wild, casting about for some rescue, even looking at Marcus beseechingly. Marcus crossed his arms and offered nothing. Long tried to run, but his steps were so unsteady it was all he could do to stay upright. He began to claw at his throat. He dropped to his knees and then, a moment later, reached for the floor as he crashed down face-forward into a sprawling heap.

Marcus didn't let him rest. He bent over him, twisted his head around. Through his coughs he asked, 'Why'd you do it?'

Long just looked at him, his eyes glazed and floating.

'Why'd you off Twitch?' Marcus said, shaking him. 'What did he ever do to you?'

'The one and only told me to.' Long sounded out of it, his mouth thick and his words strangely whimsical, as if he were drunk. 'The one and only most holy.'

'Who's the most holy?'

'Squidface.'

'You mean Father Squid? What does he have to do with anything?'

'Take it up with the squid. Take it up with ...'

Long's eyes fell shut. Marcus punched him, but to no effect. And then he punched him again, just for fun.

Then he heard the sirens.

Marcus couldn't complain about the way things turned out. He had dragged Long to safety before the fire department showed up. Boy were the cops glad to get their hands on him. There were going to be some lingering legal issues, Flipper had said, but considering all the attention Infamous Black Tongue had received recently – and the stink of police corruption around the whole thing – he didn't expect the cops to pursue any disturbing the peace or destruction of property charges. When Marcus gave Father Squid's name as a suspect, Flipper promised to use that to his advantage as well.

Reporters swarmed him, suddenly his best friends, all smiles and congratulations and a million questions. Blinking in the harsh camera lights, Marcus wished his hair hadn't looked so pathetic, singed and showing reddened scalp in spots. Oh, well, it was proof he'd taken Long out the hard way.

With that behind him, Marcus focused on another pressing matter.

Natya's performance that night was awesome. Her best yet. For a long time she danced on her own, just her body stepping and sliding, her arms sinuous, her face pure beauty, as if her mind was somewhere else entirely, somewhere wonderful. The spectral images joined her later, first just as ribbons of light, and then in birdlike forms that sailed around her, gliding on gusts of music. By the end she'd become a glowing sun, around which a swirling solar system rotated. Marcus had felt the heat of her hot on his face, and in other places as well.

The warmth faded fast once he was outside in the alley behind the playhouse. He stood there shivering in the rear of the alley, half hidden in the shadows, clutching a single flower. Occasional flakes of snow fell. He couldn't feel the tip of his tail anymore, but he wasn't gonna let that discourage him. He sported a new wool cap, pulled snug down over his ears. He'd bought it to hide his singed scalp, but was glad for the warmth of it now. Listening to Nat King Cole wafting in the night air, he wondered if they celebrated Christmas in Sri Lanka. Probably not. He should have looked that up when he Googled the place. Regardless, he was going to buy her presents. Lots of presents. He'd get her nice things, or maybe he'd make her something. He'd figure it out. Tonight, though, he'd keep it simple. A single flower.

He thought, *'Hey, Natya, how you doing? ...' No, not like that. I'll say ... 'Hey, Natya, great dancing tonight. Loved it. Hey, you ever been to Trincomalee? I hear good things about it. Been thinking about going ...'*

The door swung open. Natya stepped out. She said something back inside, a few good-byes. A burst of laughter came back out at her. A few more words, and then she let the door click shut. For a few wondrous moments, Marcus felt the world's possibilities condensed down into two beings separated by only a few steps, a few seconds. Natya exhaled a plume of mist. Marcus thought how wonderful it would be to be that warm air, coming up out of Natya's lungs, through that throat and mouth and lips. His hands, despite the cold, were sweating where they clutched the flower. Marcus slid toward her.

'Hey, girl!' a female voice called, and then sang, 'You are my sunshine, my only sunshine.'

A woman at the street end of the alley. She stood there a minute, waving at Natya, until a toddler ran up beside her and took her hand. Both of them skipped toward Natya, who had come down the steps toward them. He recognized the woman. Minal, the prostitute who once worked for Twitch.

Friends, Marcus thought. *Of course she has friends. That's okay. Doesn't change anything. I can tell them both what I did for Twitch. Maybe they'll both ...*

Then a guy rounded the corner. He took in the three greeting one another for a moment, and then walked toward them, saying something that Marcus didn't catch. Oh, shit ... Marcus had seen this guy before too! In the precinct. A cop, detective or something. He wasn't in uniform but he'd been there, talking on the phone and drinking coffee. He was black, young, and sort of goofy-looking. He had ears like Will Smith. The guy's cap didn't so much sit on his head as ride atop those ears. He also had a body kinda like Will Smith. He was no slouch, which Marcus couldn't help noticing when Natya slipped her arms around his lean torso and kissed him.

Marcus was so stunned he couldn't think, couldn't breathe. He just stood, silent, feeling light-headed. *What the fuck just happened?* Watching them walk away, Natya with her arm around Minal and the other hand gripped in the toddler's, Marcus felt the truth slide home like a bullet loading. He was alone. He couldn't count on anybody. He couldn't dream his way into a better life. The sooner he stopped thinking he could, the better.

He stretched for the nearest fire escape, grabbed it, and pulled himself free of the ground. He let the flower fall from his grasp. It twirled down to land in the snow.

Forget her, he thought. *Just be IBT. Be Infamous Black Tongue. Be a hero.*

He went looking for an ass that deserved kicking. That, he knew he could find.

FAITH

PART 5.

December, 2010

The red Santa Claus suit, much worn over the years, still fit Father Squid, though barely. It was ragged and much patched, and worn shiny at the elbows and knees, but it still had Lizzie's familiar, beloved scent. Its warm smoothness still felt like the caress of her fingers.

Father Squid waited in the wings, watching the action on stage as he did every year. He never tired of the pageant. This was his thirtieth. He'd only missed the one, back when he'd gone on the WHO tour around the world, with Chrysalis and Tachyon and Hartmann and good old Xavier Desmond. Could they really all be gone?

This one was as good as most. Old Dorian Wilde, fat and florid, sat in the front row, alternately nodding and clenching at his somewhat less thick head of hair. He updated the script every year, adding the topical reference or two, but the basics stayed the same. Yes, it had its own peculiar Jokertown sensibilities, a touch of sarcasm but never cynicism. Father Squid had seen to that. This was about peace and love, brotherhood and sharing. It was a story that had been told time and time again, and needed to be told time and time again to offer up some hope, however slim and transitory, to an audience who lived lives burdened by hopelessness.

When the end came and Baby Joker Jesus – played this year by the Ramirez twins bundled together in the same swaddling clothes, since thankfully there was currently a dearth of two-headed babies in Jokertown – Father Squid was ready to come forward as Santa and deliver presents to children in the audience.

He hoisted his sack over the shoulder, and stepped onto the stage.

'Ho ho ho,' he began ... but stopped when Leo Storgman stepped forward, the owl mask that he had worn in his role as Melchior pulled up to expose his face. He looked grim.

'Leo,' said Father Squid. 'What is it?'

'I know the truth,' Ramshead replied.

It was only a matter of time, the priest thought. *Sin will out.* 'Will the truth change anything, Leo? Can the truth raise the dead?'

'No,' Storgman said, 'but the guilty should be punished. It's what I do.'

'It's not what I do,' Father Squid said. 'I'm in the forgiving business.'

'That morning at the Rathole,' said Leo, 'the scene was horrific. Blood, gore, bodies everywhere. Yet you remained so ... detached as you viewed it.'

Father Squid nodded. 'I'd seen bodies before, many times. Some in much worse condition than those in the Rathole. And, as you may note, my face is not terribly expressive.'

'Yes, I suppose. Because of your experiences in Vietnam.'

'In part.'

'I checked around, looking into your past. It took some doing, because ... well, no one knows your name, do they?'

'My name is Father Squid.'

'I mean your real name.'

'That is my real name.'

'Is it? Then who is Robert St. Cabrini?'

Father Squid closed his eyes, opened them again.

'There was a Robert St. Cabrini in the Joker Brigade. A joker foundling, originally from Salem, Massachusetts, brought up in the St. Cabrini orphanage. Eventually drafted into the army. Sent to 'Nam. Made sergeant four times. Busted down each time.

Wounded in combat twice. When he wasn't killing Viet Cong and winning medals, he spent half his time drunk and the other half in the stockade. Must have been some career. The records say he was called Sergeant Squidface. Want to see his photo?'

Father Squid shook his head.

'He went MIA. No record of him after that, although apparently someone matching his description joined the Twisted Fists. Joker terrorists. You know about them, of course?'

Too much, thought Father Squid. *Forgive me, O my Lord.* 'That was another life, another man,' he said. 'That was before I found God.'

'That was before you found Lizzie Wallace and knocked her up,' said Ramshead. 'A bastard child would have destroyed the good Father Squid, so you whistled up Sergeant Squidface one last time, didn't you? Deedle took the fall for that, and for thirty years you thought you were safe. Then, when it seemed as though someone was about to look into the Rathole again, you panicked and hired Joe Twitch to destroy the records. Only Joe got greedy, tried to blackmail you, so you had to pay Lu Long to silence him, and that blew up in your face when IBT saw the hit go down.'

Father Squid's throat was dry. He did not answer.

'Robert St. Cabrini,' Leo Storgman intoned, 'alias Father Squid, alias Squidface, I arrest you for the murder of Lizzie Wallace and four other persons at the Rathole diner on the night of December 16, 1978.'

The church had grown deathly quiet. Father Squid could feel the blood rush through his ears. For some reason, all he felt was a sudden, great relief.

December, 1978

Father Squid sank down into his chair behind his rickety desk.

Deedle, he thought. *Deedle did it. He killed Lizzie. He killed our child. He says he is innocent, but they all say that, don't they?*

If he was innocent, then someone else had done it. Perhaps someone who had been pushed into a bloody rage by Father Squid's own actions, by his pride. That could not bear thinking about.

If he is innocent, he should prove it in a court of law. Father Squid rooted through the top drawer of his desk and came up with a card with a name and a telephone number on it. Deedle *was* guilty. He *was* lying. He needed to be back in police custody, to answer for his crimes.

The priest dialed the number. Someone picked it up after the first ring.

'Detective Pleasant,' Father Squid said, reading the name off the card. 'I know the whereabouts of someone you may be looking for …'

December, 2010

Father Squid could feel everyone's eyes on him. The silence was unbearable. It had been for decades. He had to end it, now. It was time to come clean.

He looked Leo Storgman in the eye. 'Yes. Take me in. There is blood on my hands, Leo. It is past time I confessed.'

The gasps of shock and the cries of amazed horror that burst out all around him were only to be expected. More surprising was the look of astonishment in Leo Storgman's eyes. Father Squid thought that the detective had probably figured that he'd deny everything. But he couldn't carry on with his guilt locked inside any longer.

'Sorry, Father,' Leo muttered as he took out a pair of handcuffs and locked them around the priest's thick wrists. He took Father Squid by the elbow and led him through the crowd that melted away as if he were a leper. Father Squid looked straight ahead and marched in step with the policeman. There were shocked, angry expressions on every face they passed, but it didn't bother him. Confession, he had discovered, *was* good for the soul.

A little voice cried out, 'Mommy, why are they arresting Santa Claus?'

No one could answer him.

THE RAT RACE

PART 18.

The church's storage room was a jumble of religious holiday supplies and musty choir garb. Crosses abounded, festooned with Easter declarations that 'He is Risen!' Stacks of candles with round paper holders were piled in boxes to overflowing. An old set of choir bells gleamed dully in the low light.

And everywhere, hastily stored and not precisely put away, were the remnants of the pageant.

A stable wall leaned against the basement wall, and stray sprigs of hay dusted the counters, the crates, and the floor. A plastic donkey leaned mournfully against its stallmate, a puffy white sheep with a lightbulb up its asshole so it'd glow with the help of City Light and Power, if not holy assistance. Over by the stairwell was a haloed little head hanging out of a box, the infant Jesus himself propped and forgotten for another full year. Against a huge nautical chest was pushed the manger bench, a sturdy thing made by a parishioner out of two-by-fours with an ugly brown stain.

Upon it sat Leo Storgman and a book.

Leo hunkered in the dark, breathing the old smell of paraffin wax and the sharp scents of tinsel and cheap wiring. At his feet was a box, wide but not very deep. The box was full of masks – some of the very masks recovered when the Magpie had finally been cornered and all her wares had been retrieved.

Leo held the mask he'd worn in the play.

It was tattered and rough around the edges. Not just vintage, but handmade when it'd been new. The brown and copper feathers were thin and fraying; and the interior stank of glue gone rancid and somebody else's sweat.

Maybe that part was just Leo's imagination.

But he held the mask and he passed it back and forth between his hands as he sat there in the dark beside the book he'd never finished reading, alone except for the plastic animals and choir robes and leftover holiday detritus ... waiting.

It wouldn't be long now.

The festivities had wrapped up. The aftermath of Father Squid's arrest had died down. The last of the church volunteers had finished stuffing the last scrap of pageantry into the basement, shut the door, and left. The parking lot was empty.

Leo had parked around the block.

He wanted the parking lot to *stay* empty. He wanted it to lie.

He closed his eyes and squeezed the mask, holding it by the edges and feeling the brittle papier-mâché between his fingertips. And at the edge of his hearing, he caught the soft rumble of a car's purring engine ... then the gritty crunch of its tires as it turned into the poorly paved lot, and ground its way into a parking space.

For a long moment he heard nothing. He stopped rubbing his thumb along the inside ridge of the owl's beak and opened his eyes. He pulled out his cell phone and composed a fast text message, and pressed SEND. His phone thought about it, gave him a status bar, and declared 'OK!' Right on its heels he sent another one. He put the phone away.

Out in the lot the car door opened slowly, accompanied by the pinging chime of a warning alarm – signaling that the lights were still on, or the keys remained in the ignition.

The door closed quietly and the chime stopped.

Footsteps followed.

Leo held the mask again, tracing its interior contours like there was something inside, written in Braille.

Outside the church he heard the feet find the stairs that led down to the exterior basement entrance. The footsteps faltered at the top two steps; there was no light at all, except a streetlamp half a block away. Leo knew how dark it was. He'd climbed down the damn things himself, and jimmied the door.

The newcomer didn't seem to notice the compromised door. Hands fumbled with the knob, and with the lock. The breached piece of hardware gave way. With a tiny push, the door swung open.

Though the light outside was negligible, the light within was all but nonexistent. Leo watched a hand reach inside and pat down the wall beside the door. Feeling nothing, an arm followed the hand, swatting at a larger and larger space. Still finding no handy switch to flip, a man's full silhouette rounded the frame and flailed until grazing a long string, hanging from the ceiling.

The hand seized the string, gave it a testing tug, and then firmly gripped it. The string tightened and popped.

A dim yellow forty-watt fluttered to life, revealing the cluttered room, the pageant leftovers, and Leo Storgman sitting with his knees apart and the mask in his hand. He sighed heavily. 'Hello, Lucas.'

Lucas Tate wore a suit that cost more than Leo's car, and a black satin mask that was molded to his features – or to someone's, somewhere. It covered his face down to his chin. Only his eyes were visible, and they were startled into hugeness – without lids or lashes. He replied, 'Hello, Ramsey,' because the moment seemed to require it. Then he added, 'What are ... Jesus, man. It's the middle of the night. What are you doing here?'

'I'm waiting for you.' Leo held up the mask so its front faced forward, the empty owl gazing blankly at the newspaper editor – whose fingers still clutched the light's pull chain, as if he might need it at any moment. 'And you, you're looking for this.'

'That's true, yes. My masks. The ones that batty old thief took – I recognized some of them, when people were wearing them in the pageant.' He said it with the speed of the guilty who is trying to look innocent.

'That's right.' Leo looked down at the box. 'They're all yours, aren't they?'

'Yes. It's all my property. I can come and get it if I want to.'

'Sure you can. Anytime.'

'Day or night.'

The detective said, 'Whatever.' And then with a shake of his head he said, 'Goddamn, I can't believe you kept this thing.'

'I don't know what you're talking about.'

'Sure you do. If you didn't, you wouldn't be here.'

Lucas stepped forward, his shape not quite hulking, but given a hulking look by the harsh shadows and the feeble sway of the bulb. 'That's mine. I'll be taking it with me, now.'

'To hide it again, I assume. Somewhere better this time.'

'You're crazy.'

'I'm crazy?' Leo made no move to hand over the mask. He only met Tate's eyes when he said, 'You're the asshole here at two in the morning, trying to break into a church.'

'I didn't break in. It was open.' Suddenly he realized, 'You opened it.'

'You got me there,' the man who was still just barely a cop admitted. 'I knew you'd show up eventually. You had to. Tomorrow, all this stuff goes back to the station – back into the lion's den, picked up and recorded by all kinds of cop hands, and cop paperwork. This was the last of the haul, the last stuff to be filed.'

Lucas Tate shifted his weight back and forth, like he couldn't figure out whether to stand his ground or come any closer. He said, 'I don't know what you're getting at, Leo. If this is some kind of joke – you're … you're just desperate to wrap up one stupid old case before they turn you out like Wednesday's trash!'

'Yet you knew exactly which case. I didn't even have to say it.'

'Of course not!' Tate babbled. 'You've been going on about the Rathole for months.'

Still calm. Still seated. Still holding the mask, Leo said, 'You were there.'

'No.'

'Yes,' he said, nodding. 'You killed a restaurant full of people, and you buried it. You buried it a real long time – and I don't know if you got dumber with age or maybe just more paranoid. But if you hadn't gotten so nervous, it might've stayed buried.'

Tate leaned back, just enough to take half a step away from the cop and the mask. 'You've lost it, Ramsey. They're right to retire you.'

'I've seen it before. Guys who committed crimes they should've left in the past. But they get old. And scared. And then they make mistakes.'

'Is that how it works?' He struggled to sound sardonic.

Leo told him, 'More often than not. People do stupid shit.' He shook his head. '*You* did stupid shit. You freaked out when you heard that the Rathole files were coming up for air. You've known Dr. Pretorius as long as I have. You know what kind of lawyer he is, and you can guess the kind of teacher he's become. A room full of law students, eager to examine cases for extra credit – that's the *last* thing you wanted. So you asked around and you found out Twitch would do anything for a buck. You paid him to start the fire in the courthouse.'

'You're out of your mind,' Lucas mumbled.

'Only Twitch started looking like a bad bet. He was a loudmouth and a loser, and I don't know – maybe he tried to blackmail you. Maybe you heard him mouthing off around town. So you went to Puff and you had Twitch taken care of.'

Lucas said, 'No.' More firmly, he repeated himself. 'No, that's not true. None of it's true. It was Father Squid, you said so yourself. That's what Puff said. That's what everybody said, and that's why you took Squid off to jail, isn't it? You've already got your killer. I'm sorry you don't like it but—'

'Don't.' Leo stopped him short. He shook his head. 'You're right. I didn't like arresting Squid. I've trusted him with my life and worse. That's the last man alive I wanted to cuff and book, much less on my way out the precinct door.'

'Well, that's why you're a good cop. You make the tough calls because they're right.'

'Flattery won't get you anyplace, Tate. I took Squid to make you think this was all over. So you'd figure it was safe to come for this.' He held up the mask again. 'You were wearing this, the night you shot up the Rathole.' The detective looked down at the mask and noticed something in the dim light that he hadn't seen before. No maker's marks, no brand. No label. He guessed, '*She* made it for you, before she died.'

Tate's voice was almost a squeak now. 'She?'

'Ramona Holt, the joker girl who got creamed by Contarini's car.'

'Contarini's …?'

'It's funny,' Leo continued. 'Everything I ever learned about the Rathole came back to that damned car. The Sleeper cinched it for me, when I caught up to him. He said that the shooter had come inside, demanding to know who was driving it.'

'Oh, what the fuck would Croyd know, anyway?'

'He was there. He was hiding – he'd just woke up, and the joker-ace trait of the moment made him a human chameleon. He vanished when the kid with the gun joined the party. The kid in this mask.'

Tate shook his head violently. 'All this is news to me, Ramsey.'

The detective shrugged. 'It must've looked like you were free and clear for a while there. They picked up that poor little scavenger shit – another dumb kid, one who stumbled across an open register and a bloody restaurant. Then he got loose, Squid fingered him, and the Oddity pounded him to a pulp, and the whole thing looked shut. In thirty years, nothing new happened in the case. Until you hired Twitch to start a fire at the courthouse, and then I gave it another look.'

'You wasted your time. And now you're wasting mine.'

'Nope. I've wasted some of Squid's time, and for that I owe him an apology. But *you're* the one who set him up, wearing that tentacle mask when you talked to Puff and Angel. I found it in the property room – a real expensive number, looked like one of Lovecraft's wet dreams. You must've worn it, and put another mask over it. The effect would've been close enough to draw conclusions. I don't know how you knew I was looking at Squid, but I know you keep your ears to the ground. And God knows Squid was making himself look guilty as sin.'

'Very funny.'

'Not at all. He was acting guilty about the Rathole because he was *feeling* guilty about the Rathole. He'd been in love with Lizzie, the counter girl there. She was carrying his little joker baby, and there's no telling what it would've looked like, or if it would've lived, but it was *his* – and I've got the DNA paperwork to prove it. Poor guy. All these years he kept it to himself, and no one even guessed it because she died. So he was guilty of something, yes. But not guilty of killing her. I think he would've killed to protect her, if it'd come to that. Just like you would've killed to protect Ramona.'

Tate stood beneath the bulb. He was sweating now, and the shaky light made him look all the more unsettled. 'Stop it.'

'I wish I could. Ramona Holt had been hanging out with the Demon Princes, same as you. She was about your age, hanging in your circle, and I think you fell for her. And when Contarini killed her – in that careless, offhanded hit-and-run – you lost it. Maybe you were there when it happened. Maybe it was your fault, or all this time you've felt like it was your fault. Maybe you saw the car, and caught a little bit of the license plate. And maybe, when you were running around a couple weeks later, you saw that car sitting in front of a diner, and you went inside.'

Leo paused.

Tate was so motionless that he might have stopped breathing. 'No.'

'Tell me about Ramona, Tate.'

'No.'

'Was she beautiful?'

'No. Yes. I didn't know her.'

'You *did* know her, Tate. You killed for her. Had you been drinking? Shooting up? In your book, you were pretty frank about that stuff. You had a problem with it, when you were on the streets.'

'No. Yes. Sometimes, I guess. I had a problem.'

'You must've been higher than Denver when you saw that car, and when you went inside that diner. You were wearing this mask,' Leo said again. 'Croyd thought it was a hawk mask, at first. But later he told me it was an owl instead. He was right on his second guess.'

'No.'

'Yes, he was.'

Tate mustered enough indignation to say, 'I can't believe you'd take his word over mine.'

The detective said, 'I don't have to take his word. I have your mask.'

'But it doesn't mean anything!'

'On the contrary. So thirty years go by and you set fire to a courthouse, and have a man killed to cover it,' he said. 'And when I got interested in the Rathole again, you pointed me at Esposito. You might not have known him then, but you know him now, and you know a little something about him. He could've looked good for it. A button man for Gambione, and somebody who handled a lot of drugs, coming and going – and he even had a tie to two of the victims.'

'I gave you Esposito because I thought it would help! And why … okay. If any of this is true, and it sure as hell *isn't* – but if any of it's true, why would I call you when I got robbed? Why would I ask *you, personally* – the man who's on the trail of the Rathole murderer – to go and find my masks? Why would I alert you that way, huh?'

'Good point. But by all reports the shooter was wearing a hawk mask – and you knew good and well that you didn't have any hawk masks. Come to think of it, for all your fucking epic mask collection, I don't think I've ever seen a hawk.'

'That's meaningless.'

'A meaningless omission? I guess it could be, but I don't think so. It was one more way you could kick sand over your tracks. Writing that book didn't do it, obviously. Hell, it put you in the scene at the time of the killings, even though you were real careful to leave out any mention of the Rathole – and you told me it'd all gone down after you'd left cover. But that wasn't true. A glance at a calendar told me that much.'

'I might've made a mistake. It was a long time ago.'

'Yeah, it was.' Finally now, he set the mask aside and reached for the book that had shared the bench with him all this time. It was Lucas Tate's book, *Paper Demon* – the copy Tate had left for the detective downstairs, on a day months ago when he'd been too busy for lunch.

One page was dog-eared. Leo thumbed his way to it.

He read aloud, 'For "R" … "I talk with the moon, said the owl, and the night belongs to me."' He closed the book and set it on his lap. 'Let me ask you something, Tate. Ramona, if she were still alive … is this what she'd want?'

Tate's shadowed face was dark within the mask, and his eyes were unreadable. But he whispered, 'You didn't know her.'

'No, I didn't. But *you* did.'

In a hushed, almost little-boy voice, he broke down. His eyes were wet, and he clutched at his chest like he was trying to keep something in, and failing. He said, 'She rolled around in a red wagon; she couldn't walk very well. I pulled her around the city. She was on the sidewalk.'

'Then what, Tate?'

'You know they called me "Nimrod," don't you? It was because I never paid enough attention. She … she got away from me. I let go of the handle, and she rolled. Right into the street. And I didn't see it, not before this … this black car comes tearing around the corner.'

'It wasn't your fault,' Leo assured him. 'Not that part.'

'He hit her. And for a second, he slowed down. And then he just kept driving. The whole thing happened in less than five seconds. I didn't have time to leave the sidewalk, and it was over. Goddamn.' He put his hands up to his face, trying to rub at his eyes and finding himself blocked by the mask. 'Goddamn, it's been … goddamn.'

'Stop saying that. We're in a fucking church.'

'Leo, you have to … goddamn. You have to believe me. I don't … I don't even *remember,* hardly, what happened that night. You were right, what you said earlier,' he said, talking faster with every phrase. Catching up to his own story, and seeing where he was caught. 'The drugs. I took so many drugs.'

The detective was still seated with the book lying across his knees. He said, 'You saw the car and you went inside, asking who it belonged to. You didn't know it was Contarini's car. You didn't know he'd ditched it a week or two before, and then flown back to Rome. You were wearing this mask. You had a gun.'

'I forgot I even had a gun.'

'You had a gun, and you waved it around. And Hash saw you. He thought you were there about the drugs, or to rob them. So he came out with the sawed-off, we know that much.'

Lucas Tate nodded, slower then faster. His mask slid on his face. He pushed it back up with an absent shove of his finger. 'It was self-defense. *He* shot first. He opened fire, and he winged somebody – one of the customers. I panicked.'

'Anybody would have.'

'I panicked!' He said it louder this time, and he came up closer so he was very near, in front of Leo. 'Someone was shooting at me, so I started shooting! And people were ... they were falling, and screaming. I heard somebody scream.'

'You killed them.'

'No. I didn't. I wouldn't have.'

'Lucas, you *did*. You killed them all, and now' – he sighed, and reached behind his back for a pair of handcuffs – 'it's time you answered for it.'

'No.'

'I don't want to bring you in. Believe that much for me, will you?' Leo stood and flexed the cuffs. They clicked in his hand, and shimmered in the dull yellow light.

'No,' Tate said. And this time it wasn't soft or penitent. It wasn't even defiant. It was a word that had come to a decision. 'Please, Leo, Ramsey, man – things are different now, can't you see? I've turned it around – I'm not that miserable shit anymore, I'm a productive member of society, I ... I help people! Christ, it was thirty years ago, and putting me away isn't going to bring them back!'

'Don't make this any harder than it has to be.'

'I've done good work! I've been a voice for the whole joker community – for you, Leo, and for everybody we know, everybody out there who's messed up just like us. I've fought, and lobbied, and—'

'Stop it.'

'Leo, I'm not doing this.'

'Turn around.'

'No.'

Leo knew what the decision was. He hadn't counted on it, but he'd prepared for it. 'You gonna fight me? Is that how this is going to go?'

Lucas Tate swung his head back and forth, seeking a weapon – and that's when Leo knew he didn't have one.

There'd been no guarantee he'd come unarmed, but the detective knew there were two kinds of men, and that's pretty much all: the kind who do their own dirty work, and the kind who avoid it at all costs. Tate was the latter. Upon a split second of reflection, Leo wondered if Tate's hands-off attitude wasn't a direct result of the Rathole; just *one time* he took matters into his own hands ... and look how that turned out.

Tate spied, seized, and brandished one of the painted wood poles that had previously held aloft the birthplace of Christ. The stable's support was rounded and heavy, about half the size and weight of a railroad tie. Tate struggled with it, holding it between himself and the detective – who was listening hard for something outside.

It'd been there, a moment before: a car, drawing slowly into the parking lot outside. Probably pulling into a spot right next to Tate's vehicle. Leo didn't hear it now, but he hadn't heard the door open or any footsteps. He snaked his hand into his jacket, feeling for his gun.

'Don't!' Tate warned, taking a short swing with the pole.

'Or what?' Leo asked. 'You'll kill me?' His elbow bent with a snap, and the gun was in his hand at exactly the moment Tate's weapon came whipping up from the right. The detective ducked and the pole clipped his left horn – taking his hat and smacking it against the basement window behind him. But his head and his horns had taken worse before.

Tate swung again, swiping the big piece of wood right to left – struggling to hold it up and aloft.

Leo's gun hand came up and lost to a lucky blow; Tate knocked it hard enough to strip the knuckles in an instant, and the detective felt warm blood and numbness. It was another full second or two before he realized over the stinging pain that he wasn't holding the gun. He'd lost it and it'd slid on the floor. Within reach, if he could get down on the ground.

But Tate brought the pole around again and it went wild; his arms were tired from lifting the thing, or maybe it was heavier than it looked. Leo planted his feet back and lowered his head, locking his shoulders and lunging in the old head-butting fashion that'd never failed him yet.

The pole cracked against his head and he saw stars, but he kept moving forward and he nailed Tate in the gut, which confused him. They toppled together, each one shoving the other's arms out of the way – and each one kicking at the other, elbows clattering into faces and knees ramming against ribs as they clawed and crawled sideways on the ground.

Behind everything, still Leo was listening.

He heard it when the basement door smacked open and Tate heard it too, but he didn't dare look.

By virtue of being taller than Leo and having longer arms, his fingertips were there first – pricking at the gun's butt and clawing to drag it back.

'Stop! Police!' shouted Michael, who had arrived in the nick of time like the best of the goddamned cavalry.

Leo gasped, 'Hurry!' and used a final surge of strength to grab Tate's shoulder, using the other man's weight to haul himself along the cement floor. Tate hammered Leo in the eye with his forearm and Leo wheezed, 'My gun!'

Michael had already seen it. 'Freeze!' he shouted at them both, which wasn't going to work – but it was worth the formality. He approached the writhing duo, and being both younger and taller than the detective and the editor, he seized Tate by the back of his pants and heaved him bodily off his partner.

Tate swung around with a desperate kick, trying to sweep Michael's gun away too ... and thinking what? That Leo was slow or winded, and that he wouldn't retrieve his own weapon in that intervening moment of distraction?

Leo didn't know, and he didn't stop to wonder about it.

He flung himself forward, reached his gun, and caught himself on his elbows. By the time he was up in a seated position, holding it out and forward, Tate was crouched on the ground – one hand held out to Leo, one hand held out to Michael.

Michael's feet were parted and his hands were steady, all professional precision – and this from a man who'd been summoned by a Hail Mary message in the middle of the night. Leo didn't think he'd ever been half so happy to see any other cop, maybe in his whole career.

Michael looked over Tate's ragged, fight-mussed head and he gave Leo a nod that said, 'I've got it now,' and at the same time asked, 'Are you all right?'

Leo nodded back his answer to both.

He knew Michael had it now. And he was all right.

He climbed all the way to his feet and sat back onto the bench while Michael performed the details, flattening Tate against a wall and locking him into handcuffs.

Ten minutes later, outside in the parking lot, Harvey Kant was there, and Bugeye Bronkowski too; the spinning red and blue lights of their cars were kicking holes in the wee-morning blackness. And Leo Storgman was sitting on the trunk of the lieutenant's car when a taxi pulled up to deposit Wanda.

She wasn't frantic, but you could see it from there. 'Leo! I just got your message!' She ran toward him, tripping over the small, tire-churned drifts that crisscrossed the lot and then catching herself just in time to reach him. 'Is everything all right?'

He hopped down off the trunk and opened his arms.

'Everything's going to be great,' he said. Then he gave her the biggest, deepest, most serious kiss he'd ever given anybody in public, and added, 'Fuck Florida. You ever seen Paris?'

Copyright Acknowledgments

'The Rat Race' copyright © 2011 by Cherie Priest.

'The Rook' copyright © 2011 by Lumina Enterprises, LLC.

'Faith' copyright © 2011 by John Jos. Miller.

'Snake Up Above/Snake in the Hole/Snake on Fire' copyright © 2011 by David Anthony Durham.

'… And All the Sinners Saints' copyright © 2011 by Victor Milán and Ty Franck.

'Sanctuary' copyright © 2011 by Mary Anne Mohanraj.

'Hope We Die Before We Get Old' copyright © 2011 by Stephen Leigh.

'More!' copyright © 2011 by Paul Cornell.

'The Straight Man' copyright © 2011 by Kevin Andrew Murphy.